Cast of Characters

Amanda Beagle. The no-nonsense elder Beagle sister, she's a good knitter and an ever better manager of the Beagle Detective Agency, which she and her sister inherited from their brother Ezekiel.

Lutie Beagle. The younger sister, Lutie is a crack shot who learned how to follow clues and order vintage champagne from reading detective novels.

Martha "Marthy" Meecham. The Beagle sisters' cousin, also our narrator and Lutie's reluctant Watson. She misses the good life in East Biddicutt.

Jefferson "Jeff" Mahoney. Their brash young assistant.

John Bynam. A wealthy young man about town.

Hester Gale. A nightclub singer, she's in love with Bynam.

Inspector Moore. A gentleman copper who thought highly of Ezekiel.

McGinnis. A not-so-gentlemanly copper.

Madame LaVelle. The flamboyant proprietress of *Maison LaVelle,* a theatrical lodging house, whose French accent is a moment-to-moment thing.

The Fennelli family. Mama Luisa, Papa Luigi, sons Raphaelo (Raph) and Michelangelo (Mike), daughter Lotta. Acrobats, somewhat volatile.

Dolores. Raph's estranged wife.

Floto. A trapeze artist who ran off with Dolores.

Mrs. Joffey. A retired wardrobe mistress who misses the theatrical life.

Dot DeVeere. An aging model. The years have not been kind. Nor is she.

Professor Sesame. A magician. He pulls a murderer out of his hat.

Mr. Saint John. A tragedian whose hobby is horticulture.

Mr. Smyth. An actor from Hollywood. He's not around for long.

Wilson "Bill" Paul. A dancer, not currently working.

Tabby. A cat.

Rabelais. A parrot with a colorful vocabulary.

The Beagle Sisters Duet

Our First Murder (1940)
Our Second Murder (1941)

Our First Murder

by Torrey Chanslor

The Rue Morgue Press
Boulder, Colorado

To
Caroline

Our First Murder
ISBN: 0-915230-50-X
New Material Copyright © 2002
The Rue Morgue Press

Published by
The Rue Morgue Press
P.O. Box 4119
Boulder, Colorado 80306

Printed by
Johnson Printing
Boulder, Colorado

67955054

Meet the author:
Marjorie Torrey/Torrey Chanslor

Fame is a funny, fickle thing. Marjorie Torrey, who as Torrey Chanslor wrote *Our First Murder*, was one of the major illustrators of children's books in the mid-twentieth century, achieving back-to-back Caldecott Honor awards, but today she is virtually forgotten. She was born in New York in 1899 but somewhere in the late 1950s, she seems to have quietly passed from the scene.

She wrote a few children's books herself but she was primarily an artist, whose old-fashioned style was ideally suited to illustrating books for young people. She also did the covers for the two mysteries featuring the Beagle sisters, *Our First Murder* (1940) and *Our Second Murder* (1941). Although these covers were uncredited, there's absolutely no doubt whose work it is when one compares the playful, yet extremely accurate, cover of *Our First Murder* (reproduced for this edition in a slightly enlarged form) with the delightful illustrations in her 1946 Caldecott Honor book, *Sing Mother Goose*.

The Beagle Sisters books were her only books written for adults. They belong to that school of elaborately plotted mysteries solved by very eccentric detectives popularized in this country by S.S. Van Dine and Ellery Queen. What makes Torrey Chanslor's books stand apart from her predecessors are her delightful and unusual sleuths. The Beagle sisters are two sixtyish spinsters from a small upstate New York town who inherit a New York City private detective agency from their brother and almost immediately plunge themselves into a spectacular murder case. Elder sister Amanda Beagle (think Margaret Hamilton or Edna May Oliver) heads up the firm and runs it with an iron hand, but most of the sleuthing is done by Lutie, the younger sister (think Helen Hayes), who honed her adopted craft by reading scores of mysteries borrowed from the East Biddicutt circulating library. The action is described by their Watson and somewhat younger niece, Marthy Meecham (picture Spring Byington). Their other cohorts in crime are Jeff Mahoney, a young, lanky redhead, (think a young Van Johnson on a Jimmy Stewart frame) who does some of the legwork and all of the heavy lifting; Tabby, a

cat; and Rabelais, a parrot with a colorful vocabulary (learned from his pre-
vious owner, a sailor).

The Misses Beagle weren't the first women in the genre to assume the
duties of what P.D. James called "an unsuitable job for a woman." Rex Stout,
the creator of Nero Wolfe, gave us Theolinda "Dol" Bonner in *The Hand in
the Glove* (1937), and Patricia Wentworth's Miss Silver earned her keep as
an English private detective for many years, starting with *The Case is Closed*
(also 1937) among others. But the Beagle sisters were among the earliest
and certainly the most eccentric women ever to walk the mean streets as
private eyes. Lutie, though several decades older, is as adept as Dol in her
use of and fondness for revolvers, while Amanda and Miss Silver share a
stern resolve and reliance on common sense.

Contemporary critics gave the Beagle sisters a warm welcome. "Quaint
but funny," is how Will Cuppy, a major critic of the day, accurately described *Our First Murder* in *Books,* while Isaac Anderson in the *New York
Times* gratefully acknowledged the arrival of "two such delightful spinsters."
Marian Wiggin, writing in the *Boston Transcript*, was even more enthusias-
tic: "The Misses Beagle (what a name for detectives!) are charming, especially Lutie, who has stepped up to the head of the list of my favorite detectives. These two women greatly enhance what would be, anyway, a very
neat case of hidden identity." In spite of those reviews, the Beagle sisters
returned for only one more case, *Our Second Murder*, in 1941, after which
Marjorie Torrey devoted herself almost exclusively to writing and drawing
for children because, as she once commented, "what happens to children is
the most important thing in the world, I think."

Marjorie Torrey herself began drawing as a child in and near New York
City and entered the National Academy of Design at the age of thirteen
before moving on to the Art Students League. She was inspired to draw by
her father who entertained young Marjorie and her brother with his own
drawings, which accompanied games he invented. An injury to her back
kept her out of regular school, but she spent many years at home "drawing,
painting, reading, reading, reading, and writing stories." After she started at
the National Academy, her father built her a small studio beside a brook on
their property where she could work during summer vacations.

Her favorite memories of her art school days involved winter evenings
at the Metropolitan Museum of Art when "it was even more still and magic,
and with a small group of young people—not all art students—informally
led by Nicholas Vachel Lindsay (the poet), we wandered where we chose,
gazing raptly at sculpture, at medieval tapestries, at Egyptian mummies,
discussing what we saw, trying to express what we felt." Those excursions
paid off when one of her earliest art jobs called for her to draw cartoons of
medieval ladies and their courtiers for tapestries. She longed "to make a

cartoon of modern young people on Riverside Drive, with the Palisades in the background, but was told this would not be salable…However, I sketched New York scenes, mostly of children playing, and painted from these during the weekends."

After she finished school, she married and had a son. Soon she was getting a great deal of illustration work from various magazines, which required two extended trips to Europe. Such work was mostly for the adult market and she soon gave it up. She moved to the San Fernando Valley in California with her husband, Roy Chanslor, a novelist who was beginning to get considerable screen work. His most famous novels were *Johnny Guitar* and *The Ballad of Cat Ballou,* both made into even more famous movies. *Our Second Murder* was dedicated to Roy, who died in 1964. Marjorie earned a screen credit herself (some sources credit Roy) for the 1936 screwball comedy *The Girl on the Front Page,* starring Gloria Stuart, who was nominated for a best supporting actress Oscar for her performance in *Titanic.*

From her hilltop home overlooking the valley, Marjorie Torrey was finally free to devote herself exclusively to creating books for children. She wrote and illustrated four of her own: *Penny* (1944), *Artie and the Princess* (1945), *Three Little Chipmunks* (1947), and *The Merriweathers* (1949). But it was her work as an illustrator that brought her fame and awards. Her first Caldecott Honor book, *Sing Mother Goose*, with songs by Opal Wheeler, came in 1946. The following year she earned another Caldecott Honor medallion for illustrating *Sing in Praise: A Collection of the Best Loved Hymns*, once again selected by Wheeler. A Caldecott historian wrote of her work: "The full-color illustrations reflect the solemnity and reverence seen in Torrey's Mother Goose collection, and these interpretations communicate the essence and importance of the songs' words…Torrey's gentle black-and-white illustrations possess the softness of pencil, some the sharp lines of pen and ink, and others a combination of both."

She also illustrated *Fairing Weather* by Elspeth MacDuffle Bragdon in 1955, *Far from Marlbrough Street* by Elizabeth Philbrook in 1944, and several books by Doris Gates, including *Sarah's Idea* (1938), *Sensible Kate* (1943), and *Trouble for Jenny* (1951). She deftly illustrated reprints of several classic children's books, including *Alice in Wonderland* in 1955 and *Peter Pan* in 1957, after which she seems to have vanished without a trace. Marjorie is not mentioned in Roy's obituary in a 1964 edition of *Variety* and he appears to have remarried.

All of her books are out of print today. Even her Caldecott honor books are difficult to find, often confined to rare book rooms or the special collections section of larger libraries. Ironically, she's perhaps best known today for her two mysteries, which have been mentioned in Carolyn G. Hart's popular "Death on Demand" mystery series and are sought after by collectors specializing in the evolution of the private eye novel, especially those featuring women sleuths.

Marjorie Torrey gave us perhaps the ultimate portrayal of the spinster sleuth. Amanda and Lutie's adventures on the streets and in the nightclubs of 1940 Manhattan might seem preposterous to the jaded reader of today, who associates private eye novels with gritty urban cityscapes and even grittier characters. In their joyful innocence they offer up a picture of time when people read murder mysteries just for fun. It was a period in which America was emerging from the Great Depression and not yet embroiled in the Second World War. The country certainly needed a laugh then. Who is to say that it doesn't need another one today?

Tom & Enid Schantz
July 2002
Boulder, Colorado

CHAPTER 1

IT was a beautiful Indian summer day, the sky was silky blue, without a cloud, and the air had that wonderful still clearness that only autumn brings. It was so warm that after we'd had dinner—which is a midday meal in East Biddicutt—and finished the dishes and tidied ourselves up for the afternoon, we went out and settled ourselves on the porch, just as we do every afternoon in real summer.

Amanda, tall and unbending in her straight-backed chair, was knitting, of course, and Lutie in her little rocker had her work basket of sweet grass on her lap. I knew she wanted to read her newest book from the circulating library. She'd brought it home only that morning, and it promised to be an especially delightful one; there was a crimson handprint across the black cover, and I'd caught her stealing eager little nips out of it before noon. But this time after dinner was our social hour, and she knew Amanda wouldn't like it if she buried her nose in a book. So she was crocheting another bureau scarf for me—the fourth she'd made me, and I loved every inch of every one of them.

I loved every bit of Lutie too and of Amanda, and the square, neat white house, ornamented with wooden lace and shaded by tall elms and maples, where they'd been born and lived all their lives, and the little garden that Lutie and I tended together. She had a magic way with flowers, and I was beginning to understand them too, though I hadn't known a petunia from a peony when I first came to East Biddicutt.

That was five years before. Until then I'd lived all my life in a city, and a smoky noisy factory city at that. But I'd always remembered the blissful month I'd spent one summer, visiting my third cousins Amanda and Lutie Beagle when they were young women and I was a plump shy child of twelve.

Even my memory of their Pa—Uncle Abidiah Beagle was still in the land of the living then—held a certain shivery delight; he'd had fierce black eyes and a beaked nose and a deep, thundering voice, very awesome and impressive. I've since gathered that his patients—he was a country doctor, and a very busy and capable one—didn't find his bedside manners soothing when they went to him for trifling ailments, but apparently they depended on him utterly when they had anything serious the matter with them.

Well, anyway, when my own father died and my cousins wrote and asked if I'd like to pay them another visit, thirty-odd years after that first one, I accepted thankfully, and it was like finding a long-lost dream again. The peaceful weeks went by, and I hated to think of ever leaving. Then one day they asked me if I'd care to stay and live with them; and it seems that's what they'd really thought of when they wrote me.

"But, of course, my dear," said Lutie, "we didn't want to propose it immediately. We didn't know how you'd take to life in a quiet little town—"

"Nor," said Amanda firmly, "how we'd take to you."

Amanda doesn't believe in being mealymouthed.

"But, hmm"—she cleared her throat and frowned—"you're a nice sensible child, the same as we remembered you, after all. So that's settled."

And so it was.

I'm still living with them, and I'm still a child!—though I'm just ten years younger than Lutie, who is three years younger than Amanda, and Amanda is sixty-five. But Amanda was "a great girl of eight" when their Ma died, and little sister was "knee-high to a hoptoad—just a baby," so a mere baby she's seemed ever since, to Amanda.

Now I've come in for my share of bossing, scolding and coddling—and I bask in it. For behind her fierce manner and her rugged mask of a face Amanda conceals the tenderest heart I've ever known.

Lutie is a little thing, with a soft voice and soft pink cheeks, bright blue eyes and a row of fluffy silver curls across her forehead. She has a magic hand for light pastry as well as flowers, a skillful one for fine sewing and crocheting all sorts of "fripperies, fal-lals and other useless doodads," and a keen taste for reading matter that Amanda calls trash and balderdash.

Almost every other morning she'd trot in from the library with another lurid volume. Amanda, who of course did the managing, which meant budgeting, marketing, looking after the small income Pa had left them (and now, my tiny one too), would be at her desk. From ten-thirty to eleven-thirty was her time for going over the accounts, right after she'd come home from the market and the bank. And she'd push her steel-rimmed specs down on her nose and look up over them with a snort.

"Humph," she'd sniff, *"more* folderol?"

Lutie would put down *Murders in the Morgue*, or *The Kenilworth Killings*, or *Death Deals a Hand* and proceed to take off her gloves and bonnet. Yes, she always wears bonnets—the kind that were smart when she was young, in the 1890s, with Alsatian bows or little flowers in front; she knows quite well how becoming they are, perched on her silvery fringe, and also how much more chic than the shapeless contraptions elderly ladies usually go in for. "Which," she once said to me with a giggle at some particular monstrosity, "I wouldn't be found dead in, my dear!" So she'd make a charming picture as she stood there, untying the velvet strings beneath her chin, smiling at us. And Amanda's eyes, resting on her, would glow with the pride she believes she hides behind her frowns and clucks of disapproval.

"Humph," she'd shake her head, with another snort, "dreamy and impractical, Lutie Beagle! You always were, and always will be, I s'pose!"

"I know, Sister—you've spoiled me!" Lutie would nod and twinkle. "But it doesn't matter, does it? I have you to take care of me!"

And she'd glance admiringly at the long columns of neat figures in the ledgers and account books spread out before her sister.

"I don't see how you do it—I *never* could!"

With a small contented sigh she'd tuck her latest thriller under her arm and trot off, while Amanda, with a grunt, would snap her black eyes back to her accounts, banishing the little flibbertigibbet from her mind with a stern straightening of her shoulders and another shake of her head.

If it had ever entered that sensible iron-gray head that Lutie, who likewise adores her, secretly cherishes a sweet profound indulgence for her big sister, she would have simply dismissed the absurd notion with an incredulous "Fiddlesticks!" But it is true.

And of course it's the reason Lutie hasn't the slightest objection to being clucked at and scolded. She's perfectly willing to listen to Amanda's preachments, and almost never disagrees, though now and then she'll drop into the midst of a dogmatic discourse some serene irrelevance most irritating to Amanda's prideful common sense. I used to wonder what Amanda made of it when, in the light of after events, these haphazard bits of nonsense seemed to suggest an uncanny sharpness, as they had an odd way of doing. I have frequently seen her look startled and eye little sister in a peculiar, almost a frightened manner. But then she'd shrug, "Humph! Babes and sucklings can't help hitting the nail on the head sometimes, I s'pose!" I've decided that about sums up her attitude.

And Lutie doesn't mind. That's the way she wants it. It's a kind of charming game with her. But don't misunderstand. She's not making game of her sister, I don't mean that. It's simply that they're two different kinds of people, and she's quite a bit different from Amanda's cherished idea of her, but she doesn't see why they should quarrel about that.

The nearest they ever do come to a disagreement is about their pets.

Tabby is Amanda's cat. Years ago—it was before I came to East Biddicutt to live with them, but they've both told me about it—a little white kitten followed Amanda home one day.

"Isn't she a cute little tyke?" said Amanda.

The kitten was scrawny and dirty, but Lutie didn't mind that. Amanda filled a saucer with thick cream from the top of the bottle that Lutie'd planned to whip for strawberry shortcake—but she didn't really mind that either.

"Here, Tabby—here, Tabby!" said Amanda.

Lutie said, "Wouldn't Thomas be a more appropriate name, Sister?"

Amanda snorted, "Stuff and nonsense."

Lutie didn't argue the point. Nor did she object to it. But time passed and Tabby became a huge-jowled animal with chewed ears, who prowled, battled and yowled by night and chose her finest flower beds in which to snooze by day. And Lutie did object to that.

Yet I've always suspected that she doesn't really dislike Tabby at all. I think she uses him as a sort of foil against Amanda's strong objection to Rabelais.

Rabelais is a parrot that Lutie brought home not long after the advent of Tabby. He is a handsome, angry-looking bird; she bought him from a sailor, and a fine large cage and a silk bandanna to cover it came with him.

As she hung the cage in the dining-room bay window, she remarked, "He reminded me of Pa."

"Who, the sailor?" snapped Amanda.

"No," answered Lutie.

The bird fixed Amanda with a baleful glare, opened his beak and croaked harshly, "Demmitall, you're a fool!"

Amanda didn't press the matter.

Rab's rowdiest remarks seem to go in one of Lutie's shell-pink ears and out the other, but I've seen Amanda's own large handsomely modeled pair flame brick-red at his sallies. Of course she realizes that Lutie doesn't understand half the creature's horrific vocabulary, but it's most disturbing to have her hear it, anyway.

However, those minor differences merely added to the spice of life; and on that lovely afternoon of Indian summer Rab was quiet, dozing in his cage in a sunny corner of the porch, and Tabby was curled up at Amanda's feet. Everything was utterly, blissfully peaceful. I don't suppose it will ever be quite like that again. . .

I was sitting idly in the porch swing that we hadn't yet put away for the winter. We'd had a fine dinner of meat pie, succotash, hot bread and pickled peaches, blueberry preserves and angel-food cake—which Amanda and Lutie don't think of as a hearty meal at all—and I was so contentedly replete and cozy that I was in danger of napping. So I got the garden shears and a basket—there were still some late chrysanthemums blooming along the picket fence, pom-poms, small and snowy and pungent—and began to cut a bunch for the supper table. I gathered a fine bouquet and went in and arranged it in a big blue china vase.

When I came out Amanda was saying, "Do you realize it's the nineteenth, and we haven't heard from Ezekiel?"

Ezekiel was their brother, and their only living kin, except for me. I'd never seen him, but from the faded pictures in the family album he seemed an arresting mixture of the characteristics of both his sisters, with Lutie's blue eyes and fair curly hair, Amanda's strong nose and square jaw. I knew he'd taken issue with Pa and shaken the dust of East Biddicutt from his feet some forty years ago, and his family had never seen him since, though he wrote to the girls, punctiliously if not chattily. Apparently he'd been rather a soldier of fortune for some dozen years or more anyway, so Lutie loved to think, for he wrote from all over the world, places whose very names made her blue eyes gleam with excitement. But he never mentioned what he was doing in those distant spots, and Amanda used to cluck and snort, "Hmmph. A rolling stone—"

However, he seemed to have gathered enough moss to go into business in New York, finally. He didn't say what kind of business, and his sisters never asked, for some reason that I put down to New England reserve. Anyway, on the fifteenth of each month he wrote them, and on the thirtieth Amanda answered his letter. Lutie sometimes added a postscript, mentioning the neighbors and the garden and Rabelais and Tabby.

She said now, in reply to Amanda's remark, "I've been wondering too. Poor Zekie. I'm afraid he's passed away."

Amanda looked up sharply.

"What nonsense! Why should he have passed away, as you call it?"

Lutie rocked gently.

"Because he's so like you, my dear."

"Like me? Are you crazy?" said Amanda. "That boy was never anything like me!"

"I meant, dear," Lutie explained, "that if you ever weren't dead by the thirtieth of the month, you'd write him. Wouldn't you?"

This gave Amanda pause for a moment. Then she rallied and retorted, "I must say, Sister, I don't care to be compared to Zeke. You know very well how unfilial he was!"

Lutie nodded.

"So like dear Pa—" she murmured.

Amanda stared, shook her head at this vagary.

"Ridiculous! And not very daughterly, either, Lutie Beagle." She added, "Pa never went off like Zeke, half-cocked—"

Lutie said something—I couldn't quite catch it, but it sounded like, "No, not 'arf!" and a tiny giggle.

Amanda frowned with annoyance. "What are you talking about?"

"Nothing—nothing at all!" Lutie lifted innocent blue eyes. "My wits were woolgathering—"

Amanda snapped, "Hmmph—as usual!" Her knitting needles clicked.

Just then the gate-latch clicked too, and we all turned our heads. The gate opened and the postman came up the brick path toward us.

He said, "Howdy! Letter from New York." And held it out to Amanda.

As she took it she couldn't help primming her lips, and a quick told-you-so glance at Lutie, with her hifalutin' foolishness about Ezekiel's passing away. Because the letter of course must be from him. None of us received any other mail from New York—except Lutie's seed catalogue, perhaps—and this obviously wasn't a catalogue.

Amanda held the long envelope in a sort of nonchalant way and spoke courteously to the postman.

"Thank you, Abner. How is your daughter? And the baby?"

"Thanks, both doin' nicely, Miss Amanda," he answered. And added inquisitively, "That letter ain't from 'Zekiel."

She looked at it, a swift involuntary glance. But she didn't have her specs on—she only used them for reading or doing accounts—and besides, this wasn't any of Abner's business.

"I'm very glad Minnie and little Wilbur are doing well, Abner," she said with dignity. "I'll be in to see her before supper with some chicken jelly. Very nice chicken jelly—Miss Lutie made it," she added, giving the little devil her due.

The postman said, "That's right kind of you, Miss Amanda. Well—"

He waited a moment, then added, "Well—g'day!" and turned and went down the path reluctantly.

I can't help wishing he'd never come up it.

Well, of course that isn't quite what I mean. But, anyway. . .

Because that letter changed the whole course of our lives. At least it was the beginning of what changed everything, and that's why that last exquisitely calm and peaceful Indian summer afternoon stands out with so many little details in my memory, and why I've lingered on it so.

I can't help feeling that as I stood there, under the honeysuckle and clematis vines that were so sweet on summer evenings, I had a premonition of disaster. Anyway, as I stood there I suddenly felt shivery, as if the day had grown colder all at once. Maybe that was because of the strange expression on Amanda's face, as she waited until the garden gate clicked behind the postman, and fished in her apron pocket for her spectacle case, and set her specs on her beaked nose. It was a strange apprehensive expression even before she had her first look at the long envelope in her hand. And it deepened to something like fright as she scanned the envelope. She knew then, I'm sure, that again Lutie's foolish irrelevant words were to come true, in that uncanny, incredible way they had of doing.

She picked up her scissors and slit the envelope neatly. I saw her hands shake, just a little. She braced herself, and read the letter through. She let it fall to her lap, and sat there with a bleak shocked look for several moments before she handed it, without a word or a glance, to her sister.

Lutie's bright blue eyes traveled over the letter swiftly. She drew a long breath, nodded, and her eyes clouded as she passed it to me.

She said, gently, "Poor little Zeke. I didn't really mean it. I wasn't sure—"

But it had happened. Ezekiel *had* passed away.

"...peacefully, following a stroke," the letter, from Motherwell, Krutch and Krutch, Attorneys-at-Law, informed the Misses Beagle, and went on, in an odd mixture of legal phraseology and stilted, old-fashioned sentiment appropriate to the occasion, to say that his earthly remains were now homeward bound to his sisters and East Biddicutt. "His last will and testament follows, by separate registered mail; also according to instructions placed in our hands five years ago, and never amended or revoked," concluded the epistle, which was signed, "Yours faithfully, Egmont Motherwell."

And a copy of the instructions was inclosed.

"Don't you telephone or telegraph the gals, Egmont Motherwell; and don't go traipsing out there either, unless they send for you. I don't want any alarums and excursions nor any claptrap at all. And not any fuss-and-feathers when they put me underground. But I can trust 'em for that. Just ship me home..."

My eyes blurred before I'd read the letter through, and I handed it back to Amanda. I didn't say anything, partly because I didn't know what to say and partly because I felt choky.

After a while Amanda stood up, very straight and more than usually stiff.

"No use sitting here like Stoughton-bottles. I've got things to see to," she said, and her step was firm and businesslike as she went into the house.

Lutie said softly, "She adored him, you know. And admired him too, for all her bluster. He was her big brother—"

*   *   *   *   *

But death wasn't a thing to brood over, or to be moodily sentimental about, for either of the sisters. They disliked the pomp and the parade of grief, just as their brother did.

His body came home that evening and was buried on the following day with simple quiet dignity. The funeral services were read by the Reverend Timothy Hawkins, who had known Ezekiel as a boy, and some of his old friends sent floral pieces. His sisters and I gathered all the chrysanthemums— there were three great snowy armfuls for him. And though we wore black, it wasn't the dismal crepe of ostentatious mourning.

When we got back from the churchyard where Ezekiel rested beside his father peacefully at last, Amanda led the way into the parlor. From the marble mantel, where she had laid it, she took up the long heavily sealed envelope that had arrived by registered mail that morning. She sat down in a carved rosewood Victorian chair, holding the letter in her black-gloved hands. But for some reason she didn't feel like opening it. She thrust it at me, abruptly.

"You read it, Marthy," she commanded.

I was surprised, but I took the envelope obediently. It had the address of Motherwell, Krutch and Krutch, 70 Maiden Lane, New York City, in the corner. I broke the seals. There was a communication from the lawyers, and another sealed envelope.

I said, "Which shall I read first?"

Amanda said shortly, "What Ezekiel says, of course!"

So I opened the envelope that was inscribed, "*My Will—Ezekiel A. Beagle,*" in Ezekiel's heavy black handwriting, small but very legible, and took out a sheet of paper in the same script.

It read:

I, Ezekiel Abidiah Beagle, being of sound mind and fairly sound body except for the choleric disposition and tendency to apoplexy inherited from my father, do hereby give and bequeath to my sisters, Amanda Beagle and Lutie Beagle, equally—or either of them surviving me—entirely all and everything of which I die possessed; to have and to hold, to sell, give away, dispose of or to manage. Or whatever they may damn well please.

Which is, of course, how my estate would pass if I died intestate. But I choose to record my intention and wish thus clearly, as a certain token of affection and respect.

EZEKIEL ABIDIAH BEAGLE

And the signature of two witnesses, and the date and the notary's seal.

I put down the will and looked at Amanda. Her head was turned away. She was fumbling for her handkerchief. She pulled the large white linen square out of her pocket, blew her nose loudly, and after a moment nodded at me to continue.

So I proceeded with the document from Motherwell, Krutch and Krutch. Shorn of most of its legal terminology it stated that, at the time of his demise, the estate of Ezekiel A. Beagle consisted of $15,000 in government bonds; $3,000 in a reserve account in the Farmers' Bank of America, and $1,999.01 in a checking account at the same bank. Besides which there was a separate sum of $350, to be used for his funeral expenses. To the best of their knowledge, there were no outstanding bills.

"And," the letter continued, "there is also a business, as you know, of fifteen years' growth and standing. The rent on the offices and on your late brother's apartment has been paid for a period covering the next three months, or, until January 1, 1939. The salary of his assistant and secretary is also paid for that period.

"The offices contain the usual office furniture, typewriting machines, etc. The apartment is furnished. We have not undertaken to estimate these assets.

"Concerning the value of the business, the files and records are undoubtedly important. Just how much so we cannot say. Goodwill, being so largely personal in a business such as your brother's, is quite impossible to estimate. But the license, and the number of regular and loyal clients—"

Lutie put her little hand on my arm and said, "Martha, do hurry, please."

"—will have," I read on, "a definite and considerable value in your disposal of the agency. Its long standing as a private investigating bureau of the first repute, must certainly be taken into consideration."

And the letter concluded, hoping to be of further service, etc., etc.

I put it down.

Lutie clasped her hands together.

She murmured, "A private investigating bureau . . . a detective agency. Well . . . !"

Her voice was low and soft. Ecstatic.

There was silence in the parlor.

I looked around at the marble-topped center table, the Brussels carpet, the stiff plush-covered chairs with their crocheted tidies, the whatnot filled with curios in the corner, the wax flowers under the glass bell on the mantelpiece. It was the room I liked least in the square white house. But I loved it as I looked around now, with a feeling of good-bye.

"What are you going to do, Sister dear?" said Lutie, at last, in a tiny voice.

Through the door into the dining-room where Rabelais hung in his cage there came a raucous shout, "G'wan, demmitall, get out! G'wan, you land-lubbers, get out of here!"

"Rab, be quiet!" murmured Lutie, absentmindedly. In the same tone she added, "I suppose we shall *have* to. Won't we, Sister?"

"What?" Amanda roused herself and turned toward her sister. "What are you mumbling about, Lutie?"

"Why, about going to New York. I know that's what you've decided."

She sighed. "Dear Zekie's handed us a trust, hasn't he? To you, really, of course, Sister. He knew you could manage it...though it's a little hard on us, Martha, isn't it? How will our garden grow—?"

Amanda said nothing for several moments. Finally she turned and looked at her little sister sternly. Her black eyes were glowing with a sudden, firm decision.

In a deep resolute tone that brooked no argument, she said, "After all, Sister, this is an important matter. Surely even Marthy and you can realize that. Ezekiel has imposed a trust on me. 'Gardens' indeed!"

"Yes, Sister, I know. I understand." Lutie's voice was very small and wistful. "I—I was only thinking—"

She clasped one little hand over the other, the picture of gentle resignation. I could have shaken her; and I was looking daggers at her, to the best of my ability—which is a rather poor best, I'm afraid.

But of course she wasn't paying any attention to me. She was seeing— I knew it perfectly well—quite other daggers: jeweled daggers, and poisoned darts, secret panels and veiled women, sinister men, sawed-off shotguns, murder cars and all sorts of awful and thrilling corpus delicti.

She drew a long breath.

But Amanda rebuked her. "This is no time for thinking—or sighing!" she snapped. "It's a time for action!"

The blow had fallen.

There were to be no more long peaceful hours filled with small homey tasks and pleasures, cheerful and cozy. Three days later the house had been put in apple-pie order, the shutters closed and bolted, the Spode, silver and linen stowed away. Neighbors had promised to keep an eye on things, Old Doolittle the handyman to look after the garden, and we were on our way.

In a compartment of the New York Express, with our luggage neatly stacked around us, Rab in his cage and Tabby protesting in a huge wicker basket, we sat waving from the windows at the crowd of friends who had come to see us off.

I smiled and nodded with the others, but I felt dazed and resentful. And when I thought of Old Doolittle pottering around my garden, and pictured the dear white house in its tall trees and clustering lilac bushes all left alone for the first time ever, I wanted to climb right off the train.

Of course I did nothing of the kind. I looked at Amanda, her stern face resolutely set toward her duty, and knew she'd go on with it through thick and thin without a whimper, though she was homesick already just as I was.

And I looked at Lutie, tiny and demure, her gloved hands folded meekly. Her blue eyes were bland and innocent. But I saw the delighted sparkle in their depths, and I thought, "Hmm—smug, that's what she is. This is *her* doing. She's got her way, as usual!"

Then I realized with sudden understanding that all her little quiet life she'd dreamed of adventure and excitement, and fed her dreams as best she could, and been as good as gold about it, really. Now finally she was to have her little fling, which meant at least a sight of the Big City; and probably she'd be disillusioned pretty quickly and we'd soon be back home. And my heart softened and I did hope, quite sincerely, that she wouldn't be too disappointed—not right away, anyhow.

Little did I know...

The whistle blew and the delegation on the platform began to wave wildly and shout final good-byes, and the wheels groaned and turned and the train started up and we were off.

Farewell, East Biddicutt!

CHAPTER 2

AT nine o'clock next morning we arrived at Grand Central Station.

Lutie gazed around her at the hurrying people and up at the vast blue dome above her. She nodded and smiled. I could see she had decided it was all very handsome and nearly as large and crowded as she had fancied it would be.

Amanda didn't have any time to look around because she was busy bossing the black men in red caps who had seized our shiny new trunk and the old round-topped one that had been her Pa's, his two ancient valises, my suitcase, a bundle of shawls, rugs and umbrellas and seven bandboxes all crammed to the lids with things she was sure we were going to find indispensable. But finally she had everything, including Lutie and me, herded and stowed safely in a taxi and had climbed in after us. Tabby was yowling frightfully. Amanda clutched his basket firmly, tipped the porters ten cents each, and raising her voice directed the taxi driver to 70 Maiden Lane.

I ventured, "But, Cousin Amanda, that's way downtown. Couldn't we phone them to meet us?"

She said, "Marthy, Ezekiel's lawyers suited him, no doubt. But they might not suit me. I'm not buying a pig in a poke. I'm going to see these gentlemen in their place of business."

I subsided.

As for Lutie, she said nothing. She didn't care how long the drive might be; in fact the longer it lasted the more pleased she was, I'm sure. She sat forward on the edge of the seat, her cheeks bright pink with excitement and the jet butterfly on her bonnet quivering, her eyes darting here and there, watching the thronged streets, the tall buildings, the gleaming shop windows. In his cage on her silk-clad knees Rab was quiet too—for the moment.

After what seemed to me an interminable hour of jolting, darting in and out of traffic and missing death by the skin of our tires, we arrived at a dingy building in downtown Manhattan and bumped to a stop at the curb.

Of course we couldn't leave our luggage in the cab. So Amanda motioned to the doorman and a large husky-looking fellow who was just standing around on the sidewalk, and together with our cabdriver they didn't have much trouble getting it into the lift. We managed to squeeze ourselves in too, and the car shot up to the fifth floor and deposited us in the corridor before the offices of MOTHERWELL, KRUTCH AND KRUTCH, ATTORNEYS-AT-LAW. Amanda made the men go in first with the luggage, because she wasn't going to let it out of her sight. She marched in and we followed her.

There was a nice, rather surprised-looking young woman there, who got up from the desk where she was typing when Amanda said that we wished to see Mr. Egmont Motherwell, and opened another door, and said, "Three ladies to see you, sir."

In went our trunks, bags, bundles and boxes, toppling rather dangerously as the men staggered under them a bit and grunted a good deal; and Lutie with Rab's bandanna-covered cage, and Amanda clutching Tabby's basket, which was heaving madly. I brought up the rear, carrying a morocco case that held our most special treasures.

A stout gentleman at the old-fashioned roll-topped desk swung around and stared. He had a round rosy face, a bald head and sideburns, and his tufted eyebrows were jumping up and down like startled doormats above the most astonished pair of eyes I'd ever seen.

Lutie pressed my arm and murmured, under cover of a yowl from Tabby, "Look, Martha—he's right out of Dickens!" while Amanda bowed with dignity.

She motioned to our burden-bearers to unload, watched while they did so, ordered them to wait in the outer office, and turned her attention to Mr. Motherwell.

"How do you do," she said, and as he managed to get to his feet, she continued, "I am Miss Amanda Beagle, and this is my sister Lutie, and my cousin Miss Martha Meecham."

He stammered, "P-pray be seated," and as we obeyed, sank back into his own chair.

His eyebrows were still leaping, but he was doing his best to get them under control.

Amanda settled the squirming basket on her knees, grasped it firmly, and her black eyes traveled from the gentleman's bald dome, over his immaculate waistcoat and looped gold watch-chain, down to his neatly shod and gaitered feet. She glanced around the well-appointed old-fashioned office, then back to Mr. Motherwell, and nodded.

"I am pleased to meet you," she stated.

"And now," she continued, "we will proceed to the premises of the Beagle Agency; and if convenient, Mr. Motherwell, I should like you to accompany us, with any books and papers pertaining to the business, now in your care. Naturally there are details to look into and doubtless matters to discuss as soon as possible. I wish to take charge of the business and continue it without delay."

Mr. Motherwell's eye-mats—I mean door-brows—well, anyway, they shot upward quite alarmingly.

He coughed. "A-arummph. I beg your pardon. But, er—do you mean— do I understand, Miss Beagle, that you intend to carry on the agency?"

Amanda frowned. "I have said so."

"But, er—that is, you mean personally? You, yourself?"

She said, "Naturally!"

"But—er—are you sure?"

A small voice at Amanda's shoulder put in very gently, "My sister is always sure, Mr. Motherwell. Her mind is quite made up."

He gulped. "But—er—"

"But—er, but—er, but—er wouldn't melt in his mouth!" A raucous croak issued from beneath the bandanna covering Rab's cage. "Demmitall—g'wan, get-a-move-on, blarst yer."

The cage on Lutie's knees teetered. Rabelais was getting restless.

Mr. Motherwell jumped and stared.

Lutie said calmly, "Yes, Rabelais. Be quiet, you bad bird."

Amanda drew herself up. She said stiffly, "We have discussed the matter sufficiently, and come to a decision. However, Mr. Motherwell, if you do not care to—"

A piercing "Mee-ow!" interrupted her.

"Yes indeed, we talked it all over," Lutie said sweetly. "But, after all, what else can we do? As Sister pointed out to me, it is quite plain that dear Zekie has given us a trust; that he wanted us to—ah, carry on. Of course, I'll admit I couldn't help hesitating at first. Sister is wonderfully capable—oh, she's extraordinary, dear Mr. Motherwell; you'll be surprised. But there is the matter of experience. Is it down her alley? I—I mean—"

She looked a bit flustered and blushed prettily.

"It's difficult to tell what you mean, Lutie Beagle, when you go wool-gathering down alleys!" snapped Amanda. "However, that's neither here nor there."

She rose.

"Yes, Sister," Lutie agreed meekly.

Somehow we packed ourselves into the cab again, bag and baggage—and Mr. Motherwell—and after another long ride stopped in front of a brownstone building in West Forty-fourth Street, one of those once handsome dwellings that wear a sad and apologetic air now, as if embarrassed at the nondescript uses to which they have been put. But it was in decent repair and the business signs in the windows were neat and not gaudy. It had seen palmier days, but it was still perfectly respectable.

Mr. Motherwell squeezed himself out of the taxi, and three boxes and the bundle of shawls and umbrellas toppled after him to the sidewalk. We followed, and Amanda commandeered more innocent bystanders, who seemed to have a way of collecting and gaping at us, and pressed them into service, and our caravan panted up four long flights of stairs. On the top floor at the end of the dim narrow hall was a door with a ground-glass panel lettered neatly:

THE BEAGLE AGENCY
LICENSED PRIVATE INVESTIGATING BUREAU
E. A. Beagle

Mr. Motherwell opened the door and a young man with much very red hair took his feet from a desk and stood up. He wore the pop-eyed expression with which the populace of New York appeared to favor us, and his lantern-jaw dropped as we marched in bag and baggage. But by the time Amanda had paid the carriers and cabman and dismissed them, he'd recovered his poise admirably, I must say; and he was smiling as the lawyer started to introduce him.

"Arummm—Mr. Mahoney. Mr. Jefferson Mahoney, the—er—late Mr. Beagle's—"

"—office boy—errand boy—stenographer—secretary—stooge—and chief cook and bottle-washer!" supplied the young man briskly.

He strode toward Amanda, thrust out his hand and said, "Howdy, boss."

Amanda shook his hand firmly.

"I am Miss Amanda Beagle— "

Mr. Mahoney nodded.

"Couldn't miss it. No one could. A ringer!" He pumped her arm and beamed. "You're certainly the spittin' image of his Nibs!"

A blush swamped his freckles and he stammered, " 'Scuse it, pliz. No disrespect meant to either of you!"

Amanda said, "Hmmph!" as a matter of course—and smiled! I don't know whether I've mentioned it before but she has a rare and beautiful smile. She controlled it quickly, however, and presented the young man to Lutie and me in a businesslike manner.

Mr. Mahoney beamed at us, shook hands and said, "Howdy! Please call me Jeff!" He had a boyishly engaging grin, I thought, and I could see that Lutie thought so too as she smiled up at him sweetly. "How do you do, Jeff?"

"My darnedest!" he stated blithely. And added earnestly, "I strive to please. I really do—"

"Don't strive too hard," advised Amanda dryly. "However, you might begin by combing your hair and fixing your necktie. They're a sight."

"They are that!" agreed Jeff cheerfully.

He yanked at his tie, whipped out a pocket-comb and raked it through his wiry thatch, which sprang on end again immediately. "You see? That's the kind of hair it is," he said gloomily. "Can't do a thing with it. Just like my disposition—no matter how it's squashed, up it jumps. Just like a jack-in-the-box. Just like hope that crushed to earth—"

"Just like those lovely balls of copper wool that clean pans so nicely," murmured Lutie. "I'm jealous. Mine's like the silly useless kind they put on Christmas trees—"

Jeff guffawed delightedly. "Miss Lutie, you've hit the hair on the head!"

Mr. Motherwell's hairless head seemed a bit befuddled by this nonsensical exchange, and the tufts over his eyes went down as he cleared his throat.

He didn't have a chance to say whatever he meant to, however, because Amanda snorted. "Come—that's enough tongue-wagging!"

But she turned her head to hide a funny small smile of amusement.

Jeff leaped to attention.

"My error!" he apologized briskly. "Well, first you want to mosey round the dump and get your bearings, don't you?"

Without waiting for an answer he made a large gesture, indicating the small room in which he stood.

"This cubicle is the reception room. Here I dispose of all who enter, thus—" He flicked a hand toward the hall. "Or usher them within. Thus!"

He waved us into a larger room. Amanda cast a backward glance at Tabby's basket. But it was quiet for the moment, and she followed Jeff, and we traipsed along. The room had two windows on the street, a desk and typewriter table, stiff chairs and a bench against one wall.

"The outer office," he explained. "Used for ordinary clients, routine business, and so forth. And this—" he indicated another door, "is the inner sanctum. This is where the Old Master sits and—" He stopped short, his lanky Irish face sobering. "I keep forgetting."

He opened the door quietly into a room with tall metal filing cabinets lining the walls, a great safe, shabby leather chairs, an ancient sofa, and a huge desk. Light came solemnly through a single window on a narrow court. It was an impressive room. Amanda's stern face approved it and Lutie's eyes were shining. Jeff's were fixed on the big swivel chair behind the desk, deserted now; and they were wistful.

Then he roused himself and murmured, "The King is dead. Long live the Queen."

And bowed toward Amanda, but soberly. And led us through a short hallway into a big living room, with a Brussels carpet on the floor, heavy comfortable furniture, and dark maroon rep curtains at the tall windows.

There was a hall room also, with a big walnut bed; a bath, a kitchenette, and a small room with a window on the court, which, Jeff explained, had been his lair. The living room faced south and the sun streamed in brightly. But below I saw the scrubby back yard, and beyond the thin straggling branches of an ailanthus tree were dreary rows of rear windows. A wave of nostalgia went over me.

I turned back into the room and Lutie's eyes were sparkling. I could see them in fancy pinning crocheted tidies on the chairs, redding up the place, putting knickknacks on the black marble mantel and new curtains at the windows.

Amanda drew her finger across the mantel shelf, and regarded its dust-smeared tip with primmed lips.

But she said only, "Jefferson, bring Tabby in, please. It's that wicker basket—"

She took off her flat black hat that was a sort of hybrid between a Queen Mary bird's nest and a pancake and then her cloak and gloves.

Lutie murmured, "Yes—we can put his sandbox on the fire escape. Only—I *had* thought of the Waldorf—"

"And what," asked Amanda, "would Tabby do in the Waldorf?"

"Oh, I *know,* dear," answered Lutie significantly.

Amanda's ears reddened in that way they have.

She said, "That will do, Sister!" and turned hastily to the lawyer. "We're wasting time, Mr. Motherwell!"

"Tsk, tsk—of course you are!" chirped Lutie, contritely. "You go right on now, Sister; you have all sorts of important matters to see to, you and Mr. Pickawber—I mean Mr. Micpickwick—well, anyway, I mean, dear, Martha and I will tend to all the little domestic details. And Jeff can help us—till you need him, of course."

She waved them gently toward the offices and turned to me with a blissful sigh.

"Martha dear, isn't it all wonderful?" She untied her bonnet strings. "Now, if we only have a beautiful big murder case very soon—"

"God forbid!" I exclaimed fervently.

"He doesn't, you know. Murders do happen. So we might as well have the benefit," she said serenely, and drew her gloves off from the wrists, turned them right-side-out, blew into them and pulled out the fingers carefully, as Amanda had taught her when she was a little girl.

I sighed also, though not blissfully.

But there we were, and all I could do was to make the best of it.

However, it was rather fun during the next week or so, settling the apartment.

There was plenty to do. Jeff and the Swedish janitor moved things around where we wanted them, and the janitor's wife helped with the cleaning, as she'd done for "Mister Zeke." There was a vacant rear hall room on the floor below, and Jeff moved his belongings down into it, and we fixed up the little room that had been his for my bedroom; and it looked quite cozy with some new cushions on the couch, and my green and red and purple afghan and my scarves and tidies, and some pots of ivy on the windowsill.

Ezekiel's huge bed was replaced with two smaller ones for the sisters, and there were dishes, cooking utensils and various other things to buy, too; and Amanda was busy getting acquainted with the business books and files, so she couldn't go shopping with us, and Lutie had a regular spree. The weather was clear and crisp, and she loved trotting around the noisy, crowded streets and the big stores, and even the musty little secondhand shops over on Third Avenue. We found a rocker there for her, and a straight, high-backed chair for Amanda, and a scrolled corner-whatnot for me.

"Just so you won't be too homesick, Martha dear!" Lutie twinkled up at me, and she patted my arm kindly.

Then she sighed dreamily and pointed to the pushcarts there under the El, with their dark, foreign-looking vendors and the shawled women bargaining for fruit and vegetables, neckties and cheap pink underwear.

"It's all so lovely. You can imagine you're almost anywhere." She smiled, and patted my arm again. "But I forget—you don't want to, do you, poor darling?"

I didn't, of course, want to imagine myself anywhere except back in the white house under the elms and maples. But that made me ashamed of myself. I didn't want to be a killjoy.

So I laughed and said, "Let's take a ride on the ferry to Staten Island and make believe we're going to Europe!"

Anyway, her delight was infectious.

But as for the detective business, there wasn't any.

At least none to speak of. A woman did phone hysterically that her pearl necklace was stolen and we must find it; but an hour later she called up to say she'd found it herself between the cushions of her chaise-longue. And a very intoxicated person made his way up the stairs, declaring loudly and tearfully that his wife was at a hotel with his best friend and he wanted somebody to go with him and break the door down. Jeff kept him in the reception-room while he came in and asked Amanda, "Do we take divorce cases? The Old Master nev—"

"We do not," replied Amanda. "When people get married they get themselves into trouble. They can get themselves out!"

Then there was a call from a man who wanted a guard at his daughter's wedding reception to watch the gifts, which meant phoning the staff of reliable men the agency had on call and a small percentage for the service. And that was the only actual job in ten days.

I said to Jeff—it was one rainy evening after supper, and he was helping me with the dishes—"Has the business always had flat spots like this? I understand a great deal of it was routine. But I suppose most of the regular clients have heard about Ezekiel's death, and that's why—"

"I'm afraid so," he said. "Well, anyhoo, I'm a country boy, you know! I bet I'll make a better handyman than Old Doolittle, come springtime in East Biddicutt. By that time Miss Lutie'll have had her little fling and they'll be calling it a day, I guess."

He hung up his tea towel, and at that moment there was a terrific flash of lightning and a crash of thunder that shook the house and left me shuddering. All the lights went out and Jeff said, "Zowie!" As they went on again he was grinning at me.

"Don't look so flabbergasted, Miss Marthy," he said. "After all, we'll have thunder'n'lightnin' in East Biddicutt too!"

I couldn't tell him why it seemed worse on the fourth story of a house in New York, but it did. Anyway, he was busily gathering up the ladder and a screwdriver, and I had those last little chores to do, setting the kitchen to rights for the night. By the time I'd joined the trio in the living room Jeff was hanging the ruffled curtains Lutie had bought that day and which Amanda considered a great extravagance.

She was saying so at some length, while Lutie, her head cocked like a little bird's, was directing Jeff.

"A teeny bit higher on that side, Jeffy. But, Sister dear, we haven't even touched our twenty thou—"

"Nineteen thousand, nine hundred and ninety-nine dollars and one cent," corrected Amanda. "Anyway, that is a business fund—"

"That's exactly right, Jeffy. I know, Sister, that's why I wouldn't think of spending it. In our next case we may need a large reserve to draw on for, er—well, lots of operatives and traveling expenses maybe and—and so on. 'Reserve fund'—that is what you call it, Sister, isn't it? Thank you, Jeffy dear."

Jeff descended from the stepladder, puffing slightly. He'd had three helpings of baked ham, sweet potatoes, apple jelly and hot biscuit and half a lemon meringue pie for supper, and I knew just how he felt. It's always been a miracle to me how the sisters keep thin and spry on Lutie's cooking—I know *I* can't!

And just then, shrill and startling, the telephone rang.

We stared at it rather foolishly for a moment. And somehow I thought of Abner the postman, coming up the little brick walk with the letter that had made all this change in our lives, and I felt my skin prickle with foreboding. I really did. Of course it wasn't clairvoyance, or anything like that; I was just on tenterhooks about *anything* happening. Because why on earth should we have a phone call at this hour? It was nine o'clock, with wind and rain lashing the windows. There could be no *good* reason.

Jeff said, "Must be a wrong number," and made for the phone.

But Amanda had picked it up. She held it gingerly—it was one of the newfangled kind we don't have in East Biddicutt, and she hadn't yet learned one end from the other.

She said, "Hello...Yes, this is the Beagle Detective Agency." She listened and with a slightly surprised look said, "What?" And after another pause, slowly, "I see...Yes...Yes...Yes...Certainly, Mr. Bynam, I have the address, and we will be there as soon as possible!"

She hung up and turned to us.

"A gentleman named Mr. Bynam—a client of several years' standing, as I recall of course, having gone through the B's—has found another gentleman in bed. Not in his own bed, nor in Mr. Bynam's—in a young lady's bed—or so I gathered, though Mr. Bynam seems somewhat upset and incoherent. Anyway the circumstances are peculiar; it appears the gentleman in bed is decapitated, and our client wishes us to proceed at once to the address he gave me. It is in Forty-eighth Street, West, so we can get there very quickly."

She strode to the wardrobe and had her hat and cloak off their hooks before Jeff had recovered enough to gasp, "De-decapitated—? Miss Amanda, did he say decap—? Oh, I get it. Incapacitated!" But then he shook his head and frowned. "No, that won't do either. Listen, boss, this is all wet. John Bynam's twenty-seven, good-looking; from an old family upstate, lousy with dough, but he's all on the sober side—never got in a scrape in his life. It's screwy. I tell you, it's—it's just stuff-and-nonsense!"

Somehow I had an inane impulse to giggle hysterically at Amanda's pet phrase from her assistant's stammering lips. But she, ignoring it, was putting the cat out on the fire escape.

"Hurry, Tabby—we're waiting!" she urged. And as she waited she stated firmly, "As I mentioned, Jefferson, I have gone through the B's. Therefore I am fairly well acquainted with our client, Mr. Bynam, through the cases we have handled for him . We supplied guards at his sister's wedding reception; and, later, of course, to watch her infant son during a kidnaping alarm. We also established the innocence, which our client and Ezekiel never doubted, though it appears the insurance company and the police did, of a Bynam servant suspected of theft; and traced another theft, recovering a prized heirloom; and conducted a search, which was not successful, for a missing person. Also, the files contain a very complete and satisfactory record of Mr. Bynam's antecedents and so forth."

"Have we ever," murmured Lutie, and I turned and saw that she had on her little sealskin jacket and her bonnet and was covering Rab's cage, "handled any murders for him before?"

Amanda snorted. "Certainly not, Sister! Murders do not grow on trees, even in New York City—even for wealthy young men with family trees!"

Tabby, lifting wet paws in deep disgust, stepped back through the window and his mistress shut and latched it behind him.

Lutie smiled, a small deprecating smile at her own foolishness. "Of course they don't, Sister; I was only hoping—thinking...Be a good boy, Rab!" She gathered up her gloves and her black jet reticule.

"Don't forget your galoshes, Sister!" admonished Amanda. She thrust her knitting into her capacious handbag and grasped an umbrella.

I made for my wraps and motioned to Jeff. It might be screwy and stuff-and-nonsense—and I prayed to goodness it was—but they were on their way, with or without us, and I certainly didn't mean it to be without us.

Neither did Jeff, naturally. He looked at me, shook his head and muttered wildly, "It's a crazy rib, of course!"

But he grabbed his hat, yelled, "Wait for me, baby!" and dashed after Amanda and Lutie, with me at his heels.

CHAPTER 3

IT was pouring rain, but we got a cab without delay, because Amanda stepped out in front of one and flagged it with her umbrella and told the cabdriver (who was using very bad language indeed, as he skidded to a stop) that we were detectives, and he mustn't waste words and he must make haste.

He looked as if he thought we were lunatics, but he didn't waste any more words and he did make haste. We splashed through the rain-swept streets, careened around corners, and before I'd caught my breath we were sliding to the curb in front of a narrow brownstone house much like the one we'd just left, except that instead of business placards it had a "Furnished Rooms and Apartments—Inquire Within" sign in the basement window, and it happened to be on Forty-eighth instead of Forty-fourth Street.

We hurried up the high stoop and Amanda pressed a button under one of the names and there was a "click-click" and Jeff pushed the door and we went in. A door at the back of the hall opened and we followed Amanda toward it. A tall, dark young man stood aside as we entered.

Amanda said, "The Beagle Agency." She introduced us each by name and asked, "Mr. Bynam?"

He nodded. He looked dazed and very haggard.

He said, "But where's Zeke?" He peered vaguely over our shoulders and added in a strange monotone, like a person in a nightmare, "I didn't know what to do—"

Lutie put a small gloved hand on his arm and pushed him gently toward a chair. He collapsed into it, and she drew a small flask from her reticule and held it to his lips. I recognized the bottle. It was the one she always kept in the medicine cabinet for emergency purposes and was filled from time to time out of a stock in the cellar in East Biddicutt, that Pa—I mean Uncle Abidiah—had distilled by freezing apple cider in the cask, some fifty years ago. I knew we'd brought a supply with us to New York, but I hadn't noticed Lutie slipping any of it into her reticule.

However, she was saying now, "Drink this, my dear," and the young man gulped and opened his mouth like a small boy taking medicine from his auntie. I gasped as she tipped the flask until quite half its contents had gurgled down his throat.

"There!" said Lutie cheerfully. "Now just sit quietly for a moment and soon you'll feel much better!"

If he can feel at all! I thought, knowing that brew from the one and only time I'd sampled it, when I had flu. He groaned faintly, and put his face in his hands. I wrenched my eyes away from his hunched figure—it seemed cruel to stare as I realized I'd been doing—and followed Lutie's bright gaze about the room.

This was, or had been when the house was young, a back parlor. It was furnished now with a worn rug, a shabby overstuffed sofa, and some pieces in flamboyant taste—a French desk, a tall chair with a carved and gilded back, a table with a Florentine mosaic top—that looked as if they'd come from a theatrical set. But the apartment was cozy; there were chintz curtains at the windows and the double doors leading to the front parlor, flowers, and a deep chintz-covered wing chair near the embers in the marble fireplace; beside it stood a table with an amber-shaded lamp, a telephone, a magazine and an open sewing basket.

The little clock on the desk ticked softly while we waited for the man crouched in the armchair to tell us why we were here.

Jeff, who'd been staring at John Bynam in a puzzled way, started to speak. But Amanda forestalled him.

"And now, Mr. Bynam," she said calmly, "will you please show us the body?"

He raised his face and a shudder passed over it, whether at her words or from the effects of the brandy, I couldn't tell.

He said, "But—but you can't go in there—" and looked at her childishly and rather piteously. "I wanted old Zeke. I didn't know what to do—"

"That's why we're here," stated Amanda, firmly. Lutie patted his arm. He passed his hand across his forehead and drew a long trembling breath.

"I can't think. It's a nightmare." He turned slowly toward a closed door. His face was gray with horror. "It's in there."

His hand shook as he pointed.

Amanda set her lips and marched forward. Lutie trotted after her eagerly.

My knees were weak, and I glanced at Jeff and saw that he was scared too. My feet seemed rooted as they are sometimes in dreams, and I hadn't the slightest idea they'd move. Yet somehow I found them doing so, and I was right there behind Lutie, with Jeff at my shoulder, as Amanda stretched out her hand to the doorknob and turned it.

We stood looking into a small room, dark except for the shaft of light that entered with us. Vaguely we could see a dressing table, a chair with a blue cashmere negligee trailing across it, and beyond that a bed. There was a sprawled, still figure on the bed.

Lutie pressed a gloved finger on the light switch.

And we saw that the figure on the bed was that of a man, the legs in checked trousers, the stockinged feet limp. He hadn't a coat on, and the once white shirt was horridly dark. The shoulders lay in an inky pool. And above the shoulders there was—nothing.

As I shrank back against the door-frame, I saw Amanda's face. It had turned a peculiar, greenish color. I heard Jeff gasp.

And in a kind of blur I saw Lutie step to the side of the bed, stand there looking down quietly, bend over. I saw her take off her glove, and touch one of the outflung hands thoughtfully. She lifted it, held it close to the lamp on the bedside table, scrutinized the back, turned it palm upward. An expression of surprise crossed her intent face. She peered carefully at the fingers of the hand she held, then gently laid it down, raised and examined its mate.

I heard Amanda's voice, oddly weak, "I must question our client regarding the—head—"

She backed out of the room.

Jeff whispered hoarsely, "Miss Lutie—come away! We've gotta phone the police—"

Lutie glanced up at him then.

She said sharply, "Not until I tell you to, Jeffy. Go in the other room and sit down!"

He obeyed her, precipitately.

"Martha, come in or go out. But shut the door!" she commanded.

She seemed a tiny unreal figure seen through the wrong end of a telescope. But there was complete determination in her clear tones, her pink, unterrified face, her blue eyes now darting busily about the small bedroom. I couldn't leave her there alone. I managed to reach behind me, grope for the door and close it.

I stood there leaning against it, speechless, and watching Lutie in a kind of awful fascination.

She replaced her glove and started trotting around the room, looking closely at the floor beside the bed and stepping carefully, noting the masculine coat and waistcoat flung across its footboard, the brown shoes nearby, and the small silk mules beside the slipper chair, the robe thrown over it. She peered at the negligee; then, her attention caught, removed her glove and fingered the robe thoughtfully. After a moment or two she put the glove on again, looked into a closet, and inspected the bathroom. Presently she returned to the bedside, and I nearly fainted as I saw her pick up the checked coat.

I tried to speak, to stop her—but all I achieved was a choking sound.

She said, "Sshh!" and shook a gloved finger at me, then poked it delicately into a pocket.

Deftly, swiftly, she went through the coat, the waistcoat. She shook her head.

As she stood, speculatively regarding the figure on the bed, I had a frightful moment. I knew she hated to leave the possible clues its pockets might contain.

I pleaded, "Lutie—please *don't!*"

She ignored my frantic whisper. I doubt if she even heard it. But just then a peremptory command came from the other room.

"Sister, what are you doing? Come back in here at once!"

Lutie started. But I realized that she'd decided, though regretfully, against any further search. Turning away, she pressed the light switch, opened the door, and giving me a small push closed it behind us.

"Yes, Sister," she answered dutifully.

"Boss, I'm telling you—" Jeff was saying, "if we don't get on that phone and call the cops there'll be h—"

Amanda raised her hand. Her face was still slightly greenish, but she was again in command of herself—and of us.

"Jefferson, be quiet!" she snapped, then added, "You are quite right as to the necessity for wasting no more time. We have already been here—" she glanced at the clock on the desk—"five minutes; during three of which, Sister, we have been waiting for you. But," she faced John Bynam, "we came here to help our client, and I think we should hear his report before we send for the police. Will you let us have it, Mr. Bynam, as briefly as possible?"

Lutie smiled approvingly as she perched herself on the French settee, folded her hands and fixed her eyes on the young man. I sank down somewhere and sat staring at him, too.

His hands were fists on his knees, the knuckles white. He raised his drawn face toward Amanda.

"You've just told me old Zeke is dead," he said, dully. "But you look like him. He was such a rock. Strong and wise and courageous. That's why I called him. I couldn't get Hester—Miss Gale—at the club. I'm—the whole thing is so ghastly—unreal—"

"It *is* very dreadful, of course," said Lutie gently, "but you mustn't think of that. Just tell us what you know."

"You look like my Aunt Savina in Quantucket." He almost managed to smile at her.

She patted his arm. "Tell us, my dear."

He drew a long breath.

"At about seven o'clock this evening I phoned Hes—my friend, Miss Gale—and asked if I could come to see her here at nine o'clock. She said I could. I got here a little before nine. But when I rang there was no answer. I thought maybe the bell was out of order—it had been, before—so I went down to the basement. The landlady lives there. But she wasn't in either. I was standing there in the basement area when a young man came out the upper door. He's a lodger—we'd seen each other before—so I explained about the bell and he let me in. But when I knocked at Hester's door there was no answer. And suddenly I felt terribly anxious—"

He stopped himself, glanced at us quickly, and went on, "It's utterly unlike her to break an appointment. So I felt very uncomfortable, and I decided to go in—"

He looked at Jeff, whose expression, I noticed myself, was peculiar—*knowing* is the best way I can describe it; and John Bynam flushed angrily.

"Yes, I had a key, as it happens." He kept his voice even with an effort. "I had returned with Miss Gale last night from the Harmony Club—she is a singer there—and I took her key and unlocked her door for her, and thoughtlessly put the key in my pocket. So, of course I had it with me this evening. I wanted to return it and leave a note, too; I was expecting to leave New York for a week or two; that is, unless—"

He broke off again, went on hastily, "Anyway, this evening I unlocked the door, turned on the light and started to scribble a note. Then I looked up. The bedroom door was open...the light fell across the bed. I—went in there."

His hands twisted. He set his jaw.

"That's all. I still can't believe what I saw there—"

"And then," asked Amanda, "you called us?"

"I phoned the club first—it's the only place where I thought Hester might be. But she wasn't there."

He stood up and began to walk up and down the floor.

"That's got me half crazy, too. Where is she? What's happened to her? She doesn't know anybody. She's only been in New York a few months. She hasn't any friends or—or anything—except me. If—if anything's happened to her—"

Amanda said, quietly, "There isn't anything else you want to tell us before we telephone the authorities?"

He stared at her rather wildly, started to say something, set his lips in a straight line and shook his head.

"No—no. But can't we *do* something? Can't we get that—that thing," he pointed, "out of here somehow—somewhere?"

"Yes, but where?" said Lutie in a dreamy voice.

"Lutie Beagle, don't be idiotic!" snorted Amanda. She nodded at Jeff decisively. "You may call the police now, Jefferson."

"I don't suppose it would be practical. But it would be exciting," murmured Lutie, and sighed, as Jeff seized the phone and began to dial.

I heard him say, "Headquarters? There's been a murder. Yes …Yes… Yes. No, there's no *doubt* about it—the *head's* cut off…Yes!"

He gave the address and hung up, mopping a moist forehead.

"They're on their way."

"And while we're waiting," said Amanda, "we must all try to calm ourselves." She drew out her knitting, adjusted her specs, and looked over their rims at John Bynam.

"And now, Mr. Bynam, have you any idea as to the identity of the body?"

I thought, what a foolish question! For of course he'd have told us if he had. Well, it was like Amanda to want things stated in black and white. I expected to hear an impatient denial.

But instead of that the clock ticked in a strange silence for several moments. We all stared at John Bynam, waiting for a reply.

Finally it came, slow, measured, deliberate, "I have never seen the man in there in my life."

The words dripped into the quiet of the room like icewater. I don't know why they were so frightening. I believed them, somehow, absolutely. And yet—there was something unsaid, something behind those carefully chosen words, that turned me cold.

Amanda said, slowly, "I see, Mr. Bynam. You don't wish to confide in us." Her knitting needles clicked. "I'm sorry. I think we could help you better if you chose to be frank."

He said, miserably and yet earnestly, "I have told you everything I know.

Please believe me." His haggard eyes beseeched her. Then he dropped them, stared at the floor. "It's not real—this hideous thing, here in Hester's rooms. There's no sense in it—no reason—"

"Stuff-and-nonsense!" exploded Amanda. She set her lips, and her needles, like her eyes, flashed furiously. I knew she believed him—and didn't; she was sorry for him, and angry. "Excuse me, John Bynam, but there's always a reason for what happens. And we're here to find it, with or without your evasions!"

It was very uncomfortable.

I looked at Lutie, who had left her chair and wandered to the little desk in the corner. She caught my eye and beckoned to me.

"What lovely flowers—look, Martha. Brown orchids, I think—and tame carrots, aren't they? I mean, they're not quite wild carrots—"

I joined her thankfully. She touched my arm, and, still chattering, indicated a sheet of paper lying on the blotter.

I glanced down and before I knew it was reading:

"Hester dear—Here's your key that I stupidly carried off last night. I wanted very much to see you this evening; I had a letter from Aunt Savina today and may have to go to Quantucket. But I hate to leave. Will you be very care—"

Here the note broke off with a blob and splatter of ink marking the trail of the pen beside it. I felt a guilty qualm at having read it, and an unkind desire to blame Lutie for having made me do so, which of course she hadn't. But while I was thinking that and wishing I were well out of all this mess and far away, she nudged me again, and I followed her glance and saw what she meant. If the door to the bedroom were open the bed could be plainly seen, and the light would fall squarely on its ghastly burden.

"I hope you don't mind, Mr. Bynam," I heard her say then. "I read the note to your friend. Of course I wouldn't under ordinary circumstances. But I thought we should notice whatever the police will be sure to—"

He started up with an exclamation and was about to seize the sheet of notepaper. But she grasped his arm, firmly. "No, leave it there! There's nothing they shouldn't read, and it confirms your story about the key! Don't you see? Why, you are flustered, aren't you? Poor dear! Now, do sit down. I didn't mean to upset you."

She pressed him back into a chair, and went on talking cheerfully.

"I haven't looked in here—have you? I think we ought to—" and, beckoning to me, she opened a door into a small kitchenette. There was a tiny electric stove, a sink, wall shelves with scalloped paper, a wooden table. The smooth, shining folds of a simple blue evening dress fell from a padded hanger hooked over a towel rack high on the wall, and a folding ironing board stood in the corner. It was a very clean, tidy little kitchenette, with nothing especially interesting to be seen.

Or so I thought. But Lutie's bright eyes traveled about it eagerly. She appeared to find everything interesting.

Especially the table, which I wouldn't have looked at twice except that she did, and then I noticed merely that the legs were painted blue and the top was unpainted, and looked perfectly new. Lutie stooped down and peered up at the under edge, fingered a shred of something hanging there; glanced around at the floor. I followed her glance and saw, on the clean blue-and-white-checked linoleum, several small gleaming objects—thumbtacks, of course.

Suddenly I caught her idea, and shuddered.

She stood up, opened the table drawer. There was some flat silver in a tray, a wooden salad set, a few kitchen utensils—an egg beater, a pancake turner, a ladle, a large fork and spoon and small paring knife—all with blue enameled handles. She opened the bread tin, which held half a French loaf.

Lutie shut the box, gazed once more around the kitchen.

She murmured, "No flatiron—?"

"Sister!" called Amanda. "Come in here—and sit down!" As Lutie obeyed, she added crossly, "Do stop fidgeting. It's very trying!"

"Yes, Sister." Lutie folded her gloved hands meekly. Her eyes weren't meek, however—they were excited, sparkling. I knew she thought she had discovered something. And vaguely I guessed what. But it seemed farfetched to me—preposterous, in fact. And anyway, where did it lead to?

"If," said Amanda, and I knew from her tone that in spite of herself she was on edge, "you would only knit. Besides being a useful accomplishment, it is a great help on occasions like this, as I have often told you—"

A long loud ring of the doorbell interrupted her. She jumped, then composed herself firmly as Jeff sprang to answer it.

A big policeman shoved into the room, the rubber raincoat over his blue uniform dripping at each step.

He said, "What's the trouble here? Where's the—"

Then his eye fell on Lutie, demure and dainty, wearing a bright interested smile. And on Amanda, knitting.

His jaw dropped.

Before he'd recovered, two more officers arrived. They pushed in excitedly, then they, too, paused and stared. I wished Amanda would stop knitting.

"What the h— What is this?"

Jeff said, "The body's in there." He pointed.

They glared at him angrily. I really think they believed this was all some sort of hoax. But they yanked open the bedroom door, fumbled for the light switch.

One of them said, "My Gawd—"

He came out of the room, breathing heavily. He jerked his thumb over his shoulder.

"Take a look in there, Schwartz."

Schwartz (he was the precinct patrolman—the other two were from a radio car, I learned later) stopped gaping at us as if we were lunatics, and joined the man in the bedroom.

The man who had first emerged from the "chamber of horrors" backed to the hall doorway and stood there, covering us with an eagle eye. I felt as though he were also covering us with a gun.

He said gruffly, "Nobody's to leave these premises—"

"Nobody intends to, young man," Amanda rejoined shortly. Outside in the street an ambulance clanged. "As it happens, we are here, like yourself, in the interests of—"

But she was interrupted by the entrance of a young ambulance surgeon, brisk, white-coated.

He said, "Hi, Brady. Where's the—?" And following the direction of Brady's thumb, hurried past us to the inner room.

He was still there—in fact it was only a moment later when there was the sound of more heavy footsteps tramping through the hallway. Half a dozen men—it seemed to me like many more—trooped in.

Jeff, at my side, said, "The Homicide Squad—"

Lutie sat forward eagerly. Amanda, thank goodness, put her knitting down on her lap.

The slender gray-haired gentleman who led the squad paused and stood looking gravely around. Yes, even in that moment I noticed that he was a gentleman, and that his gray suit was chosen and cut with distinction. But what I noticed most were his eyes, also a stony gray, intelligent, piercing. They took in our group in a calm, unhurried survey.

As the officer called Brady showed him to the bedroom door, Jeff whispered, "Inspector Moore." There was more than a tinge of awe in his voice.

As for me, I huddled down in my chair. Though Inspector Moore didn't look to me like a policeman, he was not less, but more, formidable for that.

I wished we were well out of all this.

I prayed that Lutie hadn't disarranged anything during her investigations.

I thought with terrified guilt of the time we'd allowed to elapse before we'd called the police. I wished Jeff's necktie was straight and his hair not so wildly tousled, and that John Bynam would get hold of himself.

And I hoped Amanda wouldn't begin to knit again, and most of all that she'd be polite to the Law.

You couldn't flaunt the Law—especially when it had eyes like that.

But I realized that my cousins were quite capable of doing so, each in her own way.

CHAPTER 4

SO I sat, shivering with apprehension, while Inspector Moore was closeted in the bedroom with the body and one of his men took our names and addresses. It was obvious that the name of John Lane Bynam caused a considerable stir by its connection, whatever that might prove to be, with a murder. But even so the oddity of our presence—three elderly and, doubtless, respectable-looking ladies in an apartment where a man lay horribly killed—was not overshadowed.

Amanda's calm statement that we were the Beagle Detective Agency, a licensed private investigating bureau acting for our client, Mr. John Bynam, didn't seem to help much either.

I caught an incredulous murmur from the background—"screwballs!"—which except for my recent acquaintance with Jeff's vocabulary I wouldn't have understood, and I'm sure Amanda didn't. But Lutie did, as I guessed from a peculiar expression that flitted across her demure face. It wasn't displeased. On the contrary, she looked as if butter wouldn't melt in her mouth, I daresay, to anyone who didn't know her. But to me she looked exactly like the kitten who's swallowed the canary—or is about to.

While my foreboding was aggravated by this realization our attention, and that of our questioner, was distracted by the opening of the bedroom door. The young ambulance surgeon came out—not quite as breezily, I noticed, as he had gone in. He shrugged his shoulders, but made no other comment; and being completely ignorant of the customary procedure in a murder case as I then was, I felt somewhat surprised to see that he was evidently departing, and without the corpse, which I'd vaguely expected would be taken away immediately in the ambulance we'd heard clanging from the street.

As he stood respectfully aside for a round, pleasant-faced little man who was just arriving, I heard him say, "D.O.A., sir—and how!"

Of course I didn't know what the letters stood for—and even thought hopefully that perhaps he was saying, in code, that the murder was already solved.

The newcomer, who wore gold-rimmed nose-glasses, a tiny patch of black mustache, a black felt hat, and carried a black bag, was taken at once to the bedroom. He certainly looked like another doctor, but even so I didn't know what Jeff meant by his murmur, "The M.E.!"

Lutie, however, noticed my uncomprehending expression and elucidated. "The medical examiner, my dear; the gentleman who just arrived," she told me kindly. And added, "And D.O.A.—that means the, er—patient was found dead on arrival."

Amanda said "Hmmph!" and I knew she was thinking, "So it takes two doctors to find that out!" as clearly as if she'd spoken the words. But she did refrain from speaking them, thank goodness, for I'd already noticed one of the squad—a bulky individual in a hideous chocolate-brown suit—frowning ferociously in our direction. I expected him to rebuke us sharply for whispering (I'll never wonder at anybody looking guilty at the very proximity of murder!). But whatever the detective meant to say he hadn't time, because just then the inspector rejoined us.

He gave some orders and two of his men, lugging paraphernalia that was mysterious to me at the time (I afterward learned the men were a photographer and a fingerprint expert), went into the bedroom.

And then I didn't notice anything else that was going on, for the person who'd taken our names passed them to his superior, and Inspector Moore turned his attention to us.

He scanned the bits of paper in his hands, while the note-taking detective waited, his stenographer's tablet opened to a fresh page. The gray man regarded our client thoughtfully.

But the first thing he said was, "I was acquainted with Ezekiel Beagle." His voice was cultivated, his manner easy and pleasant; he might have been meeting Ezekiel's sisters at home in East Biddicutt as he addressed them. "You both, I think, resemble him."

"So," replied Amanda, rather stiffly, "I have been told. For my part I see no likeness. However, people seldom do—I mean, realize what they look like—"

"Thank you, Inspector," said Lutie sweetly, lifting gentle wide blue eyes.

"Anyway," said Amanda, and folded her long steel needles inside her knitting, "I don't see what that has to do with the price of putty." She opened her capacious bag and put her work away. "We're here to help solve a murder."

She removed her spectacles, and her black eyes met the inspector's gray ones firmly.

He nodded.

"Please tell me what you know about it, Miss Beagle."

"Well," said Amanda, "at eleven minutes past nine we received a telephone call which I answered, from a gentleman who said his name was Bynam—John Lane Bynam. I had not then met Mr. Bynam; but knew him to be a client, as his name is in our files. He said—I'm not quoting his precise words, which were agitated and seemed slightly confusing—that there had been a murder in the apartment of a friend of his, a young lady. I replied that we would be with him as soon as possible.

"At twenty minutes past nine we arrived at the address he had given me. This address.

"Mr. Bynam showed us into the bedroom. We—saw the body." Amanda paused. "As—as soon as possible, we asked our client a few questions. I daresay you'll want to ask them yourself so I won't repeat them, nor his answers.

"At twenty-nine minutes past nine, our Mr. Mahoney telephoned to the authorities. That, I assume, was you.

"We have not any idea as to who committed the crime; but naturally we mean to investigate and to find out. We will be pleased to work with the police; but of course we must use our own common sense. That," concluded Amanda, "goes without saying. I mention it simply that you may know where we stand."

Inspector Moore said gravely, "Thank you, Miss Beagle." While Amanda talked he had jotted down a few notes; he regarded them thoughtfully before he continued, "What you have told me is admirably concise and specific. May I ask, for the sake of the record—" he smiled very slightly "—whether you, er, have any idea as to the identity of the murdered man?"

"No," replied Amanda.

"You had never seen him before?" The tone was casual, but the gray eyes were watching her with close attention.

"I didn't say that; how could I, under the circumstances? That," Amanda said judicially, "is a foolish question. I can only say that what I saw of the body, which may be that of a woman, so far as I know, does not suggest any person of my acquaintance."

I looked at the inspector to see how he would take this. But apparently he did not resent Amanda's outspoken opinion of his query, nor consider her reply quibbling or evasive. Seemingly he understood that she was simply being accurate, and I thought I perceived a definite gleam of appreciation—and was there a twinkle of am a amusement also?—in the narrow eyes that had seemed so formidably cold and keen.

He nodded, glanced again at his notes.

"You mentioned the hour and minute at which you received the telephone call from Mr. Bynam, and when you arrived at this address, and when Mr. Mahoney telephoned the authorities—how did it happen that you made such precise note of the time and remembered it so exactly, Miss Beagle?"

"It didn't happen," Amanda corrected him. "I considered the occasion one in which the element of time was very likely to be of importance. So naturally I took note of it. I have never known my watch to be inaccurate."

She indicated the small neat timepiece pinned securely to the bosom of her black silk bodice by a plain gold brooch.

"I see," said the inspector. He added, "Such foresight is unusual."

She knew that well enough. But she was not at the moment interested in compliments. That it was a compliment she took for granted; while I, nervously, wondered if the polite words concealed sarcasm, possibly doubt. Amanda merely primmed her lips. She said nothing.

But Lutie, beaming with innocent pride, murmured eagerly, "Isn't it, Inspector? But Sister is unusual in so many ways!"

Amanda frowned. Inspector Moore turned his attention to the little pink-and-white creature smiling sweetly up at him. I got the impression that his expression hardened—oddly enough, because that is not the effect that Lutie customarily has on people. I could only infer that he was sizing her up as a silly little thing, with her frivolous jet butterfly nodding above childish blue eyes and interjecting her inconsequential observations, and expected that she was going to be a nuisance.

Probably she was, I thought. But not in the way that he supposed.

However, he made no comment. His thoughtful glance passed from Lutie, to me, to Jeff. Then to John Bynam, where it rested.

"Now, Mr. Bynam. May I have your statement?" said Inspector Moore, and his tone, his manner, had undergone a definite change. It was still perfectly civil, but "steely" somewhat describes it, and no velvet glove disguised it as he added, "I must warn you that whatever you say may be used against you."

I was conscious, too, of the heightened interest of the detectives and policemen as they craned forward to listen. The atmosphere was tense, and every eye riveted on our client.

He, however, had pulled himself together, and though still pale and haggard, he was now quite self-possessed and his tone quiet as he addressed himself directly to Inspector Moore.

Beginning with his telephone call to Miss Gale, "at about seven o'clock," and his arrival at her residence "at nine, or a little before," the account was substantially the same as that he had given us.

He did not emphasize the anxiety he had felt on receiving no response to his ring, then to his knock on the door of his friend's apartment, but merely repeated that it was unlike her to break an appointment. So he had decided to go in and leave her key and a note saying that he expected to leave New York immediately, probably for a week or so.

He explained matter-of-factly how he happened to be in possession of the key to Miss Gale's room, without the annoyance he had shown at Jeff's significantly knowing look when he had reached that point before, and ignoring the skeptical expressions on the faces watching him now. Not, I will say, on Inspector Moore's, which remained impassive.

"I was writing at the desk when I happened to glance up and in the direction of the bedroom. The door was open and the light fell across the bed. I went in. I saw the body on the bed."

As John Bynam said this quietly, without faltering or even glancing toward the door he had just mentioned, it opened and the round little man—the M.E.—came out.

As he shut the door behind him, set down his bag, and wiped his bald head with a large white handkerchief, everyone stared at him—that is, everyone but our client and Inspector Moore.

The latter merely said, "Excuse me for the moment, doctor," and never took his eyes from the tall young man gazing back at him with an equally unwavering regard.

"And then what did you do?"

"I telephoned the Harmony Club, thinking that possibly Miss Gale had been called there for some reason, before the usual hour for her appearance. But she was not there, I was told.

"Then—my attorney being out of town—I telephoned the office and residence of Mr. Ezekiel Beagle—"

"Who croaked more'n a month ago," put in the large man in a chocolate-colored suit.

"McGinnis, I'll ask you for any information you may have, when I want it!" said the inspector sharply. "Yes, Mr. Bynam?"

"I did not know of Mr. Beagle's death," said John Bynam.

"Why didn't you telephone immediately for the police, Mr. Bynam?" Inspector Moore's tone was cold.

Jeff shifted uneasily in his chair.

Amanda opened her lips to speak, shut them again.

Our client replied slowly, but quietly enough, "It was a great shock, finding a horrible crime had been committed in my friend's apartment. I thought of old Zeke—of Mr. Beagle—as a person to rely on, to advise me. I don't know what I expected him to do, or how he could help me. I called him on an impulse."

"And when *Miss* Beagle answered your telephone call?"

Our client glanced at Amanda with a slight embarrassment. "I—it didn't occur to me that—I took it for granted it was Mr. Beagle—"

McGinnis grunted.

There was a tiny smile on Lutie's face.

"If you ever heard my sister's voice on the telephone—especially on these newfangled contraptions—you wouldn't be the least bit surprised at that, Inspector," she volunteered, brightly.

He ignored this interruption.

"You were very much agitated, Mr. Bynam?"

Amanda pinched her lips tight again.

John Bynam replied, "I was, naturally—"

Amanda opened her lips.

"Even I was, for a moment. Even your policemen, who I suppose are used to many unpleasant sights, didn't seem to take this one altogether calmly. Even the doctor there—" and she nodded her head toward him "—seemed pretty flabbergasted. Agitated—hmmph! Who wouldn't be?"

I knew who hadn't been. She sat now, beaming proudly as usual on her Amanda. But I prayed that no one else would know, or guess, the extent of her composure—her deliberate audacity—in the face of that unpleasant sight that had flabbergasted even her sister.

Jeff, as he told me later, shared my trepidation. He knew Lutie had been poking around where she had no business to; and if the chief found that out, or if the boss kept on giving him a piece of her mind when she felt like it, my hunch was that we'd be thrown out on our ears pronto, as he put it. And somehow he didn't want that to happen, even though he was heartily wishing we'd never got into this mess.

In spite of my nervousness, however, I was listening carefully as Inspector Moore went on with his interrogation of our client. The questions were asked and answered briefly, and the replies received without comment.

"How long have you known Miss Hester Gale?"

"Five months."

"Have you mutual friends?"

"No."

"Do you know any of her friends—or acquaintances?"

"No. Unless you would call a few people at the Harmony Club, and the other lodgers here, some of whom I have met in passing, acquaintances. And the landlady, Madame LaVelle, who seems to be fond of Miss Gale."

"You do not know any of these people well?"

"No."

"Have you any idea where Miss Gale may be, since she is not at the club?"

John Bynam said, "No." His composure deserted him for a moment and his terrible anxiety showed in his face.

"I am—extremely anxious about her. Where could she go—and on a night like this? Why didn't she leave me some word—or—or phone me if she knew she wouldn't be able to keep our appointment here? Only I can't imagine—"

He broke off. His knuckles were bone-white marbles across his tensed fists.

"I must phone the club again. She *may* be there by now—"

Inspector Moore said, "We are in communication with the Harmony

Club. Miss Gale is not there."

Then he asked, "Where were you, Mr. Bynam this evening, before you came here?"

John Bynam did not reply at once. Then, seemingly with an effort, he dragged his mind back from its anxiety concerning his friend and applied it to the inspector's question.

"Where was I?" he said, still somewhat absently. "Why, I came here directly from my office. That's downtown, in the Bynam Building."

The inspector nodded, glancing at the loose notes he held.

"Yes, I have the address here. You were at your office, then, since—?"

"I was there all day," answered John Bynam rather impatiently, as though this interrogation were interrupting more important matters. Then, as if realizing its trend, he smiled. "Oh, I see. You need my alibi, of course! Well, I was there from about ten o'clock this morning, with time out for lunch, but not for dinner. At a quarter to seven I had sandwiches and coffee sent in. There were some odds and ends to attend to, as I expected to go out of town tomorrow morning. At eight-thirty, I left, took the subway, and came here."

The inspector scribbled a note. He said courteously, "You had your secretary—or some of your office force—working with you till then?"

"No. I dismissed my secretary at six-thirty, and the office boy when he'd brought in the tray with my supper. That was late enough, Lord knows—the rest of the staff had gone around five, as usual—"

"You were working alone, then, until eight-thirty? Did anyone see you leave the building? You understand, Mr. Bynam, these questions are necessary. Of course you need not answer them."

The young man looked amused, rather than concerned. But he replied soberly enough, "I understand, naturally, Inspector. But I'm afraid I can't answer that one. I didn't happen to see anyone when I left. My office is only on the second floor, with a stairway right next to it—I seldom use the elevator. The night porter, who goes on at eight o'clock, may have noticed when I left—his desk faces the door. But as to that you'll have to ask him."

"Thank you, Mr. Bynam," said the inspector, and made another note. Then with no change of tone he added, "Is there anything you know which might lead you to connect this murder with Miss Hester Gale besides the fact that it was committed in her apartment?"

John Bynam's figure stiffened. He said, "No!" emphatically and quickly. I thought, with a sinking feeling, too quickly. Hastily, was the way it sounded.

And on the heels of his denial came Inspector Moore's next question. It was one that, subconsciously, I had been dreading.

"Have you, Mr. Bynam, any idea as to the identity of the murdered person?"

But this time John Bynam said, "No," and I breathed with relief. For this time there was no overemphatic hastiness, nor was there any hesitation. The peculiar manner that had seemed to mark his answer to Amanda, when she had asked that question, was entirely absent. Perhaps he had prepared himself; anyway, his "No" was a simple, positive and convincing negative. So much so that I thought I must have been imagining things before. I thanked my stars.

I thanked them again as Inspector Moore put his memorandum in his pocket, apparently finished with us for the time being, and turned to the medical examiner, who had been polishing his glasses and listening attentively to the interrogation of our client.

"Well, Doctor—"

The M.E. glanced in our direction, raised his eyebrows.

"Want my notes, or shall I read 'em?"

"Let's hear them."

The doctor put his glasses back on his nose and patted the toothbrush mustache beneath it rather as if to make sure it was still on straight. He took out a black notebook and flicked its pages.

His enunciation, it occurred to me absurdly, was like the mustache: neat, clipped, a bit bristling and pompous, as if put on for the occasion. And somehow it was so droll, yet fetching, and his round face and birdlike eyes behind the twinkling lenses so pleasant and reassuring, that in spite of the undoubtedly gruesome details with which he was about to regale us, I caught myself wanting to smile!

"Hmm." He cleared his throat and began reading, "Body, male, white. Age: between twenty and forty—probably about thirty. Height, approximately five feet eight, nine inches. Weight, not over hundred-fifty, nor under hundred-thirty-five—probably hundred-forty-three…Hmm. Approximate time death: not less than one hour nor more than three hours before time body examined. No rigor; blood—great quantity, from severed neck—not yet completely dried…Hmm.…Preliminary examination shows distinguishing marks: one-inch curved scar on back right hand near thumb, deep narrow depression of flesh circling fourth finger left hand, abrasion knuckle same finger…Hmm…Fingertips both hands heavy scar tissue, apparently burned acid; healed, no characteristic whorls as yet reforming; should say time of burning, approximately year to six months ago…"

Here he paused.

McGinnis' breath whistled between his teeth. "Fingertips burned—wheew—"

Someone else exclaimed, "A con!"

The doctor held up a slender, sensitive-looking hand.

"Death occurred instantly, no struggle; while lying bed in approximate position found by medical examiner…Hmm. Cause of death, stab wound in heart; wound made by single heavy blow, narrow sharp instrument; width of blade, approximately half inch widest part entering body, length at least six inches. Instrument missing."

He closed the black notebook, tucked it in an inner pocket, and concluded, "Body decapitated at least several minutes after death. Head hacked off, several blows large knife, not same instrument causing death...Hmm. Knife, missing. Head, missing...Hmm... And that's all I can tell you, Inspector, until the autopsy."

As the medical examiner finished his report, the photographer and the fingerprint expert emerged from the bedroom. The little doctor left then, and while he and the inspector exchanged a few words in the hall, a buzz of comment, query and exclamation broke out among the detectives and policemen. Fragments of weird jargon flew about our heads, and certainly over mine.

"Sure, two chivs, Doc says...Yeah, cold meat before they bopped his noggin...Uh-huh, we gave everything the double-oh—no dice...Must've stashed 'em-with the knob...One of 'em was a briar—wanna bet? The guy hasn't got an out...Yeah, but he's no palooka...The jane's copped a heel...Night club femme, ain't she?...Well, the stiff's a canary bird, all right...Sure, no calling cards ...A scar on one of his dukes...Nope, not a thing in his jeans...What about the old dames?...Playing with the squirrels if you ask me!...Phonies—wanna bet?...Nope, the chief thinks they're on the level...Well, it's some setup!"

As I tried to make some sense of this hodgepodge—which I don't pretend is correctly reported, and of which there was more that I don't begin to recall—I glanced across at Lutie.

She sat, with her head cocked, and two bright pink spots like wild roses in her cheeks, drinking it all in. And evidently understanding much of it too, I thought, marveling!

Then, as Inspector Moore reentered, there was the sound of the outer door slamming, and a moment later a policeman escorted in the most oddly spectacular figure I had ever seen.

CHAPTER 5

ENVELOPED from chin to ankles in a man's heavy trenchcoat streaked with rain, and topped by a huge picture hat, this apparition towered above its uniformed companion. The floppy velvet hat with its long limp ostrich plume rode a mass of frizzed orange-red hair, beneath which was a gaunt face powdered dead white, wide lips painted a deep crimson, and, set in sockets smudged with purple shadow, a pair of narrow, startlingly green eyes.

These eyes gazed around haughtily. Then, holding a dripping umbrella in one hand and a long beaded handbag in the other, the tall thin woman advanced into the room. Or perhaps I should say she made her entrance, and paused in the center of the stage.

"And what," she articulated, in a deep, musically modulated voice, "eez ze meaning of all zees, seel-voo-play? Eef you please!"

Everyone stared. Inspector Moore stepped forward. Behind him John Bynam stood up quickly. The tall woman swept across the room to him.

"Ah—Meestaire Bynam—Zhon!" she exclaimed, then paused. Her voice sank another octave. "Pairhaps you weel explain?"

John Bynam said, "Madame LaVelle, I—do you know where Hester—"

Inspector Moore cut in. "Mr. Bynam, I'll do the talking. Will you be seated, Madame?"

The lady regarded him, her chin raised, her narrow, green eyes looking down her impressive nose grandly but shrewdly. She inclined her head.

"I am Madame Juliette LaVelle."

Someone—I think it was Jeff—pushed forward a chair. It was the gilded one with the high ornately carved back. With an effect of swirling draperies she threw open her drenched coat, arranged her long bedraggled green velvet skirt, and seated herself as on a throne.

"I am seated, M'soo. And now? Pairhaps you weel favor me weeth your name!"

"I'm Inspector Moore, Madame. A crime has taken place here in your house—I understand you are the landlady of this lodging house?"

Madame LaVelle stiffened.

"I don't call it a lodging house!" She stopped short, continued, "I am ze proprietaire of ze Maison LaVelle, wee." And abruptly, "What kind of a crime? Have those Fennellis—?"

She caught herself. Then with admirable composure she resumed her former manner.

"Thees eez all most extraordinaire. But eet must be eemporrtant, eenspector, seence you are here—n'ess pah? So—I am at your ser-veece, M'soo."

She settled herself back in her throne.

Inspector Moore said dryly, "Thank you. Then you'll answer my questions as simply as possible." He paused, then shot out, "Who are the Fennellis? And what did you mean by your remark concerning them, just now?"

"Well, it just popped into my head. You see, those Fennellis—" Madame LaVelle cleared her throat. "Voo savvy, Eenspector, ze cleeontel de la Maison LaVelle eez theatrical. And so, sometimes, zey are temperamental. But I've got a pretty good eye for people, and most of my lodg-—Zat ees to say, I am a good judge of char-ac-taire; so I seldom have any trouble weez my guests, voo compren-ee?"

"Oui," said Inspector Moore. Then he bit his lip. "I understand English, Madame LaVelle; don't bother to translate. About those Fennellis—?"

"Ali, mais certainment!" She inclined her head graciously. "Zoze Fennellis, zey are vaudeville artistes, zey are acrobats, and zey are Latin. Zey occupy ze second floor aparr-rtments, just above zees one." She waved her hand toward the ceiling. "Raphaelo Fennelli eez ze star-rr of ze troupe; he eez variee talented. And supposed to be handsome, but if you ask me…Parr-rdon, I do not care for ze type, but zat eez n'importe. Voila— Raphaelo had a wife; she was also a membaire of ze troupe, and vairee beautiful and a Gr-reat Artiste.

"Some months ago she left heem, weethout a worr-d of warrning. She wrrite heem a lettaire, saying zat she have met a man who really appreciate her; zees man eez called Floto, ze Flying Wonder, and zey weel have an act togethaire wheech weel be a gr-reat noveltee and make zem both reech and famous.

"Zees eez a terreeble shock to Raphaelo. He swearrs he weel have vengeance. Sometimes he swearr he weel keel heem, sometimes he swearrs he weel keel her; onlee, he does not know where to find zose two! So zen he swearrs he weel cut heez own throat. When he gets that way Mike Fennelli, his brother, gets sore. And just last week Raph was flourishing a knife around, and Mike grabbed it—they had quite a set-to. And I tell you I'd have put 'em out, but they've been coming here for years, and Mamma Fennelli cried and said it didn't amount to anything. I didn't think it did either; of course Raph's got a kinda crazy look in his eyes I don't like, I think he's a bit nuts, maybe, but mostly bluff. Mellow, that's what he is—but just the same I don't like him cutting up in my house!"

She paused, then asked, "So—what happened? Was it the Fennellis? But what are you doing here in Hester's rooms! And who—?"

She nodded toward us, then pulled herself up. "Parr-don, who are zees ladees, seel-voo-play?"

For once Amanda did not answer first. Madame LaVelle really seemed to have taken her breath away. Anyway, she was staring, as if petrified. But Lutie replied.

"My sister, Miss Beagle." She smiled proudly, indicating Amanda. "And our cousin, Miss Martha Meecham. And our young friend and assistant, Mr. Jefferson Mahoney. I am Miss Lutie Beagle. We are the Beagle Detective Agency, my dear," she explained simply. "And we're here to—"

Inspector Moore cut in. "Never mind that, please. Now, Madame LaVelle—"

But Madame was not listening to him. It was her turn to stare at Lutie, at Amanda, at me.

"What do you know about that!" She drew a long breath, let it out again. "Well, I'll be hornswoggled!"

And suddenly Amanda's face relaxed, the puzzled expression vanished. She bowed toward the landlady.

"How do you do!" she said, in belated but warm acknowledgment of Lutie's introduction. And she smiled her rare charming smile!

Inspector Moore was not interested in these amenities.

"Madame LaVelle," he began again, "I want your attention. There are a few questions I wish to ask. You needn't answer them, of course; but it will simplify matters if you do."

"Why shouldn't I answer them?" said the landlady, with a certain acerbity. She frowned, but the extraordinary green eyes were as candid, the tone as matter-of-fact, as Amanda's own. Or so it seemed to me. And Amanda herself was nodding and smiling again at this odd, contradictory creature.

"Because," Inspector Moore replied, "we are investigating a murder. The body," he added slowly, "is in there." He made a slight gesture, indicating where.

"A—a murder? In there? In—in Hester's bedroom?" The landlady started up, and her beaded bag slipped to the floor as her hand went to her painted lips. I can't say she paled, because you couldn't tell under the mask of powder; but I'm sure she did. "Oh, God—it isn't—? You don't mean anything's happened to Hester?"

"No. No, Miss Gale isn't the victim," said Inspector Moore.

Madame LaVelle sat down again; this time without any grand manner. Her knees just gave way beneath her.

She said, "Oh—thank God!" Shakily, but with a note of deep relief. Then anger flooded over her, replacing fright. She glared at the inspector. "What's the sense in scaring the daylights out of me? Well, who was murdered, then?"

"That," he told her, "we don't know. And now, since you have no objection to answering questions, suppose you let me ask them."

While he was speaking a swift change came over the tall thin woman. The green eyes narrowed even more remarkably. I guessed that the inspector's tone when he'd said, "Miss Gale is not the victim," with a slight significant stressing of the last word, had just sunk in. But except for that momentary sharp flicker of the strange eyes her face had become more mask-like than ever, and her mien again like a queen—or perhaps I should say, the impersonation of a queen.

"M'soo, I am at your sairveece. Prrroceed. J'attend."

Inspector Moore frowned. "Can't we dispense with the—er, French? This isn't a scene on a stage, Madame."

"Par-rdon ?"

He shrugged. "Never mind, do it your own way. Now, one further question in connection with your acrobatic lodgers. Are you acquainted with Fennelli's—er, rival? Flato, the Floating Wonder—or whatever his name is?"

"Floto, the Flying Wonder," supplied Amanda.

"Ah, you have ze good memoree!" Madame LaVelle bowed graciously. "No, I have nevaire met heem," she told the inspector.

A detective, who had left the room some minutes ago, reentered and said something to his chief. The latter nodded.

"The Fennellis are not at home, it seems. Have you any idea where they might be?"

"May wee, certainment! Eef zey are not ar-rested, as I first thought, zey weel be at work! Of course!" Madame LaVelle pronounced the word "work" with impressive emphasis, almost reverently. "They play Loew's time. And they're good, too—even if they are crazy wops. They always have work."

"What time did you leave the house this evening, yourself? And where did you go?"

"Quel oor? Ah, let me reflect. May wee, I remembaire; eet was twenty-three minutes past seven, exactment, when I left ze house. Where deed I go? I went to ze ceen-e-ma. To ze Grotto. Ze peecture, *Love in the Rain*, ees not bad—come see, come sah—but, ah, zat Zhohn Barrymore—zere eez an actorrr—!"

"Twenty-three minutes past seven exactly, you say? How did you hap—how can you be so definite as to the time?"

"Because, on ze way out, I stop to speak weez ze young man who have ze parlor front—Meestaire Vincent Smeeth. I have come from here—from Meez Gale's apar-rtment. I knock on heez door. He invite me een. We chat a minute. He observes my attire—he remarks zat I go out? I say wee, I go to ze ceen-e-ma. He remark zat eet eez a stormy evening. I tell heem wee, eel pluey—may phut! Eet eez nothing—I go to ze ceen-e-ma every evening, rain or shine. He inquire ze name of ze peecture—he say he may go heemself, pairhaps—and what time does eet start? I tell heem eight-feefteen…But there was a Mickey Mouse first, and I didn't want to miss it. He'd pulled out his watch when he asked me when the show started—so I asked him what time was it, and he told me. Seven twenty-three. I had to hurry. So that's how I know. I was just in time for the Mickey Mouse—"

Lutie was leaning forward intently, bright-eyed and eager. But Inspector Moore didn't want to hear about Mickey Mouse, apparently.

He cut in, "You say you came from Miss Gale's apartment? Did you see Miss Gale? Were you in the apartment?"

"Ah, may wee. Yes, of course I was."

"Was Miss Gale alone?"

"Not aftaire I entaired," replied Madame LaVelle.

Somebody snorted. The inspector frowned.

"Go on, Madame," he commanded curtly.

"Go on, M'soo? You weesh me to—?"

"Tell me what you saw here. Could there have been any other person, say, in the bedroom? Was there anything unusual in the girl's manner? Anything you noticed?"

"No, there wasn't. And there couldn't have been anybody in the bedroom, because I went through, to the bathroom, with some fresh towels. Of course if somebody was *hiding* in the closet or under the bed I wouldn't have seen 'em—I didn't look! As for there being anything unusual about Hester's manner...When I go een she eez reading a book while she eats a sandwich and drinks a glass of meelk. Zeez young girls weez zeir diets— zey do not eat enough to keep a birrrd alive. Am I fat? I ask you!—and I don't starve myself—never have. Anyway, I geeve her a piece of pie. I scold her for not eating enough. She laugh, but she thank me for ze pie. Eet eez good pie—I make eet myself, voo savvy. So I watch while she eat eet."

Lutie and Amanda were both regarding the landlady, with grave attention, and, it seemed, approval.

She continued, "Zen, she take ze dishes in ze kitchen, wash zem, put away ze bread and ze knife, all vairee tidy, and wipe ze oilcloth on ze keetchen table. She's neat as a pin, that girl—no roaches round *her* kitchen, like some lodgers bring. Zen she ask me to parr-rdon her, but she must press a dress for ze evening. And she say she must get a new frock...voo compree, she cannot wear ze same ones all ze time, in her work. She say her favorite blue one eez torn, but she theenks she can cut off ze bad place in ze train and hem eet again.

"So she got it out of the closet and trimmed off the torn place and fixed it and started to press it. I went along then—except I stopped to tell her she must wear a warm coat and take a cab too—it was such a lou—a storrmy night. Hestaire eez not like many girls, jumping into a cab to ride a few blocks when they owe a month's room rent... She eez a vairee good girl— vairee quiet too—almost too quiet for such a pretty young thing. Anyway, she laugh and ask me eef I take a cab to ze ceen-e-ma? But I say zat eez deeferent—ze Grotto eez only three blocks, ze Harmony Club eez a dozen...Besides, I'm as strong as a horse."

Inspector Moore had strolled across the room, pausing at the small table beside the wing chair in which Amanda was installed—the table that held the tall majolica lamp, the current periodical, the sewing basket, and the telephone.

The landlady looked gravely at John Bynam. "You know, John, the child must be more careful of herself; she must think of her voice. It is very beautiful. While as for me it doesn't matter—" She drew herself up. "That eez," she gazed mournfully around at the rest of us, "Eet matters no more— seence I have re-tir-re from ze stage." She shook her head and her long earrings swayed and jingled. "I tell Hestaire zat. She keess me and say, 'Sarah, you're a darling!'—She call me 'Sarah,' voo savvy," Madame waved her gnarled hands and her bracelets clashed, "because of my resemblance to ze Gr-reat Bernhardt."

I followed the inspector's eyes. Lamplight shone softly down on the open sewing basket and its homely clutter: spools of silk and cotton, stockings rolled into small neat balls, a little red pincushion shaped like a tomato, packets of needles, a darning egg, a silver thimble.

What was he looking at so intently? He reached out, lifted the magazine, then the cover of the basket. There was nothing there—only a ragged scrap of blue silk crepe.

Then, with a start, followed by a sinking feeling, I realized what was missing.

But Inspector Moore made no comment on what he hadn't found.

He said, rather absentmindedly, "I see. Yes…Now, will you give me a short statement about the other people who live in your house, Madame? Begin, please, with yourself."

"With myself?" She drew herself up. "Well, what do you want to know?"

"I understand you room in the basement—is that correct? Do you live alone? How long have you lived here?"

"I live alone; I own the house; I have owned it and lived here for seven years. And I occupy ze entir-re basement apartment!" she replied. And so haughty was her tone and the accompanying large wave of her hand that she might have been saying, "I occupy the Tuileries!"

Then she sat back and inquired grandly, "And—what else, M'soo l'Inspector?"

"Well—that lodger in the parlor front. The young man you mentioned. What do you know about him?"

"Zat he came here a week ago; zat he say he eez an actor-r; zat he eez not wor-rking, but expects an engagement next week. Zat he comes from Hollywood—and he doesn't think it's so hot. I guess he's like a lot of 'em that can't get into pictures. But, anyway, he's paid up two weeks in advance. Because, as I told him, unless I know people I can't afford—"

"Certainly, certainly." The inspector nodded. "And on the second floor, the one above this, there's the troop of acrobats—the Finales—"

"The Fennellis, Inspectorr," she corrected him. "Mamma Luisa Fennelli, Pappa Luigi Fennelli, Raphaelo, Michelangelo, and ze daughtaire, Lotta Fennelli!"

The Fennelli family, it seemed, occupied the whole second floor. The time was, said the landlady, when they had rented the parlor floor also, whenever they were in New York. They always wrote to her ahead of time, and no matter what other guests might have these apartments, she would arrange to accommodate the Fennellis. But that was when Dolores, Raphaelo's wife, was with him. They always liked the parlor rear apartment—"theez aparrtment—" because it was "nevaire noisy."

And on the third floor, a Mrs. Joffey had the large front room. "A retired lady—wardrobe mistress until her legs went back on her; but she was smart; she saved her money and bought an annuity."

In the front ballroom there was a Miss Dot DeVeere, "a modelle—but not as young as she used to be, poor thing."

The third floor rear was occupied by a Professor Sesame, a magician.

"He's good, really high-class," said Madame LaVelle. "He always has steady work in vaudeville, though most of those ham magicians are out of luck nowadays. He's working at the Regatta Theatre, and besides, this week he's in the floor show at the Bowerie. That's a nightclub down on the Bowery—sort of an imitation old-fashioned joint. But tray chic, voo savez, ze rage. And expensive as the devil. It's certainly a feather in Sesame's cap to get on there. They laugh at him, you know, that's the idea, hooting and so on, old time stuff. But just the same he wouldn't be there if he didn't have plenty on the ball...Zat eez to say, *talent!*"

Then Madame LaVelle paused, and said gravely, "And on ze top floor resides Meestaire Sinjun. Spelled *S-a-i-n-t J-oh-n.* And a vairee gr-reat arteeste, a tragedian. He interprets Shakspear-re, Eeebson, all ze classeeks. He has been weeth me five, nearly seex years," said Madame proudly. "And I'm telling you," her green eyes flashed, "if the managers had the sense of a—" She stopped short, shrugged, and added in a flat tone, "Behind his is the trunk room, then the girl's room—"

"Girl? Name, please," requested the stenographer, glancing up from his notebook.

"Ze maid, Chloride," Madame explained. "She does not sleep here often, she prefaires to go home to Har-rlem, to her husband...Though what good he is to her—just takes her money and calls her 'Sugar.' Well, they're all alike and she's not as bad as most. She gets here at seven in the morning or I know the reason why! And back of hers is the room Miss Gale had when she first came, eight months ago. A very small room—there's a young man there now. A Meestaire Paul, a dancaire, but not wor-rking at ze moment. In fact, he hasn't worked since he came. But what can I do? He's a good kid—and a good hoofer, too. My Gawd—mon doo, times are not easy, are zey not? They are not! And that's all," concluded the landlady. She folded her hands.

Inspector Moore said, "Thank you." He added, "Madame LaVelle, what did Miss Gale use to cut the torn hem from her dress?"

"What?" Brought up short by his tone and the abrupt change of subject, the woman stared at him. "Why, the shears, of course! And a fine sharp pair they were, too—I'd often borrowed them. Why?"

She looked around at the rest of us. A sudden tense silence had fallen on the room.

Madame's voice rose. "Well, what's the matter with all of you?"

The inspector didn't answer. He was standing, looking down again at the little sewing basket there under the lamp.

She repeated, "Well? What are you staring at?"

He said, "Nothing, because they aren't here. Nor anywhere else about the place, so far as we've seen. And now, Madame LaVelle, I guess you'd better have a look in here."

The tall woman rose slowly and followed him to the bedroom door. He opened it. The light was already on...

I turned my head away and closed my eyes besides. I heard her gasp.

Then her hoarse whisper, "My Gawd—my Gawd—my Gawd! It's—it's the fellow that rented the parlor front! Oh, my Gawd—it's Smyth!"

On "Smyth" her voice rose to a thin shriek.

McGinnis said roughly, "Oh, so it's Smith! *And just how would you know it's Smith?"*

The only answer was a strangled moan.

"Control yourself, Madame. And speak up, please!" That was the chief.

I heard the bedroom door shut. I looked up then.

The landlady was backing away from that room, her staring eyes like green marbles in a chalky clown's face, her lips a crimson O encircling black horror.

"Those—those checked pants...and brown shoes...and that scar on his hand! Oh, Gawd—who did it?"

We were all standing. Someone led her to the sofa. She sank down into a corner of it. Lutie was quickly at her side, the flask of apple brandy at the woman's shaking lips.

I glanced at the inspector. He stood watching the scene—as though, I thought, it might have been taking place upon a stage.

At this moment there were more footsteps in the hall; the door opened. A large blue-coated officer stood there, a slim figure at his side: a young girl in a dripping raincoat and a wet felt hat. Light brown hair curled damply on her neck, and wide dark eyes, in a small pale face, stared around the room.

John Bynam cried, "Hester!"

His arms caught her, held her close, and she seemed to wilt against him. But only for an instant. Then she straightened resolutely.

"What is it, John—what's happened?" Her low voice was strained, but quiet. "They—they wouldn't tell me anything—"

He said, "Darling—darling! Where were you? I've been crazy—"

Inspector Moore touched his shoulder.

"Just a minute, Bynam!"

But Amanda had stepped forward. She thrust the men aside.

"Let the child alone, both of you!" She took the girl's arm firmly, led her to a chair and sat down beside her. "Now, my dear, get your breath."

The girl's eyes went slowly around the strange assemblage in her living room: the slender steely man watching her intently, the other strange men and policemen; Madame LaVelle, huddled on the sofa, her hat askew, the rouge on her lips smeared like fresh blood; the small, elderly person demurely replacing a flask in a black jet reticule; John Bynam's haggard face; and the calm woman beside her.

"Please—what's happened? Who are you?"

"Something very unpleasant, my dear." Amanda answered the questions in order. "I am Amanda Beagle." She named the rest of us quickly, concluding, "and Madame LaVelle of course you know. She has had a shock, and it seems to have knocked her galley-west." Amanda's primmed lips expressed her disapproval. "But I'm counting on you to control yourself—"

Inspector Moore cut in curtly. "Miss Beagle!"

To the pale girl he said, "I'd like to ask you a few questions, Miss Gale."

John Bynam said roughly, "She doesn't have to answer your questions! Hester—"

"Miss Gale," the inspector's smooth, crisp tones overrode this interruption, "a man has been killed. In your bedroom."

Hester Gale stared at him, a peculiar expression in her eyes. She said slowly, "Killed? You mean you—?" Then she frowned, as if puzzled, and repeated, "In my bedroom! But why had he—I don't understand it!"

Inspector Moore made no reply, and I saw, with a feeling of anger, that he was watching the girl with the same thoughtful expression he'd had for Madame LaVelle's collapse. It wasn't exactly skeptical, but quite obviously he considered that he might be dealing with clever histrionics. And I couldn't believe this girl was acting. There wasn't a hint of guilt or terror about her. She was startled, and—yes, the really peculiar look I'd noticed in her eyes was something like relief.

But that was only for an instant. Then suddenly every bit of color left her face; it became all at once years older, desperate and despairing.

She cried, "John, this is horrible! Oh, why did I—?"

John Bynam was kneeling beside her, gripping her hands. "Hester, listen to me!"

She said wildly, "What happened? Did—did—?"

He said roughly, "Hester, look at me! There's the body of a strange man in there, in your bedroom. Who he is—how he got there—who killed him—

we don't know. Only that Sarah just identified him as a new tenant. Some-one must have—"

"What? A—a tenant?" She stared at him strangely. "But—you mean it isn't—?"

"Isn't—who?" the inspector shot at her.

"Hester, don't answer! Moore, she doesn't have to answer your ques-tions!" John Bynam sprang up, facing the other man. "You can't force her!"

The inspector shrugged. He didn't reply to this outburst directly. To the girl he said, rather wearily, "A murder has been committed. It is my duty to warn you that anything you say may be used against you. If you prefer not to speak without legal advice, you needn't do so. If you have no guilty knowl-edge to conceal, however, you might save yourself a great deal of trouble by telling us frankly who that is in your bedroom—"

"For mercy's sake!" snapped Amanda. "Inspector, how can you expect the child to tell you who it is? She hasn't even seen it."

Inspector Moore turned on her sternly.

"Miss Beagle," he said coldly, "I'll have to remind you that I am con-ducting this investigation. And we are not Down East in Bidville. So, if you please—"

"Bidville!" snorted Amanda. She drew a long indignant breath, expelled it, and followed it with a vehement rush of words. "Well, Inspector, I am surprised at you. Sakes alive! You're a good, well-meaning man—that's as plain as the nose on my face; and smart enough, too, by-and-large, I dare-say. But if you can't even get the name of Biddicutt straight, how are you ever going to straighten things out around here, I'd like to know? And I don't mind telling you, since you started the subject, that the sheriff—our Sheriff Googe—has a better memory than you have. And it's too bad we aren't in East Biddicutt, I declare!" She concluded with another snort.

I looked from Amanda, fearfully, to the inspector. I heard Jeff give a kind of groan. He said afterward, "Why we weren't tossed out then and there, I don't know!" I didn't know either.

Because it was perfectly obvious there was something the girl, Hester Gale, was on the point of revealing; something John Bynam also knew or suspected, about that dreadful thing in the next room. And equally plain that Amanda's speech, simply flaunted in the face of authority, was meant to divert attention, befuddle the issue. I gathered myself together for departure.

But there is something about Amanda that has a strange effect on people. And it didn't fail this time. I actually thought I saw that momentary flicker of appreciation I had caught—or fancied I'd caught—once before in the gentleman's shrewd gray eyes.

Anyway, all he said was, "East Biddicutt. Yes, I should have remem-bered, Miss Beagle; I've often heard your brother mention the town, too."

Then he turned back to Hester Gale.

"Miss Gale, I'd like you to look in here."

He put his hand on the knob of the bedroom door.

The girl's mouth set in a grim line, and her eyes were like burnt holes in a sheet that's had too much blueing. But she stood up, holding her chin high, and walked steadily toward the door.

John Bynam caught her arm. "Hester! Inspector, does she *have* to—to look at that?"

She didn't even seem to hear him. But at a light touch on her hand she turned quickly, looked down, startled, at blue eyes under a fringe of silver curls and a quivering jet butterfly.

"Please, Inspector—it will be a shock to the child—may I go in with her?" Lutie's voice was soft, pleading.

He didn't answer, but opened the door. The girl clutched Lutie's hand.

Inspector Moore moved aside and Hester Gale took a step forward into the room.

She looked, put her hand up to her face, drawing it across her eyes vaguely, and looked again.

Her knees crumpled under her. John Bynam caught her as she fell.

CHAPTER 6

HESTER GALE sat between Lutie and John Bynam on the Victorian sofa, looking small and frail in her blue tweed suit. She was pale, with dark shadows like bruises beneath her eyes, but she looked back at Inspector Moore, who had drawn up a chair facing the couch, quietly, with composure.

As John Bynam stood in the door from the bedroom with the limp figure of the girl in his arms, Amanda had said calmly, "Put her here, John," and yanked the still dazed and shaking landlady from the corner of the sofa, shoved her unceremoniously into the winged armchair, elbowed aside the young man as soon as he laid the girl down, with the sharp command, "Don't *hover,* John, we'll tend to her!" She'd stripped off the drenched raincoat and the soaking arctics and slipped a cushion under the slim feet, while Lutie managed to get a few drops of apple brandy past the girl's ashen lips. When Hester's eyes quivered open, as memory and horror filled them, she clung convulsively to Lutie. But only for a moment. Then she'd struggled upright.

She'd silenced John's protests to the inspector when that gentleman asked if she thought she could answer a few questions.

She said, "I'm all right, John. I never passed out before in my life. I'm sorry I was so silly."

Inspector Moore said, "It was quite natural."

Then he asked her quietly if she could identify the body. She shook her head. He asked her if it suggested anybody she knew, and she shook her head again. He asked her if she had any knowledge or idea about the crime, or who had committed it, and she said, "No."

He paused then, his gray eyes narrowed and fixed themselves on the girl's face. I noticed Amanda sitting up straighter in the rococo chair in which she'd ensconced herself, and Lutie leaning forward. I know I braced myself. Of course till that evening I hadn't had the least experience with the police and only the vaguest notions about them, based on fiction, the movies, newspapers, and, I suppose, that nervous wary suspicion that even many of the most law-abiding people seem to have. And now—in spite of the courteous manner Inspector Moore had so far shown—I expected a rain of short, ruthless, accusatory questions. As Lutie said afterward, "Like a sawed-off shotgun…sarcastic, bang! bang! bang! But he's not like that. Nor heavy, stolid, phlegmatic-plodding yet competent withal. And you can't imagine him with a cigar in one corner of his mouth and the latest slang issuing from the other! No, for a policeman he's not at all according to Doyle—or Hammett or Frome or Van Dine—"

Actually his voice was easy and matter-of-fact as he said, "How did you spend this evening, Miss Gale?"

The girl hesitated. "This evening? You mean after I left here?"

He said, "Yes, but begin a while before that. And try to be explicit—and as accurate as possible, especially about time, please."

So, with a quiet question from the inspector now and then, Hester said that she had come home in the late afternoon, lighted the fire and read for a while. Mr. Bynam had telephoned, and soon after that Madame LaVelle had stopped in. They had chatted for a few minutes—

Here the inspector inquired—"for the record," he said, with a smile—what they had talked about, what Miss Gale did while Madame was visiting her, and so on?

The girl reflected a moment, and said she was reading and eating a sandwich when Madame LaVelle knocked. That her friend had brought her a piece of apple pie, and she ate that.

"And very fine pie it was too," she added, and smiled toward the landlady. "And—let's see—I mended a dress, and pressed it. We talked about Mr. Saint John, I remember, and how splendid he'd be in *Lear*; and about the last picture at the Grotto—and my wearing arctics and taking a taxi to the club because it was such a rainy night."

The inspector said, "Thank you, Miss Gale. And then?"

The girl didn't reply for a moment. She looked at the inspector thoughtfully, then at John Bynam, and back to her questioner again. She said, "May I have a glass of water?"

Someone fetched a glass, she drank a few swallows, put it down and said in an even voice, "Then I finished pressing my dress, and then I had a telephone call. It was from a man I—once knew. He wanted me to meet him. He said he had decided to go away, to some place in South America, he said. And he wanted me to meet him and lend him some money."

She paused, then continued, "I agreed to meet him at quarter-past seven— that was the time he set—if I could get there by then. I hurried, and left the house here a few minutes after his call. I picked up a taxi right away. At first we just crawled, the traffic was bad, but I don't think it took more than half an hour on the way. I—you asked me to be accurate about time, but we didn't pass any clocks and I broke my watch yesterday so that's really just a guess."

I noticed that Amanda was wearing a slight frown, and even Lutie looked a bit puzzled. John Bynam was staring at Hester as though he wasn't quite sure he'd understood her correctly. He started to speak and then didn't. I was feeling vaguely uneasy and confused, when Inspector Moore asked the question that was worrying me.

"The time you left here—can you be precise about that?"

"Oh, I thought I had mentioned that. Yes, I can be sure about it, because the time was mentioned when the appointment was made, and I checked with my clock there." She indicated the clock on the writing-desk. "It was just half-past six. Then we talked a minute or so more; then I had to dress, and as I was leaving I looked at the time again—it was twenty to seven."

I glanced instinctively from Hester's clock with the hands pointing to 10:22 to my own wristwatch, which read 10:27. I always keep it five minutes fast, so apparently hers was correct. All around the group similar comparisons with personal timepieces were being made. Amanda didn't glance toward the desk—doubtless she'd already checked the time there with her own. She still wore her frown, and I saw her fingers move restlessly toward her knitting. She didn't take it from her bag, however, but firmly replaced her hands on her rigid knees. Lutie's bright blue gaze didn't stray from the girl's face.

John Bynam spoke hesitantly. "But, Hester darling, aren't you mistaken?"

She said, "Why, no, I couldn't be. My time agreed with—with the time mentioned on the phone. Anyway, the clock's right, isn't it? It must be—it's an electric clock."

"Yes, it's correct. But there seems a discrepancy between your memory, Miss Gale, and Mr. Bynam's and Madame LaVelle's," added the inspector, glancing toward the landlady, who, all her queenliness forgotten, sat open-mouthed, staring at Hester now as if she couldn't believe her ears.

"But I'm positive about it!" Then, at John Bynam's haggard expression, suddenly troubled, "Why, John—what's the matter? Why do you—"

He said, in a low voice, "You see, darling—I thought it was about seven o'clock when I telephoned you. Perhaps I was wrong."

"Oh, you must have been, John!" she exclaimed. "Why, that was before Sarah stopped in. It couldn't have been much after six."

The inspector interrupted. "Suppose we return to that later. Meanwhile, Miss Gale, will you continue? You took a taxi, and were, as near as you can estimate, rather more than a half-hour on the way. Where did you go?"

She answered slowly, "I told the driver to go to Fifty-fifth Street between First and Second Avenue. I said I couldn't recall the number but I'd know the house and I'd tell him to stop when we reached it. When we came to one of those remodeled tenement houses I rapped on the window. I dismissed the cab and went up the stoop and pretended to ring one of the bells. I waited till the cab had driven away."

"You pretended to ring?"

"Yes." The girl's hands tightened, but she steadied her voice and went on. "The man I was to meet didn't want any witnesses to our meeting. He'd said to let the cab go before I— He said he didn't want the driver hanging around. But I thought it would seem very odd if I just asked to be let out on a corner, in the rain. So as soon as the cab was out of sight I walked east, over to the river."

My heart gave a sickening thump, and then seemed to stand still. I heard Jeff gasp, and a kind of groan from John Bynam.

Inspector Moore said sharply, "You walked—where?"

"To where I had been t—asked to go. To the dead end of Fifty-fifth Street, at the East River."

As she said those words, of course, an utterly horrible, fantastic picture sprang into my mind, as it must have to every mind present. I thrust it away—it wasn't credible. But, oh, I groaned to myself, why had she told all this?

John Bynam broke the deathly silence, echoing, it seemed, my inward cry to the girl.

"Hester, that's insanity! My God, why did you—?"

She turned to him defiantly. "John, I had to!" She drew a long quivering breath. And then she smiled! It was a wan ghost of a smile, but she did actually smile at him. "After all, there's no harm done, you see."

"No harm done!" I thought, merciful Heaven, doesn't she know what we're all thinking? Then relief surged over me. What we were thinking, then, must be all wrong. But what did Inspector Moore believe?

I glanced at him fearfully. But whatever was going on behind those cool, clever gray eyes, I couldn't make the faintest guess about it.

He just said quietly, "And then, Miss Gale?"

"Then," she said, "I waited. I'd been t—asked to wait, if—if the man I was meeting—if he wasn't there by the time I got there. He said he might be delayed, though he didn't expect to be. I'd hoped—I'd thought surely I'd be home again before nine o'clock." She looked at John Bynam, with all the defiance gone and what seemed a plea for forgiveness in her eyes. "I—if I hadn't, I would have left some sort of note for you, John."

"Please continue, Miss Gale," the inspector interrupted, though not impatiently. "You waited. And then?"

"He—the man who had phoned me didn't come. I just kept waiting—I didn't know how long it was—I thought it might be nearly two hours. But it was even longer, because when I finally asked the time it was ten minutes past ten."

"You waited more like three hours, apparently?"

She said slowly, "Yes, I suppose it must have been—"

"In the driving rain, with no shelter?"

"There wasn't any shelter, no. But I wasn't thinking of the rain."

"The place, of course, was practically deserted?"

She nodded. "Yes, naturally. That was why the—" She broke off, then added, "An officer passed once. It was when he came back, perhaps half an hour later, that I asked him the time. He'd come up to speak to me—I suppose he wondered what I was doing there. Anyway I didn't wait any longer then; I ought to have been at the club by ten. Besides," her voice shook, "I—I just couldn't bear to wait any longer."

John Bynam put his arm around her quickly, and for a moment she let herself sag against him, her face turned into his shoulder.

Inspector Moore said, "A long wait, Miss Gale—quite exhausting, of course. It was a police officer of whom you asked the time, you say?"

As she nodded, he turned to one of his squad with a low-voiced order, and the man left the apartment. But for all the inspector's courteous tone there had been something about his expression that was frightening. And then it occurred to me: suppose he were thinking that the presence of the policeman, the fact that he had obviously noticed the girl, accounted for her admitting that she had gone to the river? The thought, putting another interpretation on what had seemed to me a proof of innocence, chilled me, as the inspector turned back to the girl.

"And then, Miss Gale?"

She gently disengaged herself from John Bynam's arm, sat erect once more and answered, "Then I walked across to First Avenue and down till I saw a taxi, and rode directly to the club. Your police officer brought me here—and that's all."

"Not quite all," said the inspector gravely. "You haven't yet told me the name of the man who phoned you—the person you went to the river to meet."

She didn't reply. John Bynam started to speak, but the gray man silenced him. He said significantly, "I do not wish to doubt any part of your statement, Miss Gale; on the contrary. But I must have all the information you can give me."

The girl said, very slowly, "But I don't see how that information can help any. I—I'm sorry. I would rather not tell you the man's name."

There was a pause. Then the inspector said, "Are you withholding it because it would incriminate you in this murder? Of course, in that case—"

She said, "I didn't commit the murder, Inspector. But—"

"You are shielding someone else?"

If he meant John Bynam there was nothing to indicate that in his manner; he did not glance toward the young man. And it did not seem to occur to the girl that it might be her friend he had in mind.

She said, "Oh, no," as if her thoughts were on something else. Presently she added, "I don't—I haven't the least idea as to who—killed the man in there." Her eyes went toward the bedroom door, and her hands tightened as she repressed a shudder. "I—I thought at first that you—I mean that someone had broken in, and the police..." Her voice trailed off. She shook her head. "Such a horrible way. It—it doesn't seem real."

"I have noticed that sometimes murder doesn't seem real, even to the person who has committed it," remarked Inspector Moore, not brusquely nor pointedly, but as if stating a psychological matter of fact. He went on in the same even tone, "Hasn't it occurred to you, Miss Gale, that the man who telephoned you might be the murderer?"

It hadn't occurred to me, but as he said it a marvelous feeling of relief surged over me. I thought, of course it might be—it must be! How stupid I'd been not to think of that. Why, it explained everything, or at least many things. And I looked quickly at Lutie, wondering if *she'd* guessed right away, willing to wager that she had, and expecting to see a tiny, repressed smile of satisfaction on her face.

But to my dismay it wasn't apparent. Her blue eyes were bright with interest, and still fixed intently on Hester Gale.

And my heart sank further at the girl's startled and incredulous expression, and the blankness that immediately—and it seemed deliberately—she substituted for it.

"No, that hadn't occurred to me," she said quietly.

"But it is possible?"

She didn't answer. Her face was still empty of expression, as she gazed back steadily at the inspector, but as if she were thinking hard behind that motionless mask, and was really not seeing him, or anything around her.

He said, smoothly (and I couldn't tell what he thought, how much credence he gave to what he was saying, or whether he was testing the girl's reaction), "The phone call you received might have been a ruse, to get you away, and keep you away, while your apartment was used for a meeting place—and a murder. Naturally that still leaves many things to be explained. But when we have the name of the man who made that appointment with you, Miss Gale, and failed to keep it—we may have the name of the murderer."

She still looked at him strangely, but now as though her thoughts were traveling back, focusing on the possibility he suggested. But still she said nothing.

He said, "Hadn't you thought of that?"

Finally she shook her head, very slowly.

"Or perhaps—excuse me, Miss Gale—and try to believe I'd like to believe you in every respect—the truth is what we want—perhaps you thought it wouldn't occur to us?"

She said, "I don't understand what you mean."

"I mean—are you shielding the person who phoned you because you fear that, if his name—and possible facts about him—were known to us, he might be suspected of the crime?"

"Oh." Her eyes were wide, still with that peculiar thoughtful expression. But there was no fear in them, no vehemence of denial in her exclamation. She added, after a moment, "Oh, no—I wasn't shielding him."

She couldn't be, unless she were an incredibly clever actress. Then who?

"You are protecting someone?" said Inspector Moore.

Hester Gale looked back at him, with a weary sadness in her eyes.

"I am not protecting anyone who could have had anything to do with this murder."

"You are not trying to shield Mr. John Bynam?" The inspector came out with it now, abruptly.

The girl's lips were ashen, but they twisted in a faint smile.

"You mean—do I suspect Jo—Mr. Bynam? No, Inspector. Perhaps anyone might kill—in self-defense, or to defend someone else. Or—or other reasons. I don't know. But the person who did that—horrible thing, is monstrous, or insane. I know John Bynam is not either."

"Then, Miss Gale," Inspector Moore said gravely, "you are only injuring him, and yourself, by concealing anything that might lead to the murderer."

She looked at him with lost, hopeless eyes.

"Perhaps I am. I don't know. I can't think very clearly now, I'm afraid…" Her voice was an exhausted thread of sound.

But it only seemed to harden the inspector.

"Miss Gale, I need that man's name," he said curtly, "if for no other purpose than to corroborate your statement as to the phone call that you claim took you to the East River—"

"I told you," she answered slowly, through quivering but set lips, "that he said he was going away. Anyway, even if you could find him, I'm sure he wouldn't substantiate that phone call. It's the truth, but if you don't believe me, I can't help it. I'd rather not say any more—"

He regarded her with every trace of patience and kindliness gone now from his face and manner.

"I warn you, Miss Gale, you are making a grave mistake; or else you are simply—"

I heard Amanda clear her throat.

"Of course she's making a mistake!" she cut in sharply, with a look at Hester as if she'd like to shake her. She transferred that iron-jawed expression of disapproval to the chief.

"She ought to be spanked and put to bed with a glass of rock-and-rye and a hot-water bottle. Of all the foolish, mulish stubbornness! Just the same," she turned waspishly on the inspector, "you're as bad. If you'd let the child alone till she's had a chance to think straight, maybe she'd come to her senses. Meanwhile, you're trying to squeeze blood from a turnip and butting your head against a stone wall. Can't you see she's pretty nigh ready to drop, what with one thing and another?"

She snorted angrily. The girl looked at her. And slowly, without a muscle of that pale, small face moving, the wide blue eyes filled with tears.

I don't know what might have happened then, how the inspector might have met Amanda's scolding, if at that moment the man McGinnis hadn't come back into the room, strode across to his chief, and drawn him aside. I couldn't hear what the detective was saying, but it was evident he was excited, and he kept glancing, with a kind of grim I-told-you-so expression at the girl on the sofa. John Bynam was murmuring something to her, but she didn't answer him. She just sat there with her eyes closed now and the tears creeping from beneath the lids and running slowly down her cheeks. He took a handkerchief and wiped them gently away. But still she said nothing, and didn't even move.

Suddenly I detested McGinnis, with a spiteful fury that made me long to slap him. I hated the inspector too, as he listened impassively, merely nodding from time to time. I didn't care how civil he had been, or that he had his duty to perform. They were the enemy, and I was arrayed against them. I wasn't sorry any more that we were in all this. I looked at the sisters now in desperate hopefulness. They must get that badgered child out of this horrible tangle. I prayed they would—I told myself I knew they would.

Then Inspector Moore turned to Hester, and said abruptly, "Miss Gale, what did you carry with you on your errand to the East River, and what did you do with it?"

She opened her eyes and said dazedly, "What did you say?"

He repeated his question, pausing ominously between each word, and added, "We've communicated with the patrolman of whom you asked the time. He recalls the incident perfectly, as well as seeing you, before that, sitting on a bench there, in the rain. He says he came back, in fact, to learn what you were doing there, and was about to ask you when you spoke to him. He also recalls that you had something with you. I'm asking what that was and how you disposed of it?"

She said, slowly, "I had a bag with me, a suitcase. I threw it away afterward. There was nothing much in it. I—I looked, and when the—when nobody came to keep the appointment—I just didn't want the thing—"

McGinnis' jowled face was very red, as if he were bursting with triumph and a desire to say something. But his chief merely said coldly, "What—er—was in that bag?"

She said, "I wasn't going to mention it, because it's all so pointless, anyway." She drew a long tired breath. "You see, the man who phoned me said he had come to my apartment, this afternoon, while I was out. He said he'd left a suitcase behind some boxes in the back hall under the stairs. He'd meant to come back, he said, but then he couldn't. So he asked me to bring it with me. I—when he didn't meet me—after a while I looked in the bag. There were a couple of shirts, socks, that was all. I just glanced—I couldn't see that those things mattered much." Her voice broke, and then with a note of hysteria in it she cried, "I just couldn't bear to—to keep it with me. So I threw it in a rubbish can on my way to find a cab back to the club."

Her voice died away. She wet her dry lips and said in barely a whisper, "I'm sorry. But I'm so dreadfully tired. I don't think I can talk any more—now. Please, will you lock me up—or anything—whatever you have to. But just let me alone."

Nobody said anything. Even McGinnis looked sobered.

And then suddenly the girl's eyes dilated till the white rimmed the iris, pale circles framed in dark lashes and sockets purple with exhaustion. Understanding and stark horror looked from her ashen face.

"Oh—I see what you are all thinking. I didn't know." She stared around at us, and then with a jerky motion like an automaton, her face turned toward the bedroom door. "You mean—the head is—*missing?* And you think I—? Oh, my God!"

Her mouth twisted in a grimace, the dreadful caricature of a smile, as though she were grinning at some fearful joke with the point directed like a knife against her. And she laughed, a single short dry sound.

"Stop that!" said Amanda harshly. "Don't be a fool, girl! Nobody thinks anything of the kind. At least nobody with a grain of sense in their heads," she added, glancing pointedly at McGinnis, raking the other men with a belligerent eye and finally fixing the inspector with a baleful glare.

"Well, I hope you're satisfied!" she snorted. "You've driven the child to the verge of hysterics. Don't you think that's enough for one session?"

CHAPTER 7

THAT short sharp scolding of Amanda's broke the tension in the room, snapped the girl back from the brink of hysteria, and even had the seeming effect of turning the inspector from a harsh and ruthless inquisitor, a symbol of authority pointing the finger of accusation at guilt, to a courteous human being again. When I said something of that kind, later, to the sisters, Lutie beamed and said, "You do put things so well, Marthy dear; so—poetically!" But Amanda snorted, "That's all my eye and Betty Martin! He's just an ordinary man, quite bright and sensible on the whole; but he'd simply worked himself up, the way men do—and some *women,* too—who ought to have more sense," she added significantly. Anyway he relaxed, and even smiled at Amanda as she finished her delivery of the riot act.

"Perhaps you're right, Miss Beagle," he said. "At least as to—"

"Of course I'm right!" she snapped. "And now we're going to take this foolish child home with us and put her to bed. Maybe after she's had a night's sleep and a decent breakfast—" She cocked an eye at the pale slim girl, and there was a gleam in it at the delectable prospect, I know, of getting some good honest victuals into her. "Well, maybe she'll get some sense into her head. We'll see. Anyhow you've scared her out of whatever wits she has and you won't get anything more from her now but high strikes. That's plain as a pikestaff."

It certainly was, I thought. And apparently the inspector was agreeing as he looked at Amanda thoughtfully. Before he had answered, she continued, "If you've got any notions about whether or not she'll be safe in our charge you can put them right out of your mind. I mean to keep my eye on her— And you can put that in your pipe and smoke it, young lady," she remarked sternly to Hester, then turned to the inspector again. "She'll be just as safe and a sight more comfortable than she'd be in the lockup," she stated flatly, and gathered her bag, put on her gloves and stood up.

"Come, Sister. Marthy, don't sit there like a Stoughton-bottle! Jefferson, put your overcoat on the child. She can't wear that drenched thing of hers—she'd catch pneumonia!"

She addressed our client firmly, "Now, John, no talking to Hester—Inspector Moore won't like it—and I won't have her upset. And besides everybody's listening."

Inspector Moore, still regarding Amanda gravely, then evidently came to a decision. He nodded, and said pleasantly, "Very well, Miss Beagle. I place Miss Gale in your charge. And—"

He drew Amanda aside.

She listened, compressed her lips, then opened them to reply, "All right, you shall have them. Of course it's nonsense, but that's your own business. Goodnight, Inspector. Goodnight, John. Doubtless we'll see you tomorrow." And she herded us out.

On the way home Hester sat between Lutie and Amanda while Jeff and I perched on the small seats facing them. The rain had stopped and there was a strong wind blowing, full of the smell of the sea. I thought of the white house under the elms in East Biddicutt and how snug and peaceful it would be there. None of us spoke at all.

And after Amanda had given our charge a glass of hot milk and tucked her into Lutie's bed, next to her own, we didn't talk either. Jeff wanted to; he was popping with comments and questions, but Amanda shut him up shortly.

"What we need is a good night's sleep." She led him to the door, and added something else in a lowered tone.

I couldn't hear what she'd said, but Jeff's face looked startled—then knowing.

"Okay, boss!" he whispered.

"Mind, you'll have to be up early in the morning for once!" She shut the door. "Such tommyrot!" she muttered.

There was no use asking her what she was grumbling about, and anyway I was too weary to care.

I undressed in the bathroom, for I'd insisted on giving Lutie my room, although she protested. Presently we'd said goodnight, Amanda'd gone to her own bed, and Lutie, shaking her silvery curls at my stubbornness, tucked me up on the living-room davenport and retired to mine.

I wanted nothing but sleep. I didn't want to think, and I don't suppose the muddled questions and fantastic horror that struggled in my mind could be called thinking. But I couldn't shut the pictures out; closing my eyes only made them worse, and besides, the fringe of the afghan scratched my neck like a nest of spiders. I pushed it off and lay staring at the window, gray against the blackness of the room, with the straggly branches of the ailanthus tree swaying against a cloudy sky.

Then I heard a door open, very softly. It was the door of my own room. I turned my head. Lutie stood in the passageway. She was fully dressed, even to her bonnet and coat, and her reticule swung from her gloved hands.

As I started up she put her finger to her lips and shook her head vehemently.

I stifled an exclamation and the next moment she was beside me.

Leaning close, she whispered, "I want to see the time!"

I gasped, "Do you need your bonnet on to—"

I didn't finish, for her little hand was over my mouth.

"Ssh!" She frowned; then grasped my arm and led me into the passage. "I hoped," she murmured impatiently, "you'd be fast asleep. Do be quiet!"

"Whatever in the world—!" I said. But I did keep my voice down. "Lutie Beagle, what are you up to? What's this foolishness about the time? It's nearly midnight, as you know very—"

"Hush!" she stopped me. "You may come with me if you want to. But if you wake Sister, I—I'll be very cross, Marthy!"

I grabbed my dressing gown and pulled it around me as I followed her through the narrow passage to the inner office. Lutie closed the door after us and drew a small breath of relief.

But we didn't stop there. Feeling our way across the room we reached the front one. She pressed the switch then, and as the light went on I heard a quick satisfied, "Ah!"

I followed her glance to the large round face of the electric clock in the center of the mantel shelf. It read 8:17.

I said impatiently, "The clock's stopped. Listen, Lutie—"

She faced me. "Marthy, I have some—er, errands to do," she said quietly. "I'm going out."

"You're—what?" I said. And then, "No, you're *not!*"

"I am," she said.

And I knew she was.

I choked back questions, protest and indignation. And—could it be possible that something like a thrill as well as a shiver of excitement took their place?

"I am coming with you," I said firmly. And added, "But you must leave a note for Amanda."

"Very well," said Lutie. And going to a desk scribbled it quickly.

"Sister dear—Marthy and I have gone on a little errand. Back soon. L."

"Leave it on the living-room mantel," she said, handing it to me. "Though it's fifty-to-one we'll be home again before ever she wakes. You know how Sister sleeps. But be quiet—and hurry with your dressing, my dear. I'll wait for you here."

I made my way back through the hall, left the note, and dressed. Fortunately Amanda is a heavy sleeper, and besides I'd left my things in the bathroom, which is off the passage, and so is the closet where I hang my outdoor wraps. In less than five minutes I'd rejoined Lutie; and then, switching off the light and closing the door softly behind us, we were stealing down the four long dark flights, out into the streets of New York.

We hurried west on Forty-fourth Street toward Broadway. I didn't know where we were bound, and I didn't approve of our errand, whatever it was; but my weariness had evaporated—truth to tell, my spirits had risen, I felt exhilarated! For there was nothing gloomy or fearsome about the streets, freshened by the rain, twinkling with lights and thronged with people and the heavy traffic of an autumn Saturday night.

Somehow Lutie managed to get a taxi with very little delay, and we were soon pushing and honking on our way.

"Lutie," I demanded, "where are we going?"

Lutie's hands were clasped tightly on her reticule; her eyes were rapt.

"Marthy, look! Isn't it beautiful?" she breathed.

I started to answer grumpily, out of habit, I suppose; I didn't think this adventure ought to be encouraged. Then I looked at her little face, illuminated by the flashing lights and her own vivid enjoyment, and suddenly I saw the city through her eyes.

"Yes," I said, "it is. Wonderful, Lutie."

We lurched and jerked onward, and then the cab turned a corner.

"Here we are!" said Lutie, hardly waiting for it to grind to a stop before she had the door open and was hopping out. And then I saw that we were back again at the housewe'd left less than an hour ago! We were in front of the Maison LaVelle.

But this time, when Lutie'd paid the cabman and started across the sidewalk a large policeman barred her way.

Lutie said, "We're friends of Madame LaVelle's, officer. Excuse me—" and edging past him made for the iron gate to the tiny front yard.

"Sorry, lady." The man put a hand on the gate, firmly. "You can't go in there."

Lutie drew a card from her reticule and presented it. It was one of our new business cards and read:

THE BEAGLE DETECTIVE AGENCY
LICENSED
Private Investigating Bureau
West 44th Street
New York City
A. BEAGLE   L. BEAGLE
Assisted by
M. MEECHAM
J. MAHONEY
SUCCEEDING EZEKIEL ABIDIAH BEAGLE

The policeman studied the card dubiously.

"My orders is to keep out everyone that don't live here."

"But I am Miss Lutie Beagle!" said my little cousin, pushing gently against the gate. "We are officially recognized, you know. By Inspector Moore himself!"

She skipped through the gate, drawing me with her. The man stared after us doubtfully, but made no further protest as Lutie pressed her finger on the bell sunk in the brownstone beside the basement entrance. A moment later the door opened, a face peered through the area grille, then it swung open.

"Ah, vour-cee, mad'moiselles, vous returnez? Entrez!" Madame LaVelle exclaimed with cordiality. "Mind the steps. Come in, come in!"

She led us into a room with heavy purple velvet curtaining the low area windows and crowded with bizarre furniture. But it was clean and brightly lighted, and even had an incongruous air of coziness. We were seated with ceremony, myself in a rocker and Lutie on a Louis XIV settee. Our hostess stood back and gazed at her admiringly.

"Ah, vooz ate une petite marquise, tray jolie!" Then she lowered her voice. "And how's Hester? Is she okay? Has anything happened?"

"We left her with my sister. Sleeping like a lamb," answered Lutie.

"Ah, your seestaire—she eez magnifique! What superbe assurance—ze grande man-naire...She's swell!"

"Yes, indeed she is!" Lutie beamed.

Then she drew a quick breath. "We've returned," she explained, "to learn if anything of importance happened here after we left. You see, my dear, we must fit ourselves into our dear brother's shoes; I mean, this is our first murder, and we cannot expect the police to take us fully into their confidence as yet. Soon, I hope, we shall be hand-in-glove, but meanwhile we must work a wee bit—shall I say *sub rosa?*"

Madame's green eyes sparkled. I could see she liked the expression *sub rosa,* and she responded dramatically to Lutie's conspiratorial tone.

"Oui, oui—jay voo comprenee!" she agreed in an eager stage whisper.

"Well, then, *entre nous*—do you think we could have a little talk with the Fennellis? And I do want to see your parlor front!" As the landlady's eyes widened she added hastily, "The apartment, not the gentleman."

"Oh, I get you. For a minute I thought you meant the corpse—which, thank goodness, they've taken away. And as for the Fennellis, they're not home yet. This is Saturday night and they've got an owl show at the Paradise. But as for the parlor, you're welcome to see it. And it's some sight!"

She rose. We followed her upstairs, where she unlocked a door and ushered us into the apartment lately occupied by Mr. Vincent Smyth. As she pressed a switch the ornate chandelier shed a garish light on windows heavily draped in Nottingham lace and brown velours, an overstuffed suite, a teakwood taboret and several gilt chairs and tables grouped around the marble mantel. Madame LaVelle glanced at these with pride.

"Tray jontee, n'est pah?" she said; and then, leading us quickly toward the rear, "But—lookit here!"

The long room was divided by an archway and a tall screen with a design of storks and cattails embroidered in gold on black. Beyond this was a wide couch bed, a bureau, a chiffonier, a huge wardrobe, and two boxlike cubicles, one on either side of a dark velour curtain, with flimsy doors painted to simulate the mahogany of the original woodwork. Both doors were open, one showing a tiny bathroom and the other an empty closet. And the doors of the wardrobe were also ajar, the bureau and chiffonier drawers pulled out, the skirt of the plush couch-cover thrown up over the bed.

"That," said the landlady, waving her hands, "is just the way the cops found it. Not a single thing of Smyth's left! I went in with 'em, and they asked me what I knew about it! Of course I didn't know anything. Then they asked me about Smyth's baggage and I told 'em what he'd had. One suitcase was all, and so far's I know there couldn't't've been much in it.

"At least I never noticed anything hanging in the wardrobe, and nothing in the closet except pajamas and an old bathrobe—he didn't have an extra suit or even an overcoat. He'd had some shaving things in the bathroom, and I suppose he must've had some stuff in the bureau drawers; I hadn't looked. Fact is, I'd thought it kinda funny his bringing so few clothes, because if theatrical people own even one suitcase it's usually stuffed to the gills; but of course the poor fellow might've hocked every extra thing he had, maybe to pay me his two weeks in advance. Anyway, every single thing was gone, as if he—or someone—had grabbed it and packed it all into his suitcase in a terrible hurry.

"But," the landlady paused dramatically, "that isn't what had happened, after all!"

"No?" said Lutie breathlessly.

"No. Because they *found* his suitcase! Up there, pushed way back, where you couldn't see it—until one of the cops got up on a chair, and there it was!"

The boxlike partitions that formed the closet and the bath extended to within a foot or so of the high ceiling, leaving a space and forming a deep shelf over each. Madame was pointing to the space above the closet.

"I had those built last year, so's I could rent the front and back separate, with bath. I wouldn't have 'em built clear up to the ceiling and spoil the moldings. Well, anyway, that's where Smyth kept his suitcase."

"Hmm. What a nuisance when he wanted to get it down," remarked Lutie.

"Yes, and he'd plenty of room in the closet. But maybe he thought it would be safer up there. Some roomers are nutty on that subject; though I could've told him I've never had a thief in my house yet!" Her tone was dignified as she rapped wood and continued, "I must say it was a very handsome bag, real leather with V.S. stamped on it in gold letters."

"And what," interrupted Lutie gently, "was in it?"

"Nothing. It was empty! But devoid, parfait mong!" answered Madame LaVelle. "Yet everrrtheeng else was gone—pouf! Zen what? Where?... Don't ask me, I wouldn't know...But eet eez odd, n'est pah?"

"Very odd indeed," agreed Lutie. She pushed aside the curtain that hung between the closet-and-bathroom boxes—as I can't help calling them. Behind the drapery there were heavy mahogany double-doors.

"You see how heavy they are, and there's a curtain on Hester's side too," said the landlady, "as well as a bolt, and the key *here*. Yet some people won't take this room because they want more privacy! They say it's not the same as a real partition. But as I tell 'em—'

"Why not be neighborly?" Lutie glanced at the tiny watch pinned on her bodice with a filigree bowknot. "Dear Madame LaVelle, may we return tomorrow morning? There's a little experiment I want to make, just to be certain...though I almost am. But now if we're to catch the Fennellis we should be on our way."

She trotted toward the door and we followed. As we emerged into the hall, which was dimly lit by a hanging lamp of knobbed ruby glass, a youth was coming down the staircase.

"Bon soir, Weelly," said Madame LaVelle.

The boy stood still, staring at us over the banisters. He had a cowlick and round troubled brown eyes.

Madame LaVelle noticed their expression.

"What's the matter, Willy?" she said. Then she presented him, "Theez eez Meestaire Weelson Paul, our dansaire. Meez Lutie Beagle and Meez Marthy Meecham." She added grandly, "Zey are prrivate Investigatorrrs; Meestaire John Bynam eez zere client."

The boy said, "Oh." Then he remembered to acknowledge the introduction and mumbled, "Pleased-to-meet-you," ducking his head. "I—I was coming to—to talk to you, ma'am."

He was addressing Madame LaVelle, but his eyes were on Lutie, who was smiling up at him.

"Well, come on downstairs then," said the landlady briskly. "These ladies are just leaving."

"But not," said Lutie quickly, "if Mr. Paul has anything to say that he'd like us to hear also. Perhaps he can help us—"

The boy came slowly down the stairs. He was pleasant, ordinary-looking, with a chubby face and prominent ears; he couldn't be more than eighteen years old, if that, I thought.

"I—I been worried," he said slowly.

"Well, don't talk about it here," said Madame LaVelle. She pushed the lad ahead of us, through the hall and down the stairs to the basement. When we were once more in her little sitting room she closed the door.

"Now, Willy, what is it? Is it about the murder?"

"Yes," said Willy.

"I suppose the police have already asked you a lot of questions, haven't they?" said Lutie.

"Yes," he said. And then, his eyes still on Lutie, he burst out, "You—you're on her side, aren't you? I—I mean Miss Gale's side? You know she couldn't do a thing like that, don't you? Nor Mr. Bynam couldn't either!"

"Mr. Bynam," Lutie reminded him gently, "is our client."

The boy drew a long relieved breath. "Well, then—I'll spill it. And—and you'll tell me what to do."

He ruffled his cowlick. "You see, I lied to the cops. There was a tough dick named McGinty or something, and he began firing questions at me. I was asleep, I didn't know a thing until he banged on my door, and then I didn't know what it was all about—"

"Naturally." Lutie nodded. "That McGinty would rattle anyone, Bill. By the way, they do call you Bill back home, don't they?"

"Gosh—how'd you guess?" He beamed. "I come from Missouri. The town—" Bill turned red. Then he continued staunchly, "Well, it's called Hog Hollow. Named after a man named Hogg, double G, but most folks don't think of that and—well, that's one thing I lied about. I said I came from Kansas City; I always say that. I got a sister there. And—and I didn't give my real name either. I said Wilson Paul, like I'm known here, but my name's really Woodrow Wilson Paulson. You see, Pop's a deacon in the Baptist Church and if anything got back to Hog Hollow…He doesn't know about me being in show business."

"Dear me, how well I understand!" Lutie shook her head. She sighed. "When I was young I wanted to be a toe dancer. But Pa would have had a conniption fit, so I had to practice secretly in the barn and I never made much progress."

"But wouldn't you rather tap?" the boy interrupted eagerly. "You can do as you want now, can't you? I'll teach you. I'll be glad to!"

"Thank you, Bill. I'll think it over," said Lutie gravely. "But now I suppose we'd better get back to our muttons, as my dear sister would say. You were telling us—"

His young face lengthened again. "Yes, that's right. Well, this McGinty barged in with a couple of other cops and just began yelling at me. He shouted where was I and what was I doing at such an hour and all like that. He didn't tell me anything, and first I thought maybe there'd been a robbery or perhaps it was something about the Fennellis—Raph is always saying he's going to bump himself off—and all I could think was not to get in the papers, on account of Pop. So I just said I didn't know a thing, how could I? I'd been here in my room all evening. That was all I'd say. I told him I hadn't been off the fourth floor all day except around noon when I went to the Coffee Pot on the corner. He kept sort of snarling at me, but I stuck to what I'd said.

"All of a sudden he shot at me that there'd been a murder in the house and what'd I know about that? Of course that made me feel kind of funny and I guess I looked funny. He said he guessed I knew where and I'd better come clean! I said, well, I didn't know. I felt scared—but he made me mad too. So then he stuck his face up close to mine and sort of sneered, 'There's a man with his head cut off in the back parlor.'"

The boy's face was pale. He gulped.

"I said, 'Not Mr. Bynam?' before I thought. It was a dopey thing to say, but—anyway McGinty says, 'Yah! So you know Bynam? I guess you know plenty! What about the girl?' And he began to ask me all sorts of things about Miss Gale. I said I'd only met her in passing except one evening at Madame LaVelle's and that time she promised to speak to Sam Green, and maybe he'd give me a tryout—he's the manager at the Harmony. And she did, too. And I got an appointment to see him next week—"

The boy's face puckered. "I guess that'll be all off now." Then he squared his shoulders. "Well. So then they asked me about Mr. Bynam. I said I'd just met him going in and out of the house. Then this McGinty says, sharp, 'Did you see him going in or out of the house tonight?' And—and I said, just as quick, 'No, I didn't!'

"You see," the boy looked at Lutie unhappily, "I'd already said I'd been up in my room all evening. But besides that I thought they might be trying to pin something on Mr. Bynam."

"Of course, I understand, Bill," said Lutie. "But you *had* seen him? When?"

"It was about nine o'clock. You see—" he hesitated, and looked rather sheepishly at Madame LaVelle, "I—I got kind of low, and I thought if I could practice a couple of my routines—"

"Willy!" exclaimed the landlady, sharply. "You were at it again, after what I've said? You know you'll have the ceiling down on Sesame's head; you've cracked it already—"

"I wasn't up there!" said Willy hastily. "I—I was down in your kitchen."

She said, "Oh! Well, I told you *that's* okay."

"But I never did it before without asking. And tonight when I went down and found you were out—well, I thought maybe you wouldn't mind."

"Of course not! Why would I?" said the landlady. Then she gave him a keen accusing glance. "Willy, *did you have any supper?*" As he looked uncomfortable she exclaimed with annoyance. "Of course you didn't! And me with a big beef stew and apple pie, and you know I've told you—"

"I wasn't hungry, honest!" He squirmed and added hastily, "So anyhow, I stayed in the kitchen awhile. I thought about Miss Gale overhead but it was soft shoe and I didn't think it could bother her. So then when I went upstairs I thought I'd look outside for a minute or two; you can just see the lights over on Broadway. And when I opened the door Mr. Bynam was standing in the basement area. He saw me and he came up the stoop. He said he guessed her bell was out of order—Miss Gale's bell. And he went on in and back to her apartment, and it was raining pretty hard so I didn't stay any longer on the stoop; I went on up to my room."

The boy paused. Then he looked up at Lutie and said shakily, "And now I've been thinking. I told that McGinty a lie. And maybe it wasn't the right lie. Maybe—"

"Never mind, Bill. You just made a mistake."

"But what'll I do? I told my wrong name and—and all that, and I swore I wasn't downstairs all evening. If I tell the truth now would they believe me?"

"We'll attend to all that," Lutie soothed him. "What time was it when you saw Mr. Bynam. Do you know?"

"Yes, I do!" answered Bill eagerly. "Because first thing when I got to my room I wound my alarm, and I always check with the clock on the Belmont Tower—I can see it from my window. It was exactly nine, and I'd come straight upstairs—so it would have been a minute or two before nine when I let Mr. Bynam in."

"Yes. Well, that's nice and clear. And now we must say goodnight. Don't you worry, Bill."

"Please, ma'am!" the boy said quickly. "There's something else too."

Lutie paused on her way to the door.

"Yes?" She nodded encouragingly.

"Yes. Well, it was like this. I'd been going over my routines there in the kitchen, sort of humming a tune—I hadn't put on Madame's phonograph because, well, I didn't like to when she wasn't there. I was working out some new steps—and then I stopped and went to the sink for a drink. And I heard a kind of scratchy sound, nothing particular but it made me glance toward the laundry windows. You know, the laundry's back of the kitchen, but there're those big glass partitions in the wall between, so's the kitchen won't be pitch dark in the daytime."

Bill hesitated and blushed. "I didn't have the light on in the kitchen. I'd left the door to the hall open and some light came in that way, but not much. It—it was kind of nice like that. So anyway that's how I could see this—

well, it was just a shadow falling past the window, in the rain. And I heard a kind of squishy *plunk*. I thought something must've blown off the fire escape, the Fennellis often put things out there, so I went to the window and looked. But there was nothing there below the fire escape, and then I heard a kind of sound, like something shaking and scraping on the fence—it's kind of rickety, you know—and I thought it must've been a cat I'd heard, and it must have been up the escape to the box where the Fennellis keep things—butter and milk and stuff. So I went back and danced some more and didn't think any more about it."

He looked at Lutie earnestly. "But now I don't think it was a cat. I think it was a man. And—and maybe it was the murderer!"

Lutie nodded thoughtfully. "And do you know what time that was, Bill?"

He considered, then said slowly, "No, not exactly. I know when I left my room, I noticed then it was quarter to eight—I was hoping Madame LaVelle wouldn't have gone to the Grotto yet and wishing I'd thought of asking her sooner if I could use the kitchen. And I'd been down there a while when I heard this noise and all, and I stayed a while after. But as for just when I heard it—I kind of lose track of time when I'm dancing—"

He looked apologetically at Lutie, but her eyes were sparkling. I think the boy's uncertainty now made her sure for the first time that he was not drawing on his imagination. And his story must have fitted her theory or given her one, for she seemed greatly pleased as she patted his arm.

She said, "Thank you, Bill."

He caught her hand.

"But—but what'll I do, ma'am? Should I go straight to the cops? I—I wish you'd go with me. I don't like that McGinty."

"Suppose you just sit tight while I get on the trail of this 'cat.' " She smiled up at him. "If you're asked any more questions just say you want to talk to Inspector Moore, and tell him the truth, simply. Don't fret; I'll take care of everything."

"You will, won't you?" He followed her to the door, looking like a small boy who'd been let off a licking. "I guess I knew you would the minute I saw you. But gee, I sure made a chump of myself."

"Don't we all?" said Lutie kindly but rather absently. "Madame LaVelle, could we look around your yard just a moment, before we leave?"

"Ah, mai oui!" the landlady said graciously, and with Lutie at her heels, crossed to a curtained doorway at the rear of the room.

"Zut!" she exclaimed as she parted the drapery. "I forgot I left the kitchen dark. Wait—I'll go ahead—"

But Lutie had already stepped forward through the doorway. And then she halted. Her small figure was tense, and she was peering forward.

"Ssh!" She raised her hand in a warning gesture, and we too stood stock-still in our tracks. I had time only to glimpse a narrow cupboard-lined passage, and beyond that darkness. But no, straight ahead and in the distance there was a flicker, a flash of light tiny as a firefly…

Then Lutie jerked the curtains together behind her.

CHAPTER 8

WE on our side of it stared at each other.

We held our breath. There was no sound but the tinkle of Madame LaVelle's bracelets as her hand went to her rouged lips.

Finally she said in a deep whisper, "Did you see it—the light?"

I nodded my head, which was shaking.

Bill's freckles stood out like pennies, his brown eyes popped.

"He's—he's come back. *The murderer!"* he squeaked.

I frowned at him to be quiet, and managed to whisper back, "Perhaps it's only the police."

"No, it isn't!" the woman beside me muttered. "They searched there hours ago."

"Ssh!" I hissed sharply, for I wanted to listen. Lutie had dropped the curtain so that she couldn't be seen by the light from the room we were in; she was safe from whatever danger lurked in the yard. That is, she was safe if—if she was still standing near us there in the passage, watching. But was she? She was capable, I knew, of almost anything; even of an attempt to capture this prowler—or whatever he was—single-handed.

And with that thought came the sudden remembrance of the little pearl-handled pistol her Pa had given her on her twenty-first birthday. Which she still had, and used; for I'd seen her practicing in the woodlot back of our house in East Biddicutt; and once she'd neatly shot the poised head from a rattlesnake coiled in our favorite flower bed. On that occasion Amanda'd been away and knew nothing about the performance; she did not even know of Lutie's possession of the tiny gun, which my small cousin said would only worry her.

But I knew, and it worried me now. It would be just like Lutie to have the gun with her! And if she had, what might she not dare? And what might not happen—if the creature in the back yard were indeed the murderer?

The thought was insupportable. I stretched my hand toward the curtain. Yet I dared not part it, lest she be silhouetted—a target against the light.

"Lutie!" I said in an agonized whisper. "Lutie?"

But she didn't answer. Was she there? She could move with mouse-like quiet, I knew.

Then I heard the faint creak of a floorboard. And it was not close by. She must be creeping through the passage; perhaps she was already in the kitchen and stealing across it, nearer and nearer to—what?

I couldn't stand there, waiting, any longer. I must stop her—or be with her. Whoever was there would surely not expose himself by an attack, unless he were attacked first—or unless she came too near and he was surprised and desperate. I must prevent that, even at the risk of her anger and the more horrid risk of being shot at, or—or something!

I said, "Stay here!" as sternly as I could, and lifting the curtain as carefully and as little as possible, near the doorjamb, I edged through.

It was a moment before my eyes became accustomed to the darkness. Then gradually, at the end of the narrow hall, I could see far ahead of me square patches—gray against pitch-black—that must be windows. But no little moving shadow was near me—nor anywhere. No Lutie.

So she had traversed the passage and slipped around the doorway; she must be keeping close to the walls of the room, out of range of the light we might show by drawing the curtain. And now how I prayed that it would not be lifted—that curtain—and that I might reach her before she could creep too close to—

I had gained the end of the hall, edging forward, peering, hardly breathing, when again a light flickered in the dusk beyond the windows. For a moment a thin beam crossed my line of vision, directed diagonally upward. Then it moved down, sweeping the ground; and against it I could see stooping shoulders, a man's hat, a hunched form searching—

And where was Lutie? Had she already crossed the kitchen to the laundry beyond? Where was she? How near to that danger was she?

And then I saw her, a small shadow darting across in front of the windows. She reached the door to the yard, her left hand turned the key, moved to the knob stealthily; against the glass panes I could see her plainly as the flashlight played outside. And if it swerved a fraction in her direction, if the man who held it turned, he would see her too. And if she opened the door—

And I knew she meant to open it. She meant to—

She raised her right hand; it was sharply outlined, steady; and it clasped her tiny pistol

I plunged forward, grasped her roughly. I wanted to make no noise, I didn't mean to cry out, but I couldn't help it.

"Come back! You mustn't—Lutie, you can't go out there!" I gasped.

The flashlight went out, footsteps spattered across puddles, there was a sound of boards creaking

Lutie wrenched herself free and flung the door open, the pistol in her hand. I stumbled after her, up the three steps into the yard. But there was no one to be seen. Only the high, dilapidated fence rocking. And there was the scrape of shoes and knees against it from the farther side, then a faint wet thud.

"Lutie, Lutie, come back in the house! Please! Please!" I begged in an agonized whisper.

She looked at me briefly. I shan't forget that look. It told me I'd spoiled things, I'd failed her; it made me feel worse than if she'd called me all sorts of names.

But she merely said, quietly, gently, "I'd like you to be quiet, Marthy— if you can. I'll go in—after I've had a look around."

And she turned away. She had never spoken to me like that before. I could only stare at her miserably as she stood there ignoring me, gazing around the yard, half moonlit, half shadowy, and wholly forlorn with its few bare scraggly bushes, its muddy center plot crisscrossed by sagging clothes-lines, its lopsided fences. Above us zigzagged the fire escape, and beneath it the ground was roughly paved. From some of the uneven, broken slabs of stone the rain had drained, but there were places still deep in puddles.

Lutie, facing the fence over which her bird had flown, looked up at the battered brick rear of the Maison LaVelle. Its windows were all dark; and only a scattered few of those in the nearby houses glowed faintly yellow. I shivered; the people behind those windows were far away; they would hardly hear us if we screamed, and could not help us if they heard. And there was a presence behind the fence not ten feet away, and eyes watching us from between the gaping cracks and knotholes, I was sure.

Yet I could do or say nothing as Lutie reached into her reticule, drew out something that looked like a fountain pen. She pressed it and a tiny ray of light shot forth. Holding it in her left hand and the pistol in her right she played the thin beam over the wet pavement.

Inch by inch she went over the ground, while the minutes crawled by and I stood there, my eyes on a corner of the fence and my heart in my throat. If the truth be told I must confess I was hoping she would find noth-ing. For if she did, and it was whatever the man who had searched there before us wanted—

Suddenly she pounced, prodding deep in a muddy crack between two heavy stones with the hand that held the flashlight. Then she straightened, and the moonlight shone on some small bright object as she slipped it into her purse.

I heard the fence creak then; and as I stared, petrified, fingers slid over the boards, two hands gripping the shaky top rail. Lutie, holding her right hand close to her side, raised it.

At that moment a light went on in the house and an instant later the door burst open. Bill's voice said, "Miss Lutie! Miss *Lutie!*"

Lutie said gently, "Darn. Just another second and—"

For the fingers had disappeared from the fence. She stared at it, her lips set, her eyes gleaming. The rickety boards were still quivering. Then she turned and marched into the house, tucking the pistol back into her purse as she went.

Bill shut the door behind us. Madame LaVelle was in the center of the kitchen, her hand still on the cord of the bulb that hung from the ceiling.

Bill said, "We couldn't wait any longer. Miss Lutie, what was it? Was it the—?"

Lutie said, "Whoever it was, he's gone. And now," she patted her bonnet-strings, buttoned her jacket, "we must be going too."

She trotted ahead of us, while we tagged at her heels through the passage and the front room into the hall.

Bill said, "Whoof!" He wiped beads of moisture from his upper lip with a shirtsleeve. "Gee, it was fierce waiting! I—I should've come with you. But you said—you looked like you didn't want me to—"

"I didn't. You see, too many cooks are apt to spoil the broth." She darted a swift malicious glance at me, then added briskly, "And now, let's drop the matter, shall we? Perhaps the man with the flashlight was just an ambitious dick—a zealous detective, going over the ground again on his own, who didn't feel like explaining. Goodnight, Madame LaVelle; goodnight, Bill. We'll be seeing you tomorrow."

She opened the front door, firmly refusing Bill's offer to get us a cab.

"No, thank you. And get back in the house; you've no coat on, and it's chilly."

She closed the door quickly, and after it the area grille.

Thank goodness, I thought; now we're going home.

Then terror clutched me. For at our left, not twenty feet away, yawned the narrow black entrance to an alleyway that led between the houses—a direct route to and from the yard next door. The man who had fled over the fence, but who'd started back when Lutie had found—whatever it was she had found—might be watching and waiting for us right now in the dark mouth of that passage.

I gasped, staring; and holding Lutie tight, I shrank back into the shadow of the high stoop. The street was lonely and deserted.

"Where, oh, where, is that policeman?" I muttered through chattering teeth.

"On the stoop, up above you; and asleep, I think. Stop hanging onto me, Marthy; there's a taxi!" Lutie pulled her arm from my clasp and trotted out to the curb, signaling the approaching cab.

As it rolled to a stop and I hurried after her I saw that the officer really was there. He started lumbering down the steps toward us as Lutie hopped into the taxi, and reaching it after I'd followed her, he closed the door for us with a polite salute. His expression was heavy and a bit sheepish, as if he had been stealing a catnap, standing there in the vestibule. But that didn't matter; we were safe, now! I sank back with a sigh as the cab started forward.

It was such a relief that I closed my eyes. But the scenes in the yard came crowding back and I opened them, sitting up with a jerk.

"Lutie," I whispered, "you know that man wasn't any detective!"

"No," she said, "I don't think he was."

"Then who—?"

"How do I know? You scared him away before I could find out!" she said shortly. And then, more kindly, "And I didn't see his face. He had his coat collar up and his hat pulled down, and he kept his back to the house. I couldn't catch the least glimpse of his face." She was silent, thoughtful for a moment. Then she said suddenly, "Tell me, Marthy, did you think it—he— looked anything like John?"

"John—? John Bynam?" I repeated, aghast. "Oh, Lutie, it wasn't?"

"I tell you, I don't know," she answered. "He wore the same kind of hat John had earlier this evening. But that's nothing, of course; soft dark felt hats are common enough. Besides, it's not likely to have been John because he's doubtless being pretty carefully watched."

All the vague suspicions and fears I'd felt came rushing back.

"Lutie, you don't think either of them did it, do you? Either Hester or John? No, I can't believe it! And I didn't think you did—"

"Why, Marthy, don't you know the first rule? Never be taken in by a pretty girl's face! Or a handsome young man's, either. He is handsome, isn't he? Although as a rule I prefer blonds—"

I said sharply, "Stop it! I don't feel like being flippant. Tell me: what do *you* think?"

"My dear Watson, that's another rule you must learn: I cannot possibly tell you what I think at this stage of the game."

She patted my arm. But just then my eyes fell on her reticule and I remembered that I still didn't know what she'd slipped into it.

"Lutie," I whispered, "what did you pick up, there in the yard?"

"Ssh!" She glanced at our cabdriver, who was singing cheerfully to himself. Then she nodded, smiled at me mysteriously, thrust her fingers into her purse and withdrew them.

Within her cupped hand nestled a key. It was just the length of her palm, with a flat round head about the size of a quarter that had a small hole in it. I peered closer and read: "Columbia Locker Co." with a row of small numbers underneath, and below these, in larger characters, "J-361." I turned the key over; the other side was blank.

I felt relieved and oddly disappointed.

"Well, what's it for?" I asked.

"A locker, obviously." Lutie tucked the key back in her black jet bag.

"Yes. But what locker? Where?"

"I don't know yet," she said.

"But how do you know it isn't just any old key that anybody might have lost there? I mean—"

"It's not been lying there long or it would be rusty; and you see it's quite shiny and clean, now that the mud that was on it has been transferred to the inside of my bag! As for who lost it; whether it's what the snooping gentleman hoped to find; and if it has anything to do with our murder, I don't know. It may, my dear Watson, be the key to everything; or it may be nothing. Ah, here we are!"

I hadn't noticed where we were going. But now as the cab stopped I looked out, startled. For we weren't where I had hoped to be, in front of our own building. This street was an avenue, still busy and brightly lighted. A jostling, gum-chewing crowd, buttoning coats and lighting cigarettes, poured across the sidewalk ,and a giggling couple dashed toward our cab as Lutie opened its door.

"Gee, Al! A taxi? Gee!" The girl's thin little face was rapturous as she gazed up at the boy beside her.

"Ain't nothin' too good for you, sugar!" He swaggered happily and squeezed her arm.

"Come, Marthy; this lady and gentleman are waiting." Lutie turned from paying the driver. I clambered from the cab, the girl and boy jumped in and the door slammed. I stood on the sidewalk staring dazedly up at the flaring lights that framed the entrance of the Paradise Theatre.

I said, "Where? What?"

Lutie didn't answer. She was already yards ahead of me. A young woman in a glass cage stuck a pencil in the brass curlicues that covered her head and glanced at Lutie briefly. Her blood-red lips moved in answer to Lutie's question though I couldn't hear what they said.

Lutie called to me, "This way, my dear." She took my elbow and led me down a wide alley at the left of the theater. A single dingy bulb illuminated a shabby doorway, lettered STAGE ENTRANCE. Three rickety wooden steps led to it, and it was guarded by an old man with a sweeping white mustache.

Lutie looked up at him with a quaint expression of awe. He might have been Saint Peter! Then she rallied, fished in her reticule and presented her card. "We wish to see the Fantastic Fennellis, if you please."

He scrutinized the bit of pasteboard, then looked at Lutie with a flicker of interest.

"You ain't a cop? The p'lice've already been here to see the Fennellis. Say, what've those wops been—?"

"We are private investigators. The Fennellis have not been doing anything reprehensible, we hope.*"*

The old man eyed her dubiously. Lutie's hand went into her purse, then
swiftly it tucked something into the old doorkeeper's palm.

CHAPTER 9

A MOMENT later we were in heaven—for that was the way Lutie
seemed to feel about the dusky, musty corridor in which we found ourselves.
From somewhere to our left came thumps, bangs, the creaking of ropes, the
scuffling of heavy shoes, men's voices.

"Just think, Marthy, we're behind the scenes!" she breathed; and then,
shaking off the spell, she quickly halted a whistling youth in overalls. He
thumbed us upward, and following his directions we climbed an iron stairway and made our way down a narrow runway.

Lutie stopped in front of an open door and peered within. There were
rows of mirrors framed in naked bulbs in wire cages, and beneath them
shelves littered with powder, paint-stained rags, greasy tins and wads of
cotton. There was no one in the dressing room except one girl. She wore a
scarlet kimono; her back was toward us and her black curly head lay on her
arms.

"Miss Lotta Fennelli?" said Lutie gently.

The girl sat up and swung around.

She looked us over. Her young, broad face was streaked with tears. She
looked at us, and her black eyes hardened.

"Yeah. I'm Lotta Fennelli."

Lutie said, "The police have already been to see you, I know. And we
don't want to bother you more than we can help, but there are things we
need to know." She laid our card on the shelf beside the girl and added, "Mr.
John Bynam is our client. That is, he called us in on the case."

The girl glanced at the card. She didn't say anything.

"I know you're upset," said Lutie. "The police are so suspicious, aren't
they? But then, that's their business."

"And what's yours?" said the girl in the red kimono. She spilled a cigarette from a crumpled pack with shaking fingers.

"May I?" said Lutie, and daintily selected one herself.

The girl struck a match on the sole of a swansdown-edged slipper and
held the flame for Lutie and for herself.

"Thank you," said Lutie. I choked down my surprise. I'd never seen her
smoke before.

She said, "We only want to know the truth. Was the man with his head cut off—you know, in Miss Gale's apartment—was that your sister-in-law's friend, Floto the Flying Wonder?"

Lotta Fennelli's cigarette glowed red. She exhaled a cloud of smoke and said, "No. That punk Floto is somewheres in the sticks, so far as I know. And I hope he breaks his neck. Will you get out of my room?"

She twisted her cigarette, dropped it on the floor and ground her heel on it.

Lutie pulled on hers delicately. She said, "If you like. Of course if your brother is a murderer you shouldn't really talk with us. In that case I wouldn't expect you to. But otherwise, I thought you might naturally like to help us."

The girl took another cigarette and lighted it. She had partially removed her makeup but her full olive cheeks were thick with cold cream. Beneath it they were pale, and her bright black eyes were red-rimmed. At last she said, "Well, what do you want to know?"

"About your sister-in-law and Mr. Floto," said Lutie.

Lotta Fennelli said, "Everybody knows. Dolores beat it about three months ago. She wrote Raph—my brother—that she'd met this guy on top of a bus. That was when we were playing Cincinnati. She wrote how this Floto had seen her perform the night before and recognized her, he said. He said he was a great performer himself, a trapeze artist, but he'd had an accident or something. Anyway, she said he spoke to her in the most gentlemanly way to tell her how he admired her, and then it was love at first sight. She said they couldn't help themselves, they'd only seen each other three times, but— And that's all."

Lotta looked at us. She ground out her cigarette.

"My brother Raph don't like that Floto. But he never seen him. He don't know who he is. We never even heard of him in the profession. I tell you he never seen him."

"And he's never heard from them since?" said Lutie. "But somehow I got the idea that they—that Dolores and Floto were supposed to be in Europe."

"She wrote me once. She said they were going to Europe. But my guess is she was saving her pride. The letter sounded to me like he'd turned out to be a wet smack, a phony—"

The girl stopped herself. Then she said fiercely, "Anyway, my brother Raph didn't kill him! I tell you, he never seen that Floto! He didn't, he didn't! So how—"

The door flew open. A swarthy, stocky man entered. He wore a gaudy orange-and-green robe. He stared at us and then at Lotta.

"What's this—sob sisters?" he said, unpleasantly.

Lutie inquired, "Mr. Raphaelo Fennelli?"

"No. He's Mike," explained Lotta shortly.

"Jesu Maria!" said another voice, and another dark, wild-eyed gentleman appeared behind the other. "What's Lotta yelling about?"

"I'm not yelling."

"Shut up, both of you!" said Michelangelo Fennelli. He scowled at the newcomer, pulled him into the dressing room and closed the door behind him. "This is my brother Raph. Well, what you want?" He eyed us disagreeably.

Lutie looked at Raphaelo, who was clad in a brocade dressing gown covered with a design of peacock feathers, and was even darker and much taller and more slender than his brother.

She said, "May we sit down, please?" and did so. She waved her hand toward the rough benches. I sank down on one; and slowly Mike subsided also.

"I always think it's difficult to reach a state of rapport when people are—well, standing around and staring at each other, don't you? Won't you sit down, Mr. Fennelli?"

She smiled graciously. Raphaelo glared. Then he sat down abruptly.

She went on, "Now, of course, you're wondering who we are and why we're intruding on you."

She handed our card to Mr. Raph Fennelli, who read it and passed it to his brother. She mentioned our names, and added, "We've just had a little talk with your sister."

"And what'd you tell 'em? You—"

Mike Fennelli grabbed his brother's arm and Lotta said hoarsely, "I didn't tell 'em nothing."

"And that's what I got to say!" shouted Raphaelo. Then he checked himself. He had a small black mustache over large red lips and heavy eyebrows. He wet his lips and lowered the eyebrows.

"So what?" he growled on a lower note. "I got nothing to say—and I said it just now to the cops."

He leaped to his feet again and walked away from us.

"I'm sure you did." Lutie nodded. "I daresay they asked you right off if the murdered man was Mr. Floto the Flying Wonder. Just as if you'd tell them if it really were—"

Like a man stung by a bee—or perhaps I should say like an acrobat, and a very angry acrobat—the star performer of the Five Fantastic Fennellis bounded across the room. Landing in one tremendous graceful leap in front of Lutie he folded his arms and glowered down at her.

Lutie smiled up at him, and the jet butterfly on her bonnet quivered. It looked as if it were clapping its wings in applause.

"What a marvelous jump, Mr. Fennelli! You know, when I was younger

I often thought I'd give anything in the world to be a great acrobat! The poetry of motion...*Why* do people get excited about aviators who merely fly about in machines, while you do it all with your own muscles? That's what I really call something! But of course we can't all have talent—I should truly say genius—like yours."

She sighed.

The chest of the genius swelled beneath the brocade peacock feathers. His scowl relaxed as he raised one strong hand to his mustache. He cleared his throat.

"Yes," mused Lutie. "It almost broke my heart to relinquish those youthful dreams. But alas I hadn't the physique, so I just had to console myself with what I could do with my poor little *head.*"

She shook the poor little head sadly.

Raphaelo's frown again deepened. It was evident that, as Madame LaVelle had mildly put it, he was "vairee temperrramental!"

"Are you insinuating that I can't do much with my little—with my head?"

"Oh, dear me, no! I think insinuating is so unladylike, don't you?" Lutie rounded shocked blue eyes at him. "But speaking of heads, nobody would go to all that trouble—I mean, about that missing head. That is, if they'd taken so much pains to remove it and dispose of it, how silly it would be to speak right up and tell whose body it belonged to! Because the only reason for hiding it would be to puzzle people. Wouldn't it?"

The veins on Raphaelo's broad forehead protruded, his throat worked.

Finally he said, "I didn't do it. Lady, I tell you I don't know nothing about it. But—"

He turned to his brother and poured forth a flood of Italian. Then he sank into a chair and buried his face in his hands.

His brother shrugged and translated. "He says if that was Floto, the son-of-a— Excuse me, ladies, he don't like Floto. He says if he'd known it was Floto his face'd be there bashed to a pulp for anybody to see and that would be okay. He says he'd be proud of it. You see, he don't like Floto at all."

"Yes, I see." Lutie nodded, thoughtfully. "And I think it's so thrilling when gentlemen have strong feelings like that. But there's quite a difference between talk and action, isn't there? If we came right down to it, would your brother really be capable of such a great crime of passion? I wonder!" She shook her head rather sadly and sighed, "There aren't many men left in this unromantic world who would risk all for love."

Raphaelo had raised his head to listen. Now he dropped it again, muttering more bitter words into his hands.

Michelangelo explained, "He says love is a terrible thing. He says his life is ruined. And by—!" Mike's voice rose, then he controlled it and stated on a lower note but with conviction, "He is right. He is no good ever since that d—that double-crossing dame— Excuse me, ladies, but I don't like that Dolores since she give my brother the air. If I could get my hands on her—"

"Quite natural—brotherly sympathy—" said Lutie. But Raph jumped to his feet.

"You just try it." He glared at his brother ferociously. "I tell you, you lay a finger on her and I'll bust every bone in your body."

"Shut up!" Mike said. He added sullenly, "I never want to lay eyes on her again."

Lutie interrupted quietly, "Where is Dolores?"

"I wouldn't know." He shrugged. "And I tell you I wouldn't care—"

"Is she," inquired Lutie, "with Mr. Floto?"

There was a sudden blank silence. The three Fennellis glanced at one another, then away.

Finally Mike said, "We don't know where neither of them are. Last we heard they were on their way to Budapest or somewheres—"

"Dear me. And you won't be able to locate the? Tsk, tsk—that's a pity," murmured Lutie. "Because if we could find Mr. Floto, I mean alive, nobody could possibly wonder if you'd murdered him."

Raphaelo turned on her wildly.

"I didn't murder him! I tell you I didn't know—" He gulped, then collapsed into a chair. "What I shoulda done was kill myself."

Mike stared at him. "Keep shooting off your big mouth and they'll save you the trouble," he said shortly, then turned to Lutie. "Listen, lady, we told all this to the cops—they just left. What's the use hashin' it over? My brother's upset—"

"Poor fellow, of course he is," said Lutie. She rose. "I suppose you left the Maison LaVelle before the—before all the excitement, didn't you? The visit of the police must have been quite a shock. What time does your act go on, Mr. Fennelli?"

"Nine-oh-five and midnight," answered Mike, and added quickly, "We left the house tonight—let's see, it was about seven o'clock."

He took a few steps across the dressing room and picked up the squashed package of cigarettes. As he passed his brother he trod heavily on a slippered toe. Raph's mouth, which had opened in surprise, twisted in a grimace.

"Ow, look where you're goin'!" he growled.

Mike's eyes narrowed. He held a match to a cigarette and over the flame stared significantly back at his brother. Then he shook out the match, puffed and inquired airily, "Okay if I smoke, ladies?"

Lutie nodded graciously. "I always like to see gentlemen smoke. It gives them so much savoir faire, doesn't it? Or does it? You were saying, Mr. Fennelli—"

"I was sayin' I have to haul this big ham to the theater early and put him through his routine. Sure, he's good—too good; thinks he don't need to work—thinks he's gonna get in pitchas. Well, he ain't in pitchas yet, nor he ain't gonna be if he keeps on grousin' and lousin' around. Well, I ain't the star performer, I'm just a good hack, but it's my livin' too, ain't it?"

His brother stared at him sullenly. He opened his mouth again to speak. Mike went on quickly,

"So, like I said, for the last coupla nights I been making him run through some of his stuff before we go on." He blew a cloud of smoke and added with elaborate casualness, "Like I told the cops, we gotta dress, too, and all. That means we gotta leave by *seven—*"

At this moment the door burst open and two people plunged into the dressing room.

At least, one plunged and the other followed. The first was a short stocky woman in a bright pink dress and brown fur coat. A blue hat with a green feather rode a mass of platinum blond curls. She had large sloe-black eyes like Raphaelo's and a mustache like the faint shadow of his. The second person was a lean grizzled gentleman wrapped in a shabby raincoat. He looked mild, tired and somewhat dejected.

The lady shouted, "My God, ain't you kids dressed yet?"

She saw us and paused.

Raphaelo said, "Mamma; Mamma mia—"

She bounded across the room and threw her arms around him, drawing his melancholy head forcibly to her bosom.

"What are you doing to my boy?"

"Mamma, they're torturing me." He clutched her hand. "Mamma, I'm going to kill myself—"

She faced us wrathfully. "Can't you leave the boy alone? Don't you know he's nutty enough as it is? What you wanna do—drive him to the bughouse? Who are you, anyway? Sob sisters?" She looked us over more closely and added, "You don't look it."

Lotta said shortly, "They're lady dicks."

"What!" exclaimed her mother. "Them? *Dicks?*"

Lutie tendered our card. Mamma Fennelli held it at arm's-length and squinted at it.

"Mamma, I didn't kill him," groaned Raphaelo. "I didn't do it"

"Shut up! Of course you didn't kill him, you dumb cluck."

Michelangelo said quickly, "They're very nice ladies. They wanted to know when we left the house tonight; I told 'em seven o'clock, of course. They wanted to know where's Floto and Dolores; I told 'em we don't know."

She shouted, "Don't mention that woman's name to me after how she treated my boy! Of course we don't know where she is—why should we?

And as for that Floto, it's lucky for him he's kept out of the way or there ain't no telling what you mighta done, you big sap!" She snapped at the son whose head she still held cradled in her arms. "How many times I told you, forget it? Why should you break your heart over her? She ain't worth it! But you got no sense—I s'pose that's why you're a great artist. Ah, my little one—my poor bambino—" she crooned, and rocked his head back and forth with fierce tenderness.

"But I love her, Mamma mia," said the son very simply; and suddenly the tableau was no longer comic at all.

The sadness and sincerity in Raphaelo's voice kept us all silent for a rather painful moment. Then Papa Fennelli coughed deprecatingly.

"Luisa, can't we go home now? You know when I do not get my sleep—"

" Sleep? Sleep? Always your sleep!" His wife turned on him indignantly. "Is that all you can think of, when our poor boy—"

Lutie interrupted hastily, "Ah, but Mr. Fennelli is quite right. And we, too, really must be going. Oh, by the way—'' she thrust her hand into her reticule "—did any of you lose this?" She held out the key she'd shown me in he taxicab, the key she dug out of the muddy crack in Madame LaVelle's back yard.

The Fennellis crowded around. One by one they examined the metal object, while Lutie examined their various faces. But if any of them recognized the key they showed no signs of doing so, and they all disclaimed it.

"I found it near the Maison LaVelle," Lutie explained casually, in response to inquiring glances. "And I thought perhaps one of the guests had dropped it. Of course that wasn't very likely, was it? But one never knows, does one? Well, goodnight, Signora, Signores. Thank you for being so patient with us."

I followed her out of the dressing room and down the steep iron stairs. By the time I'd reached the bottom of them she was way ahead of me, but going in the wrong direction.

"The door's this way, Lutie!" I called, and my voice echoed in the dimly lit passage and from cavernous regions beyond, toward which she was scuttling. But she paid no attention to me. Exasperated, stumbling over tangled ropes, I finally caught up with her.

She was standing in the wings, peering up into the shadowy flies and out onto the huge stage, deserted now and darkened. Stretching out her hand she touched a rudely painted tree trunk with caressing fingers.

She murmured, "This is the very first time I've ever been backstage. Isn't it wonderful?" She sniffed rapturously. "And the smell—isn't it exciting?"

The smell was merely a mixture of dust and stale greasepaint to me, for I've never been stage-struck. But I realized now that Lutie had. She tiptoed out onto the worn boards, and stood there for a long moment, dreamily. Then she bowed deeply toward the rows of empty seats, waved a kiss, and trotted back to me.

"How many times I've very nearly run away from home to tread the boards!" she sighed, then chuckled. "Well, perhaps I should have been a dreadful flop!"

She caught my arm and hustled me back through the wings, along the musty echoing hallway to the door. A moment later we'd said goodnight to the yawning doorkeeper, clattered down the wooden steps and were hurrying toward the avenue.

Which seemed to me, suddenly, an appalling distance away. For this alley, a passage barely the width of two cars between the theater and the brick wall of a neighboring building, was lighted only by the single bulb above the stage door. And in the walls on either side, between us and the bright street ahead, were several dark recesses and doorways. The horrid feeling I'd had while we'd stood waiting for a taxi outside the Maison LaVelle a while ago chilled me again. What if we had been followed? My spine crept with the sense of eyes watching us, of a furtive, deadly purposeful presence waiting to spring from those shadows.

I grasped Lutie, shuddering. And the next moment, with relief, I realized that there was a car parked there at the end of the passage, beyond the stage door, some thirty feet behind us. Perhaps it was waiting for the Fennellis or some other dawdlers; anyway it comforted me, as I glanced back over my shoulder and saw that someone was at the wheel. We weren't alone with whatever danger might lurk in the shadows. And of course with that thought the notion of a lurking menace became immediately silly...

Then I heard the motor start up and the car move forward. It would pass and leave us deserted; I looked back again with an impulse to call to the driver, to halt the approaching car. If it were a taxi we could climb right into it. But it wasn't a taxi; it was a large black sedan, and I realized with a shock that the driver must be drunk. For the car had veered toward us, swerving to the right. We were directly in its path. It was only a yard or two behind us now, its fenders almost scraping the wall against which we stood. It was too late to dash across in front of it; we couldn't move back; in another instant we would be crushed between the oncoming car and the brick wall.

I opened my mouth to scream. Then I felt myself jerked forward, thrust back. I reeled and my shoulders thudded against heavy metal. Lutie's little body pressed against me as she stood, rigid, barely within the recess of the doorway. The black sedan plunged past us.

Lutie peered out after it. Her eyes were bright, startled but unfrightened. She said, "It's gone. Well!"

I couldn't say anything.

She brushed a streak of dirt from her skirt where a fender had grazed it. Then she straightened, took my arm. I don't know how my wobbly knees supported me, but they did. Presently we were out on the thoroughfare. Lutie had hailed a cab; we were in it. We were on our way home. Or were we?

I gathered myself together, trying to be firm, though my voice was still shaky, "Lutie, we're not going anywhere else tonight! I've had all I can stand! That crazy drunken driver was the last straw."

Lutie said softly, "That driver may have been crazy, but he wasn't drunk."

Her tone was quiet, yet there was such an undercurrent of excitement in it that I turned quickly to stare at her. Her lips were smiling, but there was no smile in her eyes, which were brilliant—and grim.

She said, "Marthy, we're on the murderer's track. I wasn't sure before, but now I *know*. Not who he is, but that we'll get him. We've missed him twice, but we won't the third time."

I gasped, "Lutie, what do you mean? We've missed him twice?"

"Well, doubtless he thinks that he missed us!" She chuckled, then added briskly, "But now we're on our way to a nice safe place, with lots of people around, and very little chance of any more strange encounters—for this evening. So be a good girl and don't worry."

Don't worry, I thought—and various other things there was no use saying. Our taxi rattled on, flinging itself around corners and threading its reckless way through El pillars, while I cringed in my seat, making myself as small as possible—which isn't very small—and vaguely praying, but without much hope, that the vehicle was bulletproof.

CHAPTER 10

THE Bowery, a down-at-the-heels and melancholy-looking thoroughfare, had kept nothing to recall the blossom-laden road that had given it its flowery name. Nor did it suggest the rowdy, gaudy revels of the 1870s that I'd seen depicted in old wood engravings. Shabby doorways and dirty windows peered dully along the street, like bleary-eyed old men watching life pass by and waiting for a handout.

But The Bowerie, a renaissance of gaiety in this doleful desert, was brilliantly lighted by flaring gaslights, music blared from the swinging doors, which were like those of the old-fashioned saloon, only much wider and taller. Taxicabs clustered along the nearby curb, as well as several expensive limousines and town cars. The uniformed doorman who escorted us across the sidewalk was at least six feet two and had the most enormous handlebar mustaches I'd ever seen, even in pictures.

So did the majordomo who led us into the long narrow room, thick with smoke, crowded with people, and raucous with music. It was a garish low-ceilinged room, looped across with pink and green streamers, lighted with gas chandeliers and brackets. At the far end, on a platform draped with crimson curtains, was the orchestra. A lady who, I imagine, was a modern interpretation of Miss Lillian Russell, was singing "She's Only a Bird in a Gilded Cage," but not in the rhythm I am accustomed to.

"A quiet table, please, in a corner," requested Lutie, and trotted after our pilot, who led us to a small table against the wall and practically under the guns—I mean the saxophones. But Lutie seemed quite satisfied.

She picked up the small menu that was placed before us. "I'll have lobster thermidor and an avocado—with lemon," she decided and passed the card to me.

I thought I might like a chicken sandwich and followed the dots across the page to . . . $1.25.

I shook my head, feebly.

Lutie said, "A club sandwich and coffee for my cousin. And—let's see—" She pursed her lips thoughtfully. "Yes; Vive Cliquot, '29."

Our attendant bowed and departed. I relaxed. In point of fact I was hungry; moreover, in spite of the smoke and heat and noise I rather liked the place. It was gay and lively; if we couldn't be home in bed at least it was cheerful and safe here, surrounded by people. And then I remembered that I didn't know why we were here.

I turned to Lutie with the question. At the same moment the music stopped. A tall gentleman with a humorously cadaverous visage advanced to the edge of the orchestra's dais and announced, "And now, ladies and gentlemen, I have the pleasure to introduce to you the Great Sesame—Professor of Magic! To those of you who have seen the Great Houdini I will say that our accommodations will not allow us to bury the professor alive, or immerse him in tanks of water; nor shall we handcuff and chain him. The professor is master of these feats, but we have not space nor time for them here. What we will show you is more subtle. It is true witchcraft. Ladies and gentlemen, the wizard, Professor Sesame!"

The announcer withdrew, amidst applause. The room was dimmed, a spotlight played on the end of the dance floor in front of the orchestra platform, and in it appeared a short rotund gentleman, bowing deeply from the waist. He wore a tailcoat, a tiny mustache and small pointed beard, and thick wavy auburn hair parted in the middle. He was greeted with a terrific salvo of hand-clapping and shouts, which seemed to me unduly raucous, and not entirely complimentary in tone. But the professor's round face remained solemn, and he continued to bow right and left. Finally the noise subsided and he began his performance.

I can't begin to describe it in detail, but it really was extraordinary.

Bunnies leaped from coat pockets—not the professor's coat pockets, but from the apparel of astonished gentlemen at their own tables. Doves flew from under the bouffant skirts of seated ladies, who shrieked prettily—and sometimes not prettily. Cards were named, to fly through the air and alight in champagne glasses before the namers, who howled with delight and amazement; yet never had a playing card appeared in the professor's hands. He glided around the dance floor, paused at a dozen tables to ask for a favorite flower; and violets, roses, carnations, pansies, orchids and gardenias mysteriously appeared where they were desired. Then he requested his audience to write whatever message they chose on the saucers that lay on their tables, collected a number, and smashed them on the dance floor. With the broken crockery still lying at his feet he lifted plump delicate hands, plucked plates from the air, read their inscriptions aloud and invited the inscribers to claim them. They did so, usually with sheepish and startled grins, while the onlookers cheered. And then an odd thing happened.

The little magician held the last saucer in his hands, and he was staring at it strangely. His small mouth hung open, and his beady eyes popped. He looked around the room excitedly.

Lutie stood up. She said, "I think that is my saucer, Professor. Will you read it?"

He ran a finger under his collar and wet the rosy lips beneath his little mustache. Then he said, with dignity, "Certainly, dear lady. Your message reads, 'Can you locate the missing head?' " He paused. "That is correct?"

"That is correct," said Lutie graciously. "May I have the saucer?"

She trotted across the long narrow dance floor and claimed it. There was a burst of applause, and the music struck up. Lutie smiled and murmured a few words to the professor, curtseyed, and made her way back to our table. The little magician bowed himself from the floor, and the dancers thronged onto it.

My coffee had been served during the professor's performance, and now waiters approached with our food. The avocado was firm and creamy, my four-storied sandwich was hot and delectable. Lutie prodded the golden crust of her lobster delicately. The wine was twirled in its bucket of ice; the cork popped.

"Another glass, please," said Lutie.

I held out my own, and drank it half down quite quickly. Of course I'd remembered by this time that Professor Sesame was one of Madame LaVelle's lodgers and realized that we were here to meet him. Perhaps he was the murderer! I finished the champagne in my glass. Well, I didn't care! There were people all around us, nice, happy, good-natured people. He couldn't harm us *here*. Only I hoped he wouldn't appear before I'd finished my club sandwich, for I like to eat without excitement.

To my relief I'd demolished the last crumb before we were interrupted. I'd also had another glass of wine when Lutie said, "Ah, Professor!" Then I noticed that the little man was standing beside our table.

Lutie presented him to me, nodded him to a chair and beckoned a waiter to fill his glass. Then she told him our names and showed him our card. Of the various people to whom she had presented it he was the only one who exhibited no surprise or incredulity.

He said, "May I keep this?"

Lutie nodded. The card disappeared before our eyes. The little magician raised his glass and leaned forward.

He said, "I have a profound respect, dear ladies, for your honorable profession. Moreover, you inspire in me a sense of confidence. For these reasons, and also, naturally, in the cause of justice, I shall be happy to assist you in every way possible."

"Thank you, Professor," said Lutie in her sweetest manner.

He lifted his glass, took a small swallow, set it down carefully.

"I think," he said, "that I should begin by giving you a resume of my own acts and whereabouts during the momentous hours of this past evening. I have, of course, already given the same account to the police, who called on me here an hour or so ago. I must admit—" he took another small swallow of wine "—that I resented the *tone* of the inquiry. However, not to digress, I was, during the afternoon, playing chess with a companion at the Cafe Royal. I arrived home, that is to say at the Maison LaVelle, at six o'clock. As I was coming in I met Miss Hester Gale, who was also entering the house. We passed the time of day. I then continued upstairs to my apartment, she went toward hers. Perhaps I should add, she seemed in her usual spirits.

"I remained in my own domicile for approximately one-half hour. Then I repaired to Mrs. Joffey's, my neighbor on the same floor, and while she prepared a most delicious repast of shrimps a la Newburg I entertained Miss DeVeere, another delightful guest of the Maison LaVelle, with a few novelties. That is to say, I experimented with one or two original creations of my art which I intend soon to introduce into my repertoire. Then we dined. At shortly after eight o'clock I returned to my own apartment; and I left it, and the premises, at eight-thirty. That is precise to the minute, since I must leave at that time to arrive at the Regatta Theatre, where my act goes on at nine o'clock. In leaving the Maison I met none of the other guests, nor any other person, either coming in or going out.

"At the conclusion of my performance at the Regatta I, er, had some time to spare. There was an hour or two before I was due here at the Bowerie, where I have been performing each night at one-thirty during the past week, and those hours I spent at a cinema. I might add that I found the show, which was called *Mr. Merlin*, greatly disappointing. It had nothing to do with wizardry. However, at midnight, or very nearly thereabouts, I repaired hither; where, not long afterward, the authorities interviewed me. Which was my first intimation of the tragic happenstance at the Maison LaVelle."

The professor frowned. Then he said, with dignity, "During the course of the police inquiry, I am happy to say, I maintained my composure, although I consider the person who conducted it, a corpulent individual in an unprepossessing brown sack suit, was entirely lacking in *noblesse oblige.* In fact he was decidedly offensive. But—" He spread his hands and shrugged. "What can one expect of the hoi polloi ? 'Honi soit qui mal y pens.' Do you not agree, dear lady?"

Lutie murmured, "I believe his name is McGinty, or some such—"

"—equivalent. Exactly!" exclaimed the professor. He sipped his wine, cleared his throat and continued, "The man's manner, naturally, I ignored. However, due to his own ill-breeding, he forfeited my esteem. *And* the benefit of information and opinions which otherwise I might have placed at his disposal!"

He glanced swiftly around him at the occupants of the nearby tables, then leaning toward us, lowered his voice, "But which, dear ladies, I shall be most delighted to place at yours!"

"That is very kind of you, Professor Sesame," murmured Lutie.

Thus encouraged he cleared his throat and began in a deep whisper, "As you may or may not be aware, dear ladies, the apartment directly below mine is occupied by the Fennelli brothers, acrobats; their parents and sister have the adjoining, the front rooms, on that floor. They are an emotional family, and a day seldom passes without their indulging in vociferous argument. Of which, alas, I cannot avoid overhearing the reverberations that arise and filter through the pipes and register grills of which the, er, *supposed* purpose is to carry hot air from the furnace to the apartments. At times the sound of battle, though noisy, is blurred; at other times the syllables penetrate with clarity, depending on the position of the speaker in relation to the, ah, transmitter."

He inched his chair closer to Lutie and continued, "When I was in my room last evening between six and six-thirty, the customary family discordance was in progress. But at the time I thought little of it, nor of the fact that when I was again in my room between eight and eight-thirty, it was still going on. Nor did I place any especial importance on what I had chanced to overhear. However, in view of the tragic event that has since transpired, portions of the conversation, which I clearly recall, acquire a significance that cannot be overlooked and should not, I believe, be concealed."

Lutie nodded. "Naturally, in the cause of justice and to prevent the possible suffering of the innocent, it is your duty to tell all. What did you hear, Professor?"

"I heard—" He took a deep breath. "I heard Mamma Fennelli say, 'Raffy, Raffy, forget it. Don't do it—' And Raphaelo shouted, 'I tell you I'll get that—' Pardon me, dear ladies, his remark is unrepeatable. But I trust I have conveyed the idea—"

"Quite, quite. And then?" said Lutie.

"Then they moved, apparently, to another part of the room, and I myself joined my friends, Mrs. J. and Miss DeV. When later I returned and was attiring myself to brave the elements there were unmistakable sounds of weeping from the room below, and Mamma Fennelli cried, 'Ah, Jesu Maria, it is awful, he is crazy! Mike, Mike, you must save him!' Then Papa Fennelli said, 'Be quiet, you're driving me crazy.' And then—" the professor shrugged "—it was time for me to leave, and I left."

"How sad!" murmured Lutie. "I mean, for poor Mrs. Fennelli!"

The professor reached for his champagne, sipped it and put it down. He patted his lips delicately, straightened his shoulders and said, somewhat defensively, "I pity Mrs. Fennelli; but I cannot help feeling that she herself is much to blame. She has spoiled and flattered that Raphaelo until, no doubt, he thinks he can get away with murder! If he does," the professor's voice rose, "it will not be with my assistance! Do you know what he had the unmitigated effrontery to tell me, only yesterday? He claimed that he could duplicate all my tricks! Yes, he said tricks."

As the little magician repeated this evidently unparalleled insult he actually choked. He buried his face in his napkin, and when it emerged it resembled nothing so much as a bright pink balloon on the point of bursting.

Lutie beckoned a waiter to refill the gentleman's glass. She said, "What a thrilling profession is yours, Professor. So much skill *and* brains. After seeing your performance tonight I am sure there is practically *nothing* you cannot do. How I should like to hear your reconstruction of the crime!"

"My dear lady, you shall. You shall!" Forgetting his momentary indignation the gentleman leaned toward her eagerly. His beady eyes gleamed; he lowered his voice again and proceeded, "As no doubt you know, Raphaelo had a wife, Dolores, whom he idolized. Moreover, she was his partner on the bars. And then she left him for another! Whereupon he vowed vengeance on her and on the man who had betrayed him. These of course are well-known facts.

"Another fact, less well-known perhaps, but extremely pertinent, is this: When playing New York, Raphaelo and Dolores always occupied the parlor rear at the Maison LaVelle; indeed, they had spent their honeymoon there. The apartment must be laden with memories for Raphaelo; and I have it, on the authority of Madame LaVelle herself, that the fellow was most annoyed at her refusal to switch Miss Gale to another apartment so that he might occupy his familiar abode during his current stay. Which, to my mind, accounts for the ruthless inconsideration he has now shown toward Miss Gale; if," the professor frowned, "it does not indicate an even more *sinister* motive—a deliberate attempt to involve her in the crime! You follow me, dear lady?"

Lutie nodded thoughtfully. "You believe, then, that the choice of Miss Gale's apartment as the site of the murder, which on the face of it does seem rather odd, can be accounted for under the various circumstances—"

"Exactly! Raphaelo is sentimental; he is also showy. To such a temperament what could seem more fitting, more dramatic, than to take vengeance on his betrayer in the very, um, ah, bridal chamber he had shared with his faithless bride?"

He paused triumphantly, then resumed. "Moreover, for practical purposes the choice was wise. For one thing, Raphaelo runs little or no risk of being seen entering the parlor rear, especially after dark, since there is a direct route by which he could enter. And also leave at a moment's notice if need be, regaining his own room in hardly more than a single leap. I refer to the fire escape! Whereas the parlor front offers no such advantage. If he had merely bearded the rival in his den—that is to say, if he had simply gone to Floto's own apartment to kill him—he might easily have been caught redhanded!"

Lutie appeared to absorb this. Then she said, "You have no doubt, then, that Smyth was Floto?"

"Dear lady, under the circumstances how can we doubt it?" said the little professor almost reproachfully.

"But why," I found myself saying, "would Floto go to the Maison LaVelle, of all places?" As the professor was about to speak I added quickly, "I'm not talking about the coincidence; of course he could have learned about the house from his—from Mrs.—from Dolores. But the Fennellis' names are there under their doorbell; he'd surely see them when he went to rent a room in the place. So why under the sun would he be such a fool—"

"Dear lady," said the professor kindly, "you are quite right, of course; it was a foolish act. But many persons are fools—especially acrobats, and particularly those who run away with other gentlemen's wives. Perhaps our Floto was sardonically amused by the idea, the audacity, of renting a room under the same roof with the husband he had cuckol—had defrauded. And doubtless he expected to remain incognito, and unrecognized, since he had changed his cognomen to Smyth, and from what I have gathered, the Fennellis had never seen him."

"But if they'd never seen him, how did they recognize him?" I said.

The professor lifted his wine glass and his eyebrows and gazed at me between them. Then he said, "Dear lady, as to that I could suggest a number of theories, but the detail is unimportant. The fact is that Raphaelo must have learned it, or Floto would not be dead! To quote an old saw, 'The proof of the pudding—' "

"The, er, morsel I find it slightly difficult to swallow," murmured Lutie, "is the presence of Mr. Floto, if Mr. Floto it was, in the parlor rear apartment. How do you account for that, Professor?"

"Quite simply, dear lady! Undoubtedly he was lured there; perhaps by Lotta Fennelli, or even by Raphaelo himself, imitating a female voice and inviting him to drop in for a neighborly visit. Why not? Had not this Floto already proved himself a willing Lothario? Meanwhile, of course, little Miss Gale herself had been lured away, to leave the ground clear—"

"By Raphaelo impersonating another voice?" suggested Lutie diffidently.

"Exactly!" said the professor eagerly. "By impersonating her friend Mr. Bynam's voice! After all, Raphaelo Fennelli is in a manner of speaking an actor; and all actors have a certain gift of mimicry. It is not a high form of art; and in point of fact Raphaelo is fairly adept at it."

The theory struck me rather forcibly. For one thing, it could account for Hester's reluctance to say who had telephoned her! If she had believed it to be John Bynam, and said so—even when later she found that it could not have been he—wouldn't the effect on the police be very bad indeed? And yet, the whole thing seemed too farfetched. For instance—

"B-but why?" I stammered. "Why would the murderer go to all that trouble? I mean, he could have taken advantage of the time when Hester was known to be at work."

"But during that time he is also at work!" the professor pointed out. "Moreover—"

"Moreover, if Hester Gale had been at the Harmony Club when the crime was committed, she would have had a clear alibi. But if she could be tricked into going to some obscure spot and the murder committed in her room, in her absence, suspicion would be diverted to her."

"Exactly!" The professor lifted his glass to Lutie. "Dear lady, you take the words right out of my mouth! Or—to phrase it more poetically—we are two minds with but a single thought! You do then," he beamed on her "agree with me that the murder is virtually solved?"

The orchestra, which had effectually drowned our words (and I thought I realized now why Lutie had accepted our particular table so contentedly) suddenly stopped, and the professor's last sentence, which had not been muted, carried to several nearby tables.

A young woman, whose head was covered with brassy snails and whose black velvet gown was upheld by sheer willpower or sticking plaster, turned suddenly toward us.

"Murder? Who's solved a murder? What murder? I always say there's nothing like a good juicy murder."

The gentleman beside her said, "Baby, you're drunk. Have another drink."

He swung her toward him, and fortunately at that moment the saxophones blared forth again.

Professor Sesame's expression showed embarrassment and relief.

"Ah," he whispered, "we must remember that the very walls have ears! Who knows? We may be surrounded by friends of the murderer! And if it gets back to him that he is suspected, the result may be fatal! We must take every precaution lest he get ahead of us."

"Indeed we must," agreed Lutie. "And speaking of getting ahead, though in a somewhat different connection, what do you suppose Raphaelo did with the—er—the one that's missing, Professor?"

"Ah, there we have, I believe, Michelangelo's fine Italian hand! Did I not hear Mrs. Fennelli cry, 'Mike, you must save him'? Of the brothers he has the soundest head, and my prediction is that after the murder he disposed of it. Um, that is to say, of the unwanted head. In short, of Floto's head." Then he dropped his voice to an even deeper whisper. "As to where, I shall put my own to the problem. And I assure you we shall soon be on the right track. I shall concentrate!"

"I am sure you will, with extraordinary results," said Lutie. She thrust her hand into her reticule and withdrew it. The key with the flat round head lay in her palm.

"Have you ever seen that before, Professor?" she asked him.

He peered, bent forward, picked up the key and turned it over.

"No, dear lady. Is it important?"

Lutie took back the key and tucked it away.

"I do not know, Professor. But if you will keep it in mind—I'm sure if you concentrate—"

"I shall, dear lady!" He raised his hand to his brow with a sweeping gesture. Too sweeping, unfortunately, for his handsome auburn locks were dislodged and slid over one eyebrow with most startling effect.

He righted them immediately. But Lutie's composure was unwontedly disturbed. She gasped, "You have been most helpful, Professor Sesame." And beckoning to a waiter, she settled our bill hurriedly. "We will certainly keep in touch with you. Thank you—we must r-run now."

And she did, literally and precipitately.

I rose and murmured a conventional leave-taking as I started to follow her. But the little magician, looking somewhat startled, detained me.

"Is she—is she going straight to the police? Is that why she is in such haste?" he whispered excitedly.

The interview, with its mixture of the gruesome and the grotesque, had unsettled me also. But I managed to stammer, "Oh, I don't think so, Professor. I'm sure she'll wait until you've located the—the, you know—"

The gentleman seemed satisfied. He performed three deep bows in rapid succession.

"Good! Dear ladies, Sesame will not fail you! Trust me, and you will see."

The last thing I did see, as I threaded my way through the crowded tables to swing time, was the little magician's arm describing a wide arc, while his fingers plucked from the air—

Nothing, of course, but my fancy supplied a most grisly detail as I hurried after my small companion.

CHAPTER 11

SO far as I was concerned, the journey home was accomplished in a daze. I suppose the champagne had something to do with it. Vaguely I remember climbing into a cab and some time later stumbling out of it and up the long dark stairs to the flat on Forty-fourth Street where all was quiet, and Lutie took the note I'd left propped up on the living-room mantelpiece and tucked it behind the embers in the fireplace below. I must have undressed, though that's a blank. But I recall Lutie tucking the afghan around my shoulders and giving me a little pat.

She said, "You scared off my murderer, but just the same you've been a darling, my dear Watson."

The next thing I knew the tinkle of glass and china awakened me to the delicious fragrance of fresh coffee.

I sat up and looked around. There was a fire already crackling on the hearth, with Tabby stretched luxuriously before it, and Amanda laying the dropleaf table, and I could see Lutie, in her crisp morning dress of gray-and-white sprigged percale, through the door to the kitchen pantry, briskly stirring batter in a big yellow bowl.

The branches of the ailanthus tree waved against a bright blue sky, and the clear fall sunshine flooded the room. It was nearly half-past seven o'clock. Lutie's big mixing spoon whisked and slapped the rich batter cheerfully in time to the breezy little tune she was humming.

There was a sharp rat-a-tat, tat, tat-tat! tat! on the door to the outside hall—our young assistant's customary knock.

I grabbed the afghan and made for the bathroom where I'd undressed the night before, while Amanda went to the door and told Jeff primly through a crack that he could cool his heels for a few minutes.

When I reappeared he was warming them before the fire and sniffing the tantalizing smells from the pantry kitchen like a hungry puppy. (I haven't mentioned it before, but I can't help being more partial to dogs than to cats or parrots. It wouldn't have fitted into our household and so I have never mentioned it, but I always had a sort of sneaking longing for an Irish terrier. I guess that's why I took to Jeff so quickly.)

Amanda had set the coffee urn on the table and followed it with a heaping platter of scrambled eggs and bacon, and Lutie came in with a stack of smoking, golden brown waffles.

She said, "Good morning, my dears—and isn't it a beautiful morning! Draw up your chair, Jeffy."

He obeyed, and almost fell into it with eagerness.

"What, do I rate breakfast?"

"Eat them while they're hot. I'll have more ready in a jiffy, Jeffy," she said absurdly, and trotted off again.

"Umm. This is the life!"

Amanda filled his plate, and there was an ill-concealed gleam of satisfaction in her black eyes as he attacked it.

"Thought you might be through breakfast," he remarked guilelessly. "'Fraid I was late."

"You are late," she said sternly. "But," she conceded, "so are we. After all, last night was a somewhat unusual occasion."

"Gosh!" said Jeff and slapped his hand on his coat pocket, jerking out a crumpled folded newspaper. "I meant to show you this first thing but the scent of vittles on the balmy morning air distracted me. Get a load of this!" And he shook the paper open, waved it at us.

I caught one glimpse of a black headline: "J. L. BYNAM QUIZZED IN MURD—" Amanda took the paper. She frowned at Jeff.

"Ssh!" She glanced toward the closed door of her bedroom. "I don't want this thing around when that child wakes up. Besides, as I've told you, Jefferson, I don't care to have this silly newspaper in my home. It's a pack of stuff-and-nonsense. Eat your breakfast. Did you deliver my parcel? And have you telephoned for it this morning?"

Jeff went meekly back to his eggs and bacon.

"Yes, boss. The cop was waiting downstairs and I gave him the clothes. And I buzzed 'em first thing this morning, but they're not through with 'em yet."

I had wanted to see that newspaper, but my attention now was diverted by this new development.

I said, "What cop? What are you talking about? Whose clothes?"

"Hester's clothes," replied Amanda, calmly pouring syrup over her second waffle. Lutie, who had just brought in another batch, listened a moment, nodded, and trotted off for more. Amanda cut a neat bite from her waffle. "That was what Inspector Moore spoke to me about, just before we left."

"But—but when?"

"After I'd put the child to bed, with her hot milk and an allonal tablet, I took everything she'd had on and wrapped it up in the office. Jefferson was waiting in the reception room—" she emphasized this bit of propriety "— and I gave him the bundle to deliver to an officer who, I understand, had followed us and was waiting downstairs. You were making up the davenport, Marthy, and didn't notice, I daresay. There are quite a few things you don't notice, my dear. Eat your breakfast, child, and don't sit there with your mouth open like a fish and nothing in it!"

I gulped, "You mean they want her clothes to—?"

"Analyze 'em for bloodstains," Jeff finished for me. "May I have some more java, Miss Marthy?"

He passed me his cup. I tried to keep my hand steady while I filled it, but some of the steaming brown liquid went into the saucer.

"You've got 'em bad, haven't you?" remarked Jeff, as he reached for the cup, dropped in three lumps of sugar and poured in cream.

I gasped, "But, Amanda! That must mean they really think she did it!"

"Tut, Marthy, you do jump to conclusions! We won't talk about the case, certainly not till you've eaten your breakfast, if you're going to get yourself all upset over it. You haven't had any of this peach preserve," she said, heaping some on my plate. "I think it's even better than usual. I must say," she went on, "it's lucky for that foolish child that *somebody's* been able to keep a head on their shoulders."

"Yes, isn't it?" agreed Lutie, putting a final stack of waffles and more scrambled eggs on the table. Jeff leaped to pull out her chair and she smiled at him as she seated herself.

I managed a swallow of coffee and tried to control my voice as I asked, "What will Hester think when she knows you've given her clothes to the police?"

"She does know," said Amanda. "I told her when I took them."

"What did she say?" I asked.

"Nothing. I told her it was all poppycock, as I'd mentioned to Inspector Moore, but that, after all, he had to do his duty as he saw it. She said, 'Then you and your little sister don't believe I could have done it?' and I told her I wasn't a fool; but of course I couldn't answer for Sister—"

Lutie murmured, "Of course not, Sister." She nibbled thoughtfully. "I don't think I had very good luck with my waffles this morning. Or do you think they are all right, Sister?"

"They're very nice," said Amanda. She added, "Lutie, you and Marthy will have to go to market this morning. I promised personally to keep an eye on Hester. Besides, I daresay we shall have a visit from the authorities this morning, and naturally I must be here. Jefferson, the child may be waking up any minute now, so if you've finished your breakfast—" She caught Jeff's glance fixed longingly on the last waffle, and her own melted. "Or perhaps you'll have more?"

He shook his head, sighing with repletion. "Guess I couldn't make it," he decided unwillingly, and rose. "Any special instructions, boss?"

"Yes; don't neglect to dust the top of the filing cabinets," she admonished him. "And don't slam the door as you go. I want the child to sleep just as long as she can—" She broke off, listened and said, "I believe she's awake now. Scoot!"

Jeff departed for the offices. Amanda went to the bedroom door and tapped on it. The girl's voice answered, "Come in, please." Amanda disappeared within the room.

"Marthy, you clear the table while I make Hester's breakfast. We'll fix her a tray, by the fire," said Lutie, bustling into the pantry kitchen.

A few minutes later Hester was installed in the big leather chair near the fire, with a little table in front of her and Tabby purring like a teakettle on the hearth. Her small bare feet were lost in a pair of crocheted slippers with cushiony lamb's-wool soles, and she was swaddled in one of Amanda's nightdresses and a gray flannel robe. Her hair curled damply from her bath, and above the tucked, bone-buttoned yoke and high ruffled neck of the muslin, gown her face had a faint trace of rosy color.

"My dear, how pretty you look this morning!" smiled Lutie, setting a tray on the low table. "Just like a little girl in her Ma's nightie! Doesn't she, Sister?"

"Hmm. Pretty is as pretty does," said Amanda firmly. "Eat your oatmeal, my dear. And your prunes. You may think you don't like prunes—I didn't when I was a child—but you'll like those. One thing I'll say for Sister, she can fix prunes to the Queen's taste. Besides, they're good for you."

The girl looked at us, and around her at the sunny room, the parrot in his cage and the cat at her feet, at the silver tray with its crocheted doily, its bowl of cereal, rich prunes topped with fluffy whipped cream, its pot of fragrant coffee.

She said slowly, "This must be a dream. I—I don't know why you're so kind to me." Her eyes filled with tears.

Amanda flushed. Tears are one thing that get her fussed.

"Kind, your grandmother!" she retorted brusquely. "We'd do as much for a starved kitten—"

"—And just look at him now," murmured Lutie. She added cheerfully, "But you mustn't cry, my dear." She poured coffee into a flowered cup. "I don't mind a bit, but Sister doesn't like it. She always says—"

"Demmitall, shut up!" said Rab.

Lutie smiled at him fondly. Tabby rose, stretched, and rubbed his arched back against Hester's ankles. The girl wiped her eyes, leaned and stroked him gently.

"Tabby's taken a fancy to you, my dear! You should feel very much flattered; he's not at all a demonstrative cat. Look, Sister!"

Tabby's unusual gesture of friendliness hadn't been lost on his mistress. But she only said sternly, "Hester, eat your breakfast!"

"How will you have your eggs, my dear? And do you like waffles or would you rather have biscuits? Or griddle cakes, perhaps?"

"Lutie, don't stand there asking the child questions! Haven't you sense enough to know she had enough of that last night? I shall make her some coddled eggs and toast, and she'll have some strawberry jam. I think she should have only a light meal now. You and Marthy run along and tend to your marketing."

"Yes, Sister," replied Lutie meekly. But the glance she gave me from behind Amanda's back was anything but meek. In fact, her left eyelid flickered in what I can only describe as a tiny conspiratorial wink.

We left Hester finishing her "light" breakfast and Amanda knitting, the fire crackling cheerily on the hearth.

It was a cozy and a touching tableau. Surely, I thought, the girl couldn't resist it; if Amanda were right and she was innocent, surely she'd tell the whole truth about her mysterious trip to the East River, the phone call and the name of the man who'd made it.

But suppose Amanda was wrong? I recalled Lutie's remark about being taken in by a pretty face. To be sure, my own impulse and wish was to believe in the girl; but I couldn't bear to have the wool pulled over Amanda's eyes.

For Amanda, who had taken the girl on trust, was the most loyal soul in the world. She was a stubborn respecter of privacy too; she might think and say Hester was a fool for holding her tongue, but she wouldn't question her. She could talk or not, as she chose. As I saw the tenderness in the stern eye my cousin was keeping on her young charge, I almost prayed that she wasn't going to be disappointed.

CHAPTER 12

AT the corner newsstand I bought three or four papers. Lutie said, "You look over them, Marthy, while I market. If there's anything really new in them you can tell me."

So while she trotted busily from counter to counter of the A&P, I tucked myself in a secluded corner behind a pyramid of canned tomatoes and glanced hastily through the lurid headlines and paragraphs of our murder. They were very sensational, and it was distressing as well as oddly exciting to see all our names there. But my hurried reading didn't reveal any new facts or developments in the case.

I had just rushed through a detailed history of John Lane Bynam's family and antecedents and was deep in a hair-raising account of Madame LaVelle's identification of the body when Lutie tapped my arm. I jumped nervously.

"Mercy, my dear, you *have* got the jitters." She smiled at me and added, "Anything we don't already know?" And nodded toward the news sheets. When I said I hadn't found anything so far, she said briskly, "Well, save them for our scrapbook. But let's hurry now. I don't want to leave Sister holding the bag—I mean the fort—any longer than necessary."

She was trotting toward the street as she chattered. "I've a notion the news hawks and the sob sisters—I mean the ladies and gentlemen of the press—will be camped on our doorstep by now."

She hailed a taxi and we climbed in.

She said, "It seems a pity not to walk on such a lovely morning but we mustn't take the time."

I said, "No, of course we mustn't." I felt no impulse to ask where we were going. Wherever it was we were on our way; and meanwhile it was a clear sunny day, with safe thronged streets all around us. The terrors of the night seemed far away.

Presently we drew up and alighted at the Maison LaVelle. Its portals were still guarded, but by another policeman. We were soon past him and ringing the basement bell. Madame LaVelle received us cordially. She wore a long-skirted, tight-sleeved green calico dress cut on what was once called the princess model. It was spectacular but crisp and spotless. A brooch with a large green stone clasped the very high collar a la Bernhardt, above which floated a wisp of emerald tulle.

She was, she said, just having her second cup of coffee, and urged us to join her. We did so and it was certainly very good coffee. We told her that we'd left Hester finishing her breakfast, and Lutie asked if there had been any new developments at the Maison.

She said, "No. The burglar, or whatever he was, didn't come back—at least that I know of. And for my part I think it was some dumb cop, poking around. Oh, there was a dick here this morning, that big sap in the brown suit; you know, the tough one. He said Miss Gale needed some clothes, a whole outfit. So I packed her suitcase and gave it to him. Did she get it?"

"Doubtless, after we left," said Lutie. "And that was all he wanted?"

"Well, he asked me a lot of questions, mostly the same ones I'd answered last night. He's a dumb cop, seemed to think if he growled fierce enough and kept asking me the same things over and over again I'd answer 'em different. But I didn't. Then just before he left he hauled a photograph out of his pocket and shoved it at me. He held his thumb over part of it, I don't know why, and asked me who it was, the part I could see. It was Vincent Smyth, some younger-looking, but it was him, all right. I asked the dick where he got it, but he said he was asking questions, not answering them. I don't like that cop."

"No, Mr. McGinnis isn't a popular gentleman," said Lutie. And added, "And now, Madame LaVelle, we'd like to visit some of your guests. May we? We've already talked with Bill, and with the Fennellis and the professor. But there's Mrs. Joffey and Miss DeVeere, and Mr. Saint John."

The landlady hesitated. "It's pretty early—" Then she considered. "Well, after all, murders don't happen every day. Come on. Zis way, seel-voo-play!"

We followed her upstairs.

Mrs. Joffey, the retired wardrobe mistress, was a plump and pleasant woman of sixty or so, with whom I immediately felt at ease. Her bed-sitting-room was cheerful, clean but untidy, crowded with bric-a-brac and with photographs of theatrical celebrities and nonentities, going back over two score of years, and all dashingly inscribed "To Polly" or "Mother Joffey" with varying expressions of love and devotion.

She received us cordially, clucking over our business card and beaming at the landlady's introduction.

"I certainly am pleased to make your acquaintance," she assured us. "Mercy me, what an interesting profession! Why, it must be just like living in the midst of a mystery story, and I do think there's nothing like a good murder to pass the time. I always like to have one in the evening. You see, the nights are sometimes a little lonely for a person like me, used to being behind the footlights during those hours. Of course, I don't mean directly behind the footlights; I should say behind the scenes, but still it's much the same thing in a way. Sometimes I can't help being sorry I gave up show business, but my legs began to go back on me—there I am running on as usual! And I'm sure you're very busy and I suppose you'd like to ask me questions, wouldn't you?"

She folded her hands comfortably over her middle and beamed at us expectantly. "Not," she added regretfully, "that I can be of much help, I'm afraid. I was right here in my room all evening, and I simply didn't hear a thing about the goings-on downstairs—that is, not until the police and then the ambulance arrived, and by that time it was all over, of course. I mean the murder was all over. That's what I had to tell the police, too, when they questioned me; I was sorry—I racked my brains, but I couldn't think of a single thing I'd seen or heard that could have had anything to do with it. They seemed quite disgusted, and I don't wonder. Such a nice, well-spoken man that inspector what's-his-name—I declare I never can remember a person's name if they're not in show business, and then I don't suppose I'd ever forget a name or a face to my dying day! Still there might be something I'd forgotten or just wouldn't even fancy had any importance at all and I'd let it slip or you'd think to ask me, and you'd know right away it was a clue because that's your business. So, as I was saying—"

At this point there was a light tat-tat-tat on the connecting door to the front hall bedroom. It opened and the blond head of a young woman in a boudoir cap smiled at us all coquettishly.

"May I come in?" asked its owner, who was not quite as young on second sight as on first, though her carefully arched brows and upcurving cupid's-bow lips made a gallant effort to disguise the fact.

Our hostess patted a chair amiably.

"Come right in, Dotty," she said. "You're an early bird this morning, dearie."

Dotty entered, trailing a slightly soiled pale blue negligee. "It's been such a very distressing night, I really couldn't sleep very well. Then I heard voices, and I just *couldn't* suppress my curiosity to see who your visitors might be. I do hope I'm not intruding? If I'm being naughty you must just say scat and little Dotty will scuttle right off."

"Not at all," said Lutie.

Madame LaVelle performed the introductions, grandly as usual, and Miss Dot DeVeere rounded her pale blue eyes and cooed, "But how too, too exciting! Now, don't let me interrupt. Please go right on with whatever you were talking about. I hope you'll pardon my appearance. I know I'm a perfect sight!"

"Not at all," Lutie said once more, with somewhat less than her customary graciousness.

Her glance traveled coolly from the rather wispy pageboy bob under the beribboned cap to the scuffed mules dangling from a very small and pretty pair of feet. It occurred to me that my cousin didn't really cotton to Miss Dot DeVeere.

But the latter certainly did not appear to be aware of this. She fluttered her lashes at Lutie.

"I declare, Miss Bugle," she exclaimed, "you and your little bonnet look just like the song! You know—" With accompanying arch gestures, but slightly off key, she started to hum.

"Thank you, Miss Veere de Veere," interrupted Lutie icily. "I hope you've breakfasted. You remember the saying, 'Sing before breakfast—' "

"Oh, dear—'Cry before night'! That's right. I forgot."

Looking quite frightened, Miss DeVeere rapped ruby-red fingernails on the arm of her chair, warding off the threat.

"Speaking of breakfast, wouldn't you all like a nice hot cup of tea? And some muffins?" Our hostess rose and started to waddle toward a screen in a corner of the room which imperfectly concealed some rather scrambled-looking culinary arrangements.

"That's so kind of you, dear Mrs. Joffey, and we'd dearly love to have a raincheck. I can see my cousin Martha and you are going to be great friends; at least *she's* quite fallen for you, as the young folks put it. But I'm afraid we should be running along now."

"But, dearie, you haven't told us a single thing about that dreadful murder—and you were all right there, too!" protested Miss DeVeere. She pouted.

"How do you know they were right there, Dot?" asked the landlady.

"Why, I read it in the papers, of course! And besides, aren't you supposed to be detectives?"

"You mean to say you been out this morning for the papers, dearie?" asked Mrs. Joffey in a tone of mild surprise.

Miss DeVeere said, rather defensively, I thought, "Yes, I have. I told you I couldn't sleep, with that awful thing happening right under the same roof, and the cops coming up and asking us all sorts of things and not really telling us anything. Not that they got anything out of me, I can tell you. I guess I know my onions! So I went out early this morning and bought the *News* and the *Mirror* to read the truth for myself! And I must say I'm not as surprised as I might be. Still waters run deep, I always say; and you know I've said it to you too, Mother Joffey, and to Julie here—"

She turned to us. "You can just ask them if I haven't. It's all very well to be quiet and refined and ladylike and I don't know who's any more so than I and neither of you can deny it. But the way you both stuck up for that girl! And speaking of stuck-up, that's what she always was, but she's had a comedown now, all right, all right—and you can't either of you say I didn't warn you! Going with that wealthy John Bynam and her just a common nightclub singer, I'd like to know what he'd want with her if it wasn't just one thing. But no, you always said she was such a nice girl!"

She pronounced the words mincingly, then finished with shrill bitterness, "What he ever saw in her is certainly beyond me! Well, anyway, I guess he's plenty sorry now he ever got mixed up with her. And it serves 'em both right, I say."

The girl gulped. Her rather pinched face was flushed, and suddenly I saw that there were tears in her eyes.

"Dearie, you are upset this morning." Mrs. Joffey shook her head and added, "There, now, it's just like Miss Lutie said, isn't it? You shouldn't have sung before breakfast! But really, dearie, you got no call to cry; you could have the professor by just crooking your little finger. Of course he wears a toupee and he's no spring chicken, but he's a kind, refined man and he makes good money and works steady and I've seen plenty girls go farther and fare worse. You could help him in his work. It doesn't take any talent or brains to be the lady in the cabinet or float around the stage on wires. You'd look very sweet from a little distance and he has to have someone. You could save him money."

"Oh, shut up!" sniveled Miss DeVeere angrily.

"Mrs. Joffey, I do think you are so wise, my dear. And Miss DeVeere, I'm sure you'll feel much better after a cup of tea. There's no use flying in the face of superstition, is there? Well—" Lutie started to rise.

"You going?" said Miss DeVeere. She wiped her reddened eyelids on her flowing sleeve, leaving a black smudge on the torn ruffle, and gave Lutie a peculiar look. "You haven't asked me anything."

Lutie raised her eyebrows. "Why, I understood you had nothing to say."

"I said the cops got nothing out of me—and they didn't!" snapped Miss DeVeere, the painted curve of her lips thinning.

"Not that I got anything to hide, but you never know. All they'd say was there'd been a murder. Not who'd been bumped off nor when nor how nor who was the guilty party—nor even suspected. Just trying to pump me, they were. So I told 'em I was up here all day—I never been off this floor except at a few minutes around five this afternoon—I went to the delicatessen for Polly. And that's the truth, so help me! I'm not such a fool as to lie. But that don't mean I have to tell every little thing I know, does it? Not before I know what's up! Least said soonest mended; I guess I know when to keep my mouth shut!"

Nobody made any reply to this for a moment.

Then Lutie said, "I see. Very discreet, indeed. May I ask what has made you change your policy? Or have you?"

"Huh?" said Miss DeVeere. "Oh. Yes, I've changed my mind, if that's what you mean. I've been reading the papers and thinking things over. And I think it's my plain duty to tell what I know! Why should I protect that Gale woman when it's sure on the face of it she's guilty of a horrible crime. And the only reason she's not already thrown in the coop is because her boyfriend's got dough and influence. Anyone can see that. And no doubt she buttered up the cops, too, just like she's done the rest of you! But I don't fall for that soft soap. Not," said Miss DeVeere, "that she ever handed me any!"

"Dotty," said Mrs. Joffey mildly, "you don't like Miss Gale. But if I was you I wouldn't let spite lead me into saying things I might be sorry for. And maybe hurting yourself more than you will her."

"Excuse me, Mrs. Joffey," Lutie interrupted. "Murder is quite a serious thing, after all, and I think Miss DeVeere would be quite right in telling anything she knew…if she knew anything."

It wasn't very subtle baiting, but Miss DeVeere rose to it.

"You think I don't? Well, I'll tell you this much! I knew when Gale left this house last night, for one thing. Because I saw her. We had just finished dinner, I and Polly and the professor, in here. I went in my room for a hand-kerchief and I heard the front door shut—a loud bang it was, as if someone had gone out in a hurry and let it slam. So I looked out the window and there was Gale running down the stoop. She beat it off toward Sixth —and I seen— I saw her wave at a taxi and get in, a couple of doors from here. And that's not all. She had a suitcase with her! Now I ask you—what's that for if it ain't—"

The landlady started to answer, but Mrs. Joffey did so instead, without vehemence.

"Dotty, you know perfectly well she often takes a bag with her evening things in it to the club, and dresses there."

"And why was she tearing off to the club at a quarter to eight? She don't have to get there till ten o'clock."

The landlady said quickly, "And how do you know it was quarter to eight?"

"Because I looked, when I came back in this room, which was right away. And Polly's clock there—" she pointed "—said so."

"Then it was only 7:40. I always keep it five minutes fast," said our hostess placidly.

"You didn't," said Lutie, her eyes on the blond girl, "see fit to give the police this information? Why not, Miss DeVeere?"

The girl looked sulky. She bit her ruby-colored lip.

"It might," said Lutie sweetly, "have provided Miss Gale with an alibi."

"Well, it don't, I'll bet!" retorted Dot DeVeere. She added, "Anyhow, I wasn't opening my trap about anything till I got the lowdown. I told you the cops wouldn't give out, didn't I? But I'm going to spill it to 'em next chance I get, I'm telling you. And that's not all I know either. Get a load of this—" She drew in a breath that hissed sharply between her teeth. "Gale swore she didn't know the guy that was murdered—didn't she?"

Her blue eyes, narrowed and defiant, challenged Lutie, waiting for an answer.

She received none, however. Lutie merely continued to regard her coolly, appraisingly.

But the landlady, who was eying her lodger with pronounced distaste, put in, "So what?"

Miss DeVeere turned on her. "You knew who it was, all right. And admitted it—"

"Look here, I've let you live here, DeVeere, without a cent of room rent going on two months now because I'm sorry for you."

DeVeere flushed. "That's right, throw it up at me! I pay you when I got it, don't I? You know I've had bad luck."

"Okay—forget it. But don't take that tone with me. Sure, I knew whose body it was, and I said so. Hester said she didn't know; said she'd never met Mr. Vincent Smyth, even to pass him in the hall. I don't know what you're getting at, but—"

Her lodger raised sullen eyes. There was a hard gleam of malicious triumph in them, and defiance. They would not meet Mrs. Joffey's.

"Well, Gale was lying. That's what I'm getting at. She did know him and I can prove it!"

That the blond girl at least believed she could make good her boast there was no doubt in my mind. My heart sank. But Lutie merely raised her eyebrows.

"Can you indeed, Miss DeVeere? And how?"

"By swearing to what I've seen with my own eyes." She glanced sidewise at her hostess. "And I guess *my* word is as good as—"

"And just what *have* you seen?"

"I've seen that man, that fellow that rented the parlor front a week ago, that was murdered in Gale's bedroom, in her bed, I've seen him going in there—going in Gale's apartment. That's what I've seen! And I'd like to know—"

"And when," inquired Lutie quietly, "was this?"

"Well, I've seen him twice. Once was about a week ago. It was after twelve midnight. I was coming home myself from the late show at the Grotto. As I opened the door I saw a man at Gale's door. I didn't know who it was then but I could see it wasn't the boyfriend—he's taller. The present boyfriend, I mean."

She set her lips, then went on, "Anyway, I thought, that's funny, because that's when Gale is out at this club she works at; but this fellow certainly knew what he was about. He just unlocks Gale's door and goes on in. If he'd been sneaking in I'd have gone down and told you, Juliette. But he was cool as a cucumber. If Gale wasn't there, he was going to wait for her— that was sure. So I should stick my nose into somebody else's business? Not much!"

Miss DeVeere's tone was virtuous, but still she did not look at Mother Joffey.

"Well," she continued, "when I was coming downstairs yesterday to go to the delicatessen I saw a man come out of the parlor front and go back along the hall. I thought it looked like this same fellow I saw going in Gale's that night. In fact, I was sure it was—the same build—medium height, slender; and the same walk, kind of jaunty but smooth—very distangay, you couldn't mistake it. I thought that was odd—it must be the new lodger, but why was the high-and-mighty Gale taking up with a chap that was renting—"

She caught herself and with a quick glance at the proprietor of the Maison LaVelle added hastily, "Not but what he was nice-appearing, he looked like a gentleman, all right enough—and this time I had a good look at his face too. I went on downstairs, and by the time I was at the front door he was opening Gale's door. He turned and looked back at me over his shoulder as he went in her room. And smiled, too, I don't mind saying, but not fresh, just pleasant, gentlemanly, like I said. I must say," commented Miss DeVeere, "I don't mind people who look at you like they was seeing you—not through you like that Bynam fellow, f'rinstance. And this chap had it all over him for looks too. Handsome, he was; pale complexion, dark wavy hair, black eyebrows, one kind of quirked up higher than the other."

Miss DeVeere broke off suddenly, staring at our hostess.

"Why, Mother Joffey! What's the matter? You look like you'd seen a ghost!"

It was true; at least, the plump woman's pleasant face seemed suddenly to have lost its rosy hue, and her eyes held a startled frightened expression. But at Dot's comment she blinked, veiled them, and a surge of color mantled her cheeks.

"Why, dearie, I've told you before it makes me mad, you peeking over banisters and putting your twos-and-twos together. I never did like busybodies."

"Is that so!" retorted Miss DeVeere angrily. Then her attention reverted and she curtailed her outburst to remark shrewdly, "Umm. Well, this time you didn't look mad. You looked scared! I'll bet you know something about Gale and this Smyth, that's what."

Mrs. Joffey shook her head compassionately.

"Dearie, you get yourself so worked up," she observed placidly, and refolded her hands. "I never met Mr. Smyth, or even saw the young man in passing. My legs—"

Lutie cut in hastily, "Could there be any question about the person Miss DeVeere saw, Madame LaVelle? I mean, this dark man, going from the parlor front to Miss Gale's rooms. Could he have been a visitor of Mr. Smyth's, instead of your lodger himself?"

"He never had any visitors so far's I know," answered the landlady. "Anyhow, Dot's description fits Smyth to a tee, especially the walk; you couldn't help notice it, as she says. But what he was doing, traipsing in and out of Hester's place—"

"Of course, it's all most peculiar, isn't it?" said Lutie. "But facts are facts, no matter how distressing."

"Puts a different face on things, don't it?" said Miss DeVeere with a

satisfied smile. "Well, seeing's believing. Though some people won't believe what's right under their noses."

She elevated her own and sniffed disdainfully.

"And if you didn't poke yours in where it don't belong," exclaimed the
landlady in disgust, "you'd be better off, as I've told you plenty of times.
Why can't you mind your own business?"

"And let people get away with murder?" retorted her lodger. "That nice-
looking fellow was murdered, wasn't he? And I saw him, just an hour or so
before, going into Gale's room, didn't I? And if you ask me, he didn't come
out till they carried him out in a basket! Anyway, I wouldn't be surprised!"

Madame LaVelle rose majestically.

"Why, you poor little fool," she said in her deepest voice, glaring down
at her lodger from that amazing height, "wasn't I in Hester's rooms after
that, and wasn't she sitting there minding her own business nice and quiet
like the lady she is? Or didn't you read *that* part in the papers?"

"And what of it?" snapped Dot DeVeere. "You knocked on her door
before you went in, didn't you? And couldn't the guy slip into a closet or
something? And, anyway," her voice rose as the tall woman started to speak
again, "what if he wasn't there then? That was just my guess and it don't
change the facts—what I'd bet my last nickel happened! I'll bet this Smyth
was an old sweetie, and she ditched him, or he'd ditched her, or anyway...
He turns up again, maybe by accident or maybe he rents the parlor front
because he knows she's living here and she's in the money—and besides,
she's got a rich boyfriend. So this Smyth—if that's his name and I doubt
it—tries to shake her down; and she plays him along and makes him think
she's still crazy about him. Maybe she still is crazy about him, and maybe
he's still nuts about her. But that don't make any difference; she can't have
him hanging around spoiling her game with the rich playboy—she might
even think this Bynam'll marry her! So she waits her chance and simply
gives Smyth the business, poor dope. And she thinks if she gets rid of his
head nobody's going to know *who* he was, so they can't connect him up
with her past, and she'll just stick to her story that she never saw the fellow
before and somebody has slipped in and got killed in her bed by accident
and it's all too, *too* bad!"

Miss DeVeere simpered mockingly. Then her thin voice dropped
and she concluded with bitter relish, "And if I hadn't happened to see
what I saw, she probably would've got away with it, I wouldn't be surprised!"

I reflected grimly on the number of things that wouldn't surprise Miss
DeVeere; but just the same what she said had got under my skin. The crude
and vulgar picture she had drawn reminded me most disagreeably of certain
vague and muddled fears that had occurred to me; and even worse, it was

only too likely that her lurid bet would be that of very many people—if not also the police.

And it seemed to me that Mrs. Joffey's plump face was troubled.

But Madame LaVelle's green eyes were fiery with disdain and anger. She was obviously gathering herself for an explosive rejoinder when Lutie quickly forestalled her.

"Mrs. Joffey, does this belong to you?" She held out the key with the flat round head.

The ex-wardrobe mistress peered at it closely. She turned it over, read the inscription and shook her head.

"No, dearie, it don't. First off I thought it was the key to a trunk that I've lost somewhere. I mean I've lost the key, not the trunk. But of course it isn't and it doesn't matter because that old trunk's in the cellar—or maybe it's in the storeroom—is it, Julie? Anyway, I don't suppose I'll ever use it again but if I do I have another key that'll fit it."

"May I see?" said Miss DeVeere jealously. She picked the key up, her little finger (that she probably called her pinky) daintily crooked.

"No, it certainly doesn't belong to me. I never saw it before in my life. Where does it come from?"

Lutie retrieved the key and handed it on to the landlady. "I don't suppose you recognize it, Madame LaVelle?"

"No. But it's one of those keys for places where you can park things—in the subway and Grand Central and Penn Station they have 'em."

Lutie nodded. "I found it on the pavement, near your house last night." She pocketed the key and rose.

"Well, good-day and thank you, Mrs. Joffey. And you, Miss DeVeere; you've been most helpful. And I'm sure your theory of the murder will be the popular one. Though I will admit it does strike me," she added brightly, buttoning her gloves, "as such an unpleasant way to commit a murder. I should push someone under a truck or something simple like that. Dear me, to choose one's own bedroom. So untidy! And not at all clever."

Mrs. Joffey, realizing that our visit was about at an end, hoisted herself from her rocker. Her expression was normally bland again.

"But," she sighed, "murders never do seem really very bright, when you think them over, do they? The murderers do something to get something or to get out of something, but all the ones you read about either in the newspapers or in stories never do get what they set out to get and they always seem to get out of the frying pan into the fire, and the pleasantest way out is to let them commit suicide in the last chapter and that always seems to me kind of a flat ending."

She rose. "Well, I do hope you'll come again. Do drop in any time; I almost never go out because of my legs, and we can have another nice chat when you ladies aren't so busy; I know you are, but I've enjoyed it so much."

Murmuring vaguely appropriate responses and farewells, we backed out of her door.

It closed behind us. But immediately reopened, and Mrs. Joffey's round face appeared.

"Sssh," she whispered, and oozed her rotund self into the hall, closing the door behind her. "That poor Dotty, she's so unhappy she's very mean sometimes. I wouldn't want her to know I'm keeping anything from her."

She leaned closer to Lutie.

"I said I didn't know a thing about this murder, and no more I do. But there's something I've just made up my mind I'm going to tell you, dearie. I wouldn't breathe it to another living soul, though goodness knows it may come out, anyway. That's what's bothering me. You see—"

She cupped her hand to her lips and brought them closer to Lutie's ear, as I moved off, joining Madame LaVelle at the rear of the hall.

Lutie listened intently.

Presently, she said softly, "Thank you, my dear. I'm so glad you told me. It's our little secret; and even if it does come out, as you say, it has given me exactly what I need to work on. Yes, indeed." She nodded and smiled, her blue eyes sparkling. "So don't you worry!"

"I won't, dearie," whispered Mother Joffey, cheerful again. Aloud she said, "Ta-ta, dearies. Come again soon."

She reentered her room. As the door opened, poor Dotty's voice could be heard, shrill with bitterness,

"Telling them not to pay any attention to anything I said, weren't you? Poor Dotty—she don't mean any harm—and I suppose you even told those two silly old dames I'm jealous, too, didn't you? Jealous, indeed! What of, I'd like to know? I'll tell you I wouldn't be in that Gale's boots, not for all the John Bynams in *Who's Who* and not if he was strung with diamonds! Not that I ever saw any diamonds he gave *her.*"

"There, dearie, don't take on so. It's so bad for the complexion, especially a fair thin skin like yours. You know when you get upset you get all puffy under the eyes. I'll just make you a nice hot cup of tea."

The door closed.

CHAPTER 13

WE followed Madame LaVelle up the last flight of stairs. She led us along the hall toward the front, paused before a door and rapped gently, almost reverently.

"Alexander, it's Juliette. And two ladies," she called.

A deep, perfectly beautiful voice replied, "Come in!" and we were ushered into a small room, with a sloping roof and half-windows such as attics have. It was shabby, the plaster of the walls was cracked, but there was about the small room a strange charm. The faded colors, the relation of table and chairs, couch and bookcases, lights and windows, was right. And all were centered around a coal fire in a tiny grate and a tall figure that rose from a chair beside it as we entered.

Mr. Alexander Saint John wore a black velvet smoking jacket and baggy trousers. His age was perhaps sixty, and he had a head like an aristocrat sculptured by Praxiteles. But instead of a tight mat of ropy carven locks it was crowned by a shaggy mane, thick, straight and pure white. He was easily the most handsome man I had ever seen or imagined. In fact he didn't seem quite possible.

Madame LaVelle presented us; we were seated and he resumed his own chair. He studied our card for several moments.

"I am afraid I can't be of any help to you." He shook his magnificent head. "A dreadful thing. That pleasant young woman..."

"But she didn't do it, Alexander!" said Madame LaVelle.

"It doesn't seem probable," he agreed.

I wished he would say more. I didn't much care what; his voice was so rich, so resonant, yet so exquisitely natural that I simply hated it to stop. And it seemed to me that such a voice must produce words of wisdom.

But he didn't say any more.

Finally Lutie ventured, "Could you—will you tell us what you think about it?"

"I'm trying not to think about it," he said gravely.

He stood up—a majestic figure—and smiling down at us he asked, "Do you like growing things?"

He opened the door into a small hall room, and I got up and stood beside him. The room was full of potted plants, on shelves and benches, hung from wall brackets and ranged along the windowsills—begonias, ferns, Japanese lilies, amaryllis, cactus and ivy. There were no unusual blooms, but it was unusual that anything could thrive in that small cubicle with its tiny window, and somehow very lovely.

"I see you do like them," he said, evidently enjoying my surprise and pleasure, and in his beautiful voice he began telling me things about his garden, of how well his children (as he called his plants) could thrive on artificial light and in very little soil if they were fed certain chemicals. "They want understanding, a little attention—like everybody else," he said.

He spoke not so much to me as to them, as if they were alive, which of course they were, but I mean as if they were beloved companions who could hear, understand and almost reply to him.

I could have stayed for a long time in that tiny bower with its worn green linoleum floor and sky-blue walls against which the varying greens of foliage made such charming patterns, looking, and listening to that splendid voice, even if I hadn't been so interested in what it was telling me. And Lutie did allow me a few minutes.

Then she said, "Well, we must really run along. By the way, Mr. Saint John, is this yours?"

She reached into her reticule and drew out the key.

He glanced at it. "No," he said, without comment.

"Thank you," said Lutie, returning the key to her purse, and we took our leave. Mr. Saint John detained the landlady for a moment in the doorway.

I caught a few words: "—too bad to trouble you with it now, my dear. But I thought I should mention it before I forgot or they might do damage again. I should have told you sooner—I heard them several nights ago."

"Thank you, Alexander. I'll have the traps set," said Madame LaVelle; and closing the door she muttered, "Drat it!"

"Drat what?" Lutie pricked up her ears.

"Rats," explained the landlady. "They're in the storeroom again."

She indicated the door we were about to pass.

"Oh. May we look in?" asked Lutie, with interest.

"Yes, but there's nothing to see."

The tall woman stooped and lifted an edge of the threadbare runner in front of the door. She fished out a key, inserted it in the lock and opened the door.

"The cops were in last night. I don't know what they expected to find— anyhow they saw nobody'd been in for weeks. More like months, I guess," she added, standing aside. "I don't know what anybody'd expect to find, but go on in if you want to."

Lutie, however, didn't go in. She stood in the opening, gazing around eagerly. I looked over her shoulder.

It was a small space, crowded with the usual oddments that collect in such places. There were a few battered trunks, packing boxes, hatboxes and miscellaneous cardboard boxes, suitcases and valises, two old kerosene lamps and a basket of dilapidated artificial flowers on a shelf. Everything was thick with dust and cobwebs, and one industrious spider had spun an enormous pattern across the entire front of the cubbyhole; the gray light from the small dirty skylight shone down on this delicate testimony that no one had been in the place for some time, as evidently even the police had decided at one quick glance, since two steps into the room would have broken the frail barrier.

Lutie stood, examining with bright intent eyes the floor, the walls, the spiderweb and the dusty array behind it.

She closed the door and locked it and we trooped downstairs, the land-lady saying that she supposed she really ought to keep a cat but she didn't like them; her mother had been scared by a cat before she was born and naturally that had marked her. And speaking of cats, she believed that was what Willy had heard last night, as many's the time she'd thought there were burglars and she'd gone to look and it was just that dratted animal scrambling about over the fence or the fire escape.

Lutie listened rather absently, and when we arrived at the parlor floor she interrupted. "My dear, I've just recalled that question about the degree of privacy between the front and rear apartments. Shall we try a little experiment?"

Amiable as usual, the landlady unlocked the door of the parlor front and ushered us into the room which, though it had been put in order and was swept and clean, still seemed, to my mind, uncomfortable and gloomy. Be-sides, it was the room of the man who had been murdered.

Lutie said, "Marthy dear, just skip into the parlor rear—"

I backed away from her. "Lutie Beagle, wild horses couldn't drag me in there."

"Oh, the body's gone, there's nothing to bother you!" said the landlady cheerfully. "Here's the key."

She took it from a capacious pocket and held it out.

I shook my head with determination.

" 'Fraidy cat," said Lutie, smiling. She took the key, gave me a little push toward the double doors between the rooms and parted the heavy curtains.

"You stay here then, my dear Watson, and listen very carefully for a few minutes. Then go back toward the middle of the room and listen in an ordinary way."

She flitted out of the room. Obediently I applied my ear to the crack where the doors came together. The landlady, much interested, hovered near.

Presently there was a sound, the key in the lock to the back apartment I guessed, the sound of the door closing, then Lutie's voice, "How do you do …Come in…Good afternoon…Dear me, how ridiculous, I can't think of a thing to say…Life is real, life is earnest…Drink to me only with thine eyes, and I will pledge with mine…Sixteen men on a dead man's chest, yo ho ho and a bottle of rum…Can you hear what I'm saying, my dear Watson? Just go on listening for a minute while I telephone…Then move off and listen…"

There were light footsteps as she moved across the room; then her voice, from a little further away, "Hello…Hello…Hi diddle diddle, the cat and the fiddle, the cow jumped over the moon, the little dog laughed to see such fun and the dish ran away with the spoon…Goodbye…That'll do; now step back in the room and listen casually, and after that ask Madame LaVelle to stand where she stood when she dropped in to chat, and both of you talk a bit just in ordinary tones."

I let the curtains fall back into place and moved off.

"Well," said the landlady, "you can hear, all right, if you take the trouble. But why should anyone—"

"I don't know," I said. "But wait, please; we're supposed to find out now what you can overhear without particularly trying."

So we were quiet. There was the murmur of a voice, the words indistinguishable. Then faint sounds, barely enough to tell that someone was in the other room, moving around, opening and closing doors. This, I supposed, was all that Lutie wanted to ascertain, so I obeyed orders and drew the landlady toward the front of the room.

"Well, I don't think that's anything to complain of," she said.

Without explaining that I didn't imagine this experiment was being conducted for her benefit (though I didn't, myself, know just what it was about), I asked her to stand where she'd been when she'd dropped in last night.

She looked puzzled, but moved near the front door.

"Why, right here," she said. "What's this all about?"

I shrugged. "I don't know. Go on talking, please."

"What'll I say?" she asked, and stared at me—the garrulous Madame LaVelle, suddenly tongue-tied!

"Anything!" I told her, and waited. Exasperated, I rattled, "Mary had a little lamb, its fleece was white as snow...This is some sort of experiment, Madame LaVelle. It doesn't matter what you say. Repeat Shakespeare—or what you said last evening."

Then I wished I hadn't said that, as she replied, "Oh! Okay," and addressed me with a kindly smile, "Bon swor, Meestaire Smeeth. I have brought you a piece of apple pie..." She handed me an imaginary piece of pie and went on, "Eet eez good. I make eet myself"

The parlor door behind us opened, and Lutie tripped in. But Madame was now so absorbed in her role that she went on with it.

"Now, don't you set it down on the mantel! I won't budge till you finish it. That's right. Didn't I tell you it was first-rate pie? Here, give me the plate. I'll take it with me and leave it downstairs on my way out. You say eet eez a vairee rainy night to ventur-re out? Phut—me, I do not mind zee rain! Rain or shine, eet eez all ze same."

"Oh, splendid, Madame LaVelle!" cried Lutie. "What a comedienne you are! As well as a tragedienne, I'm sure! I can absolutely see that young man eating the pie! And to the last flaky crumb, I'll bet."

"Merci!"

The tall woman bowed graciously, accepting this compliment to her dramatic and culinary talent. She added, "I'll say he ate it. He polished the plate."

"I hope you'll treat us to some of your pie some day, will you, Madame LaVelle?"

As the landlady beamed, Lutie turned to me. "Tell me, my dear Watson, how much could you hear of the silly things that were all I could think of to say?"

I repeated a few of her inanities.

She twinkled at me, handed back the key to the rear apartment and said, admiringly, "Marthy dear, you have one of the best memories I've ever met for whatever you really hear! Dear Madame LaVelle, I think that was a very profitable little experiment, don't you? Thank you so much. And now we won't bother you any more for the time being."

After a further exchange of amenities, and after declining a pressing invitation to stay for midday dinner, roast pork and sweet potato pie, we again took leave of the Maison LaVelle.

CHAPTER 14

I HAD been accumulating questions all morning. I was fairly bursting with them, and the moment we were clear of the lodging house I began, "Lutie, what *did* Mrs. Joffey tell you?"

"Sshh!" she said.

She was trotting swiftly eastward. I tagged at her heels, finding it none too easy to keep up with her.

"Where are we going?" I asked rather crossly. For we were not headed toward home and dinner, and I'd been looking forward to both, as well as to some satisfaction of my curiosity.

I was several paces behind her, puffing slightly, when we reached the corner of Forty-eighth Street and Sixth Avenue, and she darted into a drugstore. I followed as she hurried toward the rear, seized a phone directory, and thumbed swiftly through it. Fishing in her reticule she pulled out her tiny violet leather memo book, scribbled in it, tucked it back in her bag and popped into the phone booth. She placed a nickel in the slot and dialed.

I heard her say, "The County Morgue?…This is Miss Lutie Beagle… Yes…Yes, we are working with Inspector Moore and Dr. Throckmorton on the Headless Murder Case. I wish to speak to—"

She pulled the door shut, and I heard no more. But as the light went on in the little cubbyhole I could see her lips moving, close to the mouthpiece. Then they stopped, she cocked her head eagerly, listening. Her cheeks were bright pink, her eyes gleaming. I saw her nod, nod again, murmur a word or two and place the receiver on the hook.

At this moment a minor commotion occurred at the front of the drug-store, as a small man, dashing in at the door, collided with a customer on her way out.

"Why don't you look where you're going?" snapped the irate female.

"A thousand pardons, dear lady!" begged a familiar voice. "I was in something of a hurry."

The gentleman swept off his jaunty pearl-gray Fedora with a deep bow. Then he hurried and came scuttling toward the back of the pharmacy.

"Why, Professor Sesame! So we meet again!" said Lutie, in the door-way of the phone booth.

He stopped short. His face was mottled, his beady eyes popping with excitement.

"Dear ladies!" he exclaimed breathlessly.

Swiftly he glanced around him. Leaning close to Lutie's ear he whis-pered tensely, "It is as I thought! I now have the proof! I am about to com-municate it to the police. You will pardon me?"

He indicated his desire to replace her in the booth. But Lutie, without moving from it, looked up into his face, her own filled with admiration and sweet, appealing interest.

"Have you actually found the proof? Really and truly, Professor?" she cooed softly. "How wonderful! I suppose you mean the missing head, don't you?"

"Sssshhh!" he hissed.

Lutie glanced at the solitary clerk, who was engaged in arranging a dis-play in the front window, and at the white-capped boy yawning behind the soda fountain. There were no customers in the store. She smiled trustingly at the little magician and murmured, "I'm sure it's safe to speak here—if we're very careful. Now, do tell us. Where was the head?"

Thus baited the little gentleman replied, "Dear lady, I have not yet lo-cated the head. But I have discovered something of far more importance! I have found out that Vincent Smyth, the mysterious lodger in the parlor front, the, er, ex-owner of the missing head—in short, the murdered man—was Floto! Incontrovertibly, indubitably, and without a doubt; he was Floto!"

"Oh, have you, really and truly? How did you discover that?" asked Lutie, in a thrilled whisper.

"By keeping my ears open, and waiting beside the register, like a cat at a rat-hole! After all, the murderer is a rat, and the end justifies the means; the police use dictaphones! Reasoning thus, this morning I took up my position as soon as stirrings below told me that the Fennellis were awake, and waited patiently—for hours, it seemed—for the family, alas, then, for some time congregated in the parental apartment, the front room. Eventually, however, the brothers returned to their room, and Lotta, the sister, was with them.

"Well, the girl was crying, not loudly, but as if her heart would break. I heard her say, 'Oh, why did I ever tell you, Raffy? Why did I?' And Mike said, 'Shut up, you little fool.' But she went on, 'I know—I know I was a fool. But it struck me all of a heap yesterday when I saw that Smyth walk in the house—and there he was, the guy I'd seen in Cincy with Dolo! I tell you I thought he mighta come here to get rid of Raffy—I don't know what I thought! But how'd I know this would happen?' Mike said, 'Listen. What you gotta do now is keep your mouth shut, both of you. If you don't you're in the soup, Raph; I'm telling you!' Then Raph said, 'You don't think they'll find out it was Floto? They will—they'll find out somehow!' Then he said why didn't they beat it, skip the next two weeks' work in New York and go on the road right away? And Mike said that was just like his dumb way of figuring—that would be a fine way to make the cops suspicious.

"So," said the professor, who had been carried away by his story and rendered a very effective impersonation of the Fennellis, with appropriate gestures, "—so I left them arguing. I needed to hear no more, and I realized the imperative necessity of haste!"

Again he made a move to enter the phone booth, adding urgently, "A thousand pardons, dear lady. I must inform the police. You will appreciate, there must not be any delay! If you will excuse me—"

Lutie stepped backward into the booth and slipped a coin from her glove into the slot. Rapidly she dialed a number.

She said, "Professor, that's marvelous! But you know, in cases of murder the police receive so many calls from fanatics they might not pay attention to what you have to tell them. Whereas, we are official, in a sense—Hello!"

She broke off, pulling the door partly closed. Through the opening came her voice, speaking loudly and quickly, "Headquarters?…This is Miss Lutie Beagle, of the Beagle Detective Agency. I have important news for you. I didn't make this discovery myself—all the credit is due to Professor Sesame …Very important…No, we will not risk telling you on the phone—walls have ears…Yes, at once…Do you wish the professor to come with me?…Oh, you prefer him to wait until he hears from you?… Oh, no, I'm sure you can place implicit trust in him—he won't reveal what he knows to anyone…Yes, he'll hold himself at your service. He's most anxious to cooperate…Certainly, I'll lose no time. Goodbye, Inspector!"

Lutie hung up the receiver and pushed open the door, all in one gesture.

"You heard?" she smiled at the little man, who was beaming with pride and fairly shaking with excitement.

"Yes indeed, dear lady!" He bowed deeply. "And I shall await a call from the inspector; I will be home in my apartment, or at work, at the theater. Meanwhile, not a word passes my lips."

He placed his finger delicately across them.

Then, inflating his chest, he whispered exultantly, "You agree, then—the case is solved?"

"Yes, I think it is," said Lutie brightly. "But there's no time to be lost. I must run!"

She did so, and I followed, leaving the professor executing a series of profound bows.

Out on the street again, Lutie hastened around the corner and toward a cruising taxicab. She waved and called, but the driver's attention was elsewhere. With an annoyed exclamation she turned, scurrying in the direction of another cab, beckoning wildly.

"Taxi—taxi!" she piped, dashing through the noonday crowd that thronged the sidewalk, toward the curb. As she stepped from it a pedestrian bumped heavily into me. I staggered against Lutie and, nearly losing my balance, clutched at her. But Lutie had caught the cabdriver's eye this time; the taxi slowed, halted. She darted to it, pulling me with her, and hopped in while I clambered after, jolted, bruised and irritated.

"For goodness' sake, Lutie!" I exclaimed, plumping into a seat as the cab, prodded by impatient vehicles in the rear, jerked forward.

"Where to, lady?" asked the driver, over his shoulder.

"Marthy, my reticule! It's gone," said Lutie, in an odd voice.

"Oh, dear—you must have left it in the phone booth," I exclaimed.

Then I remembered that I'd seen it swinging from her wrist as we hurried out of the drugstore.

"No, you didn't. You must have dropped it."

"No, I didn't drop it," she answered, still in that strange tone. Then, brightly, she added, "Well, anyway, I recall the address perfectly," and leaning forward, said, "Driver, go to 1542 Broadway, please. And try to make as good time as you possibly can, won't you?"

He said, "Okay, lady," and barely missed a big delivery wagon as we barged around a corner.

I groaned. "Lutie, aren't we going home yet? We're already late for dinner. If you're not going to try and find your reticule—"

"Marthy," said Lutie softly, "my reticule was stolen. When you grabbed me, someone grabbed my bag."

I stared at her. Her eyes were gleaming; color blazed in her cheeks.

"What luck!" she murmured.

'Luck?" I repeated, bewildered.

She nodded. "Yes. Because the person who stole my purse wanted this!"

She unbuttoned the glove on her left hand and peeled it back. Curled in the palm was the key she had found last night in the back yard.

"Of course, I knew that's why he tried to run us down last night; he saw me slip this in my purse. If there'd been an accident in that dark alley he might have got it! But there wasn't. And then, this morning I'd almost begun to fear he'd given up. Dear me, I was really worried. Ah, here we are!" She hastily fastened tiny black glove buttons over the key as the cab lurched to a stop and was out on the sidewalk before I'd collected my wits.

"Marthy, pay the cabby, please," said she. "And give him a good tip— half a dollar! We're charging it to expenses!"

As I climbed out after her I protested, "But, Lutie, that's too much— he'll think we're greenhorns."

"Tut—this is my lucky day!" chirped Lutie.

I fumbled in my bag. The chauffeur pocketed his tip with surprised thanks, and I tagged after Lutie, across the sidewalk, into the building.

An elderly man came forward and asked what he could do for us.

Lutie looked up at him appealingly.

"Oh, dear. Such a silly thing has happened, Mr.—er—"

"Smith, ma'am," he supplied politely.

"Thank you! Dear me, what an odd coincidence! We, er, know another gentleman named Smith, too! That is, he used a 'y' and maybe you use an 'i'—and we don't exactly know him, but still—it's a small world, isn't it? as I often say to my cousin! This is my cousin, Mr. Smith; we're from out of town and rather lost in this big city. So you see, that's why I came to you. Oh, dear, I've been so stupid. I hardly know what you'll think of me."

The gentleman murmured that he would be glad to be of service, and Lutie drew the key from her glove and handed it to him.

"Well, this morning my sister, who resides here in the city, gave me this key when Cousin and I were going out. She said, 'I wish you'd attend to this for me, my dear. And I'm sure she must have explained what I was to do with it. Or did she? Perhaps she just took it for granted I'd know! But—poor rattle-gated me! I don't—and if she told me I've forgotten! So, I came to the address on the key, to ask you! What do I do with it, Mr. Smith?"

She gazed earnestly at Mr. Smith, who scratched his head.

Presently he said, "That is a key to one of our lockers."

"Oh, yes, of course we know that! But where," asked Lutie, "is the locker? Here, I suppose?"

"No, we don't have lockers here." He smiled at her naiveté. "This one would be in the Times Square subway."

"Oh, yes, of course! I remember now—dear me, I must be getting ol—things go right out of my head, you know! But then, at a word, they'll pop right back again. Sister was shopping at ...Meecy's, I think she said. Anyway, a very big store, and she had…yes, it was a feather comforter and some blankets—my cousin does get so cold at night, you know…and they made such a big package and Sister had to go to the library—that's over on Fifth Avenue, isn't it? Such a handsome building, though I must say we have a very nice one in our little village, too. Well, anyway, Sister left the comforter and forgot all about it till she got home—she's very absentminded, though she wouldn't like it a bit if she heard me say so."

"What time was it," asked Mr. Smith, "when your sister left this package? Because if she left it more than twenty-four hours ago it won't be there. We collect anything that is left longer than that."

"Oh, what a lot of bother to put you to! But I'm quite sure—yes, she didn't go out till two yesterday—so she couldn't have even bought the things before then! So it will be all right." She reached for the key and tucked it back in her glove. "And I'd hate to be any more trouble. I've already taken your time and I know you're a very busy man, but still I always believe it pays to go right straight to the person higher up! Thank you again, Mr. Smith, ever and ever so much. And good-afternoon. It is a beautiful afternoon, isn't it? I hope we'll meet again. You've been so kind, and it's so nice to see a friendly face in this great big town. Of course, at home we know everybody, but here it's different. Well, I mustn't keep you any longer; I'm a terrible chatterbox when I get started, Sister always says! Let's see—Times Square, that's quite near, isn't it? Well, good-bye, Mr. Smith!"

We left Mr. Smith looking benevolent but slightly dazed.

"What a nice man," said Lutie when we were once more out on Broadway and headed south. "Now for our last errand!"

I was tired and hungry and my shoulder had begun to ache where I'd been bumped into.

I muttered crossly, "I hope it's not a fool's errand!" And then I gasped. For then—and somehow not till then—the significance of what she'd said about our last night's accident struck me in full force! So the driver of the black sedan wasn't simply drunk; he had deliberately meant to run us down! Which meant that he was the murderer—or a confederate. And a killer too, who, she believed, was luckily still on our trail!

It was a paralyzing thought. After all, crimes had been committed in broad daylight. In a city like New York anything might happen. Fear and terror flooded back over me. I stood stock-still.

"Hurry, my dear!" said Lutie.

I winced as she tugged briskly at my arm. But I didn't budge. She turned and looked at me then, and of course my face must have shown her the fright I was feeling.

"Now, Marthy—" she pleaded gently.

"Lutie," I begged her, "please let's go home. I'm frightened! I've just realized—"

She said gravely, "Marthy dear, you won't fail me, will you? I really need you. I think perhaps it may be dangerous; but not if you'll do as I tell you. And everything depends on it."

Of course I couldn't resist her when she talked like that.

"But what is it all about?" I faltered.

"I don't know, exactly," she said.

Taking my arm she led me quickly down Broadway and across the great triangle where we'd gone, one night, escorted by Jeff to see the sights—the towering buildings and enormous placards flashing blue and red and green and gold against a black sky, the swirling after-theater crowds, the crawling, honking, pushing traffic.

Now at noon Times Square was just as clamorous, though not as glamorous, as at midnight; but in spite of the bright fall sunlight, the fresh pleasant smell of orange from the Nedick stand and the warm odor of pot roast, pie and pancakes from the restaurants we passed, the busy commonplace crowds around us, I was shaking in my shoes. I stiffened and glanced fearfully over my shoulder at each quick footstep behind us, and, holding tightly to my small companion, shrank from every approaching figure.

But as we came to the subway entrance I held back once more. Up here on the great street it was at least sunlight, there were policemen within call; there below it was dim and gloomy, the cold dank air that blew up into our faces chilled my marrow, the scream of trains over the deadly third rail was a shriek of menace and warning.

I said, "Oh, Lutie—"

She gripped my arm, urged me forward. Down the stairs we went, into that echoing, roaring vault.

"Here it is," she said, her voice low, tense; and stopped.

We stood before a bank of lockers. They were in vertical tiers, painted olive green, and above them a gold shield displayed the name and address of the Columbia Locker Company.

Lutie scanned the lockers. Still holding my arm, she moved in front of one. Printed large, in red on gold, I read, "J-361."

"Marthy," said Lutie quietly, "don't look around you. I am going to open this locker. And whatever I find, I am going to take it out. And we are going to take it away with us. We will both hold on to it—whatever it is— and if anyone shoves us, or hits us, or tries to take it from us in my way, hold on for all you're worth and yell like—*Yell!* Simply hang on and YELL! Can you do that?"

I swallowed. I was shaking all over. But I managed to say, "Yes, Lutie."

She peeled back her glove, extracted the key, inserted it in the lock and swung open the locker door, all very quickly; and with a jerk pulled out a small suitcase. Without bothering to close the locker, she shoved it toward me.

"Now, hold on," she said.

I grasped the handle of the bag obediently. Both holding it, we ran toward the subway steps.

"Don't forget. If we're pushed or anything—scream!" said Lutie loudly.

I saw faces turn in our direction. My knees felt weak, and I stumbled as I ran. But I did run. And I held on to the bag.

"Let people look. I want them to look!" said Lutie gaily. "It's perfect, Marthy. We're going to make it My dear, you're wonderful!"

We were up the stairs, out into the bright sunlight of the street.

And there Lutie caught the arm of a young man coming toward the subway entrance.

"Oh, my dear, will you call a taxi for us? We've just come to town and we're so confused! Please, will you stop that cab?"

Startled, he looked down. Then seeing the small creature smiling wistfully up at him, his face relaxed.

"Sure, ma'am! Hi—taxi!" he bawled and waved vigorously.

A cab drew up in front of us and the young man assisted us into it. I still kept my grip of the bag, and so did Lutie.

The young man grinned.

"Thank you so much, my dear," cooed Lutie.

"Don't mention it, ma'am," he said, doffing his hat.

And then, at the spectacle of the elderly ladies from the country each still desperately clutching the handle of their shabby suitcase, he added cheerfully, "Must be something pretty important in that there!"

"Yes, indeed, there is!" said Lutie, smiling at him gratefully.

CHAPTER 15

THE cab lurched and slithered through the traffic. We had only a few short blocks to go, for at last we were actually on our way home. On learning that, I'd drawn a deep breath of relief; but fear struck me again almost at once.

"Lutie," I whispered, my voice trembling, "suppose we're being followed now? And on our way upstairs, in those dark halls, if we're overtaken—" I shuddered.

And just then, as we turned the corner into Forty-fourth Street, I saw before my eyes the stolid, comforting back of a large blue-coated figure. By leaning from the cab I could have touched the policeman's shoulder.

And Lutie or no Lutie, I was going to do it, to claim his escort and protection. I edged forward.

But small strong fingers fastened on my elbow.

"Stop that, Martha!" said Lutie sharply. "If you call that policeman I'll explain that you're a lunatic cousin with a mania of persecution! Do you want to spoil everything? Keep quiet. I know what I'm doing!"

I sank back in the cab. A moment later it was drawing in to the curb. The driver climbed from his seat, opened the door for us and reached for the suitcase. He was a heavy young man with a broad amiable face.

Lutie allowed him to assist her from the taxi. But she clung to the suitcase with both hands.

I climbed from the cab, almost missing the step in my nervousness.

"There, there!" chirruped Lutie. She looked up at the taxi driver. "We're both so upset! You see, we're from the country; and my purse has just been stolen! Will you mind coming upstairs for your money? Come, Marthy."

I followed her up the stoop, the burly young fellow at our heels.

As we pushed open the door he said, "Let me carry that for you, ma'am."

"No, thank you, it's not heavy!" said Lutie. "But," she lowered her voice, "will you stay just behind us, and keep an eye out for—well, for anyone who may come up the stairs? You know, don't let anyone push past you and get near us. I daresay it's silly, but after what happened we're so frightened."

The young man looked slightly surprised. Then an indulgent grin turned up the corners of his wide mouth.

"I'll take care of you, ma'am. Betcha life!" he assured her kindly.

So up the stairs tripped Lutie, with me puffing in her wake and our guard lumbering in the rear.

At the door of our living room she tapped smartly. The door opened and Lutie darted past Amanda into the bedroom. She was back in a moment minus the suitcase but with Amanda's flat black handbag

"Thank you so much!" she said breathlessly, and pushed a crisp bill into the cabby's brawny paw. As the man departed she turned to me happily.

"You see, Marthy? That was simple, after all, wasn't it?"

"Lutie Beagle," demanded Amanda, shutting the door crossly, "whatever in the world! Are you crazy?"

"No, just marvelously lucky, Sister dear!" She sighed blissfully. "I lost my reticule, but there was only a dollar in it and nothing else of importance. I shall crochet myself another. I've seen the prettiest model—isn't it funny the way things come back in style? The purse I saw was just like one of Grandmother's and it was at Bergdorf-Goodman's! And we picked up such a bargain—not, of course, at Bergdorf-Goodman's! My, I'm hungry!"

She untied her bonnet-strings and unbuttoned her jacket.

"Hmmph, I should think so! You're forty-three minutes late for dinner. A fine time you chose to go gallivanting, I must say!" Amanda said.

She turned her back and stalked away.

It was the first chance I'd had to catch my breath. Something was missing.

"Where's Hester?" I exclaimed.

Amanda went on into the kitchen without answering. I hastened into the bedroom. The girl wasn't there, nor in my room either. I threw off my wraps and went back to the living room.

Lutie had taken off her bonnet and jacket. She shook her head at me significantly.

"Sister is upset. Didn't you notice? Something disagreeable has happened. But don't let's bother her by asking. Sshh!" she cautioned me, as Amanda came from the kitchen with a laden tray and put our dinner firmly on the table.

We drew up our chairs meekly.

"Jefferson and I have had our dinner," said Amanda. "Don't blame me if the lamb's ruined and the peas spoiled. Hester's gone. Arrested, I suppose you'd call it."

She sat down and reached for her knitting.

"Arrested?" I repeated feebly.

Amanda said, "Eat your victuals while they're hot. Or I'll tell you nothing."

Suddenly I didn't seem to feel hungry any longer. But there was no use arguing, I knew. I picked up my fork. Lutie, like Werther's Charlotte, calmly went on eating bread and butter, also lamb and mint sauce and green peas.

Amanda said finally, "Hester has been taken to headquarters, but before I tell you any more, I'd like to know, Lutie Beagle, what you've been up to? What in the name of nonsense did all that balderdash mean on the telephone?"

"This sauce is really delicious," said Lutie. "That telephone call, Sister dear? Why, you see, there was a gentleman, a Professor Sesame, a magician. He is quite sure the murder is solved, and he wanted to phone the police. But I preferred him not to, at the moment. So I did; only I didn't!" she finished brightly, and took another roast potato.

"You mean to say you were just pretending, Lutie?" I gasped. "You—you mean you actually phoned *here?*"

She nodded, smiling at me.

"And what," snapped Amanda, "was the purpose of this shenanigan?"

"Well," said Lutie thoughtfully, "I just didn't want things stirred up."

"Hmm," said Amanda.

She eyed Lutie suspiciously. The latter helped herself to caramel custard.

"We must give that nice Madame LaVelle this recipe," she remarked. "What happened, Sister—about Hester, I mean?"

Amanda began to knit furiously.

"Two men arrived here, soon after you left. Two members of the homicide squad, I believe. The inspector was not one of them; a man named McGinnis seemed to be in charge. They came to the office, and Jefferson, who had done very well at keeping the representatives of the press from intruding on me, did not manage so well with these two persons. In short, he seemed quite impressed with them, and without a word of warning, before I could prevent it, he'd allowed them in here, when the child hadn't even finished her breakfast!"

Amanda scowled resentfully. "And goodness knows she needed it. She'd have eaten another egg and more toast, if she'd had a chance, and maybe then she'd have got some sense into her and told me—" She broke off, and added grimly, "How's anybody to think straight on an empty stomach, I'd like to know? However, there they were, and she lost her appetite at the first sight of them. Just the same, I told 'em they couldn't come in till she was dressed; and how was she to dress, I asked them, when she hadn't anything to wear? So McGinnis handed me a suitcase, and said all right, let her get dressed then, but to make it snappy. I was annoyed at the fellow's manner but naturally did not show it; I merely remarked that I hoped they'd satisfied themselves with their damn foolishness about the child's clothes.

"Yes, I said 'damn.' I did not consider any other expression suitable. McGinnis replied with what I can only describe as a leer that he was pretty sure they'd be satisfied, all right; they were not yet through with the clothes the girl had worn when she committed the murder. This conversation took place while Hester was in your room, Marthy, putting on the garments which, it seems, Madame LaVelle had packed this morning at the request of the police."

Amanda put down her knitting and picked up Tabby. She stroked him sternly as she continued.

"When the child appeared McGinnis thrust a photograph at her and growled most uncivilly, 'Who's that man?' She answered that he was a man she had once known, an actor. McGinnis shouted at her, 'Yes, I'll say you knew him! And he's the man that was murdered—isn't he?' "

Amanda paused grimly.

After a moment she continued. "The child didn't reply at first; then she said she didn't know. He shook the picture at her and sneered, 'You might as well come clean. That's Vincent Smyth; that's the fellow that had the parlor front, and we know it.' But Hester merely replied very calmly that she had not seen the man who had rented the parlor front, and therefore she didn't know it. And that was all she would say. McGinnis asked her the name of the man in the photograph, and what she'd had against him, as well as various other idiotic questions. She was white and shaking, but she simply told McGinnis coolly that she didn't care to talk to him. And this time she was right, and I was proud of her. McGinnis is not worth talking to. So finally he gave up and said that his orders were to take her down to Headquarters, anyway. She said she was quite ready to go. And they went. But," said Amanda, "not before I'd had a look at that photograph."

She set Tabby on the rug.

"There was an address on the back, The Stoll Studios, Chicago, Illinois, and a date of five years ago. And it was a picture of Hester and a young man. And I must say that it answered the description of the lodger in the parlor front."

Lutie nodded. "McGinty held his thumb over Hester," she murmured. "Of course they found it in the suitcase."

"What are you muttering about, Lutie Beagle?" asked Amanda sharply.

"Nothing, Sister." Lutie dropped three lumps of sugar in her coffee. "That is, it was only something I happened to think of. You might call it foolishness."

"Hmm. Never mind what I'll call it. You may as well come out with it. And then we can get down to facts," said Amanda.

She folded her hands to listen as patiently as possible.

"Well, you see," began Lutie, stirring her coffee, "Marthy and I did the marketing. And then, it was such a pleasant morning, and it seemed much better to leave you alone with Hester, you were so cozy and it was plain she'd taken a fancy to you. It was just bad luck you were interrupted before she'd had a chance to tell all, for I'm sure she would have, and that might have been quite a help, mightn't it? Well, anyway, Marthy and I thought we'd call on Madame LaVelle. Such an odd soul, isn't she? With her airs and graces, and a heart like a rough diamond, in a manner of speaking, as the English lower classes say. Or do they? At any rate, she was very pleasant, and before we left the Maison LaVelle, as she calls it—that's so touching, isn't it? And I think she comes from Brooklyn!—as I was saying, before we left we'd practically dropped in on most of her guests."

"You mean you'd dropped in on practically all her—"

"No, Sister dear. I really meant what I said. It did seem to me like a practical idea, to drop in and just let them talk, and try to listen and remember very carefully. Most of them loved talking, though of course their first impulse when the police shot questions at them was to be a bit cagey—I mean, well, not chatty, you know. But with a good listener…Well, it's a temptation even to you, isn't it, dear? And as for me, I could just go rattling on by the hour—"

"So I've noticed," said Amanda dryly. "But we haven't got hours to rattle on in, as it happens."

Lutie finished her coffee and put down the cup.

"Why," she murmured, "there's plenty of time to talk now! We can go all over everything. I'll tell you the things I heard, and you'll tell us what to think. That's practical, isn't it? And then—"

She was interrupted by Jeff's knock on the door, the one that opened on the inner hallway to the offices.

Amanda said, "Come in," and Jeff entered with John Bynam.

"Our client wishes to see you, boss," he said. "I thought I'd better bring him in here. Not much privacy out in front," he gestured. "The ladies and gents of the press keep barging in."

Amanda nodded at him. "Go back and take care of them, Jefferson. And do not allow anyone else—anyone, mind!—in here. Good afternoon, Mr. Bynam. Please be seated."

Jeff obeyed, though reluctantly, and John Bynam took the chair my elder cousin had indicated. We exchanged greetings. Then Lutie rose quietly and began clearing the table, and I followed her example.

In the kitchen, however, she whispered that we would leave the dishes for the time being, since this was quite an unusual occasion.

We returned to the living room to hear our client saying, "They've found out the whole story. It would have been best if she'd told them in the first place. But how was she to know? So they're holding her on suspicion of homicide."

Lutie settled herself quietly in the background and motioned me to a chair beside her.

There was a short silence. Amanda cleared her throat.

But she didn't say anything, and presently John Bynam said quietly, "Also I am under surveillance myself. I suppose the police are waiting to tighten up their case, but before the day is over I expect I'll be held on the same charge. I certainly had motive, and so far as they know, opportunity; also apparently I lied—the young man who let me in the house has denied that he did—I don't know why, but it doesn't much matter."

He shrugged, then added bitterly, "The trouble is the evidence against me won't clear Hester. Their case will be that we acted together; probably that I committed the murder and that she took the—"

He broke off. "Imagine Hester making that trip to the river, calmly carrying the bag containing—what they think it held."

He laughed, a short harsh sound without mirth. "It's insane, of course—but it all fits in, apparently. Makes a pretty picture!"

He stared into the fire and added, less to us than to himself, "If I'd had the chance I'd cheerfully have killed the rat. Now someone else has done it. And Hester..." He shook his head. "What a hideous mess!"

Then he squared his shoulders. "My attorney's on his way back to New York. We'll hire the best defense lawyers in the country. But meanwhile she— It's devilish to think of their holding her. Finding that photograph clinched the case against her."

"Where," asked Amanda, "did they find that photograph?"

He said, "In a suitcase on top of a closet in the parlor front. It was marked V.S. and was apparently empty. The police took it with them, and later found the picture slipped under the lining. They showed it to Madame LaVelle. I'm told they kept part of it hidden. I suppose they thought she might lie out of friendship for Hester if she saw the whole photo. Anyway, she identified the man as her lodger—as Vincent Smyth."

A coal dropped in the grate. Tabby rose from the rug, stretched, and went to the window that gave on the fire escape. But for once Amanda paid no attention to his demands.

John Bynam said, "So that ties her up with the man who was killed in her room. And there's her trip to the river with a suitcase—which she threw away. And her mistake about the time she left the house—which I can't figure out. There's something queer about it, but I suppose to the police it looks like a deliberate lie."

He got up and walked across the floor, then back again.

"Of course they won't find any bloodstains on her clothes, but that won't help much. I daresay they'll figure that she committed the murder dressed in her cellophane raincoat!"

He laughed again, harshly.

"Or that you did," murmured Lutie.

"Don't talk poppycock!" snapped Amanda. "Who," she demanded, "aside from being the lodger called Vincent Smyth, identified as the murdered man by Madame LaVelle and by Hester as an actor she once knew, is the man in the photograph?"

John Bynam did not answer for a long moment.

Then he said slowly, "His name, when Hester knew him, was Victor Shaw. He was the man who phoned her last night. He was a convict—a murderer. He was Hester's husband!"

CHAPTER 16

"THAT'S hell to tell the captain!" remarked Rabelais, as he woke from a nap and ruffled his green and scarlet plumage.

Lutie said, "Be still, Rab." She had obviously not been startled by John Bynam's revelation.

But Amanda was, I could see.

The cat meowed and she went to the window to let him out. She walked rather heavily, but by the time she'd resumed her seat she'd regained her usual poise.

"I think," she said, "you'd better tell us the whole story, John. I daresay you won't find it pleasant, but that can't be helped. Begin at the beginning, please—and try to be as matter of fact as possible."

"Do smoke!" murmured Lutie gently.

He said, "Thanks," and drew a case from his pocket.

He lighted a cigarette absently and, leaning one arm on the mantel, stared down into the fire.

"When Hester was a child," he began, "her mother, who was a very fine pianist and had been a concert musician before her marriage, started her musical training. Later she decided the girl had a real voice and took her to Chicago—they lived in a nearby suburb—for lessons. These came to a stop when Hester was sixteen; her mother died, and soon afterward her father married again. He had no sympathy with her music, and the sound of practice gave her stepmother sick headaches, she said.

"So Hester used to practice at the home of a friend of her mother's, who had a piano and encouraged her to use it. The friend's sister visited Evanston now and then; she was also very fond of Hester—Hester called her Aunt Polly. She was a wardrobe mistress and passionate about the theater. She used to take Hester to plays in Chicago, and frequently they'd go backstage to visit some old crony of Aunt Polly's.

"One evening they went to a musical comedy called *High Time,* and after the show, in the star's dressing room, Aunt Polly had Hester sing for him."

John Bynam paused.

He didn't look up as he continued, "While her friend and the actor were talking over old times Hester wandered out into the corridor. A young man spoke to her. He was a minor actor in the show. He'd overheard Hester singing. He told her she had a great voice. He—"

Bynam threw his cigarette into the fire.

He said abruptly, "A week later they were married."

His voice fell into a monotone as he went on, "Hester was just eighteen then. She wrote her father about her marriage. She said that Victor Shaw was a fine pianist. Shaw had told her that, explaining that he had injured his hand and the small part in *High* Time was a fill-in till he could use it again. Hester's father wrote that he'd always known her mother's crazy ambitions would lead to no good end, and so on—pretty cruelly, I gathered. Anyway, he was through with her, and she wasn't to come crawling back to him when she got in trouble. The stepmother wrote that she'd broken her father's heart. Nice people!" remarked John Bynam. He added bitterly, "That didn't make things any easier later. Poor kid."

Amanda cleared her throat.

He glanced at her and said, "I know. It's no use going into that—" His voice resumed its flat tone as he went on rapidly, "The day after their marriage Shaw told Hester he'd left the cast of *High Time.* They went to San

Francisco. He told her there was a great teacher there she was to study under. He painted glowing pictures of the future. When her voice was ready
and his hand was well, they would get concert engagements together and
she would become famous. And so on and so forth.

"In San Francisco he did take her to a good teacher. He also got her a
job in a cheap cabaret, singing. He said it was good experience and would
give her confidence. It was rather distasteful, but she was grateful for her
singing lessons, worked hard, and didn't mind the cabaret work too much.
What she did mind was the change that came over Shaw, abruptly."

John Bynam lighted another cigarette, with hands that shook a little.

He said, "Apparently the fellow was a good actor—off the stage, at any
rate. Hester says that her first impression of him was of a gentle, idealistic
person. He was boyish, affectionate but not ardent. In fact, he treated her
shyly—as something too precious to touch. She was just a kid and that seemed
wonderful to her; what she wanted was a companion.

"Then suddenly he turned on her. He began to tear her to pieces; to find
whatever faults and weaknesses she had and never let up on them. The only
thing he encouraged was her singing. He said she was a damn fool who
happened to have a voice like an angel, if she ever learned to use it. And he
meant to see that she did!

"By this time Hester knew that though he had taste and some technical
knowledge of music, he wasn't a pianist and never had been. The injury to
his hand was real enough; and one day he told her the scar had been left by
a woman who had tried to kill him and then killed herself. Hester didn't
really believe that story. She'd found that he liked to boast about the women
who had been madly in love with him. And add, 'Funny, isn't it—when I
don't give a damn for any of 'em! In fact I hate every woman I ever knew.'
That, she felt, was true. There was something twisted about him. And though
his treatment of her, which grew more subtly vicious day by day, revealed
an intimate understanding of her nature and how best to hurt her, there was
something impersonal in the hatred back of it, she felt. At least, until...

"She told him that she was going to leave him. He seemed amazed at the
idea. He reminded her that that was impossible, that she was his wife and
had promised to obey him, then dismissed the subject. But, though she didn't
know what to do or where to go—she had no money, not one cent, as he
collected her salary from the cabaret—she was waiting for the first opportunity to get away from him where he could not find her and bring her back, as
he'd warned her he would do.

"Then one night he didn't come home. When, at five in the morning he
did come in, he told Hester that, if she were asked, she was to say that he had
been with her all night. She asked him why? He gave her no answer.

"She learned the answer next day, when he was arrested with another man for a robbery during which an old watchman was killed, shot in the back. Shaw smiled at the idea that he had anything to do with the crime; he had been home with his wife all night, he said. He was tried, with the other man, and both were found guilty on the evidence; the confederate was sentenced to death, Shaw to prison for life. Hester refused to testify. She does not believe that she could have averted the verdict by lying as he had ordered, and kept warning her with threats, to do. But apparently Shaw believed she could have saved him. Anyway, his last words to her were that she was the second female Judas in his life, and she would pay for it as long as she lived.

"He was— She told me she used to wake up, for years after that, seeing his face when— Damn!" John Bynam struck his hand on the mantel. "I'm sorry."

He ground out his cigarette. "Shaw was sent to San Quentin. Hester's pictures had been in all the papers, of course. She'd had offers to sell her story, to go on the vaudeville stage, and so on. She'd been deluged with crank letters, some threatening, others wanting to marry her. And she'd had one short bitter letter from her father, for though she'd been using the name Dawn Shaw (her husband's choice) to sing under, her own name had come out during the trial. Anyway, all she wanted was to crawl away somewhere, away from California and not too near Chicago.

"She'd sold a necklace that had been her mother's and had a few dollars left. She took a bus and got off at a town in Texas. She called herself Edith Edwards and managed to get a job in a music store. After several months the owner called her into his office and showed her a letter he'd received. It was crudely written, unsigned, and said that she was Dawn Shaw, her husband was a murderer, that she had double-crossed him and skipped with the dough.

"Hester admitted her identity. She was dismissed. She went to Tennessee, and within a few months the same thing happened again. Her employers were informed, they said, that she was mixed up with gangsters and had barely escaped prison herself.

"She went to St. Louis, got a job doing housework, and kept it for a year. Then she found a rather pleasant position as a governess-nurse—and there was another letter."

John Bynam said slowly, "By this time she believed that she'd be molested in whatever halfway decent work she might find to do. So she only tried for the most menial jobs. She worked in a laundry. She washed dishes in a cheap restaurant. She scrubbed floors. That went on for nearly two years.

"Then," John Bynam straightened his shoulders, "after more than four years of being sick with self-disgust at the mess she'd made of her life, and being ridden with fear, suddenly she decided that she was through with hiding away. She took her own name, came to New York, and found a good music teacher. She'd saved a little money; when that gave out she got a job in a store, trying out sheet music for the piano. She went on studying, evenings. She made no friends, but she was happy because she wasn't frightened any more.

"Then one day her friend Aunt Polly—Mrs. Joffey—chanced to come into the shop where she worked. That's how she happened to go to Madame LaVelle's to live. And it was Mrs. Joffey who got her a hearing at the Harmony Club. She was engaged for a week, and later given a contract. It's a rather exceptional place of its kind. And after what she'd been through it seemed like heaven. I—we met there. And—"

He looked into the fire.

Then he said abruptly, "I wanted Hester to marry me. She wouldn't. So I kept on asking her. And she told me her story."

He drew a deep breath. "My God, as if it mattered in the way she seemed to imagine it would! Of course it was horrible to think what she'd been through. But it was all over. I told her that she must get a divorce, which was perfectly simple, and after we were married she could study or anything she liked. But she kept saying it wouldn't be fair to me and all sorts of things that seemed merely silly to me. The thing is, she's the only girl. I knew that the minute I saw her. Nothing else has anything to do with it."

He stopped short, then smiled.

"Well, that's beside the point, isn't it? She—"

The smile was gone.

He said, "Then, four months ago, we learned that Shaw had escaped from prison, killing a guard. It brought the whole ugly past alive again for her. But it just made me more crazy to marry her, right away. I was frightened about her, too, with that creature loose. I put Ezekiel on his trail—"

Amanda nodded. "A brief record is in our files. I place it now," she remarked. "Unfortunately, the search was not successful."

John Bynam said, "Hester wouldn't listen to me. I begged her to go away, to Europe, if she wouldn't marry me. If she only had gone!

"But she said she was through with running away. And she said she wouldn't see me any more, unless I stopped talking about Shaw—and about marrying her...

"Which wasn't easy, but I tried. If I didn't, she'd just freeze up. She said she didn't want to think of anything, feel anything very much; fear—or anything else. So that's how things were when he—when she got that phone call last evening."

He paused and steadied his voice. It was low, barely audible, when he spoke again.

"She had just one thought: to find out where he was, to get the police there. And she heard him laugh. He said, 'Get those ideas out of your head, baby. I know how much you'd like to double-cross me again. No dice. If you do, my friends'll get the boyfriend. And what they'll do to him won't be pretty.' He mentioned details. They weren't pretty.

"Then he told her that he'd called on her that afternoon and left a suit-case behind a trunk outside her door. She was to bring it, and any money she had and a check made out to cash for whatever she had in the bank, and he told her where to meet him. He said he was going away. He wanted to say good-bye.

"Hester says she believed he meant to kill her. But his threats against me had made her helpless." John Bynam set his jaw, his eyes were haggard. He added angrily, "And irrational! It was an insane thing—to go to that deserted place to meet him."

"Well, since he wasn't there, there's no harm done, as she said herself!" remarked Lutie brightly.

She rose and trotted from the room..

He said, with a groan, "When I think what might have happened—"

Lutie returned with the flask from the medicine chest. She poured apple brandy in a tumbler and held it out to him. He accepted the glass and stood staring at it blankly.

"You drink it, you know," she prompted him. "That's right! Now, you mustn't brood. As Sister often says, that gets us nowhere."

He set the glass down sharply on the mantel shelf and shook his head like a man coming out of a daze.

"But what does?" he said violently. "Why was he killed in her room? How—"

"You, John, were the logical person to be killed," said Amanda.

We all stared at her. But she was not looking at us. Her eyes held a strange gleam, and there was a flush on her rugged cheekbones.

"From what you have told us of Victor Shaw, I do not believe he meant to kill Hester there by the river where he told her to go. Maybe he meant to meet her, take his suitcase and her money, and watch her face while he told her that you were dead and he had killed you. Then he would have left her; it would have been easy and doubtless a satisfaction to leave her uncon-scious with a blow, while he made his escape. That, of course, is surmise; we can't know exactly what he planned; but I believe he did plan to kill you."

Lutie murmured, in delighted surprise, "Why, Sister!"

But Amanda was intent on her own thoughts.

Turning to our client, she said, "Can you remember just what Hester said in response when you telephoned her last evening?"

"Yes, she said, 'Nine o'clock? Of course I'll be here, John. Be seein' you!' I remember her exact words and her tone because later I kept thinking back to them, wondering."

Amanda nodded. "The doors connecting the front and rear rooms are probably not soundproof. By eavesdropping, Shaw could doubtless overhear her words to you. He could then telephone her. When she had left the room and the house, he had only to wait till you, John, came. He and, of course, his confederate—"

Lutie, her blue eyes wide, said, "His confederate, Sister?"

John Bynam said, "Miss Amanda, I had some such an idea! Only I thought perhaps it was too farfetched. Please go on!"

Ignoring this, Amanda addressed herself to Lutie. "Being a bully, naturally he was a coward. Therefore, to help him overpower John, he would most likely have had a confederate. A rough, heavy creature, to stun him with a blow, especially since firearms, which are noisy, would be inadvisable. The idea would then be to murder John, to leave his body for Hester to find when she returned; possibly with the hope that she would even be blamed for the crime."

"Sister dear, that's marvelous!" breathed Lutie.

"But," continued Amanda, "Shaw was an unpleasant man. It is reasonable to believe that his confederate actually hated him. And took advantage of the situation to kill him. Perhaps while they awaited John in Hester's apartment, or perhaps the initial blow was struck in Shaw's parlor, after which he was carried into Hester's rooms and—and the crime completed there."

"But why did he cut—Why the obvious attempt to make the body unidentifiable?" said John Bynam, pushing his hair back from his forehead in an excited gesture. "If Victor Shaw were found—where he *was* found, Hester would be the first suspect! *She* would seem to have had the strongest motive in the world for killing him."

"Perhaps not," said Amanda gravely. "He was not a nice man. He may have had many enemies, who wished to avoid any suspicion. I think we should make an immediate effort to learn about everyone associated with him."

She turned to Lutie. "Are your investigations of this morning likely to give us any practical information—any rational light on the subject?"

Lutie didn't reply at once. At last she said quietly, "Yes, Sister. I think so. I think I know who the murderer is. The only thing, though—"

Our client turned abruptly. He stared at her calm bright blue eyes and her soft pink cheeks. And Amanda stared at her little sister, sitting there with her hands folded and her small neat shoes barely touching the floor, and in the eyes of the elder was a familiar mixture of startled and incredulous awe. And I stared at my tiny cousin, wondering—was it true? Did she really know? Or was she being the mysterious detective in a storybook?

John Bynam said, "You don't—you don't really know?"

Amanda cut in sharply, "Lutie Beagle, if you're fabricating—"

Jeff's knock sounded on the door. He stuck his red thatch into the room. "Inspector Moore," he announced. "In the inner office, boss! Do I allow him in here—or will you see him there?"

"In the office!" snapped Amanda, waving him out. And as he closed the door she turned firmly to Lutie.

"Sister, you cannot go to the inspector with some foolish cock-and-bull story! So if you're letting your imagination run away with you—"

Lutie gazed back at her with round innocent blue eyes.

Then, "Perhaps I am, Sister dear," she murmured meekly. "Anyway, I promise not to tell the inspector my suspicions. Or anybody—"

"But if you believe you know something that may help—" exclaimed John Bynam desperately, and clutched her small hand.

She patted his large one, smiled at him kindly and shook her head.

"You heard me promise Sister, John. What I think I know will keep."

His shoulders sagged. His eyes were still fastened on her sparkling blue ones. Then the light died out of his face, and disappointment filled it. He turned away, found his hat, and strode toward the outer door without another word.

Amanda said sharply, "John, haven't you sense enough to wear an overcoat? This is just the kind of weather for pneumonia. I declare."

"Excuse me. I—" He opened the door, and without looking back at us said shortly, "Goodbye."

Then he went out.

Amanda said, "Hmmph. Well, I don't blame him for being upset."

She glared at Lutie. Then her gaze narrowed.

"What," she snapped, "did you smuggle into the bedroom, Lutie Beagle? More foolish fal-lals that we don't need and won't ever use? Did you think I didn't see you? And I declare it looked like luggage! Whatever do we need of more luggage, I'd like to know?"

"Why it isn't new, Sister; and I got it for nothing, really!" Lutie giggled.

She looked at me significantly. "Marthy tried to stop me, but you know, sometimes I just can't resist things. But hadn't you better scold me later? We're forgetting that nice Inspector Moore cooling his heels out there—just because I picked up a secondhand suitcase! Or maybe it's third-hand—"

"Of all the foolishness!" snorted Amanda.

But with relief. Little Sister was back in her character of frivolous flibbertigibbet again. Which was as it should be.

And yet had there been another of those uncanny flashes, as though a cherub were about to display an unbelievable, almost an unholy sapience?

Amanda gave her one more quick, not wholly comfortable glance, said, "Hmmph!" and squaring her lean shoulders, marched toward the inner office and Inspector Moore.

As Lutie trotted after, and I followed, my small cousin twinkled up at me impishly.

I felt like shaking her. Was she playing a game? I thought of poor John Bynam's face. It was cruel to hold out hopes that couldn't be fulfilled. But perhaps she did know something important. Then she ought to tell what she knew, I thought indignantly.

Was it about the Fennellis? But Smyth was Shaw—that was proved. And so how could he be Floto? And—

And had her reticule really been stolen? And even if so—had the theft any connection with the murder?

And the suitcase she'd stolen from the locker? What was in it? And why think that it had anything to do with the case? I'd been frightened silly, of course; but that was by her mysterious manner, and actually there was nothing to show we'd been followed, or—or anything, I concluded feebly. There was simply nothing to show.

With a feeling of muddled doubt, hope, and bewildered exasperation, I tagged through the dim passage at her heels.

Then I felt a little hand steal into mine.

"My poor Watson—you're all in a pother, aren't you?" she whispered and grinned at me fondly. "But just the same, I really do know who committed the murder!"

CHAPTER 17

INSPECTOR MOORE was restlessly pacing the floor of the inner office when we entered. Jeff, who had been perched on a corner of the desk, removed himself and withdrew to the background while Amanda enthroned herself in the large swivel chair, with Lutie on her right and me on her left. The inspector seated himself across the desk from Amanda and addressed himself to her, rather as if he were hardly aware that the rest of us were there at all. As on the night before, he was dressed in gray and he was spruce and immaculate, but today he looked tired. The effect of steely hardness that had intimidated me was gone or in abeyance; he looked troubled.

He said, "I daresay you know, Miss Beagle, that Vincent Smyth was Victor Shaw, murderer, escaped convict, and Hester Gale's husband?"

Amanda answered that our client, Mr. Bynam, had just told us the whole story, and the inspector said, "You know then of Shaw's threat against his wife, her fear of him, and so on?"

Amanda nodded.

She was about to say something when Inspector Moore continued, "The threat was made after Shaw's sentence, before witnesses, and the girl, wisely enough, makes no attempt to deny it now. In fact, she admits that her terror of him had its inception during their brief marriage and persisted for years; she even seems to believe that he managed to persecute her while he was still in prison."

"Admits?" interrupted Amanda. "You mean she has told you—"

"Enough to show a very strong motive for killing him," said the inspector.

"Yes," said Amanda.

Inspector Moore gave her a surprised, and, I thought, a somewhat disappointed glance. Then his eyes fell to a glass paperweight on the desk. He sighed, picked it up, and turning it watched the miniature snowfall swirl about the tiny landscape in its crystal depths.

He murmured, "Good old Zeke. He told me he'd carried this around the world with him. Said it reminded him of home—of East Biddicutt." The inspector smiled, then sighed again. "I miss the old boy." He set the glass globe down with a thump. "Well, that pretty well ties up the case against the girl, doesn't it?"

"No," said Amanda.

He said sharply, "What! But you yourself just admitted—"

"I agreed," Amanda corrected him, "that Hester Gale had a strong motive for killing the man. And it is possible—I don't say I believe it, I haven't had enough experience to form an opinion—that ordinary decent people may kill, at a pinch. But they do not cut off people's heads under any circumstances. That's poppycock, Inspector; you do not believe it yourself, or you would not be here talking to us!"

From the keen glance he gave her I knew this was a shrewd thrust.

But he shrugged rather wearily and said, "Well, the D.A. believes it—"

"The D.A.?" inquired Amanda.

"Gorman, the district attorney. He's sure the girl is guilty. I—yes, I'll admit I think he's being precipitate. But John Bynam—the very fact of his wealth and position will make it a big case for Gorman, whose code and polit— Anyway, it will be a big case for him, if it stands up. He thinks it will; as he says, Bynam also had motive and opportunity. And he has no alibi, unfortunately. The old night porter at his office building does confirm his statement that he rarely uses the elevators, and the old man says he was probably running them when Bynam left. But he did not see Bynam leave. So there it is; he may have left any time after a quarter to seven, instead of at half-past eight ,as he claims."

I surprised myself by putting in eagerly, "But there's a young lodger who let him in the house at nine, just as John said—"

The inspector favored me with a brief glance.

He said, "Yes, so one of them—young Wilson Paul—says today. But he denied it when first questioned. Meanwhile, he's read the papers; and I'm afraid he's a partial witness. He's not a very convincing one; first he said that he hadn't been out of his room on the top floor all evening, and now he claims that he was in the basement kitchen, alone, and in the dark, for an hour or so—during which he thinks he heard a mysterious marauder in the back yard!—and on his way upstairs he happened to go to the front door and look out at precisely nine o'clock.

"The landlady, by the way, also has a yarn about a prowler during the middle of the night. We get these fanciful tales frequently during murder cases. Some people like the limelight—and in the Maison LaVelle, you must remember, they're actors—also vairee temperramental."

He smiled slightly.

"However," he added, "even if young Paul's present statement proves to be reliable—that is as to seeing Bynam in the basement area at nine—it means little. Bynam might have been leaving the house, actually—having gone down the inside stairway; and being seen and recognized thought best to say that he was trying to get in, and so on." He shrugged. His slender well-kept fingers tapped the arm of his chair restlessly.

"Anyway, Gorman figures—"

"—what he chooses to, that's plain!" said Amanda shortly.

She dismissed the D.A. abruptly.

"Inspector Moore, what, if anything, have you learned about the so-called victim? I have been led to believe the police have extraordinary means of unearthing pasts, especially of persons with criminal records."

He said, "Oh, yes, we uncovered Shaw's history very quickly after we'd found that photograph. The burned-off fingertips pointed to an ex-convict; and we found the man's photo in our rogues' gallery. He had a record for theft here in New York, dating some nine or ten years ago. That led us to his conviction in California, his imprisonment in San Quentin, his escape. And his wife—"

Amanda nodded impatiently. "Yes, I know. But have you looked into his antecedents, found out anything about his associates, and so forth?"

"Yes," he said thoughtfully, "I've talked with the lawyer who defended him when he was tried here for theft. Victor Shaw, or Rex Heyward—to use his real name—wasn't an ordinary type of criminal. That is, he came of what's called a good family. And a comparatively wealthy one. His father died when he was an infant; he was brought up by his mother, luxuriously, it appears; he was educated by tutors, spoke French, German and Italian fluently, and had some musical training. According to his mother he had a great talent for the stage; but she said the poor boy was too fastidious for that life. At any rate he didn't do anything about it seriously—or about anything else. Then in 1929 or 1930 what remained of Mrs. Heyward's fortune—she'd probably squandered and mismanaged it—went up in smoke.

All she had left was an annuity of fifty dollars a week. She lived on half of that and gave the rest to her son. He was disgusted with this puny pittance and indignant at the disappearance of the fortune he'd expected to come into at twenty-one, and proceeded to get into various scrapes—forgery, and two or three thefts of money or jewelry. They were perpetrated against rich friends of his mother's and she managed to square them.

"Finally, however, he stole a valuable piece of jewelry, was apprehended, tried, convicted, and sent to Sing Sing for three years. His mother had hired the best defense she could get, wept and denounced the owner of the neck-lace for prosecuting. 'After all,' she said, 'that mean woman could easily afford to give the poor boy the necklace—it was only worth a few thousand and she's worth millions!' But her son wasn't touched by all this devotion, or whatever you want to call it.

"In a last scene with his mother—the attorney was present and described it to me in detail and with comments that I'll omit—young Heyward told the tearful woman that the whole damn thing was her fault; she'd lost his money, she was a fool; but he wasn't finished with her yet. Whatever that meant, the poor woman was just about finished; she renounced her erstwhile friends because they hadn't come to the fore when poor Rexie needed them, and died soon after poor Rexie was released from jail. Whether or not she ever saw her son again—he wouldn't see her when she visited him in prison—my informant didn't know."

"Hmmph," said Amanda, as the inspector paused. "Spare the rod—"

"Makes a fairly complete picture of a spoiled brat, doesn't it?" said the inspector. "But fortunately most of them don't turn out to be murderers.

"Well, to bring things up to date, Heyward apparently cleared out of New York when his jail sentence was up—anyway, there's no further record of him here. His conviction in California was a year later; meanwhile a few months before that he'd married Hester Gale. As for his associates, Miss Beagle, evidently he did that San Francisco robbery with the one other man, who has been executed for it. There's no record or suggestion of association with other known criminals or gangsters. He had no visitors while in prison, though I understand he occasionally received letters from some silly woman who'd apparently never met him—sentimental, schoolmarmish letters such as prisoners, especially murderers, often get. He was a model prisoner, though unpopular with his fellows; he didn't fraternize. It was a shock to the prison authorities when he escaped."

"Alone?" asked Amanda.

"No. There were three other men with him. Two were killed in the attempt; the other eluded justice as successfully as Shaw. More successfully, it seems. Why, Miss Beagle? Did the girl tell you anything that might lead—"

"Hester told me nothing whatever," replied Amanda curtly. "She might have done so if she'd had time. And I do think the child should have been allowed to finish her breakfast. However, that's spilt milk. I inquired because I am interested in any information that might lead to the murderer."

Inspector Moore looked at Amanda thoughtfully. He picked up the crystal paperweight and tipped it gently. He said with seeming irrelevance, "Your brother Ezekiel was an extraordinary judge of character, Miss Beagle. I've known him to refuse to accept as clients extremely wealthy and reputable persons because he didn't like them, and frequently events did prove them to be crooked or mistaken, pigheaded and ruthless. And I've known him to go to bat for numbers of poor bedeviled creatures, petty clerks, servants, scrubwomen fired from their jobs on suspicion—even tramps, drunks, or prostitutes accused of some small or great crime. He'd work tirelessly to prove their innocence, if he believed in it. And he always formed his judgment on his first look at a person. It often seemed to me uncanny. And yet..."

The gray-eyed man paused and frowned.

"Zeke was wrong once. He cleared a gentle-looking woman of a murder charge, and she later killed three people for their insurance money. But it was the single flaw in his record, so far as I know."

He put down the glass sphere. His fingers tapped the desk top nervously.

Amanda said, "Ezekiel was a generous, warmhearted lad, and bright enough in his way; but it does not surprise me to learn that he remained a hot-headed boy as long as he lived. His lack of balanced judgment is neither here nor there. Please stop wiggling your fingers, Inspector. As I've told Sister many a time, fidgeting never accomplished anything. It is distracting in all its stages, from thumb-sucking to chair-rocking."

The gentleman hastily thrust his hands into his pockets. Then he smiled and withdrew a small meerschaum pipe.

"Is smoking in the same category, Miss Beagle?" he asked.

She snapped, "That depends on how it's done!" Then she too smiled. "Don't mind me, Inspector Moore, when I sound like an old curmudgeon. I daresay that's my way of fidgeting. Go ahead and smoke your pipe—we like it. But," she sobered, "let's get back to our muttons." `

He proceeded to fill his pipe.

He said slowly, "The truth is, I had a habit of talking over peculiar cases with your brother. He often gave me valuable suggestions. He was, of course, utterly trustworthy. I knew that nothing I told him would ever be used by him except to establish, or help me to establish, the truth."

"Naturally," said Amanda, with a hint of impatience.

He pressed the tobacco in the bowl of his pipe.

"It is somewhat irregular, you know, for a policeman to discuss a case in which..." He struck a match. "After all, the suspects are your clients."

Amanda's lips tightened.

Then she opened them to say, very formally, "What you choose to discuss with us is entirely a matter for your own discretion, Inspector Moore."

He held the match to his pipe. His head was bent, but his gray eyes, narrowed, went swiftly from Lutie, to me, and back to Amanda over the small flame, spurting, sucked down, flaring again. He flipped out the match and laid it carefully in an ashtray.

He nodded. "I'll trust yours," he said. "So, suppose I state certain facts. You may know of others, or you may be able to suggest another way to look at them. I have a feeling that the D—I don't think the case should be rushed. But…Well, anyway, I'll line it up, shall I?"

"If you wish, Inspector Moore," replied Amanda, still rather stiffly.

He drew on his pipe. "We'll take the landlady's statement first. She says that at about seven o'clock she dropped in to visit her tenant, Hester Gale. She found the girl, dressed in a negligee, reading a magazine and eating a light supper.

"While Madame LaVelle was there Miss Gale took the dishes into the kitchen and put away the bread—and the bread knife. After that she brought out a blue evening dress and trimmed the torn hem with a fine sharp pair of shears. Then she started to press the dress.

"Later," he went on, making a gesture with his pipestem as though scoring the point, "we find an open sewing basket, a scrap of blue silk near it, on the living-room table. But no scissors. And no bread knife in the kitchen. They've both disappeared. The medical evidence points clearly to two such weapons having been used in the commission of the crime."

He paused, and Amanda said, "I daresay. But excuse me. Go on, Inspector."

"Yes. Well, then the landlady, after leaving Miss Gale's rooms, stopped in to visit Smyth, the lodger in the adjoining apartment. They chatted; after a few minutes she asked him the time; he looked at his watch and told her it was twenty-three minutes past seven. Which we can pretty definitely accept as being correct, because Madame LaVelle then went to the Grotto, about a five-minute walk, and was just in time for Mr. Disney's cartoon, which we find went on at seven-thirty. So Vincent Smyth was alive at seven twenty-three. That's that."

He paused, puffed on his pipe, considered. "Well, let's see. At about nine o'clock John Bynam phoned you—"

"At eleven minutes past nine," Amanda corrected him.

"At nine-eleven, then. You arrived at the address he gave you soon after—"

"At twenty past nine."

"Thank you. Then, I understand, Bynam showed you the body and gave you an account of his coming to the house at nine, of finding the murdered man, and so on. After a while you telephoned the police—"

"After nine minutes. It was exactly nine twenty-nine when we called you. But," said Amanda, "we know all that."

"And what transpired during that nine minutes, and while you waited for us, naturally you know better than I do," he said quietly.

"I think I've told you what occurred, as accurately as possible," said Amanda. "It's true that—er—several minutes elapsed after we saw the body during which I—" She flushed, but continued firmly, "I—just sat down. In the living room. Er—presently I called to my sister and my cousin, who were still in the bedroom; though what they were doing—"

"I know, Sister dear," murmured Lutie soothingly. "You never could bear the sight of blood. But it was so interesting."

The inspector took his pipe from his teeth and wheeled to face her. He said sharply, "What was?"

She looked at him, her blue eyes bright and wide.

"Why, everything, Inspector! All the little details. The stab wound that had caused death before decapitation, since there was no sign of blood having spurted as it would have done while the heart still pumped. And the acid-burned fingertips, the scar on the left hand and the mark on the finger left by a tight ring. The fact that the murder was very recent, too, of course; the body was still warm. Oh, I know such things are an old story to you, Inspector. But you see, this is our first murder—"

He said, "Do you mean that you noticed those things yourself, there in that room?"

"Of course. How could I help it?" said Lutie mildly. "And the other thing that would strike anybody—what a very tidy job it was. The blood wasn't tracked around, there were no signs of haste or flurry. Whoever did it was certainly cool and careful. There was one wet towel in the bathroom, with traces of blood on it, naturally; but it was neatly hung up on the towel bar..."

Her voice became dreamy. "The floor wasn't splashed either, and there's no shower, and the tub was dry. I mean, at first I hoped—that is, it's so intriguing, the idea of people without any clothes on—not ordinarily, of course, but in committing that type of murder. Still, it's never really been done, has it? At least that one can be sure of. I always did think it silly to imagine Lizzie Borden running around the house like that even on such a warm day. She'd never have risked it, I'm sure, even if she hadn't been too modest—"

"Lutie Beagle," said Amanda sharply, "what are you babbling about?"

"Oh, dear—just meandering, Sister! I only meant that our murderer was probably clothed, you know. Then, as John suggested, there's the raincoat theory, very plausible in this case; slipped on back-to-frontwards like a surgeon's tunic would be best, wouldn't it? But of course," she gave herself a little shake and murmured regretfully, "those notions passed through my mind before I'd noticed the negligee—"

The inspector's pipe clicked against his even white teeth.

"The negligee?" he exclaimed. "What about the negligee?"

"Why," said Lutie, her eyes round, a little startled at his vehemence, "it was there on the chair in the bedroom, so naturally I examined it! I do want to tell you right now, Inspector," she said earnestly, "because I know how important such things are; that was the only time I took my gloves off, except of course when I felt the body to get a rough idea of its temperature and the time of death. It was significant, wasn't it? I mean the robe. Of course the other things were too, and the little details I noticed afterwards, while we were waiting for you, Inspector. John's note on the desk—and when I called his attention to it he was going to tear it up, which doesn't look as if he'd planted it, does it? Though of course you can't be certain, can you? And the scissors that weren't with the sewing basket; and the half loaf of French bread in the bread tin, but no bread knife; and the wooden tabletop that obviously had been covered with oilcloth, which would make such an excellent wrapping for the missing head when it was taken away; and the ironing board with the freshly pressed frock hanging nearby, but no iron—and what domestic utensil could possibly be more handy to use for a weight? Which would make anyone think of the head being thrown in the nearest river, naturally. But first, it was used to press the sleeve of the dressing gown...I mean the iron, not the head, of course."

She glanced at Amanda, apologetically. "Dear me, Sister, I certainly do mix things up, don't I!"

CHAPTER 18

INSPECTOR MOORE'S meerschaum had gone out. He drew on it deeply, then unclenched his teeth on the amber stem and placed the pipe in the ashtray without taking his eyes from the small demure person facing him. He appeared to be going over the fantastic words he had just heard, delivered so calmly in that soft rippling voice. His expression was peculiar; Amanda would have called it flabbergasted, and later Jeff described it very graphically. Anyway, for several moments the gentleman in gray seemed quite unable to speak.

Presently Amanda vouchsafed, in the gruff tone that she used to conceal pride, "Sister was always an observant child, in her way."

As such a meed of praise needed to be qualified, she added severely, "If she would mix fewer fancies with her facts we could get on faster. Sister, you started to tell us something about a negligee."

"Oh," said Lutie meekly, "I mentioned it in passing. Inspector Moore knows all about it."

"But I do not," Amanda reminded her.

"Excuse me, Sister; I forgot that. Well, Hester's negligee was laid neatly over a chair in the bedroom, and I noticed there was a scorched place on it. I looked closer and saw that the sleeve had been very roughly pressed on the wrong side, and there was a big crease squashed down by the iron, which had been too hot and left its imprint. So I felt the sleeve then, and it was still dampish, but even if it had time to dry anyone could tell that the sleeve had been washed and ironed, not the whole gown. And of course I knew why, when I saw the slit near the bottom of the sleeve. Or, at least," she murmured, "I knew the obvious reason. But the gown should have been dry-cleaned, or thrown away; it was quite ruined. So—"

"Don't ramble," said Amanda. "I suppose it was a loose sleeve?" As Lutie nodded she said, "I see. So you figure that the shears were concealed within it, and when the blow was struck, they penetrated the material, leaving it bloodstained—hence the hasty laundering. Umm—well, that's a logical deduction, Sister."

She turned to the policeman. "Doubtless it is yours also, Inspector?"

He said, "Yes, it is."

"Oh, good!" exclaimed Lutie. "That means that the analysis has already revealed the bloodstains! It's so thrilling, isn't it, when one's guess is proved to be correct! Because once in a blue moon appearances are deceptive and one could be wrong. But it is odd how the most careful criminals are supposed not to know about such things—chemical analysis of bloodstains, I mean, and how difficult it is to impose on the police in that way. Or don't they, do you think? I can't help but wonder."

She stopped herself and shook her head.

"Mercy, I've been babbling ad infinitum or perhaps I should say ad nauseam. So thoughtless of me! Won't you, Inspector, for a change?"

Inspector Moore looked back at her steadily. Then he reached for the glass paperweight and suddenly grinned.

"Another chip off the old block," he chuckled. "Well, Miss Lutie, you've pretty well marshaled the evidence. Maybe I ought to be annoyed, but—go ahead. What else do you know? I suppose you searched the corpse's pockets? What did you find?"

"Nothing," said Lutie gravely. But she did blush. She added, "I—I only looked in the coat and waistcoat. But later, of course, we heard your men remark that there wasn't anything in the other pockets either. And today we learned that everything belonging to Smyth had been taken from the front parlor, except, of course, the suitcase with the photograph, which was out of sight. And also, we've learned that another lodger, Miss Dot DeVeere, twice saw Vincent Smyth going into Miss Gale's apartment, quite coolly. And—well, while we were talking to the various tenants, my dear Wat—my Cousin Martha and I chatted with them this morning, you know—we gathered all sorts of other interesting information. At least it was interesting to the visiting firemen, but I—I think that's all that's relevant to your case, Inspector. Or isn't it?"

He took a black-and-gray-striped silk pouch from his pocket, reached for his pipe and began to fill it again.

"How about Hester Gale's statement that she left the house before seven o'clock? We know she couldn't possibly have done so, from Madame LaVelle's statement, and the DeVeere woman actually saw her leave at 7:45, it develops. That lie is a pretty damning bit of evidence against her."

"Such a silly lie, though, wasn't it?" murmured Lutie. "Why, even John Bynam didn't back her up."

"Yes, I know. But people make strange slips when they're lying," he said. "They'll grab at straws to try and establish an alibi."

"Even when they've planned and executed all the other details so carefully?" mused Lutie.

Then a thought seemed to strike her and she nodded. "Still, apparently that's true—murderers do some foolish things. At least the ones who are caught."

Amanda interrupted this truism impatiently.

"Don't you know a liar when you see one? That girl was telling the truth, so far as she went. There's some funny business there, mark my words."

But the inspector wasn't marking them at the moment. He had noticed something in Lutie's manner, something behind her trite reflection.

"What's on your mind, Miss Lutie?" he asked her quietly.

"Oh," said Lutie, blinking and shaking off her abstraction. She smiled deprecatingly. "I wouldn't like to tell you that! If I babbled about my various imaginings I'm afraid you'd laugh or something. But the case against Hester, and John too, is quite clear, isn't it?"

"Is it?" said Inspector Moore. "Well, you've started very well; suppose you sum it up."

"I'm sure you'd do it much better, Inspector," murmured Lutie.

"I'd like to hear your ideas, just the same," he replied.

She said, "Oh, I don't claim they're my ideas."

Amanda said, "Sister, don't beat about the bush. I know what you mean, but never mind. Just get on with it."

"Very well, Sister," said Lutie meekly. She clasped her hands in her lap. She thought for a moment and then she began, "Hester Gale met a young man, married him within a week, and soon afterward discovered that he didn't love her and was a ne'er-do-well and a vicious person. He was mean to her during the short time they were married, he was involved in a murder and was sentenced to prison for life, and he threatened vengeance on her because she had refused to lie for him during his trial. He even found a way to hound her after he was in prison. Anyway, she thinks he did, and that's the important point against her, isn't it? But finally she threw off her fear, resumed her own name and her career as a singer, and met a wealthy and handsome young man of fine family who wanted to marry her.

"Then her husband escaped from prison. And after a few months he tracks her down and a week ago he rents the apartment adjoining hers. Perhaps he hoped to blackmail her, threatening to expose her to her rich suitor, not knowing she had told him her story. Or the convict husband may have tried to blackmail John Bynam, believing the respectable young man would pay to suppress the past of the girl he wished to marry. Or perhaps Shaw demanded her back as his wife. Which would explain where the body was found. And, back of all that, is his threat of vengeance against her, her hatred and fear of her husband."

Lutie paused. Then she said in a practical tone, "Of course she *should* have turned him right over to the police, who would have been only too pleased to lock him up. But that would have involved her and John Bynam in an open scandal, shocked his family and so on." Her tone became dreamy again. "So she plays a part, pretends to be frightened or compliant... allows her husband to retire to the inner room...and then, snatching up the shears from beside her sewing basket and hiding them in her flowing sleeve, follows him in and kills him."

There was silence for a moment. Then Lutie said, "And then there was his body in her bed. She really hadn't bettered the situation. So awkward. But people don't think of that when they're desperate, do they? Then John comes in.

"Of course we're just supposing he did, partly because it's hard to imagine a young girl planning and carrying through the rest of it, all alone. Though there was that young woman out west in '31, whom the newspapers called the Tiger Woman—"

"Sister," snapped Amanda, "will you stop talking about Tiger Women and all such poppycock and get on with this nonsense?"

Lutie came out of her reverie with a little start. "I'm sorry, Sister! Where was I? Oh, yes—John comes in. And there's that dreadfully awkward situation with Hester's husband's murdered body in her bed. But there's a saving element. Shaw's fingertips are gone—burned off! Of course he'd done it for his own ends, but how well it served theirs! Now all they had to do was to remove the other identifying appurtenances and dispose of them, and what was left might be anybody. Not that this was ideal; one must expect some unpleasantness when even a stray body is found murdered in one's bed. But it was the best that could be done Anyway, it must have seemed like a good idea at the time..."

Lutie's voice trailed off. Then she gave herself a little shake.

"Well, anyway, there are still some details to be attended to—and quickly. Let's suppose that while Hester washes and presses her bloodstained robe, John has removed the contents of the dead man's pockets, a ring from his finger, and his head. Then she gathers Smyth's belongings from his room, which she could do with no risk of being seen in the hall by other tenants by using the doors between the front and back parlors—I noticed this morning that they weren't locked on his side—and while she's doing that John is making a bundle of the head, the shears, the knife, the ring and whatever he's found in the victim's pockets. And—Hester having finished with it— the flatiron.

"Then everything's packed in a suitcase, either a bag of Hester's, or possibly Smyth had two, even if Madame LaVelle doesn't think so. Meanwhile Hester has dressed for the street; and now, at 7:40, if we believe Miss DeVeere, who noted the time by Mrs. Joffey's clock which she keeps five minutes fast, just like my dear Wat—Marthy—she leaves the house, with the bag for the river."

Lutie's brow puckered thoughtfully. "Let's see; Smyth—Shaw—was alive at 7:23. Then he went to his wife's rooms, removed his coat, waistcoat, necktie and shoes, lay down on the bed, was stabbed and decapitated; his clothes and his rooms were searched, his various belongings packed up, Hester's negligee was roughly laundered, she dressed and departed—all in . . ."

"Seventeen minutes," said Amanda.

Lutie, who had been moving her lips and fingers as she struggled with this problem in arithmetic, nodded in relief

"Yes—just seventeen minutes! Well, it could be done, I suppose."

Jeff, from the background, burst out for the first time.

"What gets me," he scowled, running his fingers through his carroty thatch, "is why Bynam let the girl make that trip to the river with the—I mean, even if all the rest of it happened just like that?"

"Well, you see, Jeffy," explained Lutie, "if it did happen something like that—if Hester was busy with the other details while John, er, wielded the bread knife and made up the oilcloth bundle, she wouldn't even have had to see what was in it. So she might have preferred to carry it away, rather than to stay behind and tidy up, and then remain with the remains. Isn't that reasonable, Sister?"

Amanda said, "Hmmph."

I put my oar in (and I might mention that, while Lutie had talked, the whole awful thing she was describing had become engrossing, like a puzzle, and in some odd way not real at all!).

I said, "But, even if John stayed behind to tidy up, that would take only a few minutes! What was he doing for over an hour and a quarter after she left, and before he phoned us? Why didn't he leave long before that?"

Lutie turned to me and nodded. "Good for you, Marthy dear! That could be a point, couldn't it?" Then she frowned. "But maybe he did leave. And then remembered some incriminating detail he'd overlooked, and came back. That could be, couldn't it? As Reggie Fortune—"

She blushed, for some reason, and sat back in her chair. After a moment she murmured apologetically, "Dear me, I *have* chattered, haven't I ? But you did ask me to, Inspector."

"Yes," he said dryly. And added, "You haven't yet expressed your opinion of the case—overtly."

"Oh," said Lutie, clasping her hands demurely while the pink in her cheeks deepened, "I—I wouldn't think of doing that! I was just mentioning some of the things I'd noticed or—or learned—all things you already know, Inspector! and fitting them together."

"And quite neatly, Sister, even if you did meander a bit and use some hifalutin' language here and there. That comes from all those silly books you cram your head with; but I must say you use it pretty well when you've a mind to," said Amanda, her tone severe and her eyes gleaming with pride. She turned abruptly to our visitor. "There's your case, Inspector Moore. What do you think of it?"

"Admirably covered," he said, not taking his eyes from Lutie. "Your sister has also found some plausible answers for several rather puzzling little points. For instance, the last two, made by Mahoney and by Miss Meecham. And she doesn't believe a word of it. Why not, Miss Lutie?"

He picked up Zeke's talisman, but he continued to watch her steadily. "What do you believe? What do you know that I don't?"

Lutie's eyelids fluttered and she made a little deprecating gesture.

"Oh," she murmured, "it would take too long to tell you that." She bit her lip, and added hastily, "I—I mean, about my flights of imagination! If— if we really find out anything new, Sister will tell you. I've already babbled enough, haven't I, Sister?"

"I daresay," said Amanda, "you could go on for some time, Sister. But I doubt if we'd get any further at the moment." She glanced at the big clock on the wall. "It is four-thirty, and I, for one, am going to have some tea. Will you join us, Inspector?"

He put down the paperweight and the snow flurry settled softly within the crystal.

"Thank you, some other time." He stood up, and Jeff leaped to help him with his overcoat. "I've enjoyed our talk, even if—"

"—we don't agree with your D.A.?" said Amanda. "Well, neither do you, in your soul. And that's not a bad place to look for the truth," she informed him in a practical tone; and added, "As for your D.A., he'll do well to hold his horses or he'll find he has a mare's-nest on his hands. But I don't suppose there's any use in your telling him that; he sounds like the sort of person who won't listen to reason. So the thing to do is to find the actual murderer just as soon as possible, which is really your business, but apparently in the interests of our clients we'll have to make it ours too. I am sorry you cannot stay for tea; my sister makes very good scones."

"Thank you, Sister," said Lutie.

Then, as our visitor, politely repeating his appreciation of Amanda's invitation, turned to depart, she touched his sleeve, gazing up at him earnestly.

"I know," she murmured rather breathlessly, "that Smyth was Shaw... but what if he were Floto, too? That might change the—the whole setup, mightn't it? And then there's Madame LaVelle, such a strange person, so melodramatic, yet so anxious to feed people... And Professor Sesame, he's a magician, and they're so skillful at making things disappear...And then, the DeVeere girl, who certainly has it in for Hester Gale! Of course I don't mean anything definite against any of those people; but in a murder case you're supposed to suspect everybody possible, aren't you? And there's Sister's idea of a confederate with whom Shaw meant to murder John, but who murdered Shaw instead which, of course, would be the nicest thing of all! Well, we're sorry you won't stay. If—if you'd care for—for something stronger than tea—men often do, I know—we could offer you some apple brandy our dear Pa barreled many years ago."

"Thank you. Thank you; some other time," replied Inspector Moore, looking rather wildly for his hat. Our assistant handed it to him and escorted the gentleman out.

"Whew!" remarked Jeff, rejoining us. "You sure had him on the ropes, Miss Lutie!"

Which, I understand, is a term connected with the prize ring, meaning that one combatant has delivered a blow that has dazed his opponent. I must say, these modern slang idioms are often very expressive; and as I've pointed out to Amanda, even if she doesn't like them, they are frequently not a bit more brusque than many of her own old-fashioned phrases which are really slang, too, in their way.

She didn't deny it, either, though she shook her head and said, "Marthy, what will they think of you back in East Biddicutt!"

But, as I told her, there doesn't seem to be much hope of our going back to East Biddicutt.

Well, there I go, chattering, as Lutie would say. To continue with my narrative...

CHAPTER 19

WE had scones and cinnamon toast and chocolate cake with tea, which we consumed with hardly a word between us. Amanda was silent and thoughtful; Lutie quiet and dreamy; while as for me, my head was whirling wearily with bewilderment and questions.

Who *did* Lutie really believe was the murderer? Was she, like Amanda, convinced that Hester and John were innocent? She had never said so. And our adventure with the mysterious suitcase in the subway—what was that all about?

But I knew there wasn't the slightest use in asking and, truth to tell, I was so tired I didn't for the moment much care. So I made up for my scanty dinner and ate as though I were famished, and drank three cups of strong hot tea in thankful silence.

When we'd finished, Amanda went back to the office. But in the doorway she paused, looked down her nose at Lutie and said gruffly, "Sister, in spite of your habit of getting off the track, I must say you had some very interesting things to tell us today; and you made some valuable points. I shall think them over."

She shut the door quickly behind her.

Lutie was touched. She gazed after her fondly and murmured, "Dear Sister. Such a rock, isn't she? A darling rock..."

Then with a swift change of manner she said, "Quick, Marthy! Let's have those newspapers before she comes back!"

I got the bundle of papers and gave them to her, then I went and changed to the comfort of a house dress. When I came back to the living room she was busily engaged clipping paragraphs, headlines and pictures. I set about preparations for supper, and presently a blaze in the fireplace proclaimed that she'd culled what she wanted and disposed of the remains. I caught myself thinking in those very terms and shuddered. But Lutie was humming a little tune; with her clippings spread out before her, and a scrapbook and paste-pot on the table, her silver head pored happily over her task. I returned to my muffins.

She'd tucked the scrapbook away before Amanda and Jeff joined us for supper, during which my elder cousin quelled any attempt to discuss the case. But she allowed our assistant to chatter along about his encounters with the press, though she was still intent on her own reflections and didn't pay much attention to him. Lutie, however, was interested, and encouraged him to describe his visitors at length.

She was amused when he told us about one reporter who thought the best part of the story was the old ladies from Biddicutt.

"He said he wanted to cover that angle," said Jeff. "And it was a relief—the others all tried to pump me about what I knew, specially about Bynam and the girl, of course. So I told this chap I thought he had something there. I didn't think a little publicity would do us any harm, so I showed him around the offices and gave him an earful. Told him you and the boss had the real lowdown but naturally you were keeping it under your hats! Of course he wanted to see you both, but I said no dice. I painted a pretty picture for him, though, complete with Rabelais and Tabby, etcetera, and had his mouth watering when I described your suppers. Ought to make a good story."

Lutie laughed, and asked him what newspaper the young man worked for and if the story had had time to be printed yet. Jeff said the reporter represented the *Star* he hadn't seen the late edition and offered to get it after supper; but Lutie, with a quick glance toward Amanda, signaled no, some other time!

She said hastily, "Was he a nice young man, Jeffy? What did he look like?"

Jeff said he hadn't noticed especially what the fellow looked like; he was just an ordinary guy with specs and light hair; yes, he was nice enough "Or," he added firmly, "I'd have thrown him out on his c—ear."

"Well," said Lutie, "publicity isn't supposed to be good for detectives, Jeffy. But I won't scold you—this time!"

Actually, I thought, she was quite tickled.

After supper while Jeff and I were doing the dishes he returned to the case.

"What do you make of it, Miss Marthy?" he asked me. "The boss just sits tight and says, 'It's all poppycock.' It's swell the way she sticks to it—makes you believe she's right, in spite of h—heck. But has she really got anything? When you go over the evidence, like Miss Lutie did today—"

"I know," I sighed.

He said, "I can't make her out. What's on her mind? Or," he eyed me shrewdly over a platter decorated with forget-me-nots, "is she just being the mysterious little sleuth?"

I had an impulse to tell him about the key that Lutie had found, and the adventure of the suitcase, but I thought I shouldn't. I said I didn't know what she had up her sleeve. I was just as much at sea as he was, which goodness knows was true. He asked what we'd been up to all morning, and I gave him some account of the lodgers at the Maison LaVelle.

He chuckled over Sesame, and was amused by the professor's theory that Smyth was Floto and the Fennellis had killed him and had framed Hester; but he believed the little magician's imagination had run away with him and that he had invented or twisted what he had heard through the hot-air flues from the room below to fit his theory.

Likewise Jeff dismissed "Weelly's" yarn. But when I got to Dot DeVeere, her expression of envious spleen against Hester Gale, and Lutie's evident dislike of Dotty, he became very much excited.

He was in the midst of a lurid reconstruction in which Dot DeVeere and the professor committed the crime when he heard the telephone ring. Amanda answered it, and Jeff stopped to listen. Whoever was at the other end of the wire talked for some time, but there was little to learn from Amanda's monosyllabic queries and responses.

But the moment we returned to the living room, having finished our task, I could see that she was disturbed. She had Tabby on her lap and was stroking him vigorously, and there was a vertical furrow between her eyebrows. Lutie was placidly crocheting a pair of blue bedroom slippers.

I sank into a corner of the davenport, reflecting thankfully that I could sleep tonight in my own bed and planning to retire to it very promptly. Jeff squatted on a hassock and began to mend the fire.

Amanda said abruptly, "We have just had a telephone message from John's attorney. John has been taken into custody. The suitcase that Hester threw away last night has been found."

Jeff dropped the fire tongs with a clatter.

He said, "W-where?"

"Where she put it," snapped Amanda. "In a rubbish can."

"N-not in the river?" stammered Jeff.

Amanda frowned. She repeated, "In the rubbish can where she put it, as you heard her say."

She set her lips, then after a moment added, "An item of the contents, according to the police, incriminates John."

"The—head?" Jeff gulped.

Annoyance reddened Amanda's cheekbones. She said coldly, "I have mentioned that the bag recovered is the one Hester disposed of. The head, therefore, is not a part of its contents; neither are the bread knife, the shears, or the flatiron."

She turned to her sister. "The article which the district attorney regards as definitely compromising John is a handkerchief, marked with his initials."

Lutie glanced eagerly up over her blue wool.

"Bloodstained?" she inquired.

"So it seems," snapped Amanda. "Idiots!"

"Good Lord!" groaned Jeff.

"Tsk, tsk," said Lutie. "What does John say?"

"He says, of course, that he didn't put it in the suitcase and doesn't know how it got there. But they do not believe him."

"No, I suppose not. What a thorough fellow, our murderer!" murmured Lutie.

She looked up and asked quickly, "And the ring?"

"Ring? What ring?" said Jeff.

"Have you forgotten the mark of a ring on the victim's finger, Jeffy dear?" asked Lutie kindly.

"They *have* found a ring, yes," said Amanda. "It, and John's handkerchief, was under the other things in the suitcase—the shaving implements and the few articles of men's clothing that Hester mentioned last evening. The ring is a plain gold band, obviously much worn, and engraved on the inside, 'V.S.-H.S. 1933.' "

"Holy smoke. Victor Shaw-Hester Shaw and the date of their marriage!"

"Obviously," snapped Amanda.

"Whee-ew," said Jeff. "So this guy, hating his wife like poison—according to her—wore their wedding ring all this time! My gosh! What does she say to that?"

"She says," replied Amanda coldly, "that he did not wear it when she knew him, nor possess it then, at least to her knowledge and belief; she had never seen it before. But," said Amanda, in a tone of annoyance, "the child is exasperating, I'm bound to say. The suitcase is hers."

"Rats!" whispered Lutie, her eyes sparkling. She shook her head. "Thorough, yes. But risky…"

"Wait—wait!" Jeff exclaimed. "Boss, this gets screwier by the minute! She denies knowing anything about the ring, you say and John wouldn't know how his handkerchief got in the bag; yet she admits the suitcase is hers."

"It is hers—naturally she says so!" replied Amanda.

"Dear me, I suppose she was too upset to notice that last night," remarked Lutie.

Amanda nodded shortly. Then she glanced at Lutie and a slightly defensive note crept into her gruff tone.

"Well, she was upset and not without some reason. And it's an ordinary looking bag. She'd put it in the storeroom months ago and all but forgotten it; she only recognized it definitely as hers when she examined it closely this evening. Still, it puts me out of patience. I declare I can't imagine even you, Sister, for all your flightiness, or even Marthy, being so silly."

"I suppose," Jeff interrupted, "LaVelle identified the suitcase?"

"She did not," answered Amanda. "She states that Hester had stowed some things away when she moved from the top to the parlor floor, at least that she'd asked for permission to do so. But the landlady doesn't know just what things. She says she seldom goes into the storeroom."

"She doesn't," I agreed. "The place is thick with cobwebs and dust." Then I exclaimed, "Why, Hester couldn't have taken a suitcase from that cubbyhole just yesterday! Nobody could. When we glanced in today there was a spiderweb right across the doorway."

Lutie darted me a swift bright glance.

"Rats, my dear Watson!" she whispered, very softly.

Amanda turned on her. sharply.

"Lutie Beagle, that's the second time you've said 'rats.' Do you mean something by it, or are you merely being rude?"

"I—I'm being mysterious, Sister, I'm afraid," murmured Lutie. "You see, when I looked into that trunk closet I had a notion—"

But Jeff, intent on his own point, cut in, "Well, anyway, the girl must have thought the landlady could, and would, identify the suitcase. Or why would she have acknowledged it was hers?"

Then he unwound his long legs and shot up from the ottoman. "But what I can't see, what makes no sense at all—why didn't she chuck the whole d-darn bag in the river? Where was the point?"

"In carefully removing the oilcloth bundle with the shears, the knife, the flatiron and the head, you mean to say?" Amanda carried on his thought, "while overlooking—"

"The handkerchief and the ring, yes!" said Jeff. "And then, after all," he raked his carroty thatch and shook his head in bewilderment, "she goes and confesses that the bag is hers when she might have taken a chance and got away with denying that. *Why?* It's nuts, boss, if you ask me."

Amanda set Tabby on the rug.

"I did not ask you, Jefferson," she said.

Her tone was cold and her assistant should have taken warning. But he didn't.

"Do you s'pose she figured that the flatiron wouldn't be heavy enough to sink the whole suitcase? Or—or maybe she thought, in case anybody was watching, it would be less conspicuous to slip the bundle out of the bag and toss it away. She could be standing there, with the bag resting on the rail, lift the lid and slide the thing out and just let it fall."

"Jefferson," said Amanda, her face stony, "you *had* put your finger on a point of absurdity that sticks out like a sore thumb. I thought—or hoped— you were going to keep it there. But no. Like all the other perfectly simple facts that establish the innocence of our clients, you must argue it away, with specious folderol that nobody but the most gullible sophist with an ax to grind could swallow."

She paused, then standing very straight she said, "Once and for all, I will name a few more of those facts. First: John Bynam called for Ezekiel when he found a murdered and headless body in Hester's room. Would he have done that if he were pretending to find it? He knew Ezekiel. You knew Ezekiel. Would he have called in Ezekiel, if he had killed, or helped kill a man, and cut off his head? I am asking you; would he?"

Jeff sat abruptly down on the ottoman.

"It doesn't seem likely," he said slowly.

"It does not. He would have telephoned the police. Second: Do you recall what he said when I asked him if he had any idea as to the identity of the body?"

I said eagerly, "I remember, Amanda! He said, 'I have never seen that man in there in my life.' But he said it very strangely."

"Yes. Because, though it was true, he believed the murdered man was Victor Shaw. He had Shaw on his mind. But he didn't want to say so, even to us. Third: Do you remember Hester Gale's manner when we first saw her?"

"She was scared—scared stiff!" exclaimed Jeff.

"Yes, she was. She had been through an ordeal, hearing from her convict husband, waiting for him for hours in the rain. And probably, when the police found her and while they brought her to her apartment, thinking that he had killed John or possibly that John had killed him. When she saw John her first and worst fear was gone; and his manner dispelled the second. Then Inspector Moore told her that a man had been killed in her bedroom. Her first feeling was relief—"

"Yes—yes, it was!" I put in excitedly, as the scene came back to me. "I thought it was strange at the time. But then she seemed bewildered."

"Naturally. As to why they had killed him, how he had happened to be in her bedroom—"

"But—but they, she and Bynam—they were both scared to death it was Victor Shaw and the police would find it out!" exclaimed Jeff.

"Precisely," said Amanda. "It appears you noticed it yourself, Jefferson; they didn't *know* it was Victor Shaw, which they would have been aware of if they'd murdered him."

Amanda stood up.

"If," she said, "anything more were needed to prove their innocence there are several points which have since developed. A clever, unslovenly girl like Hester Gale would never have done a stupid bit of laundering that anyone would notice on her dressing gown. Under the circumstances you are imagining she would have thrown the gown away with the rest of the incriminating evidence. And we have just been over the absurdity of her supposed maneuvers with the suitcase. I will not waste time recounting them. Obviously, as you say, that is screwy, which, I believe, means nonsensical. But while you recognize that you still stubbornly stick to it!"

"But—but, boss," stammered Jeff, "if they didn't do it, who did?"

"That," said Amanda, "is beside the point. However, I daresay we shall have to find out. At the moment I think further discussion is useless. I am going to bed. Goodnight."

She turned and marched from the room.

Jeff stared after her.

"Gosh," he muttered ruefully, "she was sore at me, wasn't she?"

"She's grand!" said Lutie softly. She tucked her crocheting away in her sweet-grass basket and rose and patted Jeff's arm. "And," she added with a little yawn, "she's quite right too. We won't talk about it any more now, and perhaps all these little quirks and puzzles will be straightened out in the morning."

Jeff said, "Miss Lutie, do you mean to say you still believe—?"

"Sshh," she whispered. "You heard the boss—no more chatter! Now be a good lad—" She steered him gently toward the door. "Pleasant dreams, Jeffy dear!" said she, and closed it after him. She turned to me, smiling.

"She said screwy. Did you hear her, Marthy? Such a cute expression— from Amanda, I mean! Not very new, of course—still it's the only addition to Sister's slang in half a century!"

She chuckled happily.

But I was too tired to feel very much amused—or anything except a great longing for my bed.

Ten minutes later Tabby had had his airing, Rab's cage was covered and the fire fixed for the night; Lutie had waved a kiss to me from her bed-room door, Amanda had retired to the bathroom and was running herself a hot tubful. I crept under my soft quilts, hoping I'd dream of East Biddicutt, but thankful at any rate to lay my head at last on the cool lavender-scented pillow.

And then I lifted it—I mean my head, not the pillow—startled. On the other side of the wall against which stood my couch there had been a faint bump, a scraping sound. I sat up, listened. Someone in the inner hallway, of course. But who? And why? And where were they going?

I thought furiously, "I don't care!" and lay down again and pulled the covers up over my ears. But my heart was thumping; the terrors of the night before came flooding back. I thought, "We'll all be murdered in our beds or worse, in our baths!" as I heard Amanda now vigorously splashing. I told myself crossly it was just Lutie, of course, up to more of her pranks.

But it was no use. Muttering to myself, I found my slippers and threw on a dressing gown. If it *were* Lutie I was going to see what she was up to and also I was going to give her a piece of my mind!

"It seems to me we've been through more than plenty for one day!" I grumbled to myself; and trying to talk myself out of being scared stiff, I opened my door stealthily, poked my head out and peered into the passage.

Sure enough, there was a light showing in the crack beneath the door to the inner office. A steady light, which reassured me; and besides I was over my first fright, and quite certain now that it was my younger cousin up to goodness knew what. So, pulling my wrapper close around me and shivering only a little, I hurried quietly through the hallway.

Lutie was standing with her back to me, before the big safe. It swung open just as I entered. She turned with a little start.

"Oh!" she said. And then, sharply, "Come in, Marthy, but quick—and shut the door."

"What in the world—?" I began.

"Sshh," she said, and bent over something at her feet.

I closed the door, and backed against it, and stared. There was a suitcase on the floor. It was in the shadow and half behind the desk and I hadn't noticed it at first. It was the suitcase we had stolen from the locker in the subway, and it was open. But as I looked, and before I'd caught a glimpse of its contents, Lutie had flipped down the lid and snapped the clasps.

As she straightened up she threw me a quick inquiring glance.

I had a sudden, perfectly ghastly thought.

I shrank against the door. Lutie picked up the bag and slid it into the safe. I tried to speak, but could only point, with a trembling finger.

Finally I managed to gasp feebly, "What's in that?"

She didn't answer.

"What's—in—that?" I repeated, hoarsely, and my voice rose. "Lutie Beagle, you tell me! *What's in that bag?"*

"Sssshh," she said.

She pushed the thick door of the safe. It shut with a muffled thud. She twirled the combination. Then she turned to me with a small impish grin and a finger against her lips.

"Hsst, my dear Watson!—Cheese," she replied sweetly. "Merely... *cheese!"*

CHAPTER 20

TWO minutes later she was tucking me into bed. But not another thing would she tell me, and I was scared and sulky.

"Come now, Marthy dear—a little shuteye is what you need."

"And I suppose you think I'll get it after all this!" I retorted bitterly.

"Well, don't go gadding any more, dear, you'll catch cold, you know, traipsing around—"

"I traipsing!" I spluttered. "I like that!"

She giggled. Then she patted a tiny yawn.

"Dear me, I'm sure we should all sleep tight tonight. Such a busy day!"

"I don't expect," I said angrily, "to sleep a wink!"

"Mercy, Sister mustn't catch us chattering like schoolgirls. She'd be mad as a hornet." She dropped a light kiss on my forehead. "Why, you're asleep already!"

"I'm nothing of the kind," I muttered. "I'm—I'm..."

But before I'd finished I must have been. At any rate I didn't hear her go; and indeed I didn't hear, or know, or dream another thing until—

Suddenly, with a perfectly horrible feeling of fright and dread, of some appalling danger hanging over us all, I sat straight up in bed. I didn't know—I don't know yet—what had wakened me. I hadn't been tossing and dreaming, as I'd done the night before; I wasn't conscious even of having been asleep; nothing had startled me. Yet there I was, stark and rigid, icy cold but with the blood pounding in my heart, caught in this nameless terror, pressed down by it, yet forced to struggle upright, to thrust away the bedcovers as if they were bonds holding and strangling me, keeping me from something I must do, somewhere I must go.

"Lutie!" I whispered hoarsely, and groped for her in the darkness.

I don't know why I did that—perhaps because she'd been there when I fell asleep. But as I realized she was no longer in the room it seemed to me my terror reached a climax. It was Lutie who was threatened, I felt—I knew! And I had to get to her, to warn, to save her.

As I shoved my feet into my slippers and grabbed my robe I recalled, though dazedly, that when I went to sleep there had been a pale glow, reflected from moonlight on the brick wall facing my window across the narrow court. It was gone now; by that I knew that some time had passed. Hours, perhaps.

The passage was pitch dark. No thread of light showed beneath the door to the office. I turned to the rear, feeling my way along close to the wall. Presently my outstretched hand struck against the living-room door. This was usually left open at night, and now, as I groped for the knob, dread almost paralyzed me. Who had closed it? And what would I find?

But I managed to turn the knob, to pull the door toward me, to slide through into the living room. From the embers in the fireplace a faint radiance revealed Tabby curled on the hearthrug. As I moved across the floor a board creaked, a coal dropped through the grate, and the cat lifted his head and blinked at me drowsily. His eyes gleamed red as they caught the fire-glow; he yawned, then tucked his head down again and went back to sleep, a sleek fat lump, luxuriously indifferent as only a cat can be. His familiar lazy unconcern comforted me; I was still shaking, but I reached the door of the bedroom quickly.

Then relief surged over me, and the warm delightful reaction of anger. Several of Rab's most emphatic cuss words occurred to me; with great relish I called myself a demned fool, a blarsted idiot and a chump.

For the cool, lavender-scented bedroom was sweet with peaceful slumber—nothing whatever was amiss. Each in her own narrow bed the sisters slept, the covers tidily smooth, as usual, over their quiet forms.

Amanda, who was nearest to me, lay on her back, straight as a ramrod even in bed; the patchwork quilt with the sheet neatly folded over was drawn snugly under her chin, and in the dim light from the open window I could see its slow rise and fall as she breathed, deeply and regularly.

Amanda was a good sleeper. So good that she had no patience with my own occasional plaints of wakeful hours or nights and scolded me roundly for exaggerating, while feeding me hot milk or herb tea. As I leaned against the doorframe now, recovering from my scare, I could very well imagine what she'd say to my silly alarum and excursion. I'd never dare confess it to her.

As I turned to make my way back to my room, I glanced again at Lutie in the farthest bed. She was curled up on her side, apparently, facing away from me, with her head deep in the pillow and the covers pulled up over it. In fact, not even the tip of a nightcap-ribbon showed.

I looked closer, and my heart seemed to stop beating. There was not a motion, not the tiniest movement of those covers; the small mound beneath them was still. Utterly still. As still as—as—

"Lutie!" I cried, and was at the bedside, bending over. No breath stirred the patterned quilt. "Lutie—Lutie!" I called loudly, and put out my hand and touched her

"For the land's sakes, Marthy!" said Amanda. She opened her eyes, glared at me. "What's the matter with you? Have you lost your senses?"

I was tearing at the bedclothes, stripping them wildly back.

"She's gone—look, she's gone, she's disappeared—she isn't here!" I babbled hysterically, and I pointed to the bolster where Lutie should have been.

Amanda sat up. She stared. Her rounded eyes and the tight iron-gray pigtails falling straight on each shoulder gave her momentarily the look of a little girl. She reached out, rather foolishly, and prodded the bolster with a finger. Then she drew a long breath and squared her jaw. The reaction of annoyance set in; she shook the bolster, furiously, rather as if it had been Little Sister herself.

"The little—little devil!" she snorted. "This is some more of her tricks!"

"But—but where is she?" I stammered. Amanda's scolding tone warmed me; but suppose— "Maybe *she* didn't put the thing there," I whispered, trembling. "Maybe someone—someone else—"

"Fiddlesticks!" snapped Amanda sharply. "Of course she did it, to fool me! She's up to some nonsense."

"But—but you don't know about—about—"

About the prowler in the back yard, searching for? About those clutching fingers on the fence and the drunken driver who had almost run us down, who *wasn't* drunk, perhaps! Of Lutie's reticule torn from her wrist, and the suitcase we'd stolen with its fearful secret and our run from the subway, with my knees almost buckling under me and my heart in my mouth and Lutie, utterly fearless and gay, beside me.

The reality of all that, and the vividness of my fright at the time, had been partly obscured and dulled during the day. I'd told myself it was probably quite irrelevant, had nothing to do, in all likelihood, with the murder and the murderer.

But now, if that bag held the awful thing I had imagined might be in it, how could I have gone to sleep, as I'd done, right after that horrifying thought? I'd gone out like a light directly afterward, as if I'd been stunned or something. Perhaps that's why I'd waked as I had, with the memory of some portentous thing, the belated realization that there was danger near, like a charge of dynamite in the flat.

Of course all this went through my mind in a flash, while I stood there staring at Amanda and stammering that she didn't know…

"Don't know *what?*" she demanded harshly, and grasped my arm. "Don't stand there gasping like an idiot, Martha Meecham! You *tell* me!"

But there wasn't time to explain what, without understanding any part of it, I was thinking and fearing. I shook my head. All I could say was, "Hurry!" as I thrust my cousin's dressing gown at her.

She was already out of bed, her feet in her slippers; she took another look at my face, grasped her flashlight from the bedside table. Holding it like a truncheon, she girded her robe around her, and marched into the living room.

I stumbled after her. Tabby rose from the rug, stretched, yawned and came to rub against her ankles. She hissed a warning to him to behave and he subsided, obedient but sulky.

We glanced into the pantry kitchen—I didn't think why, except that the door was closed, and we had to look. But it was empty.

Then we made for the hallway, passed my door and peered into the bathroom. Lutie wasn't there. There was a big closet or storeroom next to it; Amanda yanked at the door. It stuck.

"Amanda!" I choked. I knew the same fearful picture was in her mind that was in mine—that was why we had to look. A small figure, perhaps bound, perhaps—

But she muttered angrily, "She used to sneak out of bed and hide—to read her storybooks, when she was little!"

The closet door came open. Amanda flashed her light on the floor, into the corners. There was no sign of Lutie.

"She's in the office, of course!" snapped Amanda, more to herself than to me.

"Without a light?" I groaned.

My companion didn't answer.

She opened the door to the inner office. For a moment, I think, she was afraid to look. Then she pressed the button of her flashlight.

"For mercy's sake!" said a small, exasperated voice.

We couldn't see her, but the whisper came from the shadow beside the big safe. And it added, sternly, "Put out that light! And *hush.* Do you want to spoil everything?"

Amanda exhaled a deep breath. It sounded as though she'd held it for minutes. But she obeyed the command to switch off the light. She stood stock-still for several seconds. Then she crossed the room, stretched out a hand and felt for her little sister. I was at her shoulder.

"What's happened? Are you all right?" she asked in a gruff, shaken whisper.

"Of course I'm all right. And nothing's happened—yet," said Lutie.

I was close enough to see her now, just barely, in the dim rays that filtered through the small skylight. She was sitting stiffly in a chair, dressed in her flowered robe. Her hair was not put up in curlers tucked beneath the lace and ribbons—silver curls peeped from beneath the filmy nightcap. In her hand was her small pearl-handled pistol. Her eyes were bright and annoyed.

She said rapidly, "I am waiting for the murderer. I haven't time to tell you about it now. I didn't expect this interruption. I wish you would both go sensibly back to sleep."

Amanda found her voice. But she kept it low. There was no fright in it, however, and no surprise. Merely impatience as she retorted, "Don't be ridiculous. I shall stay right here. As for Martha, she can do as she likes."

As for me, I'd rather have stayed right there and been killed in my tracks than to be anywhere else and alone. But I hadn't a chance to say that, or anything else.

"Will you both be quiet!" hissed Lutie.

My teeth chattered, my lips were dry. But I managed to beg, "Lutie, won't you call the police?"

"And ruin everything?" she replied. Then her eyes widened; she put a finger to her lips, listened.

We held our breaths, too. But there was no sound. And after a moment Lutie relaxed.

She said, "If you're going to stay, Marthy, you get behind the desk on the floor. And, Sister, you sit there, on the other side of the safe. Get back as far as you can. And take this.".

She drew something from a pocket of her dressing gown, handed it to her sister. I could just make out the outlines, as Amanda took it. It was the big revolver from Zeke's desk.

"Just point it, Sister. I'll do the shooting, if necessary; though I hope it won't be. And I warn you—we may have a long wait. Or it may be any moment, so we mustn't make a sound."

I shivered. But I crept to my place behind the desk without a word. Amanda nodded grimly as she took her position on the other side of the huge metal box.

It was just barely before midnight then, for I'd seen the wall clock by the light of the flash as we came in the office. Strange to notice and remember, at a moment like that, but I had; the hands stood at three minutes to twelve.

Then what seemed like an hour passed—and the clock struck twelve times!

After that, as I huddled there in the silent room, I almost prayed for whatever was going to happen to happen soon. At first, I'd hoped that nothing would happen at all. That the time would pass, hours, or even the whole night, and morning would come, and the nightmare would be over. Then, if Lutie wasn't convinced that she'd got on the wrong track, if she wouldn't tell us what it was all about, or even if she did, I was going straight to the police. I wouldn't care what she said; she could be disappointed with me if she chose to, but I would tell about the suitcase, and how we'd taken it from the locker in the subway, and what I was certain, now, was in it. But would morning ever come? Better to face the threatened danger, to have it over, no matter what. Better than this ghastly waiting...

The big clock ticked, ticked, ticked. Would it never strike again?

And the sound of its measured beating began to sound alive. I felt, oddly, that its large round face, there on the wall behind me, was grinning maliciously. It was holding the time back perversely, and watching us with a spiteful leer. Surely another hour had passed—it must have!

The beating of the clock grew so loud it seemed to me that it must drown out every other sound. Whatever we were waiting for, whatever Lutie expected to hear, to warn us of its approach, would be lost, overlaid in that heavy thud, thud, thud. Time and again I held my breath, listening for my cousins' breathing. I could not hear them, nor the faintest stir.

Strangely enough, I did not wonder what, or who, we were waiting for. Lutie had said it was the Murderer. I write it that way because that's the way I felt about this nameless creature.

I had had all sorts of notions, suspicions, wild ideas as to the person who'd committed the murder.

Only in horrid, unreal flashes, of course, had I thought of Hester Gale and John Bynam doing the awful thing—only as my imagination, straining away and actually incredulous, had been forced to follow the discussions, the gruesome details that connected them with the crime.

But my mind had been open, had brooded over the picture of Raphaelo Fennelli, swarthy, wild-eyed, insanely vengeful, plotting and executing it.

And I had thought of Dot DeVeere's pinched, envious face and had tried to figure out how she might have done the thing in a kind of crazy petty rage against the girl she obviously hated.

I'd even fancied Professor Sesame accomplishing the murder by a kind of legerdemain and throwing the blame on Fennelli, the handsome acrobat who had arrogantly belittled his magic.

But none of these people occurred to me now. What we were waiting for was the Murderer. Something inhuman, featureless, faceless.

Suddenly, crouched there on the floor, I realized what I was dreading. It seemed to me that what was approaching, on stealthy footsteps that must be noiseless, was a deathly Thing. A featureless, faceless, headless Thing…

I had to speak. I had to hear a human voice. I had to.

But I couldn't make a sound. I opened my lips, but nothing came through them. The shock of formulating this ghastly terror had paralyzed my throat, frozen my tongue.

But I managed to stretch out my hand, to touch Lutie's skirt…

And then we heard it—the smallest possible sound. It was in the main hall; it was at the door to the outer office. Some Thing was fumbling at that door. Some Thing was opening it. Some Thing was in the room next to us— was moving toward us—was putting Its hand on the doorknob of the room where we waited.

Then the door opened. Some Thing came in. The door closed behind It. And It stood there, Its back to the door, for a second. Then It moved forward.

"Don't move," said a gentle voice, very softly.

A sudden small beam from a tiny pocket-light struck full on a figure standing still, its back to the door. (I could just see it beyond a corner of the desk.) It was only a slight, blond young man. His face was smooth, expressionless. His hands were at his sides.

Then he raised one. And there was a sharp report, a flash. And his hand dropped.

"I said, don't move," said the soft voice again. And it added, "Marthy, reach up and turn the light on."

I don't know how I did it, but I obeyed that calm command. A greenish radiance filled the room, from the student lamp on the desk. It showed Lutie, in the angle between the safe and the wall. She had risen from the little wooden chair on which she'd been sitting, and the tiny weapon in her hand pointed at the blond young man standing there against the door. His arms still hung motionless against his sides. Then swiftly the right arm swung toward the left—something passed from the right to the left hand—there was a gleam of metal.

Then another shot, a spurt of flame. I didn't see what happened that time. I shut my eyes. It was dreadful. This was just a blond young man, hardly more than a boy; good-looking, harmless-looking. I didn't know what Lutie was doing to him, or why. Maybe she'd gone crazy. But I didn't want to see...

Then I heard her say, almost kindly, "Drop the gun. You can't shoot with it now anyway. Sister, there's some rope right here. I was going to tie him up but since you're here—"

I managed to open my eyes.

There was a clatter as something dropped from the man's flaccid fingers to the floor.

Amanda came from the shadow where she'd waited. She was holding Ezekiel's big revolver straight out in front of her with both hands. Her lips were locked and her face gray. But her black eyes, fixed on the man against the door, were without fear. I thought they held a kind of grim pity, as she laid the gun gingerly on the desk, picked up the neatly coiled rope that lay on the floor at Lutie's feet and went toward our visitor.

Lutie said, "Don't bind his arms. I've shot them both, right above the wrists. Just wind the rope around his ankles. We don't want him trying to run away."

Not lowering her little gun she added, "Marthy, get up, dear. You can call the police now. Spring 7-3100. And tell them we need a doctor too."

She gazed at our prisoner. He stared back at her.

And then I knew he was that Thing I'd feared—the Murderer. For if ever such evil could look from human eyes, they were no longer human. I saw that behind those pleasantly modeled features, that smooth youthful mask of a face, there was hate. More loathsome and deadly than the venom of a snake, because that has no malice behind it. The soul that had distilled the poison behind those long-lashed, large and handsome eyes was cruel and vicious, twisted with dislike for all its fellow creatures.

And Lutie's quiet voice held no ruth as she told him, "I didn't wish to shoot you. But you left me no choice. If you hadn't moved when I warned you—"

Then she said sharply, "Marthy, what's the matter with you? Don't you see he's suffering? Never mind!"

Feebly I scrambled to my feet and reached for the phone. But she'd forestalled me. She dialed the number rapidly.

Amanda had finished her task and the man's feet were bound. His face was white, contorted; and he swayed now against the doorframe. But he braced himself; and still his hating eyes glared back at Lutie.

She said into the phone, "Homicide Bureau? I want Inspector Moore, please...The Beagle Detective Agency...Yes...Yes, Inspector, we've got the murderer...Right away, please—and we want a doctor...Yes, I'm afraid he's hurt. I had to shoot him..."

She replaced the receiver with a click, and went toward our captive. His eyes had closed.

"Quick, Amanda, take his shoulders! Marthy, help me—we'll take his feet. Put him here—"

Again, seemingly without volition, I obeyed her. We got the limp figure on the worn leather couch.

Then his eyes opened again, and for the first time his pale lips. The ugly stream of words, spoken softly in a low, well-modulated voice, was directed at the small person who, with her back turned to him, was now swiftly tearing long strips from the hem of the muslin gown beneath her flowered robe.

I don't want to remember what he said. Such quietly uttered brutal epithets, such smooth, egotistical, malevolent threats—

Lutie said briskly, "Sister, take off his coat. Dear me, we really should keep a first-aid kit in the house, shouldn't we? But this will do for the nonce. Here, you were always so much better at bandages, Sister."

And she handed Amanda the pieces of muslin.

Then she turned to the man on the couch and said briskly, "Tut, tut. Sticks and stones will break our bones, but words will never hurt us! So save your breath to cool your porridge, Mister—Floto!"

CHAPTER 21

ON the following night an eager crew was gathered in the kitchen of the Maison LaVelle.

We were assembled in the kitchen because that was where our hostess always held what she called her soirees; and certainly no other room in the house was so large, yet so cozy. The time was midnight, and the occasion, as described in an invitation elegantly written on pale green paper and delivered to us by young Billy Paul, was, "To partake of a little rifreshment, for all those conected with the recent Trageddy to meat eech other, and to here Miss Lutie's acount of how she Solved the Mistery."

Somewhat to my surprise, neither the lateness of the hour set nor the rather fantastic nature of the occasion had brought any real protest from Amanda. Her "hmmph" was perfunctory; apparently she had taken a liking to Madame LaVelle, and I thought she was curious about many of "those conected," who were still only names to her.

But her strongest motive for accepting the invitation was obvious as, her eyes resting on her little sister, she said gruffly, "Hmm. I daresay it's only civil for us to go. I hope, Sister, you'll do yourself justice."

"Oh, Sister, do you think I can, before all those people? Suppose," faltered Lutie, "I have stage fright!"

"Fiddlesticks!" snapped Amanda. "You did quite well in presenting your report to the inspector."

"But—but I was only telling him the bare facts," said Lutie. "I—I wasn't trying to—to—"

"—to put on an act?" said Amanda shrewdly, while I gasped at the expression, another addition to her vocabulary.

Lutie was startled too, and a tiny delighted grin touched her lips.

But she only said meekly, "Well, I'll do my best, Sister dear."

So now she was receiving the congratulations and the excited queries with becoming modesty. The newspapers had come out with spectacular accounts of last night's arrest, of course, and had given some report of Lutie's part in it; and it was evident that Madame LaVelle had embroidered these, yet had done so with a keen sense of drama, revealing and concealing just enough to whet the curiosity of her guests to a fine edge. And now she held it in check; she would not allow Lutie to be besieged and shooed us to our places with the firm command, "Please to be seated at the Festeeve boarr-rd, everrrybodee! We weel eat, drrrink, and afterrrwards, Meez Lutee weel be so kind as to spik!"

The festive board ran down the middle of the long kitchen and consisted of several tables of different widths and somewhat varying heights. It was laden with platters of ham and chicken, mounds of jelly, biscuit, cake and pie. Candles glowed along its length, flowers decorated it, and bottles of red wine. Also there was champagne—presented by Inspector Moore.

Since our hostess had banned discussion of the subject uppermost in all minds "teel laterrr, seel-voo-play," conversation lagged, just at first. But she carried it on with commentaries in her grandest manner on "ze current offerings in ze theatrrrical worrrld"; Mrs. Joffey contributed rambling but piquant anecdotes of life behind the footlights; Billy Paul compared the technique of a Mr. Draper and a Mr. Astaire; Lutie and Mamma Fennelli reviewed the latest fashions; Papa Fennelli and Amanda grew eloquent on the care and feeding of felines; while I found myself deep in a fascinating talk about plants and flowers with Mr. Saint John. Jeff was amusing Lotta Fennelli; her brother Michelangelo and Inspector Moore were animated about the chances of Notre Dame against USC (whatever that meant) and Professor Sesame and Dot DeVeere coyly whispered together.

Hester and John were very quiet, though they smiled and looked at each other, from time to time, with eyes that said more than words could ever do. And Raphaelo Fennelli, seated next to a thin dark girl, heaped her plate with tidbits and filled her wine glass, leaving his own almost untouched. They too had little to say; but they were sitting near me and once I overheard a low-voiced interchange.

She said huskily, "You are good, Raph. I don't deserve it." Her large sad eyes filled with tears. "That letter to Lotta—he made me write it. I didn't mean it. I wanted to come back to you right away."

Raph said, "Every night I prayed you'd come. I prayed it on my knees. Ah, Dolo mio—"

She whispered, "I dasn't. He—he said he'd kill you." She shuddered, and touched her husband's arm. "But I came as soon as I read in the papers where you was. And when I knew he was—when he could do no more harm—I thought you would hate me. But I came, anyway."

"I love you, my Dolo. Nothing else don't matter," he said softly, and drew her hand against his cheek.

And I wondered, with a tight feeling in my throat, how I could ever have cast Raph Fennelli for the role of villain, even for a moment...

I was thinking this and furtively dabbing my eyes with a table napkin while I nodded in response to Mr. Saint John's tender eulogies on the crimson rambler, when our hostess grandly rose.

"You are all craz-ee, I know, to hear just how our Mademoiselle Lutee have solve ze terr-reeble crime wheech fell, like a bombshell, in our meedst, just two nights ago. You have been patient. And now eez ze time for your rewar-rd, I hope...Meez Lu-tee, weel you tell us ze storr-ry, seel-voo-play? We're all ears!"

She sat down. There was a stir of excitement, an eager murmur, as all ears and eyes turned toward Lutie.

Her cheeks were very pink, her own eyes the blue of periwinkles as she smiled shyly at her attentive audience.

"Why, I'm only too delighted to Tell All, you may be sure! This was our first big case, you know. And the outcome has been gratifying in several ways."

She beamed at Hester and John, at Raphaelo and Dolores, then went on earnestly, "But you mustn't say that I solved the mystery, because indeed you all did. First, and last, if it hadn't been for my dear Sister's staunch conviction as to the innocence of our clients, I might not have got, and kept, on the right track. But she is always able to see the bright needle of truth in the haystack of nonsense."

Amanda's grunt at this florid tribute was covered by Professor Sesame's appreciative murmur, "Ah, exquisitely phrased, Miss Lutie!"

Lutie turned to me. "And if it hadn't been for my dear Watson—I mean my dear Marthy— Well, she was splendid!"

She paused, suddenly overcome by diffidence (or so it seemed). "Sister, how shall I begin?"

Amanda, far more nervous, to a discerning eye, than her small sister, answered gruffly, "Hurr-rum. At the beginning!"

"Yes-s," said Lutie meekly.

She clasped her hands and drew a deep breath. "You know—you've all heard, I'm sure—how, on a dar—on a stormy evening, the evening before last, we received a telephone call from John, and came to this house in response. John had wanted and thought he was calling our brother, and he was surprised when we appeared. But he was much more upset for another reason, and no wonder. After a moment or two he showed us the cause of his concern...

"Well, I've always had a habit of noticing all sorts of little things, and of course this was the time to see how useful that habit could be. So I took special note, first, of everything about the headless body he showed us on the bed in the bedroom. Naturally several things were apparent at once. For instance—"

She enumerated the stab wound that had caused death, the evidence that death had been recent, the absent fingertips, and the empty pockets of the coat and waistcoat on the foot of the bed.

"I—I had to assume that the other pockets would be empty too," she admitted. "But—well, the inference was plain: a murderer taking advantage of the lack of fingertips to get rid of all other clues as to the identity of the victim. There was a scar, however, on the left hand—a very noticeable and peculiar scar. Also the mark of a ring on one finger. The next thing I noticed was a negligee lying on a chair."

And she described the damp scorched spot on the sleeve that suggested a hasty attempt to eliminate bloodstains.

"And that was when I had my first hunch—I mean, it was evident that the girl who lived in those rooms was a meticulously dainty person. I didn't believe she would ever have expected that ineffectual piece of laundering to pass unobserved. It was too crude. She would have thrown the gown away— especially as any intelligent person nowadays knows that chemical analysis would reveal the stains anyway—you can't fool the police that way. No, that sleeve was meant to be noticed. And that meant, you see, a deliberate frame—fraud. As Sister also saw, the minute she heard of it—"

"Just the same," put in Miss DeVeere with a slight sniff, "some of us couldn't afford to throw away a perfectly good gown."

"Pipe down, dearie. Miss Lutie simply guessed that. Hester wasn't sloppy nor a dumbbell," said Mrs. Joffey placidly. "Go on, Miss Lutie."

So Lutie went on. She recounted John's story of how he'd come to the house, and found the body.

"And later it turned out that he couldn't establish an alibi for the hours before that. But even while he was talking to us, it was perfectly plain that he was concealing something that worried him awfully. And I'll admit that I did begin to get all sorts of odd notions. I won't quite call them suspicions, but—"

"I know," said John, "I should have been quite frank. It would have saved a great deal of trouble."

"Trouble?" reflected Lutie dreamily. "Well, I don't know..." She took a tiny swallow of champagne. "Anyway," she said cheerfully, "Sister knew that you were just upset. So I paid no attention to my silly fancies. As I told you all before, everything worked out beautifully when I really trusted her intuition—that is, her judgment"

Amanda said, "Hmmph! Intuition! Horse sense, you mean. But never mind. Don't wander, Sister!"

"I'll try not to, Sister," said Lutie meekly. "Well, then," she continued, "while we waited for the police I went on looking around, and of course I noticed that a pair of scissors, a bread knife, the oilcloth from the kitchen table and the flatiron were all missing from where they should have been. And presently, when Madame LaVelle came in, she mentioned every one of those things, as it happened. And again I'll confess that struck me as odd; and I even began to wonder if she could have had something to do with the murder! But Sister wasn't wondering anything of the sort. So I stopped imagining, and just took what Madame LaVelle said as the simple truth. That is, as to her intentions. Of course she did make a mistake. But—"

"I certainly opened my mouth and put my foot in it!" said our hostess ruefully.

"And who wouldn't!" cut in Miss DeVeere. "I'm sure nobody blames you! I could have sworn—"

"So you did," Lutie reminded her. "Anyway, then Madame LaVelle viewed the body, and was shocked, especially to recognize her lod—her guest from the parlor front, Vincent Smyth. And then Hester came in..."

She smiled down the table at the quiet girl. Hester sent her a look of affection and gratitude. (I knew it was only these feelings, toward Lutie and Amanda and her friend, Sarah, that had allowed her to be present this night.) Her face glowed warmly as Lutie went on, "She looked just as I'd thought she would, somehow. And the idea of her having done that dreadfully unpleasant thing was even more preposterous. She was too—too—"

"Far too pretty, and little, and sweet!" agreed Professor Sesame gallantly, with a deep bow that brought his auburn locks so close to the candle flame that I gasped. Miss DeVeere's pale blue eyes darted an annoyed glance at him but melted as he turned to her with another courtly and dangerous genuflection and added, "She could be no more suspect, my dear, than your own charming self!"

"Aw, go on, Sessie," simpered Dot. "I'll bet you say that to all the girls."

"Not at all!" said Lutie, addressing the gentleman. "I am little and pr— I mean to say, that has nothing to do with it! I've seen plenty of sweet little women who—But never mind. Where was I?"

"Hester," said Amanda, "came in."

"Oh, yes," said Lutie. "Well, and besides being a nice girl, as I was trying to say, she was all in, er, I mean, she'd been through a great strain. And it was also plain that she and John were trying to say something to each other. They feared something that they didn't want anyone else to understand."

Hester said, in a low voice, "That was stupid. But—"

John said quickly, "It was my fault. I was afraid—"

Inspector Moore said, "Quite understandable."

"Of course it was!" cried Miss DeVeere, defensively. "I'm sure no one can blame Mr. Bynam for standing by his friend, no matter what he thought! I'd have done the same. I mean, f'rinstance, if it was Sessie," she gave him an arch glance, "and I suspected him."

"Shut up, dearie," suggested Mrs. Joffey, mildly. "John never thought anything foolish like what you're hinting. He just didn't quite trust the police, that's all. And no more do most folks, when you come right down to it, and I'm sure Inspector Moore won't take that amiss, it's nothing against him personally, it's just human nature and it can't be anything new to him; is it, Inspector?"

"No, it is not, Mrs. Joffey!" agreed Inspector Moore with a rueful grin, which was reflected a bit self-consciously by several other faces around the table. Lutie glanced at him wickedly.

"That's where we Beagles have the advantage over you, Inspector!" she chuckled. Then she sobered and resumed. "Well, then Hester had to be shown the dead man, and besides being horrified, she recognized that scar on the left hand. Of course, it was obvious to us from her manner that she believed the victim was...someone she had known; and also—I felt sure—the same person who had been in her mind when she'd first come in, when we'd first seen her, so distressed and frightened. But she was very brave and replied to Inspector Moore's questions quietly and fully, except for one thing she wouldn't tell."

Lutie gave Hester's account of where she had been during the evening.

"And," she said, "then one thing was clear. I mean, plainly someone had got her out of her apartment on a fool's errand. She wouldn't say who. But she said she wasn't shielding that person; and when Inspector Moore suggested that it might even be the murderer, the notion obviously struck her as incredible. It was puzzling.

"And so was her conviction that she'd left the house at twenty minutes of seven. Because John had phoned her at seven, and Madame LaVelle had dropped in to see her after that. They were positive as to the time, and so was Hester; she said the man who had called her mentioned it, and she'd checked with her electric clock—her watch was broken. And she called our attention to her clock. It was correct.

"And then I thought of something; you see, we live in the same district, and I recalled how, right after supper, there'd been a terrific, lightning flash and all our lights had gone out for an instant. That same flash would have stopped Hester's clock.

"Well, when we got home I checked with our office electric clock, and it had stopped at 8:17. Which meant that someone had started Hester's running after that. Who?

"Next morning I learned from Miss DeVeere that Hester had been seen to leave the house at twenty minutes to eight—an even hour later than she believed to be the time, according to her statement. Of course there was nothing to prove that she hadn't returned, after 8:17, and set the clock or that John hadn't done so. Nothing except the fact that that made no sense. But suppose the man who had phoned her and made such a point of the time— the wrong time!—had hoped to entangle her in a lie when she was later questioned? I had no doubt that he was connected with the crime in some way. Suppose he had entered her rooms while she was out that afternoon— for instance, when he left the suitcase she took with her to the river hidden near her door—and set back her clock? Then later, when the murder was committed, the clock had been reset. Why not? At least that did make sense!"

"Most perspicacious, indubitably!" murmured the professor.

"My goodness, I never would have thought of it, I'm sure!" said Miss DeVeere.

"However, Miss DeVeere," remarked Lutie, "you were most helpful; more so than you expected, I shouldn't be surprised. You did see Hester leave and noted the time; and it was your vivid description of Vincent Smyth that struck Mrs. Joffey—"

"All of a heap!" agreed that lady. "It did indeed. I'd never seen that Smyth, you know, on account of my legs, but when Dot described him, especially that odd walk—well, I'd seen that Shaw just once, but it was behind the footlights, and I never forget a person I've seen on the stage as long as I live—"

"I knew," piped up Dotty, "you were knocked for a loop about something! Didn't I say you looked like you'd seen a ghost?"

"No one would ever deny that you are observant, Miss DeVeere," said Lutie.

"Well, er—" she hesitated, glancing toward the Fennelli "—from this and that, I learned about Raphaelo and Dolores and their unhappy separation. You know, I needed to learn things—it wasn't mere gossip."

"Why not? Everyone gossips," said Mamma Fennelli, with a shrug of her sturdy shoulders. "Anyhow, we never made no secret of it."

"I'll say we didn't!" Lotta said, frowning and reaching for a cigarette.

"You should talk!" cut in Mike. "Getting Raph all hot and bothered telling him this Smyth was Floto! But what I wanna know—who spilled that, ma'am? We didn't tell nobody."

"Ah, but the walls have ears!" Lutie replied. She didn't glance in the direction of the little professor, who was looking uncomfortable, as she explained, "And it is my business to listen. I hope you'll forgive me, since it's all turned out for the best. And besides, maybe you did raise your voices a wee bit."

"My family, they always yell," said Papa Fennelli.

"Somehow it seems to be becoming to them, Signore," Lutie commented thoughtfully. "Well, anyway, I learned that Smyth was Floto, according to Lotta. And at first I didn't know quite what to make of that, because from the photo found in his suitcase he certainly appeared to be Victor Shaw. But then from John we learned Hester's story; and between it and Dolores' there were certain peculiar and interesting similarities. You know, I can't tell you exactly the order in which I learned things; but we all chatted, and—and things came out and fitted together. For instance, there was Bill's part in the actual tracking of the murderer." She smiled at him. "If it hadn't been for his sharp eyes and ears—"

With great effect she told us of the Something that had leaped down past the laundry windows while Bill was in the kitchen.

"And that," she said, "naturally made me want to look over the ground. For a clue. Suppose there'd been a shred caught on the ladder, or—or something. So we started back to the yard, and by the most wonderful fortune, there was someone with a flashlight prowling around out there. But, though we tried to creep up on him quietly, we weren't quite quiet enough. When I opened the laundry door he was off over the fence in a jiffy. It was a little disappointing—"

Lutie paused. She didn't look in my direction, but I felt my face reddening with chagrin. She went on, "However, we looked around, and in a muddy crack that had been deep in puddles I found a key. And the moment I picked it up there was a noise on the other side of the fence. Hands appeared, gripping the boards; someone was starting to climb back over!"

Bill's eyes popped with excitement. He gasped, "And then I bust out, and scared him away! Gosh! But you never told us, Miss Lutie! You said—"

"Well, he was gone, there was nothing to do about it at the moment. If we'd set up an alarm he might have flown for good. So I put the key in my reticule, and soon after that we left the Maison LaVelle. We called on the Fennellis then, at the Paradise Theatre. It was late, and I feared we might miss them; but," she blushed slightly, "I've always wanted to see the really inside of a theater, so—so we went.

"And afterward, as we were leaving the stage entrance, we were almost run down by a car."

She described our hairbreadth escape in the alley, while a ripple of awe and excitement went around the table.

"Of course I realized that the car had come at us deliberately; it didn't wobble or swerve at all. There in that dark alleyway, with only the old door-man to see or hear, it should have been easy to run us down, to kill us or get something we had that the driver wanted. But he didn't *quite* do it. So... Well, then we went to the Bowerie and saw Professor Sesame's marvelous performance and chatted with him; and then we went home. Next morning we called again at the Maison LaVelle, during which a number of interesting things transpired. And we conducted a little experiment, Martha and Madame and I, to find out what could be heard between the back and front parlors."

She described it, and concluded, "By a charming accident, while Madame was talking, I learned an extremely significant fact. In connection with which, at the corner drugstore, I made a phone call. I'll come back to that later. Anyway, then we hailed a cab, and when we were in it I discovered that my reticule was gone. You see, someone had bumped into Marthy in the crowded noon street, and she'd grabbed me—that's all I noticed; I was in a hurry and my mind was on something else. I was certainly caught napping! But it was really lucky, after all; because I realized at once, of course, that the murderer was still on our trail. And he'd finally got my purse."

She took a sip of wine. Her cheeks were pink with remembered excitement.

"Of course it was the *key* he wanted. But I'd taken it from my bag and put it in my glove. So I still had it. All I had to do was to find out what it was for."

She told how she'd discovered that, and how we'd gone to the Times Square subway and opened the locker.

"And we found a suitcase." She drew a deep breath. "Do you know, when I saw that bag my imagination quite ran away with me—I fancied quite gruesome things about what was in it; but we had to have it, though I knew it would be a ticklish business, getting it away, because there was someone standing quite near and watching us, from behind a newspaper. I couldn't see his face, but I could tell—"

I gasped, for this was news to me.

I said, "Lutie Beagle, you didn't tell me that!"

"Of course not," she replied. "I just told you to hold tight and yell if anyone tried to grab the suitcase from us, and I said it loud enough for our watchful waiter to hear, so what could he do? He couldn't afford to risk a commotion, even if he did get the bag. We ran, and he followed, but we foiled him!" She beamed at me. "Dear Marthy, you were splendid!"

A ripple of excitement went round the table. When it subsided Lutie went on briskly.

"Well, when we got home I put the bag in our bedroom closet. But I hadn't a chance to get a peek into it for hours. I knew it would take a bit of time to force the lock; and so many things were going on ..."

She described the afternoon and evening, the various things that had happened and transpired. It hardly seemed possible to me that it was only yesterday!

"And so," she explained, "it was bedtime before I had an opportunity to see what was in that bag. And then—well, I was relieved, I'll confess. For instead of what I'd expected, it was full of money!"

Papa Fennelli said, "How much money?"

"Sixty gran—thousand dollars, we later learned. I could only tell there was a lot. So I believed it would be called for by the murderer."

"But—but how did you guess the money had something to do with the murder?" asked Dotty, excitedly.

"I did not guess, Miss DeVeere," answered Lutie coolly. "By that time the whole plot was clear, naturally. The one thing that had bothered me was—how would he come? But that was simplified by something Jeffy had told us at supper..."

She described the reporter who had been so curious about us, and Jeff cut in ruefully, "Gosh, he was a smooth customer! And what a sap I was, showing him all around—"

"It was very useful indeed, Jeffy," said Lutie, smiling at our assistant, "because I'd been afraid he might come up the fire escape, and I didn't see how I was going to watch there and the front way too. But when I knew he'd had an opportunity to see how easy it would be to pick our simple locks—"

"Creepers, yes!" exclaimed Jeff. "I'll see to having those locks changed first thing tomorrow."

"Oh, no, Jeffy!" said Lutie. "Another similar occasion might arise. Well, anyway, I put the suitcase with the money in the obvious place, in the safe. And we waited, Marthy and Sister and I, and the murderer came, and we caught him—"

"You caught him," said Amanda. She turned to the enthralled gathering and explained, "She disabled both arms by shooting them just below the elbows. Though how she ever learned—"

"Why, you see," Lutie said shyly, "Pa gave me a little pistol on my twenty-first birthday. He said it would take the place of a man in the house, after—after he was gone, and he told me I'd better learn to use it, because Sister was too tenderhearted to hurt a fly."

"Hmmph!" snorted Amanda. "And I thought it was those Bayly boys shooting at squirrels in the woodlot!"

"I know. And you used to be so angry with them," Lutie murmured. "But I gave them molasses cookies to make up for their scoldings."

Amanda snorted again. But she couldn't help a reluctant chuckle, as everyone else laughed.

When we'd sobered again, Mr. Saint John said, "But what a terrible risk to take, Miss Lutie! Why didn't you ask for police assistance?"

"Oh, but that might have queered the—I mean, that might have kept the murderer away! I was sure he was watching the house. That's why I couldn't tell *anyone,*" she explained meekly, "what I knew."

"And did you *know* who the murderer was?" inquired Mr. Saint John, "before you actually captured him?"

"Oh, yes!" replied Lutie brightly. She drew a long breath, and I could tell she was going to enjoy spinning this out a bit. "I knew that the murderer had to be a person who could hate, coldly, venomously, viciously."

"He was—he was! The most cruel, cold-blooded thing that ever lived!" cried Dolores Fennelli. "I—I wanted to leave him a week after we—" She cowered against her husband's arm, her eyes dark with remorse and remembered terror. "But—but I dasn't. He didn't like me—he didn't like nobody. But he had to have somebody to be mean to, and he made me work for him. Night after night I thought I'd break my neck—I almost wanted to—he'd be standing there in the wings watching me."

"Don't you think of it no more," said Mamma Fennelli, patting the trembling girl.

"I shoulda killed him," muttered Raph, his hands clenched.

"No, bambino—no!" cried Mamma. "Not in a nice lady's room like that you couldn't—"

"Well, he didn't, Mamma, so don't argue!" said Lotta, and added, "Forget it, Dolo!"

The dark girl shivered. "He—he wasn't human—"

"No," Lutie agreed. "And I'd learned that from Hester's story. Floto, and the man who had trapped Hester into marriage, who had lured her to the river with threats against John—those characters fitted the inhuman character of the crime. But what clinched my suspicions as to the murderer was a piece of apple pie."

She sipped her wine.

"You see, by that charming chance I mentioned, during our experiments in eavesdropping, Madame LaVelle repeated the tableau with her parlor front tenant, just as it had happened an hour or two before the murder. And I learned that she had taken him a piece of her apple pie, and that he had eaten it to the last crumb.

"And soon after that I telephoned the morgue. I do appreciate the courtesy that has been shown us, Inspector Moore. They were simply lovely to me—and, after all, this is our very first murder—and gave me the autopsy report at once. And of course, as I'd hoped, the dead man hadn't eaten any pie."

There was a silence, as this sank in.

Then our hostess said, "Well, I can't help being pleased, on account of me being so cocksure about who the dead man was, that afterwards I did help prove who he wasn't—"

"Yes," said Lutie, smiling back at her, "and that made it all simple. Because the logical person to have committed the crime was Victor Shaw. So when I knew he could have, I was sure he *had*. It all fitted!"

"Of course, it would have been a relief to Hester and John if I'd told what I'd found out, right away. But I was afraid if I did, something might slip. And we did seem to be right on the murderer's trail by that time. So I thought I'd just keep quiet, and see if my luck would hold. And, as you know, it did."

She looked modest and appealing. But there was an amused twinkle in the inspector's eyes, and I noticed the dry smile he covered as he raised his wine glass to his lips. He knew quite well that she'd meant to have all the thrill and the satisfaction of catching the killer for the Beagles—and her own little self. She wasn't fooling him for a moment!

CHAPTER 22

THEN everyone began talking at once, in the midst of which John took Hester away (she was staying with his Aunt Savina, who had come to town to be with her), and Dolores and Raphaelo also said their goodnights.

And their going seemed to be the signal for a certain loosening of tension.

As Madame LaVelle exclaimed, settling back into her chair, "Now, Miss Lutie, you can tell us all! What kind of a bird was—I mean is that Smyth-Shaw-Floto—what's-his-name ? My Gawd, to think what a nice young chap he seemed. And I thought I knew a thing or two about people!"

"Well," said Lutie, "he is a peculiar bird. For example, this is the way he starts his confession: 'When I went to prison for the first time,' he says, 'I told the woman who was to blame that I wasn't through with her. She'd squandered my fortune and ruined my life. So the next time I saw her I convinced her that she had no right to her own. She took an overdose of sleeping tablets. Of course that isn't on the records; but I killed her, as certainly as if I'd fed them to her. The point is, I keep my promises.'

"That woman," said Lutie, "was his mother."

"His own mamma?" cried Mamma Fennelli. "Dio mio! How could anyone be that mean!"

"The man was an egomaniac, obviously," commented Mr. Saint John.

"And maybe that was partly her fault," said Amanda sternly.

"You never can really tell, though, can you?" said Mrs. Joffey thoughtfully, "in spite of this Frood or whatever his name is, it's like the chicken and the egg. Anyhow she paid for it, poor creature."

"And she's dead now," said Lotta, impatient at this diversion. "So he confessed, did he? That ain't in the papers yet. Why did the sap do that? I'd think, from what you say, he'd be more hardboiled!"

"Maybe," said Miss DeVeere with a giggle and a meaningful glance at the inspector, "they gave him the business."

Lutie snubbed this suggestion with a cold glance.

"Victor Shaw knows," said she, "that he is doomed, without question or quarter, for the killing of a guard during his escape from San Quentin. Besides, he is extremely proud of his brilliant crime. He confessed to it not only willingly but with gusto. Of course, he wasn't feeling very chipper for a while. I'm afraid I rather hurt him, spiritually as well as physically. But his ego is very resilient, and he had soon recuperated enough to spend several evidently gratifying hours dictating the smallest details of the murder. The gist of his statement will be in tomorrow's papers."

"Gee, Miss Lutie, do we have to wait?" exclaimed young Bill wistfully.

"Come on, Miss Lutie, give us the lowdown now!" urged Lotta eagerly.

"'Seel-voo-play, Meez Lutie," coaxed our hostess. "After all, it's the shank of the evening."

"But I've already chattered so much!" said Lutie.

Amanda said, "Hrrmm. We might as well be hung for a sheep as a lamb. Go on, Sister."

Lutie said, "Very well, Sister."

She reflected. "Well then," she decided, "I'll go on as he does himself.

"It seems Mr. Shaw—*né* Heyward—lays great store by promises. He follows up his opening announcement thus: 'Yes, I committed the murder you are interested in. I don't regret it, and I expect to suffer for it. But just the same, you can lay it all, first to the woman who ruined my chance in life, my mother, and then to the woman I married. She also betrayed me, and I was sent to prison for life. Remember, she'd sworn to honor and obey me. But she did not. When I needed her she let me down. Well, I told her that she would pay for it. And she has.'

"Then he goes on at some length concerning his grudge against Hester," said Lutie, "and tells how he immediately started making good his threat. You see, after his sentence to life imprisonment Hester went away and tried to hide herself, but wherever she went she was followed by anonymous letters..."

Lutie described them and continued. "Shaw explains how he managed that piece of persecution. There was a woman who had helped him with several forgeries, whom he could have sent to prison. But he agreed not to, as long as she was useful to him. He ordered her to keep on Hester's trail, to write those letters. And, as he boasts, 'it was a h—' it was a bothersome job, but she had to do it or else.

"So from time to time she sent him reports of Hester's whereabouts and activities and how she had interfered with these—in letters that were apparently innocuous, but actually contained a code that she and Shaw had used for years. Shaw's code letters in reply held orders to keep up the good work and the assurance that he had no intention of remaining in prison.

"Which was true, too. From the first he grimly planned his escape and revenge. Meanwhile he was pleasantly confident that he was making Hester's life wretched.

"Then several months ago he received the information that his wife had stopped hiding, had resumed her maiden name, and was singing at the Harmony Club. He also learned her address, and about her friendship with John Bynam.

"Shaw's informant—he describes her as 'a smart dame, not to be judged by the phony illiteracy of the billet-doux she concocted to impress the yokels'—would make a valuable adjunct to our agency." Lutie interrupted herself to comment rather regretfully, "However he refuses to disclose her identity. 'She obeyed orders, I'm not squealing. I keep my word,' he affirms proudly. Anyway, his return orders were 'to keep him wise, but leave things alone.' The reason was that he now meant to attend to them himself. Because he'd at last, and as he felt most opportunely, received the inspiration he'd been looking for.

"A new prisoner was lodged in the cell next to his. Victor Shaw says he was," Lutie wrinkled her brow, then quoted. " 'A poor addle-cove who had been a good pickpocket till he was roped in on a killing and got the book.' Which means, I understand, a life term in prison," she explained. "These colloquialisms are so trenchant, aren't they? And Shaw goes on to say that this man—his name was Joey Futz—was 'a natural fall guy. He had no chin and his head should have been in a circus.' But Victor Shaw had no use for his head. What had interested him was a scar on Futz's hand, which was practically identical with the one on his own; and also Futz was of the same build and complexion. Shaw felt that 'heaven had sent him.' So our hero exerted his charm. And in no time at all the two were buddies.

"Shaw had a plan of escape already worked out. In a few weeks he put it into execution. He says, 'Needless to remark, it worked. And by the way, I'll mention that I neither wished nor expected the two mugs who helped us to get away themselves. I'd handed them the hard part. But I took good care of my buddy. And after that, naturally, there was nothing he wouldn't do for me.'"

Lutie took another small swallow of champagne.

"Well," she continued, "then Shaw brags at length of how he eluded the cops, but I won't go into that. Except to mention that the lady of the letters helped him. She hid him and Futz, fed them and got clothes for them.

"And during that time Shaw burned off Joey's calling cards—fingerprints, that is—and his own.

"Also he bought a lucky ring for Joey, and another for himself. Joey's was too tight, as Shaw had meant it to be, but there were tears in his eyes as it was solemnly placed on his finger. At the same time, his pal placed a similar gold band on a corresponding finger of his own hand.

"Shaw had bought both rings at a pawnshop. He'd had Joey's engraved 'Until Death.' His own, though Futz did not know that, was marked with initials and a date that had nothing to do with Joey."

"My gosh, what a lousy trick on that poor Joey!" said Mike Fennelli furiously.

"An imaginative fellow, however—" Mr. Saint John commented.

"Yes. And thorough, in his way," agreed Lutie.

She went on, "It was then, too, that he bleached his hair and eyebrows a nondescript straw color and cultivated a sedate walk instead of his own naturally arrogant gait."

She smiled at Lotta. "I congratulate you, my dear. You only saw the man, and not closely, in that disguise; yet you recognized him later when he'd resumed his own characteristics."

"It was something about his expression, I guess," Lotta said, frowning.

"It was clever of you," repeated Lutie.

"Well, it was soon after that, while on their way east, that Shaw met Dolores. She was beautiful, and it pleased him to exert his charm and find that it hadn't failed him. He told her that he was a great trapeze artist and that as soon as his injured hand was well they would become a famous team. He kept up that pretense only long enough to impress her; then he resorted to threats, especially against her husband, to keep her with him. He needed the money she earned and also someone to dominate and torment.

"Meanwhile he was waiting for a chance at some real cash, as he puts it. And after a few weeks it came. With Futz's help he robbed a payroll and stole sixty thousand dollars. He left Dolores then, with threats which still kept her intimidated, and came to New York, bringing his buddy.

"He rented a rear attic room for Futz, two doors from where Hester lived. Joey needed no persuasion to lay lo'; as Shaw says, 'He was scared of his shadow.'

"Next, Shaw resumed his own dark coloring by applying a quickly removable dye on top of his assumed blondness. Then, as Vincent Smyth, in a purposely rather striking getup of the so-called Hollywood type, he rented the parlor front in the Maison LaVelle. And for the following week he watched, listened, and took note of whatever might further his great scheme. It amused him, he remarks, to find that Dolores' husband was rooming on the floor above, and he played with the idea of incidentally involving him in the murder he was planning but regretfully decided to discard the notion. He couldn't afford to confuse the issue.

"He was soon acquainted with Hester's hours for being at the Harmony Club, of course; and by eavesdropping he could tell when she was out at other times—and so forth. And he had no difficulty in fitting a key to the simple old lock on her door, and getting a look around her rooms during her absence.

"It was during his first visit that Miss DeVeere surprised him entering her apartment. But he kept his manner casual and nonchalant, and Miss DeVeere assumed, naturally, that he was a friend of Miss Gale's with a key to her apartment and a perfect right to use it."

"What I don't see yet," interrupted Madame LaVelle, "is why Dotty kept that juicy bit of gossip to herself as long as she did."

Dotty flushed. "Well, I did mention it to Mother Joffey."

"And," said that lady, "I didn't believe it. And anyhow as I told Dot it was none of her business. And I said, if she went around saying naughty things about Hester I wouldn't be nice to her any more."

Mother Joffey's pleasant lips looked firm, and it was evident that the plump woman could exert her will, when she chose to.

"Yes. Well," Lutie went on, "anyway, Shaw soon gathered that Hester had not learned about his call, which was all that mattered, as it would have forced his hand. On the afternoon of the murder he deliberately allowed Miss DeVeere to see him going into his wife's rooms, figuring that her testimony would actually be damning to Hester later, as, indeed, it did seem to be.

"Meanwhile, he observed the layout of her rooms, noted the shears, the bread knife, the oilcloth on the kitchen table and the flatiron. And he picked up a handkerchief that John had left there. He also unbolted the connecting doors on her side—a curtain covered them, so there was small chance that this would be noticed and he wanted them ready for the great moment. He kept the doors unlocked on his side too, for an emergency.

"And while he chatted with Madame LaVelle, taking care that she got an eyeful of the scar on his wrist and the ring he was wearing, he was gathering information. For instance, he learned that Hester had stowed some luggage in the storeroom."

"I certainly gab too much!" said the landlady, reddening. "But that Smyth—I mean Shaw—I must say he did have a way with him. I can look back now and see how he pumped me but at the time he just seemed like a kinda lonesome young fellow, friendly and interested in what a person had to say."

"A talented actor—offstage, at any rate," Lutie agreed. "And how he gloated as he worked up the details of his plot! It seemed like such a clever and ironic touch, to get Hester actually to carry her own suitcase with her on the incriminating fool's errand he meant to send her on! And what a subtle place in which to put John's handkerchief and the wedding ring. Much better than planting them in her apartment as he had first intended. It amused him to wonder just what she would do with the suitcase when he didn't claim it. Would she have it with her when the police apprehended her? Or would she have thrown it away? All the better, he thought, if she had; even if she dropped it in the river it would probably be recovered."

"But," objected Jeff, "the oilcloth bundle wouldn't be in it. That always did seem queer to me."

Amanda looked at him. "However," she said, with meaning, "doubtless he counted on some sort of theory being invented to explain its absence."

Poor Jeff looked uncomfortable. Lutie said hastily, "Yes, so he says. You must remember he was like a painter lingering over a masterpiece—a bad painter, of course, who spoils his work with last touches. So—"

"I must say," put in Miss DeVeere, "it still seems odd to me, Miss Gale not knowing her own suitcase—"

"That's right—and just suppose she had?" said Lotta. "Then she'd've *known* something was pretty fishy."

"So what?" Mrs. Joffey replied. "She wouldn't have known what Shaw was up to anyhow and she'd still have been afraid not to do as he told her, after what he'd promised would happen to John."

"That was what he counted on," Lutie agreed.

"Gosh, he took a chance," said Bill, his brown eyes round, "getting Miss Gale's suitcase outta the storeroom! S'pose I'd'a seen him! Then afterwards—"

"But," said Lutie, "he didn't take that chance. He went over the roofs from Futz's room and down through the skylight. And he had the good luck to recognize Hester's suitcase. Because it was one he had actually bought himself, when they were first married and went to California."

"And so that," said Mr. Saint John slowly, "was what I heard in the trunk room! And I thought it was—"

" Rats!" nodded Lutie, smiling at him. "And, when we peeked in, the morning after the murder, there was a cobweb right across the door. But beyond it, and around the skylight, the dust did look as if it had been disturbed. Of course that didn't seem to have any special importance at the moment; but later, naturally I remembered it, when we heard about Hester's bag."

"The murderer," said the professor, shaking his auburn head, "was indubitably most painstaking!"

"No—pleasure-taking," said Lutie. "He was delighting in these last details of his perfect crime, even prolonging the exquisite anticipation of revenge he'd cherished for years. When the time came for the final act, I think he was almost regretful, not, of course, of what he was about to do, but as at the ending of a dream. However, he realized there were dangers in too much delay. So at last he decided on the evening, and approximately the hour, for the murder.

"The night before, he procured Hester's suitcase from the trunk room. At the same time he told Futz to come to the parlor front apartment at eight o'clock exactly. Meanwhile, Futz was to pack his own valise but to leave it in his rear attic room. He, poor fellow, thought they were about to make their final escape to one of those charming islands without extradition laws that he had often seen in the movies, where they would live in peace and luxury on their sixty thousand dollars. Indeed they would have even more than that, because his pal had told him they were 'pulling another little job before their getaway, and not for Mexican jumping-beans, either!' Poor Futz had protested against this risk—they already had plenty of money, to his mind. But it wasn't a very strong mind, and what there was of it was entirely under Shaw's control. So was the sixty grand they'd stolen together. Futz didn't even know where his friend kept it. Altogether, without his buddy he was lost. Therefore, Shaw knew Futz would arrive according to orders at precisely eight o'clock. And he was sure he could handle him after that also.

"So on the afternoon of the fateful day Shaw nicked his own leg with a penknife, staunched the blood with John's handkerchief, and put this, and the wedding ring, with the few things of his own from the closet and bureau jammed on top of them in Hester's suitcase.

"He knew that she had an appointment at the hairdresser's, having overheard her make the appointment. So as soon as she'd gone out he hid the suitcase at the end of the hall.

"A few minutes after that he took his final look around her rooms. And it was then he conceived another bright idea. She had left her wristwatch, and he found that it was out of order. She would have to depend on her electric clock for the time. So he set it back an hour.

"Presently, watching from behind the heavy lace curtains at his windows, he saw her come home. Then he took up his listening-post at the double doors. A while after that he heard her talking on the phone. He gathered that John would be at the house at nine o'clock. Which, of course, was just the bit of luck he'd hoped for. It meant that John would definitely be on the spot—in more ways than one.

"Soon afterward Madame LaVelle dropped in to chat with Hester and then with him. But, since he was acquainted with her invariable custom of visiting the early show at the Grotto every evening, rain or shine, he felt no worry that she might overstay her welcome. So his manner was easy and his enjoyment perfect as he consumed her excellent apple pie. As he bade her au revoir, and a minute later saw her leave by the basement way, he turned to the phone and dialed his wife's number, never realizing that he had committed his first fatal error.

"Well, Hester was affected by his threats against John—exactly as he had expected she would be. He hung up the phone and presently saw her hastening from the house with the incriminating suitcase.

"He smoked a cigarette while he waited for Futz. Also, he threw open the closet doors and yanked out the bureau drawers—there must be the appearance of a hasty ransacking. He set the connecting doors barely ajar.

"On the dot of eight he let Futz quietly into the house, into the parlor front. Then he told his buddy they were to exchange clothing.

"Poor Futz was naturally puzzled. But when he ventured a feeble question Shaw said, 'Look, pal; have I ever let you down yet? I've got a job to do, and I need your duds. You needn't put on mine; if you want to be stubborn you can stay here and shiver. Or you can climb into my jeans and scram back to your dump and wait for me. If I don't join you in a couple of hours—here—' and he handed Futz the key to the locker in the subway and told him all about it.

"So Futz stopped protesting, though he was still bemused and reluctant. What should he do if his friend were nabbed? Shaw told him, 'Not a chance, kid. I'll be seein' you. And we'll be on our way. But you hang on to the key, just in case...'

"It was when Futz had stooped to lace those bright brown shoes so easily recognized later that Shaw hit him, swiftly, deftly, just behind the ear. And then carried him, unconscious, through the connecting doors to Hester's rooms, and laid him where he was later found.

"And stabbed him. With the scissors, as he had planned to do, but it was another flash of inspiration that made him catch up Hester's negligee, lying there on a chair beside the bed, and thrust the weapon through the sleeve before he struck."

Lutie paused.

Mike Fennelli said grimly, "I don't like that Victor Shaw."

Lutie said, "No...

"Well, after that he washed out the bloodstains, ironed the sleeve roughly, removed his victim's lucky ring and the part of him that he didn't want discovered, made an oilcloth bundle of these, and the weapons and the flat-iron; washed his own hands; removed the brown shoes from the body and put them on the floor. He hadn't given Futz time to dress fully, so he only had to throw the waistcoat and coat across the foot of the bed—of course he'd already emptied all the pockets.

"Next he turned off the lights in the parlor front and bolted the connecting doors from Hester's side. He glanced at his watch and noted complacently that it was not quite half-past eight, yet he hadn't had to hurry. And that made him recall the electric clock that he'd set back. Its hands pointed to 7:37. He reset it by his own watch and started it running again. If," remarked Lutie, "he'd connected its stopping with the lightning flash that had dimmed the lights for an instant, and merely put it ahead an hour without starting it …But that didn't occur to him.

"Which," she said contentedly, "was his second fatal error. The third— But I'm coming to that.

"He was now ready to leave. He picked up his bundle, switched off the lights, stepped from the window and closed it behind him. A few minutes later he'd dropped from the fire ladder, scaled two fences, gone through an alley to the street, and, using Futz's keys, was safe in that rear attic room where he'd kept his friend; all with little or no risk of being seen after he was 'dead.'

"There he took off Futz's shabby clothes, washed the removable dye from his hair and eyebrows, applied a coat of artificial tan to his face and hands, and dressed himself in a clean white shirt, a dark blue suit, black shoes and horn-rimmed spectacles.

"He put the oilcloth bundle in Joey's cheap valise. The meager possessions it already held left plenty of space. Soon it would go into the river, and a blond, tanned young man in neat inconspicuous clothes and glasses, with an unnoticeable walk—and sixty thousand dollars—would be on his way south.

"He picked up the shabby gray suit he'd just taken off and thrust the trousers into the valise. Then he reached into the lower right-hand pocket of the jacket. But what he was looking for was not there. Yet he knew that was where it should be—Futz, while he dressed, had kept the key in his hand, and Shaw had taken it from his limp, unconscious fingers and slipped it into the pocket of the gray coat he himself was wearing. But it was gone now. He tore at all the other pockets, pulled them inside out, crushed the coat, felt the lining, almost ripped it out. Then he went through the trousers in a last vain hope. The key was missing. He had made his third fatal error.

"Well," said Lutie, "that was the worst moment of Victor Shaw's life. So he says—and I'm sure it's true. But he is very proud of keeping his head and his nerve. He was sure the key must have dropped from his pocket as he jumped from the fire ladder, or when he climbed the fences. He *had* to have it—he knew he couldn't force that locker—and before three o'clock of the following day. He must go back and search for it.

"Of course he knew that by now—or soon—the police would be all around the Maison LaVelle. So he must wait till the coast was clear.

"He finished packing Futz's valise and hurried—but deviously, cautiously, by cab, crosstown car, and on foot—to the East River. He knew the city and chose a lonely spot to slip the oilcloth bundle from the bag and into the dark water. Probably, he figured, it never would be recovered; but if it were the head could by that time be mistaken for his own! So much the better—and the worse for Hester.

"As for the valise there was nothing, he well knew, to identify it. So he simply left it in a doorway.

"Then he went back to Joey's room. Passing the Maison LaVelle he saw the crowd of policemen and pressmen and curious people around the door. And from Futz's window he could still see flashlights circling the back yard. He waited until they disappeared—he waited for almost an hour after that. Then he crept through the alley next to the Maison, climbed over the fence and searched for the key. And then we came out, and he ran. But he stayed there, watching through a gap in the fence, and saw me pick up something. My little flashlight gleamed on metal—he saw the key.

"He waited for us, in the mouth of the alley, but only for a minute or two. There was a policeman guarding the house; he couldn't hope to waylay us there. When the officer had turned his back, Shaw left the alley. There is a place with cars to hire in a nearby block; he went there and hired a black sedan and drove it to within a few doors of the Maison. When we came out he followed us. And parked the sedan in the passage next to the Paradise.

"But he didn't hit us. And he didn't dare to go back—if he'd left his car and . . . Well, you see, he couldn't risk any hue and cry. All he could do was to trail us, after that."

Lutie paused. Then she went on, "He says that he followed us home, and he would have attempted to raid the house and make us give him the key that night. But there was an officer guarding the place, it seems—You know, Hester was with us. But early next morning he returned and trailed us. He saw us go into the Maison and come out, and his chance to steal my purse came on that crowded corner of Sixth Avenue at noon.

"And still he hadn't got the key! I think, then, he might almost have given up, but fortunately I'd scribbled the address of the Columbia Locker Company in my memo book, which was in my purse. So he figured we were still going after what he wanted. And the rest you know."

But there was something I didn't know. I leaned forward across the table.

"Lutie," I said, "was he really there in the subway, waiting for us, watching us? Or was that your imagination?"

Lutie smiled at me. She wrinkled her silvery brows and thought for a moment.

"You know, Marthy dear, I do believe I can quote that part of Victor Shaw's confession. He says, 'I was standing there with a news rag up in front of me and along came those two old dames. My chance! I edged closer. They opened the locker. Then the little one, with a nasty look in her eye, told the fat one to hold on and yell if anyone tried to grab the bag. I could have strangled her. But all I could do was to beat it after them and see where they were taking my money.'

"And," said Lutie, "he goes on, 'Well, I saw. And that afternoon I paid their place a little visit and the redheaded sap'—of course, Jeffy dear, he meant to say *chap*—'swallowed my line and gave me the dope on the old maids and showed me around. The rest of the day and that night I kept an eye on their place. I still thought they'd tip the cops. But when, toward midnight, no cops had appeared, I figured the old girls were counting on using those sixty G's themselves. Naturally I figured they'd be a pushover.' "

Lutie sighed contentedly.

"But we weren't," she said, "thanks to Pa and his little pistol!" She finished the one glass of champagne that had lasted her all evening and commented, "Well, Mr. Shaw has added me to the list of ladies he is mad at. His boast—I mean his confession—winds up, 'Mine was one of the most brilliant crimes ever conceived. Only bad luck prevented the killing of three birds with one stone. I would have been dead for the books; Futz gone the way of all flesh and I in sole possession of sixty grand; and my Judas wife would have taken the rap she once let me in for. But of course another d— ahem—female had to queer it. Which makes the record complete.' "

"And so it does," stated Amanda firmly, rising. "Come, Sister—"

And indeed it was after three o'clock by that time!

So we said our goodnights and wended our way homeward, tired but— of course it sounds dreadful to say—satisfied and exhilarated after the fact of a murder and all the distressing things that had happened in connection with it. Still, several lives had been straightened out, after all; and one could be thankful for that.

And in the time that has passed since then I have been thankful, too, that life has become almost tranquil again. Not that it is like being home in East Biddicutt, of course. But we have made pleasant friends; I enjoy many a comfortable chat with Mrs. Joffey, and frequently go to the movies with Madame LaVelle, while best of all are the pleasant hours spent helping Mr. Saint John in his garden. The Fantastic Fennellis are on the road, and so is Professor Sesame, with his wife, *neé* Dot DeVeere; Hester and John are to be married soon; Billy Paul is working at the Harmony Club, a very happy lad, and often drops in to see us.

As for the experience that introduced us all, I daresay it was broadening in its way, but I certainly hope we shall never have another like it. Lutie, of course, doesn't share that hope. On the contrary, I catch an eager anticipatory gleam in her blue eyes whenever the phone rings. Meanwhile, she has been widening her acquaintance with New York, learning a new crochet stitch, and completing the records of the case in her scrapbook.

The routine business of the agency has picked up considerably and keeps Amanda's hands full. But time seems to hang rather heavily on mine, now and then. Lutie likes to tease me by saying that I miss the excitement of the days when we were in the thick of the mystery! Which is absurd, of course.

But I will admit that my mind does dwell on them rather persistently. It's for that reason I've set down these recollections, drawing on Lutie's record to corroborate them or to fill in blanks, and hoping to finish with them once and for all and really get back to normal.

But I do shiver a little with foreboding whenever I take up Lutie's scrapbook, with its lilac-colored cover significantly labeled in her delicate slanting script:

Our First Murder

Rue Morgue Press Books

We specialize in reprinting mysteries from the 1930s through 1950s, releasing one new title a month. All books are quality trade paperbacks, usually with full-color covers. To find out more, to get a catalog, or to suggest titles, call 800-699-6214 or write to P.O. Box 4119, Boulder, CO 80306.

Titles as of August 2002

Cannan, Joanna. *They Rang Up the Police.* An English village mystery set in 1937 featuring Inspector Guy Northeast. **Cannan.** *Death at The Dog.* An English village mystery set in late 1939, the second and final book featuring Northeast. **Carr, Glyn.** *Death on Milestone Buttress.* Murder on a mountain in Wales. **Clason, Clyde. B.** *The Man from Tibet.* A 1938 locked room mystery set in Chicago with Prof. Westborough and a mysterious Tibetan manuscript. **Coggin, Joan.** *Who Killed the Curate?* The vicar's wife turns sleuth with hilarious results. **Coles, Manning.** *The Far Traveller.* A 1950s comic ghost story in which a long-dead German nobleman returns from the grave to star in a movie being made about his tragic death. **Coles.** *Brief Candles.* The first of three comic ghost stories featuring the Latimers, two Victorian gentleman and their pet monkey, who, as tourists, were killed during the Franco-Prussian War and who rematerialize in a small French village.**Coles.** *Happy Returns.* 2nd Latimer. **Coles.** *Come and Go.* 3rd Latimer. **Davis, Norbert.** *The Mouse in the Mountain.* A comic private eye novel in which a P.I. and his Great Dane solve murders in Mexico during WWII. **Davis.** *Sally's in the Alley.* 2nd Doan and Carstairs. **Dean, Elizabeth.** *Murder is a Collector's Item.* A 1939 screwball mystery set in the Boston antiques world with Emma Marsh. **Dean.** *Murder is a Serious Business.* 2nd Emma Marsh (1940). **Dean.** *Murder a Mile High.* 3rd Marsh. **Little, Constance & Gwenyth.** *The Black Gloves.* From the queens of the wacky mystery, this one is set in East Orange, New Jersey. **Little.** *The Black Honeymoon.* **Little.** *The Black Stocking.* **Little.** *The Black Paw.* **Little.** *The Black Coat.* **Little.** *Black Corridors.* **Little.** *Black-Headed Pins.* **Little.** *Great Black Kanba.* **Little.** *Grey Mist Murders.* **Little.** *The Black Eye.* **Little.** *The Black Thumb.* **Millhiser, Marlys.** *The Mirror.* Our only non-vintage mystery, this is a wonderful time travel (sort of) novel set between 1900 and 1978. 6th printing. **Norman, James.** *Murder, Chop Chop.* Set in the 1930s during the Sino-Japanese War and involving the eccentric foreign community. **Pim, Sheila.** *Common or Garden Crime.* An Irish village gardening mystery, set during Wold War II. **Pim.** *A Hive of Suspects.* Irish mystery. **Pim.** *Creeping Venom.* Irish village mystery. **Pim.** *A Brush with Death.* Irish art and gardening mystery. **Russell, Charlotte Murray.** *The Message of the Mute Dog.* Spinster sleuth solves murder at a defense plant on eve of WWII. **Sheridan, Juanita.** *The Chinese Chop.* Lily Wu and Janice Cameron solve a murder in a Washington Square boarding house. **Sheridan, Juanita.** *The Kahuna Killer.* Lily and Janice return home to Hawaii. **Sheridan, Juanita.** *The Mamo Murders.* Lily and Janice find murder on a Hawaiian ranch.